DOCILE

DOC

A TOM DOHERTY ASSOCIATES BOOK NEW YORK

K. M. SZPARA

CILE

DOCILE

Copyright © 2020 by Kellan Szpara

All rights reserved.

Edited by Carl Engle-Laird

A Tor.com Book
Published by Tom Doherty Associates
120 Broadway
New York, NY 10271

www.tor.com

Tor® is a registered trademark of Macmillan Publishing Group, LLC.

Library of Congress Cataloging-in-Publication Data

Names: Szpara, K. M., author.
Title: Docile / K.M. Szpara.
Description: First edition. | New York : A Tom Doherty Associates Book, 2020.
Identifiers: LCCN 2019046668 (print) | LCCN 2019046669 (ebook) |
    ISBN 9781250216151 (hardcover) | ISBN 9781250216144 (ebook)
Subjects: GSAFD: Science fiction. | Dystopias.
Classification: LCC PS3619.Z68 D63 2020 (print) | LCC PS3619.Z68 (ebook) |
    DDC 813/.6—dc23
LC record available at https://lccn.loc.gov/2019046668
LC ebook record available at https://lccn.loc.gov/2019046669

Our books may be purchased in bulk for promotional, educational, or business use. Please contact your local bookseller or the Macmillan Corporate and Premium Sales Department at 1-800-221-7945, extension 5442, or by email at MacmillanSpecialMarkets@macmillan.com.

First Edition: March 2020

Printed in the United States of America

0   9   8   7   6   5   4   3   2   1

For my family, who are embedded in me.
And for Faith, who is embedded in this book.

DOCILE

ELISHA

After today, I will have seven rights.

"One," I whisper. "Retention of the right to vote in a public election. Two: the right to adequate care: food, water, shelter, hygiene, and regular medical attention."

Abby rolls around in her little bed. The old wood squeaks as she settles back under the covers. That's the only right that would've done my younger sister any good. Here, she'll make do with the occasional medical clinic and home remedies.

"Three: the right to anonymity of surname." I squeeze my eyes shut. Pressure builds between my brows. After today, I won't be a Wilder.

"Four." I pluck the photo of my family from the windowsill. "The right to one personal item." It's the same one Mom took with her. She won't miss it. She probably can't even remember it.

That visit was the last time she was anything like herself. We had our picture taken by a man at the fair. His camera had an old-fashioned lens that reminded Dad of his childhood.

It was years ago, anyway. Abby was only a baby, all wrapped up in swaddling. Dad still had his beard, a smile nestled in the middle. I'd just grown one tiny hair on my chin and couldn't wait to show Mom how manly I was becoming.

"Five." I resume my count. "The right to personal physical safety." My heart beats a little faster. "Six: the right to sexual health and protection from pregnancy." A breeze cools the heat on my face.

Between school and work and helping around the house, I've

never had time for relationships. And I've certainly never had time
for sex. Where would I have done it, anyway? On my mattress on
the floor, next to my little sister's bed? I know a few guys who use
the community barn, but between the squawking and cow shit I
could never bring myself to join them.

Besides, I'm counting on Seventh Right to save me from anyone
who tries to violate Sixth. "Seven: the right to refuse or demand
Dociline, and at any time to change your mind."

I rise from bed as quietly as possible and pull on my jeans. No
sense in changing my shirt. I put on an old pair of sneakers, leaving my good boots for my sister. She'll grow into them eventually. I
doubt they let Dociles keep their clothing.

One personal item.

I slip the family photo into my pocket and tiptoe out of our room
without waking Abby. Regret tugs at my heart as I close the door. I
didn't even say goodbye, not a word or a kiss on the cheek while she
slept. Nothing. Not for her, not for Dad.

I linger at his bedroom door for a moment before going to the
kitchen. Mom doesn't look up from the floor. She sweeps back and
forth over the same worn-down spot, even when I put my hand on
her shoulder.

"Hey, Mom, it's Elisha."

"Hello, Elisha."

I hold on to the moment when I can pretend she remembers
I'm her son, and that it's not ten years of Dociline bending her to
politeness.

"I miss you so much."

"That's nice," she says, her voice smooth as fresh-churned butter.

"I wanted to let you know I'm not mad at you." I take the broom
with no resistance and lean it against the wall.

"Okay." She smiles, but her eyes are empty, expressionless.

"And I love you."

"Okay."

"I understand why you left us. And when you're better, someday—"

"Okay."

I pause. It would be easier if she didn't reply at all, rather than in that monotone voice, following the same script, over and over.

"Someday, I hope you'll forgive me for doing the same."

"That's nice."

"I need your signature." I flatten the Office of Debt Resolution form on the table and find her a pen. My parents aren't married—not legally, anyway. Get married and you—and your children—inherit your partner's debt. Like each of them don't have enough separately. No, this is the form that signs both of my parents' debts over to me, so I can sell it. Sell it all.

Dad already signed, assuming it was for Abby, like we'd discussed. It was that or wait for the police to drag us all off to debtors' prison. They only send out so many notices.

I trace the scar tissue that patterns the inside of my left wrist. The mark stands out, dark and ropey from years under the sun, a fat "S" with a "U" slicing down its middle. If I close my eyes, I can still smell the dollar sign burning into my flesh, hear the cop calling me a drain on society.

Mom finishes her signature, dots the i's in "Abigail," and stares at me, still smiling. Waiting for my next order.

"Thanks, Mom." I kiss her cheek.

"You're welcome, Elisha."

I fold the paper and hold it tight, afraid to lose it. One more stop before the ODR. I lock the door behind me and bury my key in the flowerpot on the porch. When I look up, I see the Falstaffs' front door open and close, one house over. Dylan stuffs her socked feet into oversized boots. She crosses her arms to secure an old crocheted blanket over her pajamas and hops over, still squeezing her shoes into place. "Where're you running off to? Can I come?"

The two of us have snuck out more times than I can count. Midnight swims in the reservoir; talks on the bridge, our bare feet dangling over the edge; that time we walked to Hunt Valley for a party in one of the old office buildings and ended up sleeping in an abandoned unit overnight, talking about what we'd do if we didn't stand to inherit our parents' debts. I'd go to the University of Maryland, get my teaching degree, put all the tutoring I've done to good use. She'd travel to an elephant sanctuary in Thailand that she read about in an old textbook. I told her it probably didn't exist anymore; she told me to mind my own dreams.

I smile at the memory, but hers fades when she sees the forms in my hands. I tuck them under my arms, but it's too late. Dylan knows me better than anyone; she's practically my second sister. After her father took his life and it became clear that my mom was no longer herself, Dad and Nora began spending more time together. We have three surnames between us, but we're still a family. Even after what our parents went through—what we're dealing with, now.

"I have to." I have trouble looking into her eyes. "We received a final notice. The interest is—"

She wraps her arms around me before I can finish. Warm together inside the blanket, I never want to leave.

"I don't want you to go," she says, voice muffled against me.

"I don't, either, but it's me or Abby."

"I know," she says. "Just seems like everyone's leaving, lately, and too few of them come back. Even fewer like their regular selves."

"Don't worry. I won't let that happen to me."

"Well, do what you have to, but if it gets too hard, talk to your caseworker." Her father hadn't. He didn't make it.

"I will."

"And I'll see you in six months, okay? For your visit." Dylan drapes her blanket around my shoulders. "Don't fucking freeze to death on your way."

She shouldn't waste it on me—I'll have to give it up—but I'm too cold to refuse.

When I slide out of her grasp, I know I can't go back for another hug or I'll run back inside and do the same with Dad and Abby and then I'll never leave. There's no time to waste. Last I heard, the walk from Prettyboy Reservoir to Baltimore City took twelve hours.

/ / /

I don't have a watch, but the moon hangs high overhead when I make it to the entrance ramp for the interstate. A single strip of undisturbed pavement lines the center of 83 South—a path barely wide enough for a car and mostly used by bikes and pedestrians. I doubt the pockmarked road has seen much action since the last police raid.

I count the few cars that pass instead of thinking about how I'm going to miss my sister growing up or wondering whether Mom will ever snap out of it. I'm up to thirteen—the last car sunflower yellow and shaped like a cat ready to pounce—when soggy fields transition to neighborhoods and the pavement to a darker, smoother texture. My fingers are numb where they poke through the crocheted blanket.

South of Exit 20, cars crowd 83. I fall into line with the other pedestrians who exit onto the local road. A metal sign reads: "Welcome to Hunt Valley!"—one of a few struggling towns along the way. A diverse group of smiling cartoon people wave at me; I do not return the sentiment.

I thrust my hand into my pocket and rub the wad of cash, worn soft by too many hands. The only thing I need in order to register with the ODR is a state ID. The amount of money and red tape that stands between me and one of those isn't worth the hassle. I started saving for a fake one the day Dad told me his plan to register Abby with the ODR.

She'll fetch the most, Dad said. *She's got the most life ahead of her.* But I'm twenty-one, old enough to consent. I've heard stories about trillionaires fucking their Dociles, and trillionaires? They pay. If I could sign with one of them, I might be able to sell off all our debt. I might be able to keep the collectors and cops from ever coming for my family again.

So, while Dad's smile faded and his energy dropped, I pocketed a few dollars from our take at the Hunt Valley farmer's market and stayed out late tutoring kids who couldn't make it to their "local" schoolhouse an hour away; a dollar per hour isn't bad, out here.

Our neighbor Shawna's the only one who goes into Baltimore

City regularly. She and her wife have a tandem bicycle, and since they both work for the government, it's not too bad of a deal. She hooked me up with the forger in the city. Fifty dollars, she quoted. I re-count my money as I pass the patchwork houses that pop up the closer you get to the city. Dad told us they used to be called Mc-Mansions. The ones out our way crumbled to the foundations, long ago, before everyone with money moved into the center of the city. We built them up with logs and stones and makeshift cement and what house parts we could scavenge from abandoned neighborhoods. Here, the first floors are still intact and squat looking without the former second floors to top them off.

Locals inhabit abandoned chain stores and restaurants. Office buildings house people instead of corporations. A grocery store spills out into the parking lot where folks trade and donate canned goods. And an Empower Maryland banner hangs over an old movie theater advertising supplemental education, daycare for working parents, skills training, and public assistance. They've come to our farm a few times. Donated winter boots, blankets, a bike every few years. They help some, I suppose, but we sure haven't felt it in Prettyboy.

Buildings thicken the closer I get to the center of the city, and corporate-sponsored clothing thins. People in these neighborhoods can afford to buy their own. Cold claims the sweat on my back, as I fold Dylan's blanket over the TruCare Insurance logo on my shirt. It was free.

No one seems to notice, all too busy speed-walking to work or breakfast or whatever they do for fun in the city. I've only been a handful of times and never for fun. Heard they ride bicycles that don't move and soak in bathtubs full of chemicals. Along the city blocks, trees grow from predesignated holes in the ground; their branches are trim and tidy, their roots don't sprawl. Pink and yellow flowers—colors you shouldn't see yet in January—hang from streetlamps in metal baskets with some sort of fake brown grass. I wonder if anything here is real or if it's all plastic. Like I'm walking through some child's play set. Even the buildings look unreal, the marble shaped into arches and frills and angels, painted baby blue and gold and red.

Ahead, a hand-painted sign reads: "Eddie's of Mt. Vernon." My destination. I didn't think people worked until 9:00 a.m. in the city, but the clock tower in the distance only reads 8:00 and already shops are opening. It smells like filth and perfume.

I walk around back of the grocery store until I come to the dumpster. When she sees me, a woman nudges the man beside her. He stomps out his cigarette and heads inside.

"You Shawna's friend?" she asks, wiping her hands on her coat. She looks more like a butcher than a forger.

I nod and hand her the fifty dollars.

"She told me a guy from the county was coming in for a fake." She counts the cash and pulls out a tablet. "Stand against the wall. Don't smile."

No problem, there. I stare at the tablet, while she takes my picture, then glance left and right.

"Stop looking so suspicious," she says. "We're just two friends taking pics."

Easy for her to say. Someone is bound to see us, and I cannot get arrested. Not when I'm so close. She shoves a plastic card into her tablet, then pulls a stylus from her coat pocket and moves it over the screen, like she's writing in a foreign language.

"Write in your full name, address, age, and so on. Skip whatever you don't know and I'll make it up."

The stylus slides too easily over the tablet, but I know most of the answers, and hand it back to her when I finish. After a few more minutes, she rips the plastic card out and hands it to me, still warm.

"There you go, kid."

I examine her work because I feel like I should, not because I know what to look for. "This'll fool the card readers?"

"Yeah."

"Thanks."

"Don't mention it. There's only one reason someone from the county buys an ID." She pushes up her sleeve to reveal a scar that looks like mine did ten years ago.

"The ODR's about a mile down Charles Street." She eyes the blanket Dylan gave me. "You going to make it?"

"Yeah, thanks," I say, pocketing the ID.

"Maybe I'll see you around." She opens the back door of the grocery.

"Probably not."

We share a shrug and I leave in the direction she pointed. The only things I look forward to are the heat and sitting down.

2

ELISHA

A middle-aged white man at the front desk gulps his coffee. "Welcome to the Office of Debt Resolution; how can I help you?" Little brown drops stick to his graying beard. He dabs at them with his shirt sleeve.

"Checking in."

He taps at his computer. The keypad flickers under his touch. "ID?"

I pass the fake over the counter. The man scans it without a second look.

"Elisha Wilder." He pronounces it "E-lish-a."

"E-lie-sha." I correct him, but he doesn't seem to notice. Probably no one will, from here on out.

"Twenty-one years old, biological child of Abigail Wilder and David Burns. Are you here to represent both lineages?"

"Yes."

"Multilineage Debt Resolution Consent Form, please."

I dig the signed paper from my pocket and hand it to him.

"All right." He stamps it and scans it into the system. "How much debt do you want to sell off?"

"All of it."

For the first time, he looks at me—all of me, like he's buying me. "Not sure you'll fetch three million. Maybe with some cleaning up." He checks my ID again. "Well, you are over eighteen. That'll boost your price."

I've never been so conscious of my appearance. No one in the county cares about scraggly hair or freckles. Only that you're strong enough to help raise a barn or dexterous enough to patch up clothes.

"Sign here." He pushes a clipboard in front of me. "And initial next to the life term clause, in case someone goes for it."

The words "life term" send a chill through me. Mom sold almost a million in debt for ten years. Of course, terms must go longer—I knew that deep down—but hearing someone say it? With a breath to center myself, I do as instructed, and the man scans it alongside my consent form.

"You will receive your ID back upon completion of your service term. Hold on to this"—he hands me a new card—"for now. It contains your rights, calendared alerts for all forthcoming elections in compliance with First Right, a copy of your parental consent form, and the agreement you just signed." He punches a hole in the top of the card and hooks an ODR lanyard through it, then continues in the same droll tone. "Report to the second floor for the remainder of processing. Per Third Right, all interactions from this point forward are anonymous. Disclose your surname at your own risk. If at any time you feel your rights have been violated, please contact this office per the information on the card. Thank you and have a nice day." The man returns to his computer, as if bored by the speech he's forced to give over and over.

"Thanks," I mutter, and head for the stairs. I expected the inside of the ODR to be marbled and bright, like the rest of the city, but the carpets are worn and the only elevator is out of order.

On the second floor, a Latina woman with warm skin and a bob of shiny black hair takes my new card and scans it. Age lines frame her smile and eyes. "Confirm your name, age, and gender, please."

"Elisha—" I stop with the Wilder "W" formed on my lips.

"It's okay," she says. "Everyone does it. I promise to forget your personal information."

I return her smile. "Elisha, twenty-one, male."

"You passed the quiz. My name's Carol; I'll be your case manager." She pulls up one of my documents on the flimsy little card. "Says here you're trying to pay off three million."

I bite my lip to stop myself from making excuses. Not all the debt's ours, personally. According to Dad, everyone in our family used to attend college, graduate school—for generations they became doctors and artists, professors and architects.

But when the Next of Kin laws went into effect, all their debt passed down to their kids after they died, and to their kids, accumulating over decades before people got smart about that kind of thing and stopped getting married. Combine that with credit card debts, student loans, utilities, mortgages, and healthcare, and suddenly you're living in the outer counties of Maryland, four million under. It's taken us years to get even this far—to fend off debt collectors and the threat of debtors' prison. Took Mom ten years and she only sold off one million. Look what that got her.

But Carol doesn't react like the man downstairs. "It'll take the right Patron, but we might be able to make that happen. Come on." She takes my hand like I'm a small child.

I hold tighter than I mean to.

"First, a shower. Changing room's over there; you can drop your clothes in the donation bin and put on a pair of scrubs when you finish. Place your Docile card and personal item in this resealable bag for safekeeping." She holds it open.

I hesitate.

"You'll get them back after you're cleaned up, I promise. Fourth Right."

I breathe deeply and forfeit my belongings. After Carol closes the curtain, I do the same with my clothes. I wince as I pull my shoes off, exposing my blistered feet to the air. They go into the donation bin first. Each item of clothing, one at a time, another part of myself gone.

Only the crocheted blanket remains, still on the bench where I tossed it. It's going to be donated. Someone cold will feel my family's warmth. I hug it tight against me one final time, breathing in the scent of the wood stove in Dylan's house and the cat her mother, Nora, refuses to kick out during winter.

I drop it into the bin and force myself to get in the shower. From now on, all my needs will be provided for. That's exactly what Dad was clinging to when he suggested Abby. But what good is a comfortable house and new clothes when you're drugged out on Dociline?

"Scrub everything real good in there!" Carol shouts over the rush of water. "Rinse and repeat. And use conditioner; I don't care how short your hair is."

I haven't used a conventional shower in years, much less all these products. Seaweed and saltwater shampoo? I could have jumped in the reservoir before trekking down here.

I step out smelling like minerals and chemicals, an imitation of the beach. The scrubs I put on are loose and comfortable; still, I glance at the donation bin. What's left of my life is in there.

"There you go, much better." Carol squats down to examine my blistered and bleeding feet. "Grab your personal item and Docile card and follow me."

There aren't any licensed doctors in my town, just people who know what to administer for a broken bone, or burns. I've had to drag my family into the city for regular checkups—Mom for blood tests—every year, despite Dad's objections. What's the extra medical debt when you're millions under? But this ODR doctor applies medicine and real bandages for free. He draws blood and injects vaccines. By nightfall, I feel like one of the farm animals.

"I'll be back for you in the morning." Carol leaves me in a room full of metal-frame bunk beds.

A few men look up when I enter. Some look freshly scrubbed like me, others tired and rumpled from a long day of interviews. I discard any notions of solidarity or conversation and settle into an empty bed. In a few days, they'll all be loaded up on Dociline, happily serving out their terms.

"There," Carol says, smoothing my hair into place. "Who knew you had a face under that shag?"

I never cut it in the winter. Warmer that way. But I smile for her in the mirror.

I've spent all morning imagining home. No one's called to report me; Dylan must've told them, but, if not, Dad will find out when the ODR sends him notice of all debts cleared.

"Please let him make it," I whisper.

"What was that?" Carol finishes scrubbing the calluses down on my hands.

"Nothing, sorry."

She puts down the pumice, rinses away the dead skin, and rubs thick lotion into my palms.

"Today, someone is going to inspect every inch of you to determine if you're worth the price you're asking for. They're going to ask you a bunch of personal questions you aren't prepared for, and if they decide to take you home with them—" She holds my chin and forces my eyes onto hers. "—you will spend the rest of your life speaking when spoken to. So, for god's sake, son, if you have something to say, say it now."

A thin layer of tears seals my lashes together. When I open them, her face runs like rain before my eyes. She called me son. Her voice didn't sound much different than Mom's in that moment.

"I'm scared."

"It's okay. The Dociline makes it easier." She touches her wrist like so many debtors do. "Seventh Right."

"Can I tell you a secret? You won't tell the Patrons or write it down in my file?"

She nods and holds my hands, still tender from her cleaning.

"I'm going to refuse."

"Refuse what?"

"Dociline."

Carol flinches, then laughs. "No."

"Yes."

Her smile fades, lips thin to a line. "You shouldn't tell anyone that."

"You're not going to—"

"No, and neither should you." She nudges me onto my feet. "It's for everyone's good, you know. They want a happily obedient drone, and you don't want to be too aware of what's happening. Trust me."

She pushes me into a room full of clothes and starts throwing them at me. "Put these on. Hurry up."

I duck behind a curtain, too shocked to move.

"No one's going to buy a sluggish Docile."

"I don't have any underwear here." I sift through the pile.

"You won't need any. Go on."

I hike up the jeans. I've never worn a pair so tight before. The shirt hugs the lines of my arms and chest in ways that would make farmwork uncomfortable.

"I've seen a lot of Dociles, Elisha; I know how to sell them." Carol yanks the curtain aside. "You have a nice body. Let the Patrons touch you. Don't aim for three million; aim for five. Don't speak unless spoken to, or do anything unless you're told. Don't lie, but definitely don't tell them you're going to refuse Dociline. Got it?"

I barely nod. The clothes are only the first chip off any notion of dignity I'd brought with me.

Carol checks her watch. "The Patrons should be arriving. You ready?"

"Yes."

She pinches my cheeks until they burn. "You look like a ghost."

The slam of the heavy metal door still echoes in my brain. Carol's left me in a room with two chairs across a small table. I step toward the closer chair, then stop.

Don't do anything unless you're told. Aim for five million.

I clasp my hands behind my back to still them.

A loud buzzer signals the door. I straighten to my full—though unimpressive—height. My heartbeat radiates through every inch of me.

The door bursts open and a white woman with an unnatural-looking tan saunters in, still eyeing a tablet. My file, probably. She sits across from me and looks up, lips pursed, eyes darting every-where.

"Turn around," she says.

I move slowly, dropping my hands to my sides. Feels more like I'm trying on clothes in a fancy boutique than selling myself.

"You're twenty-one?"

"Yes, ma'am."

She swipes to a new page on the tablet, her inch-long fingernails scraping the glass surface. "My daughter's going to the University of Maryland. I don't want her getting involved with anyone she shouldn't. You know how college is." She waves her hand like my answer is "yes." It isn't. "Take your shirt off; let me see your muscles."

I comply, draping it over the free chair.

"Yeah." She smiles. "Not bad. We'll bulk you up. But my daughter, she's into those punk skinny boys anyway, so whatever. You know how to handle a girl, right?"

"Handle, ma'am?"

"You know, in bed."

Does she want me to have sex with her daughter? "No, ma'am."

"Eh." She winks. "We can fix that, too."

I picture myself smashed between this woman and her daughter, in bed at some fancy university. I realize then that I might cave. I might take the drug.

She walks over and squeezes my arms. Then my crotch. I tense under her touch, trying my hardest not to recoil.

"Three mil, huh?" She plays with a strand of my hair.

A buzzer sounds and the attendant opens the door. After the woman leaves, I let out a sigh so big I think I might pass out.

The next Patron has salt-and-pepper hair and looks like he hasn't seen the sun in a decade. He wears a vest and pressed slacks. He doesn't sit; he walks right over to me. I haven't even put my shirt back on.

You have a nice body. Let the Patrons touch you.

"How much can you lift? From the ground."

We don't have weights, at home, so I hope my answer doesn't sound off. "Around two hundred pounds, sir."

"Any experience with manual labor?"

I nod.

"Well?"

"I've worked on a community farm most of my life, sir."

"That'll do," he says, and walks out, not waiting for the buzzer. Him I could live with. It would be like back home, except without my family or friends, or hope for a future.

Three others interview me, but I immediately dismiss them as options: a young woman who silently measures various parts of my body; a couple, who ask if I have experience raising children, because they've just had screaming triplets; and an older man who asks about my threshold for pain.

After him, I wait—five minutes, ten, fifteen. Cold air tickles my skin. I want to put my shirt on and sit down, but that would probably cost me three million dollars.

Finally, the door opens. This man is younger than the others, white, probably late twenties or early thirties, and dressed in colors as bright as the flowers outside.

He sits opposite me and casually unbuttons the top of his shirt, the fluorescent light glinting off a ring on each of his fingers. "Put that shirt back on and have a seat." He brushes his blonde hair out of his face, but it falls across his tan forehead, like the model on the shampoo bottle I used this morning.

It's inevitable that I'll hate anyone on the other side of this table—anyone who could make my family's debt vanish with a single paycheck. Yet I relax in his presence. It's the way he treats me—like I'm an equal part of this interview. Then, I imagine him fucking me. If he's a trillionaire, like I suspect, it's inevitable. Despite his money, he is attractive. And I realize, out of everyone I've interviewed with today, I want him to pick me.

3

ALEX

I arrive at the boardroom before everyone else. Our meeting isn't until 8:00, but the sunrise looks even better through the Smart-Glass that surrounds the space than it does outside. Nanotech enhances the burnt-orange and red-wine sky against the gray-blue ripples of the harbor. Sensors warm the room slowly and strategically so that the brisk transition from Baltimore winter to climate-controlled office doesn't shock my body. I only really notice that I've warmed up when I remove my jacket.

A Docile takes it, disappearing into an alcove and returning with a petal-pink porcelain cup and saucer. I take it, the coffee already doctored to my taste with cream and sugar, cooled to a temperature that won't burn my tongue. He silently returns his attentions to the plants that decorate the hallway.

Though most of Bishop Laboratories is underground, the boardroom is situated on top of the Maryland Science Center. The institution was nearly bankrupt when my family stepped in to save it, several generations ago. Dr. Alexandra Bishop I, my grandmother, all this is her legacy. I sit in the warm leather chair where she first declared her intentions for Dociline. Where my father, Dr. Alexander Bishop II, developed Formula 2.0, and where I will soon begin work on Formula 3.0.

I breathe the coffee so deep I'd swear the caffeine absorbs directly into my bloodstream through my lungs. One perfect cup, every morning. With a few taps of my fingers, my SmartRings bring up monitors where the sunrise once was. Fifty-three minutes, I note, then review my presentation.

Board members trickle in at the top of the hour. They shed their jackets, exposing colorful sweaters and scarves and pocket squares. Sitting in brown leather chairs, they look like rows of neatly planted flowers. I smooth down my tie, slide my fingers over the engraving on the white-gold clip my grandmother gave me. *Legatum nostrum futurum est.*

To be a Bishop means to shape society—the future. That's the charge I received from my grandmother, along with my name. It would be hard to expand our fortune by marrying into a wealthier family—few exist—and yet the pressure remains, not only to preserve our legacy but to enrich it.

My friends Dutch and Mariah enter together with only a wink in my direction. The two of them stayed up all night, listening to me practice, helping me refine my points, until we'd gone through half a dozen bottles of champagne and as many rewrites of my plans for Dociline. It doesn't hurt having the support of the CFO and a shareholder who also happens to control most of the country's media.

My father arrives last—on purpose. When he enters the room, it falls silent, the meeting begins. And, for once, I'm nervous. He sits opposite me, each of us crowning one end of the table. Out of habit, I trace a groove in its underside that's grown slowly smoother and deeper over the years.

"Welcome, everyone," I say, "and thank you for joining me so early. I am excited to share my vision for—"

Dad raises his hand. My presentation vanishes from the surrounding monitors. "There's something we need to discuss before you begin, Alex. If you don't mind me interrupting."

My smile contracts, nerves hum with anxiety. "Of course, my apologies." I sit and adjust my tie again for want of something to do. If I settle my hands, I'm afraid someone will see them trembling.

With a tap, my father draws up a file and slides it into the middle of the table. Though I can't read the font from where I sit, I recognize the form: Termination of Intent to Propose. I clasp my hands under the table. I know where this is going.

"You broke things off with Dr. Madera?" Dad leans on the table and stares directly across it, at me.

"Yes."

"Why?"

I glimpse the horror frozen on Dutch and Mariah's faces. I have to fight to keep the same off of mine. I'm dizzy and cold and warm and light-headed, suddenly and simultaneously. I clear my throat and breathe deep, sit up straighter.

"Is this something we need to talk about here? I don't want to take up any more of the Board's time than necessary." I smile for good measure.

"Yes, Alex, I'm afraid it is. As I and others have explained many times, who you partner with affects not only our company's reputation, but also its finances. The stability of your personal life has direct bearing on your potential as CEO. Now, we are all allowed to figure ourselves out, determine the kind of person we want to partner with."

"Dad, please," I say more sternly than I should in front of others. But for goodness' sake, he's embarrassing me. Dutch and Mariah avoid my eyes when I look to them. Did they know about this? If there was discussion—no, they wouldn't have.

"You're turning thirty, this month, Alex. You've worked at Bishop Laboratories all your life and will see it into the future. From that seat, you will influence the lives of billions of Americans. They will look to you to make responsible decisions, both for the company and your private life."

"I am aware," I say, stiffly. "There are plenty of other options that we can discuss later—"

"Our lawyers don't see as many options as you'd think. Fortunes are fragile. The wrong match could easily topple everything we've worked for." Dad folds his hands and looks thoughtfully at them. "Given that, we are willing to give you more time—the public will understand that recovery is necessary after a breakup—but meanwhile, we, the Board, would like you to invest in a personal Docile as a symbol of your commitment to this company."

As if my work doesn't follow me home enough—and I do like my work, but a man needs a break. That's one of the reasons I terminated my relationship with Javier. He was always over or out with me. Always around and never engaging enough that I wouldn't rather have spent the time alone. So what if he was perfect on paper? I'm the one who would've had to live with him for the rest of my life.

"I don't need a personal Docile. I work with thousands of them, every day."

"Then," Dad continues, "you're welcome to review the remaining, eligible partners—"

"No."

"Appearances matter, Alex. You know that. The CEO of Bishop Laboratories will be perceived as incompetent—naked—without a partner or a Docile on his arm." Dad stands, pushes his chair back, and motions for the waiting Docile to bring his jacket. "If you cannot handle dating, and you cannot handle a Docile, then you cannot handle Bishop Laboratories." He adjusts his scarf and dons his hat. "For now, I suggest you think about what this company, and your place within it, means to you."

As he leaves, I suppress the urge to defend myself. To pull up progress charts and statistics, all my carefully crafted plans. If he isn't going to listen, I'll have to adjust. I can do this—I can play along, prove how serious I am about the company's future and that I can work with the Board. I can use this opportunity to invest in a personal Docile whom I can inject with Formula 3.0. Use him to show everyone what I can do. What my legacy will be.

I've been waiting at the ODR for fifteen minutes when a white woman dressed like a flight attendant enters the lobby through a door marked "Employees Only." She approaches me, then squeezes the handle of her white cane and retracts its laser length. "Dr. Bishop?"

"Yes. Call me Alex," I say, extending a hand.

"I'm Charlene Williams, your Patron Liaison." She shimmies
the lanyard of her white cane into the crook of her elbow and we
shake hands. "I hope I haven't kept you waiting too long."

"No," I lie because I'm polite. "Not at all." I would've sat, but
the plastic-covered chairs were not encouraging. Like most government entities, the Office of Debt Resolution is housed in a
half-restored historic building. Though the façade is painted mint
green and the decorative floral architecture restored, its insides
are furnished with unraveling carpets, outdated filing systems,
and the slight scent of mildew.

Luckily, Bishop Laboratories has a bid on an exclusive contract
with the ODR for renovations. Looking around, I see the need
is more dire than anticipated. If corporate representatives and
people of means don't feel welcome at the ODR, fewer will become
Patrons, and debt will spiral out of control, again, which is the opposite of our aims. But Charlene seems kind and eager to help and
none of this is her fault, so I don't mention it.

"Your father's asked me to work as an intermediary between
the ODR and Bishop Labs, so I've compiled a list of Docile profiles
based on the memo your assistant transmitted." Charlene hands
me a thick tablet with a rubbery case, squeezes the handle of her
white cane, again, and leads me down the hall, the laser scanning
side to side.

"Thank you." I scan the selected men's photos and those statistics that preview alongside them. I tap the profiles of those I find
physically unattractive and delete them from the queue, followed
by those who never attended an accredited school and those without much debt. If I am going to do this, I'm going to do it right. I
fake my enthusiasm for enough people that I lack the energy to do
the same for a partner or Docile.

"Have you made your selections?" Charlene opens the door to a
room marked "Patron Lounge."

I glance at the few remaining profiles and feel disinterest stirring in me. "Is there a master database I can browse?"

"Yes. Technically." She takes the tablet from me. "Though I've been advised that you're supposed to select from the prescreened profiles I showed you."

"I'd love to do exactly that, Charlene, but . . ." I search for the right words, not wanting her to tell my father—or the Board—that I was being difficult. I have to assume they tapped her, directly, to handle my case. "This Docile will be injected with the developing Formula 3.0, so I can't pick just anyone. He needs to be in enough debt to accept a life term, smart enough so that I can subject him to periodic tests when he returns, sober, from family visitations, attractive enough to accompany me from political functions to Board meetings, and after-parties. If I'm going to accomplish the tasks set forth by my father and the other Board members, I must be allowed to select my subject."

I swallow hard, hoping she buys my speech. Why do I feel like I'm back in high school, bullshitting a paper? I'm better than this.

Charlene pushes the tablet back into my hands. "I must not have given you the correct selections. My apologies." A smile tugs at the corner of her mouth.

It takes me longer than it should to understand. Charlene is ambitious. I'm the Bishop who'll oversee the ODR's renovations, should we win the contract with them, and I'll be the one to appoint capable employees to help us. I accept the favor and file it away for later, as she intends.

Charlene waits patiently while I scroll through the full database, narrowing down my options, then sorting by the most recent arrivals. I see him right at the top of my results—the one I want. I know because I find myself thinking, when I tap his profile, even if he's a bit too skinny or attended an unaccredited school, that I can still work with that.

His photo isn't like the others'; it's not staged. Strands of dark brown stick up from his freshly cut hair, like someone had just run their fingers through it. Probably a caseworker—not him. He stands in his clothes like he's not wearing any, slightly hunched, arms crossed in front of his body. Covering himself as if his tee shirt and jeans are painted on his bare skin. Unlike the Board's selections, he's imperfect. His white skin is freckled and pink, if not sunburnt despite it being winter, and though a thin layer of gloss coats his lips, they're cracked and dry.

Not all Patrons can afford to pay off as much debt as he has, but I can afford all of his time. Long enough that his lips will heal and soften. The Board wants me to invest, and this one will be an investment on multiple levels. "I've made my selection, Charlene, thank you." I hand her the tablet.

She runs her fingers over the surface, then cocks her head. "Only one?"

"Yes." I anchor myself with the word, remind myself that I'm Alexander Bishop III and not only do I get what I want, but I know what I'm fucking doing. "Only one. Only Elisha."

Elisha's not wearing a shirt when I enter the small, windowless room. He tenses, still standing, as I take the chair opposite him. It's different being in the room with him. I have to remind myself of my confidence. He's no different from the Dociles I work with every day.

Except I have to win this one's favor.

I take a deep breath, then beckon him over with the crook of my finger. "Put that shirt back on and have a seat."

He breathes out—possibly for the first time since I entered the room—and scrambles to comply. I do my best to examine his body without being too obvious. I'm either the hero offering him comfort and privacy, or the stranger making him feel uncomfortable, and wouldn't he rather sign with the former?

"My name's Alex; what's yours?" I ask, even though I already know.

"Elisha," he says.

"Nice to meet you." I hadn't decided whether I was going to keep his name until I heard him say it. Most Patrons don't, and at Bishop Labs we assign them numbers. On-meds don't know the difference and it helps to distance Patrons from their Dociles' pasts. It's a business relationship. There are boundaries.

"You too," he says, probably a lie, and right now I need him to be honest if I'm going to make an informed decision. Debtors have been known to lie to fetch a higher price, but that's not my only motivation. I want a feel for his voice, his demeanor—before the Dociline smooths it all down. Formula 2.0 only does so much; it makes people more willing, more at ease, more comfortable. It doesn't invent skills or knowledge, and strong negative personality traits have been known to pierce through. Otherwise, I wouldn't even bother talking to them; I'd just pick the prettiest one.

"I'm going to ask you a few basic questions and I want you to answer honestly."

"O-okay."

"I work with Dociles, so there's nothing you can say that'll surprise me. I just want to make sure we're a good match. Does that work for you?"

He nods.

"I'd appreciate if you'd answer me out loud."

"Yes—sorry." He squeezes his eyes shut and shakes his head, berating himself. "Yes."

"No big deal," I say, hoping to put him back at ease. I pull up his profile on the tablet and review it.

"You have no criminal record outside your debt history—complaints from creditors, a few police citations, including a home visit fourteen years ago—is that correct?"

"Yes."

"Good." His record is standard, cleaner than most debtors'. Plenty resort to theft and violence in their desperation. I will not have one of those types in my house, even on Dociline.

"I see you attended an unaccredited school." My only reservation about him. Schooling in the counties is often spotty at best. "Would you mind elaborating on your education?"

Elisha rubs his left shoulder with his right hand—a guarded position. He remains that way while he explains. "We were only unaccredited because we couldn't afford to pay state-certified teachers, but I learned the basics: reading, writing, math, local history."

I wouldn't describe those as "the basics," but it's better than nothing.

"How long did you attend?"

"I completed all the compulsory grades, first through eighth. After that, I attended night classes. Had to work during the day."

"What kind of work?"

"Whatever was asked of me." He shrugs. "Clearing weeds, cutting wood, tending the animals, mending clothes or houses. In my free time, I tutored those who couldn't make it out to the schoolhouse."

"And you're healthy?" People with chronic illnesses have been known to scam the system, selling themselves for the required medical care. Sometimes a Docile's healthcare costs the Patron more than their debt. I'm not looking for *that* much of an investment.

"Yes."

"Good. Do you have domestic experience? Cooking, cleaning, that sort of thing."

"Yes. I managed most of the household while my—" He stops and bites his bottom lip, unsure if he's supposed to continue.

"While?" I can't make him tell me anything about his life, but now I want to know.

Elisha sits up straighter. "While my mom was serving her term. For ten years."

I force myself to say, "Good," rather than probe. This is a business relationship, I remind myself. His history won't matter once he's on Dociline. "I only have a few more questions; then you can ask me yours."

"Okay." He tucks his hands under his legs and leans forward, opening himself up to me. For the first time he appears interested.

"Are you attracted to any specific gender?" The more the better, to be honest. Not only do I plan to fuck him, but it's expected I'll share him with others at social events. Already I'm not looking forward to it.

"Men," he says, tentatively.

Too tentatively. I wait while he reconsiders.

"Men?" It's almost a question. He looks up, lips moving slightly, as if he's counting to himself. "I notice men."

"Sounds like you don't have any sexual experience."

He shakes his head and tucks a stray hair behind his ear before remembering he's supposed to answer me out loud. "No. I do experience sexual attraction; I've just never had a chance to . . ."

Elisha blushes as he forces his eyes to meet mine, and suddenly I'm imagining him shirtless, in my room, on my bed. I wonder what he looks like naked, what all those freckles and muscles would feel like against my skin.

I hold his gaze. "Had a chance to what?"

"Have sex."

I let the word "sex" hang in the air.

"Are you attracted to me?" I ask, finally. A dangerous question. If he says no, I'm not sure I'll be able to proceed, and then I'll have to resort to one of the Board's picks. For the first time during this interview, he holds the power.

After a few seconds of consideration, he says, "I find you attractive."

"Good." I let my breath out slowly to hide my relief.

I debate asking what he thinks of me as a person, but it's clear he's torn and I don't want to tip the scales out of my favor. Elisha has more debt, less education, and less experience than the pre-approved Dociles my assistant sent over. But under his calluses, I see an opportunity to show my father, and the Board, what I can do. That I'm capable of handling my personal and work life. That with enough determination, I can turn a desperate debtor into the perfect Docile. With Formula 3.0, Elisha will become my legacy.

4

ELISHA

"Elisha!" Carol waves me into her cramped office. A mixture of papers and tablets crowd the desk and filing cabinets. "Sit down. Glad you found me in this maze of a building. I have good news."

I can't return her smile, because any good news also means the end of my freedom. A small piece of me had hoped to drag out the process, unwind my nerves.

"Each Patron who interviewed you made an offer, though I have a feeling you'll only be interested in one." She hands me a tablet—the nicest one I've ever held.

I grip the sides tightly, afraid to drop something I can't afford to replace. "What do I press?"

"Oh, right there, hon." She taps a spot on the screen and it lights up. "Move your finger up and the page will follow."

I forget how to read for a moment. The letters are jumbled squiggles. What am I looking for? A name, an amount, a term length.

I see it underlined: <u>William Barth, three million dollars, thirty years.</u> I'll be fifty-one when I'm free.

"Thirty years is an extremely generous offer for three million."

I tap Barth's picture and it fills the screen. He's the one who asked about manual labor; I recognize him now that I'm less nervous, now that I can put a name with a face. The work doesn't scare me—I do enough, already—but, staring at his name, now, I realize I've heard it before, from folks at the farmer's market. How he'll buy anyone's debt—quantity over quality. Then it doesn't matter if a few can't keep up. If they get injured or die.

At least my family would get to keep the money. Patrons are supposed to take care of your health—Second Right. They break it, they buy it.

"By law, you're required to view all offers before making a decision," Carol says. "And you're allowed to wait if none of these appeal to you. But I don't know if another like Barth's will come around again. He doesn't usually bid so high."

"Where are the others?" I set the tablet down and Carol taps to a window with Patron photos, each representing a different offer.

My fingers slip across the glass surface, slick with sweat. There he is. Alex—I read his last name aloud—"'Bishop.'"

"Hm?" Carol cranes her neck to look as I touch his picture.

I skim his offer the second it appears. <u>Dr. Alexander Bishop III, three million dollars, life term.</u> My whole life. I'd die in this stranger's house, without my family.

My fingers brush the screen and another underline catches my eye. "'Docile's immediate family will receive a monthly stipend of one thousand dollars for the duration of his life, revocable at the Patron's discretion.' Is that normal?" I ask Carol.

Her face twists in discomfort. "No. And, paired with a life term, I admit, I'm suspicious of his intentions."

"What do you mean by that?"

"Elisha, do you know who he is?"

"A trillionaire?"

"Not just any trillionaire. His family owns Bishop Laboratories." When I don't react, Carol leans across the desk. "They make Dociline."

"Oh." *Oh.*

And I'm going to say no. Can I say no to him? *Will I,* when it comes down to it? If I can, this might be my best offer. I shudder remembering the woman who wanted to buy me as a pet for her daughter.

I take the tablet and read the entire contract again. With a thousand dollars a month, my sister might be able to afford the University of Maryland if they saved properly and she took a job. It might incur some extra debt, but it would also get her a real job in Baltimore City, where she might make enough to pay it off.

"I get two visits home per year," I say. I've already memorized every Docile-related law and regulation; I know the answer's yes.

"Yes," Carol says anyway, "but keep in mind this is a life term. With Barth's offer you'll be free by your fifties. You can retire with your family."

"On what, my nonexistent savings?"

Carol sits back; hurt creases her face.

"I'm sorry, I didn't mean to snap at you."

"I've had worse. People aren't at their best once they've registered with the ODR, and I can't blame them."

We both look at the contract in my hands. "If I live until I'm eighty that's about sixty years of stipend. With twelve months in a year it comes out to . . . seven hundred twenty thousand dollars." Alex Bishop is exactly what I came looking for: a trillionaire who'll use me for sex rather than dangerous labor, and is willing to pay extra for the privilege. "How do I accept his offer?"

Carol waits with me on the sidewalk. The others who've signed contracts boarded the bus for delivery hours ago, but Alex left instructions that he would send a private car.

"Stop playing with it." She swats my arm away from my back before I can scratch between my shoulder blades again. That's where they implanted the ID and GPS microchip. People do the same thing to dogs.

"I can't stop thinking about it," I confess.

"You will shortly, trust me." She wrangles my hand into hers in order to hold me still.

I squeeze back. People in brightly colored suits brush past us, not giving me a second look over their pastel ties and floral scarves. If they stand still too long beside the painted ODR, they clash with it. None of them know where I'm going or what's just happened to me. It hasn't even hit me, yet.

When a black car pulls up, Carol tightens her grip. It parks and an older white man exits the driver's seat. "I've never ridden in a car before," I say, because anything else I'd express would be pure terror.

Carol hugs me before I can let go. "You'll be fine; I know you will."

I nod in the crook of her shoulder. "I have the ODR's contact just in case."

"Call me if there are any violations of your rights." She stands back. "I don't usually say goodbye."

"What's the point?" I shrug. The driver opens the back door for me. "Most people won't remember you anyway."

She looks like she's going to cry. I feel like I'm going to throw up. Somehow, I get in the car. The driver closes the door and I immediately start swiping my fingers over the panels on the door. A lock clicks; lights dim. One of these has to— The window rolls down.

"I'll remember you, Carol," I say.

Her waving figure is cut off as the window rises, not by my doing.

"Windows up. For your own safety," the driver says. "And fasten your seat belt."

I look at the seat for a belt. Finding nothing, I meet his eyes in the mirror again.

"Behind you, on the right."

It's exactly where he says. A belt stretches out when I pull, clicking into a metal end on my other side.

"Thank you," I say, trying to get comfortable. It's not hard. The leather warms beneath me, the air around me. The strap is a little annoying, but I don't dare remove it.

People rush around outside, swinging briefcases and drinking coffee from paper cups. I've never understood why someone would throw away a perfectly good cup after using it once. Everything is disposable here, even people.

I watch through the window as families wait at crosswalks that look freshly painted in order to reach towering glass buildings on the piers along the harbor. Beside the water, there's a giant building people call the Power Plant. It's not a plant, anymore. All the working-class people must've been pushed out so the rich could gut it for fun. Restaurant signs are attached to the painted brick— salmon colored, probably to remind folks of the sea—with a giant guitar fixed to the top. It's not like the ones my father and his friends play, but sleek and shiny, like it might launch into space.

We stop at several shops and spas before reaching a tall red building that faces the water. Its painted marble is shaped into flourishes and flowers along the doors and windows, not unlike the buildings that surround it. This time, when I get out of the car— still raw from the waxing and plucking and scrubbing—the driver unpacks the bags of clothes and hands them to a doorman. Standing on the sidewalk, I tilt my head back until I'm staring almost into the sun. Beneath the roof, human figurines guard the building's corners—or they hold it up.

I want to ask if this is Alex's house, but I've barely spoken a word since leaving Carol behind at the ODR. For all I know, these people will report my behavior, and I don't know my new Patron well enough to gauge his reaction.

"Dr. Bishop left this for you." The doorman hands me a small, sealed envelope, then resumes loading my shopping bags into a trolley.

I take it and press my finger under its seal. "Thank you." The paper's so nice, it takes me a minute to rip the envelope open.

I read the handwritten script quietly to myself: "'Take the elevator to the top floor. Stand beside the window and look over the harbor. Do not turn around—wait for me. Alex.'" I fold the thick note between my shaking fingers, hoping there is only one window, and that I don't suddenly have to pee or need a drink of water, or anything that requires me to turn from the window.

When I look up from the note, I realize I am alone. The doorman's gone. I could run. I'm free and undrugged. The only thing that can force me to follow Alex's instructions is myself.

I step into the waiting elevator.

The microchip in my back would be used to locate me the instant

I ran. They'd find me. Alex would be unhappy with me, and the rest of my life would begin miserably. He could withhold the monthly stipend—even if it's pennies to him. That's what the contract said.

When I press the button for the highest floor, it lights up and a soothing, electronic voice says, "Welcome, Elisha."

I almost reply before telling myself it can't hear me; it's a machine. And, yet, it knows my name.

"Penthouse," the elevator announces with a ding.

When I walk forward it's not with dread but wonder. The entire outside wall is glass. I feel like a god looking out over the city. Ships in the harbor look like toys, floating in a bathtub. I can see right down through the triangular glass of the Aquarium's rainforest exhibit; I asked Dad to take me so many times as a kid, but even when we all had bikes to travel into the city, the ticket price was too steep.

My new shoes slip on the polished hardwood floor as I wander closer for a better look. Every step I take forward is another I can't take back. *Don't turn around.* My eyes wander over marble countertops, plush navy furniture, soft light from invisible sources. As soon as I reach that glass, I'm committed to the view until Alex shows up. I close my eyes and breathe deep, clinging to the last few second—minutes, hours?—that are my own.

But the light scent of vanilla and wood invades my nostrils, reminding me I'm in someone else's home. And not just four walls to keep out animals and a roof to stop the rain. This is not a shelter; it's for pleasure. And I'm another decoration, picked out to complement the space.

I wait. Outside, the sunlight moves across the water.

The soft ping of the elevator might as well be thunder. I stare even harder at the ant-sized people below, determined not to turn around. Behind me, footsteps echo off the high ceilings.

Don't look. I can't look. I want to look. I have to remind myself to breathe. My heart races faster than a car. Even when the room falls quiet, I know I'm not alone.

5

ALEX

Elisha stares out the window, hands clasped formally behind his back. His skin is still pink from the salon, but the clothes do him justice; they're colorful, pressed, formfitting. He should be comfortable, and yet he's so stiff, I imagine he'd tip right over if I prodded.

I shrug off my coat and open the closet as quietly as possible, like he might run away if I make a noise. I can't scare him off—he can't even leave. He's my responsibility, now. The realization settles into my body like the first shot of alcohol on a night out: warm, invigorating, dangerous. I can do this—want to do this. This is not a punishment; it's an opportunity.

Quietly, I close the closet door and roll up my sleeves as I go to join him. Continuing to follow my instructions, he doesn't turn around. I linger behind him. What do I say, *Hope you had a good ride? How was the spa? Good to see you?*

We're still strangers.

"What do you think of the view?" I ask, unsure whether small talk is the right choice.

"It's beautiful." The natural timbre of Elisha's voice throws me off.

He's not on Dociline—not until tonight. Maybe that's why it feels so weird, standing next to him like we're in a bar and I'm trying to pick him up. After I inject him, it'll be easier. He'll be happy simply standing there, waiting for my next instruction. Fulfilled rather than stiff and nervous. It's making *me* nervous. I chose a Docile over a husband because the latter requires emotional labor that I don't have time for and now I'm pulling my weight, anyway.

Get over it, Alex. It's just for one night.

"The inside's not bad, either," I say, finally. "Follow me. I'll show you around."

He follows me into the kitchen, where I point out appliances camouflaged into the room's woods and whites, all clean for this evening's party. I slide a recessed wine rack out from between the pantry and the refrigerator, grab a bottle of red—don't even check the label. Elisha watches while I set a wine glass down on the kitchen island.

Before I know it, I'm asking him, "Do you want one?"

I set down a second wine glass, not waiting for his response.

"Um." He looks around like someone's going to catch him drinking on the job. There are no other rules here, besides mine. "Sure, I guess."

By the time he's answered, I've already filled both glasses. I down half of mine in one gulp. The lump catches in my throat and I feel it push down my esophagus. Across from me, Elisha brings the rim of the glass to his nose and sniffs it, but not like I would at a restaurant, more like a dog sniffing another dog's ass. After watching me finish my glass, he puts his own to his lips and sips.

I pour myself another, store the rest of the bottle in the rack, and push it back into hiding. "You don't need to know much about the kitchen. I've hired a caterer to manage tonight's party."

When he doesn't ask what kind of party, I go on, anxious to fill the silence. "A birthday party."

More silence.

"It's my birthday."

For the first time, Elisha's face relaxes. He almost smiles. "Happy birthday."

"Thank you." The wine is already absorbing into my bloodstream and loosening me up, excising my anxiety. I take advantage of it and explain: "After we finish the tour, I'm going to run a few last-minute errands while the caterers set up. I'll be back in time to introduce you to . . ." No point in explaining to Elisha who everyone is. He won't really remember once I inject him. "Everyone."

"Okay," he says. Clearly, that was enough for him.

Elisha follows me upstairs, silently and slowly, trying not to spill his wine, his glass still almost full. I wait at the top of the steps, looking down on my home, out its floor-to-ceiling windows, and at the younger man whose debt I purchased.

He glances up at me and smooths back a strand of hair threatening to liberate itself from its new sleek style. His lips are slightly reddened with wine, face slightly flushed. I remember why I picked him and how this won't be *all* work. Once he's dosed up, we will definitely play.

"This is my bedroom." I wander in, at ease in my most private space. Though the bed is made and my clothing hung, my personal laptop still rests on the blue-gray down comforter and a rocks glass sits on a coaster on the nightstand. Remnants of last night's Scotch stain its bottom.

I glance over my shoulder to see Elisha lingering at the threshold. "You are allowed in," I say, though he knows that. He eyes the bed with trepidation, standing as far away as he dares.

"You'll sleep in here with me." I walk to the left side of my bed frame and kneel to point out the adjustment I had made. "This is your bed." When I wave my hand over a sensor, the trundle glides out silently, already fitted with matching bedding. Elisha doesn't react to our sleeping arrangements, which, I admit, are more intimate than the capsule bed setup Mariah keeps, or the separate rooms Dutch's Dociles sleep in.

"The only other rooms, up here, are the bathroom and my office." I point to both of their doors in turn. "The latter of which is always locked when I am not using it. Do you have any questions?" I ask. He looks nervous, still, though I feel much better with twelve ounces of wine in me. "I'd rather you ask now. I'll be busy entertaining guests later, and will expect you to handle yourself."

Thirty slow seconds pass.

"Yes," Elisha says. "What do I do, tonight, exactly? Follow you around? Wait upstairs? Are there any guidelines . . ."

I blanch like a schoolboy who's forgotten his homework. Rules. I should've thought up rules. I finish my wine and set it on the nightstand. "Yes." I can make shit up on the fly. I do this kind of thing all the time for investors and reporters and people who ask me how I'm doing.

"I'll put the rules up on the wall for you to study while I'm running errands. Memorize them." I sit at my small writing table, pull a touch keyboard up on its surface, and begin to type.

1. Always answer aloud when people address you, and do so honestly.
2. Do not speak unless spoken to.
3. Consult me, first, if someone makes a request of you.

I hesitate, debating whether that is enough, before adding one more.

4. If you require my attention for a non-emergency, say, "Excuse me, Alex," and wait for me to address you. Always speak up in an emergency.

There. That'll last the night. Good job, Alex. "If you have further questions about any of the rules, now is the time to ask them."

Elisha bites his thumbnail while he rereads the rules.

"Don't do that," I say. "I just had them manicured."

He removes his finger from his mouth and forces his hand to his side. "Is there a certain way you want me to stand or sit when I'm not doing anything?"

Good question. "Yes," I say before even having thought of the answer. Thank god he won't remember any of this once he's on Dociline. This time, I take a cue from Dutch, who treats his two Dociles more like pets than sex toys. "Unless otherwise directed, you are to sit on the floor beside me or stand with your hands clasped either in front of or behind your body. And look at me when we speak to each other."

"Okay," Elisha says, reviewing the rules one last time. "Will I be . . ." He hesitates, trying to form his question.

I'm enraptured simply watching him think.

"Will I be expected to do *things* at the party?"

"Like, entertain?"

"No, like . . ." He shrugs, looks between the bed and the ceiling, stuffs his hands in his pockets.

Oh. I know where this is going. "Say it."

Elisha flushes rose gold. "Like, sex?" He sets his half-full wine glass on the writing table and folds his hands together to quiet their trembling. He can't even look at me. "I've heard stories."

Once Elisha gets some Dociline in his blood, he won't be so nervous. Correction: he won't be nervous at all. I almost wish I'd been on Dociline for my first time. I'd gladly forget a few of my first partners.

He straightens as I walk toward him, hands still in his pockets, eyes on the floor, then me, then the floor, and then me, again—I draw so close he startles backwards. I reach out, instinctively, to catch him. This is the closest Elisha and I have ever been. I can feel the heat from his skin, hear the arrhythmia of his breath.

"Have you ever kissed anyone?"

"No," he says.

I hadn't been planning on being intimate with Elisha until he injected Dociline, until he was obedient and eager. But a selfish part of me wants him to remember this. To feel it fully.

I tilt his head back until we're looking into each other's eyes, and then at each other's lips. His are flushed, like rose petals beneath mine, and part easily when I kiss him. He nuzzles my hand when I rest it against the side of his face. Suddenly, I'm struck by how much trust he's placed in me. He anticipated this—and more. Sought it, even. And I've barely thought through tonight.

I pull back first. His cheeks and lips ripen with blood.

"Now you have," I say.

I release him and walk to the door, pausing at the threshold. "The caterers are due any minute. Do not go downstairs or interact with them. Guests will begin to arrive in two hours. I expect you'll have memorized the rules by the time I return." I check my watch. "Be here, in this room, at six forty-five."

I leave without the option for further questions. If I stay, I worry I won't be able to improvise any longer. And that I'll want to kiss him, again.

ELISHA

My eyes bounce between the rules and the clock. It's 6:40, and Alex doesn't seem like the type to be late. Everything here is so neat. Nothing stands out—even my bed is tucked away. Invisible, silent. Nothing takes up space in this immaculate house. Not for long. Not once I refuse Dociline.

6:41: I wonder if I should be standing when he arrives.

Alex said, *Be here*. Technically, I'm here.

He didn't say to sit down. I don't want him to think I'm too comfortable or lazy or—

Did it say anything in the rules about standing and sitting when he's not around?

I skim them again, glance at the clock, run a finger over my lips. I can't stop thinking about the kiss—about how warm and sure his lips were against mine. How I liked it. How I shouldn't have liked it.

The elevator dings. I'm suddenly light-headed. What if I forget a rule? Did I decide to stand up or keep studying? I can't remember.

I stand and push the armchair in, so it looks like I've been standing the whole time. My heart beats against my eardrums as Alex climbs the stairs.

I'm supposed to stand with my hands clasped if he's around. My hands close behind my back.

The door opens.

Alex walks right past me and sets a black box on his nightstand. I immediately wonder what's inside, then bite my lip to stop myself from asking. Rule number two: don't speak unless spoken to. I glance over my shoulder as Alex rustles through a bag. He catches me when he surfaces, holding a pile of folded clothing and a pair of shoes.

"Put these on." He presses them into my arms.

"Okay."

"And it's unbecoming of a Docile to peek around. Suppress your curiosity, for the night."

How am I supposed to do that? Elisha Wilder: the first man to suppress hundreds of thousands of years of human instinct. I hold the shoes so tightly, the laces dig into my arm. "Sorry," I manage to say. "I will." A lie. I'm not supposed to lie, but it's what he wants to hear.

"I know it's difficult," Alex says, and I momentarily feel better, until, "The Dociline should help."

My lips part—just enough to fake a breath and not betray speech. I'm torn between Carol's advice not to tell anyone I'm going to refuse Dociline and Alex's first rule, that I always answer honestly.

He hasn't directly asked.

This is the one thing I can hold on to. It's my right to refuse.

"You may change in the bathroom," he says. "And don't touch your hair."

"Okay, thank you," I say, still unsure how to respond to commands. But it satisfies Alex, so I disappear into the bathroom and turn the lock. I barely have time to set the clothes down when there's a knock on the door. I open it to Alex.

"Don't lock doors," he says, then pushes it closed.

I clench my hands into fists, but resist slamming them against the door. This is how it's going to be, from now on. Following Alex's rules, living to his standards. *Don't lock doors*—I want to tell him to fuck off, but I suppress my feelings. Good practice for the rest of my life.

I pull off a shirt that isn't mine and replace it with another, wiggle into sleek pants that fit tighter than any I would own. My hair doesn't belong to me. I wouldn't have touched it before he had it styled, but I don't touch it now because I can't. This is Alex's hair, Alex's shirt, pants, designer underwear.

"Elisha" can't exist in this form, anymore. Not if I want to survive. I have to retreat into this body—into the few parts of the mind that aren't Alex's. The parts where my heart beats and memories live.

The door startles me when it swings open. "Finished?"

I nod, quickly followed by a verbal "Yes." Rule number one.

"Come here; let me see." Alex beckons and I follow.

He adjusts the seams of my button-down shirt, lining them up with my shoulders. It unbuttons lower than I'm used to, makes me feel naked even though it's only my collarbone and a hint of chest. I don't dare try to cover up.

I suck my stomach in when Alex grabs my belt. He unbuckles it, tightening the leather a notch. The khaki pants sit right above my hips, crisp and soft, with a line pressed down the front of each leg.

He tucks the shirt back into them. "What's rule number four?"

"I should say, 'Excuse me, Alex,' if I need your attention, and wait for you to address me. Unless it's an emergency."

"Good. What if I sit down to eat?"

"I should sit beside you, on the floor."

"Good. Stand like you would if I were speaking with a group of people."

I clasp my hands behind my back. The stance makes me feel exposed, even though I'm only with Alex.

Only with Alex? Did I really think that? He's still a stranger, one who holds my life and my family's finances in his manicured hands. I'm stupid to think I'm safe around him.

"Excellent," he says.

At least I've passed the oral exam.

"How do you feel?"

The polite response is *good, thank you.* It's what I'd have said to any Patron who interviewed me. Not Alex, though. I give him the honesty he says he wants.

"Nervous."

"Why?"

Why does he think? "I'm afraid I'll forget a rule."

"Don't be. You have them memorized."

If we were really having a conversation, I'd say, "*Doesn't matter. I'm still terrified.*" But he hasn't asked me any further questions, so I can't speak up.

I bite my lip.

Alex catches the movement like a skilled hunter. "Don't do that in public."

"Sorry."

"One last thing." He glances at the door. Voices have begun to fill the downstairs. "Not everyone is like me. Some of my guests may have different expectations of you than I do. Their expectations do not matter. They do not hold your contract and they are not the ones who will discipline you if you do not live up to their standards. I am. I'm the only one whose opinion matters. Remember that."

"I will."

"Good." Alex takes a deep breath, like he's about to jump off the rocks into the reservoir. "Then, let's go."

I clasp my hands so tightly behind me, my fingers numb. My whole body tingles, as if my heart has sucked up all the blood in my veins. That's why it's throbbing in my chest—like a blood bomb waiting to explode.

Electronic music rises to meet us as we descend the stairs. I don't know the artist; we only get the news radio station out where I live. *Lived.*

People stand in groups around tall tables with tiny plates on them. I ignore my stomach when it growls. Haven't eaten since the ODR this morning.

That was only this morning? Sixty more years . . .

"Alex!" My head turns at his name, because I'm not my own person, tonight. I'm his shadow.

"Dutch, hey!" Alex shakes hands with another white guy who shares his shade of tan, topped off with slicked-back brown hair that's so dark it's nearly black. Green and white stripes trim his navy-blue blazer. His smile unnerves me.

I was counting on standing beside Alex quietly, so it catches me off guard when his friend Dutch points at me. "Who's this?"

"This is my new Docile." Alex steps aside so this man can see me. "Elisha."

He didn't teach me how to introduce myself, so I say nothing.

"Elisha, huh?" Dutch says. "You mind?"

Mind? Mind what?

"Not at all." Alex gestures to me.

What does he not mind? I look to him for any hint, but Alex is only watching. He's on their side, not mine. Dutch runs his hand through my hair—the hair I'm not allowed to touch—traces his hands down the sides of my neck and out across my shoulders, stopping only to squeeze my arms.

He makes a smug, satisfied face at Alex, then continues. I purse my lips and let my eyes drift upward as he circles my waist. "Not bad," he says. It's almost clinical when he runs his hands over my ass—like he's checking to make sure I have one—except for the slight squeeze.

I grit my teeth and force myself not to flinch. Not to slap his hands away.

"How is he in bed? Bet those lips feel like crushed velvet against your dick."

I expected that Alex would fuck me. I didn't expect that he'd talk about it with other people so openly. As if it isn't hard enough ignoring all instincts to protect myself, I have to pretend I'm not here while they discuss it.

"Remains to be seen," Alex says.

He doesn't meet my desperate glances, but doesn't deepen my humiliation, either, changing the topic. "How's Opal? I heard there was a pregnancy scare."

Dutch's mouth gapes in shock. "I would never violate Sixth Right. Opal is always on her happy pill. Well, my happy pill." He laughs.

I hold down bile. I assume they're talking about his Docile, in which case Dociline is that girl's "happy pill"—whatever her real name is. Can't possibly be Opal.

I try not to listen to the rest of their conversation, tuning my ears to the music and nose to the smell of seafood and spices. Abby and Dylan will be setting the table, about now. Dad and Nora finishing dinner—chicken soup, maybe, if there's any meat left from the weekend's slaughter.

My stomach gurgles again.

"Whoa, I think he's trying to tell you something, Bishop!"

"I wouldn't mind some food, myself," Alex says. "After you, gentlemen." He turns to me. "Elisha, wait for me by the window."

"Yes, Alex." As I turn to obey his "request," I hear Dutch and his buddies joking.

"On a first-name basis already? Are you sure you haven't fucked him, yet?"

I focus on a cruise ship, below. Inside, figures move amidst colorful, strung-up lights. They don't look like they're dancing to the thumping beat of Alex's party on board the boat, but I pretend because any sound is better than people talking about me.

"Well, well." The smooth voice belongs to a familiar-looking East Asian woman a few inches taller than me, with sleek brown and black curls, and bright pink lips. She blends in with the rest of the guests, wearing a fitted short-sleeve dress that matches her lipstick, patterned with neon-green palm leaves. The colors are so bright, I can't look directly at them.

"Looks like Alex went through with it."

I don't reply because she hasn't asked me anything. I do look twice over my shoulder, hoping that Alex will appear.

"Though I don't remember seeing you among our selections," she says. "What does he call you?"

I have to answer. "Elisha."

"Is that your given name?"

"Yes, ma'am."

She smiles, clearly amused. "This your first day? Must be. You don't sound like you're on Dociline."

"Yes, ma'am," I say, skipping over her implication that I'll be drugged before the night's over.

"You are in for quite a night."

"Yes, ma'am." My response doesn't quite fit her statement. I sound like my mother.

I startle when Dutch bumps into me from behind. "Bishop, you can't just leave your toys lying around." He makes a show of repositioning himself, brushing a flat hand across my crotch.

Alex catches the momentary horror that flickers across my face, but doesn't return it. He sits on a love seat beside the woman in the neon dress.

I can't afford to panic. What am I supposed to do with myself? Sit. I'm supposed to sit on the floor beside Alex when he's seated, but that means walking past his friend Dutch. The one who can't keep his hands off me.

"Your Docile looks lost," she says.

Alex glances around the room, then lowers his voice as if he might be found out. "I can handle him, Mariah."

As soon as he says her name, I realize where I know her from. Mariah VanBuren, VanBuren Media. Her name and face are on the billboards that line 83. Of course, she didn't introduce herself to me. Why should she? My world consists of sirs, ma'ams, and Alex.

"Elisha." He calls me to his side like a pet.

I go, grateful for the direction, and settle on the carpet beside the sofa. Around me, their conversation carries on. My stomach rumbles again. If I could quiet it, I would.

Suddenly, Alex's hand appears poised in front of my mouth, holding a little ball of crab meat. He's barely paying attention to me, still laughing at whatever joke Mariah has told.

He must want me to take this. It's right in front of my face, and he knows I haven't eaten all day. I reach for it, but he stops me with a slight shake of his head. What am I supposed to do?

Alex lowers the food to my mouth again and I understand. As if it isn't enough to sit at this trillionaire's feet while his friends ogle and touch me, discuss my body and what they'd like to do with it. I eat out of his hands like one of their million-dollar designer dogs. I cost about the same.

Lumps of crab stick to my throat like bugs in sap. Another appears and my jaw drops to accept it. I close my eyes as my lips close around Alex's fingers. He lingers, waiting while I chew. I'm meant to suck his fingers clean. They taste like spices we never had access to on the farm.

"Look at him!" someone says.

A laugh, then, "He loves it."

"Crushed velvet." I hear Dutch's voice over the others.

When Alex draws his hand back, I bury my face in the side of the couch. I'm on fire. The corners of my eyes burn. I want to cry. Tears would feel so good, like ice against my cheeks.

I hate myself, my decision, for keeping my objections to myself, for enjoying Alex's touch, for eating his expensive food and wearing these overpriced clothes.

A hand strokes the side of my head, sliding down the back of my neck. I should jerk away, but instead I lean into Alex's touch. No guests are looking at me, anymore. I close my eyes and relax my forehead against the couch, focusing on the slow circular motions of his fingers.

"Elisha," he says, eventually.

I look up.

"It's time. Come on."

"Coming." I follow him.

The party has only grown. Dead-eyed Dociles glide through the crowd handing out little plates of food and colorful glasses of alcohol to guests dressed in navy, salmon, canary, jade—bold colors crammed together in plaids and stripes, on scarves and belts. I remember the dull TruCare Insurance shirt I ditched at the ODR. Everything is brighter in the city.

"Stay here," Alex says. "I'll be right back." He goes upstairs.

I watch him the whole way, staring at the door even when he disappears through it. I don't think I can handle another guest roping me in for conversation and touching me. Luckily, Alex is quick and no one so much as looks at me.

When he rejoins me, he's holding the black box from earlier. I barely have time to wonder what's inside, before he calls for attention.

"Friends." He raises his glass of bubbly alcohol. "I want to thank you, first, for attending this"—he smiles—"self-indulgent shindig."

The crowd laughs.

"I hope you're all enjoying remaining young while I age."

More laughter. I am expressionless.

"And I want to share an inaugural moment with all of you." He puts a hand on my back. "If you haven't yet had the pleasure of meeting my new Docile, allow me to introduce Elisha."

Now everyone looks at me. I want to duck behind Alex, but he positions me in front of himself.

"This is our first day together, and I look forward to many more."

I'm relieved I'm not forced to agree.

Behind me, Alex is quiet. Though something rustles, I don't dare look. I lift my arms as he reaches around from behind me to un-buckle my belt.

My ears ring, hands tremble. Is he planning to fuck me right here? In front of everyone? An involuntary gasp escapes me when he pushes my khakis down around my thighs.

I can only hear my heart beat; I miss when Alex pulls a chair up behind me.

"Elisha, sit down," he says, as if he's repeating himself.

I can't reply like I'm supposed to. I can barely bend my knees.

Alex rounds the chair, finally, holding a glass vial of yellow liq-uid. He inverts it and stabs a needle through the stopper.

He's not going to have sex with me? That's some kind of medi-cine. What medicine could I possibly need? The ODR vaccinated me against everything.

"This won't hurt." He draws back the plunger.

"Excuse me, Alex?" I say.

A yellow drug fills the plastic tube. He doesn't answer.

"Excuse me, Alex," I say louder, in case he didn't hear me.

Instead, he flicks away any bubbles and opens an alcohol swab. It's cold against my thigh.

"Excuse me, please, Alex." This time I don't wait. He can scold me if he wants. "What is that?"

"Dociline." The accompanying look is meant to quiet me.

But it's my right to say no. This is my one chance to speak up and he can't stop me.

"You need to relax your muscle or this will hurt." He places one hand on my knee to steady me.

I close my eyes and muster up a deep breath. "I respectfully refuse."

"What?"

I open my eyes on his and try not to stutter, but words tumble out of my mouth without thought. "I don't want it. I don't want Dociline. It's my right to refuse."

"Do you know who you're talking to, Docile?" Dutch steps into our space and I recoil, nearly toppling my chair.

"I—"

"This is Dr. Alexander Bishop the Third."

"It's—"

"The CEO of Bishop Laboratories." He stops only inches away, red-faced and pointing.

"Dutch, you don't have to—"

But Dutch grabs the syringe from him and holds it in front of my face. Tiny bubbles pop and disappear inside the translucent yellow drug. I turn my head and, like a photograph, the syringe blurs and the lined faces of Alex's guests come into focus. They murmur among themselves. The woman in the neon dress cringes.

"Bishop Laboratories invented Dociline," Dutch says. "You're going to refuse what this man created for you? After he bought your whole family out of debt?"

"That's enough," Alex says, in the same tone he uses with me.

It affects Dutch similarly. He caps the needle and slaps it down on a side table before disappearing into the crowd with a huff. Alex ignores him as he turns to address his audience.

"All Dociles are guaranteed seven rights, the last of which is the right to refuse or demand Dociline. I knew that when I bought his debt—everyone knows that about any Docile. Elisha's decision is not up for debate. Elisha," Alex says, looking only at me. "Put yourself back together, go stand in my room, and wait for me."

"Yes, Alex." I hurry to my feet, turn away from the crowd, and fasten my pants. They all watch as I go upstairs.

I close the door as quietly as possible and stand there for a minute with my face pressed against the wood, still holding the knob. A few nervous tears rim my eyes. I wipe them on my sleeve and run my hands through my hair before remembering I'm not supposed to touch it.

I'm about to flop down on the bed and curl up on the unwrinkled covers when Alex's words come back to me: *stand in my room.* Does he actually want me to stand, or was it an expression?

When has he used any kind of expression or euphemism with me? Not once since we met. Alex always says exactly what he means. At least that doesn't force me to guess.

I stand in the middle of his room with my arms clasped behind my back. White numbers glow on the wall opposite Alex's bed: 8:30 p.m.

By 9:00, my shoulders ache from the backwards pinch. I stretch my arms over my head and around my chest, then switch, clasping my hands in front of me. The other acceptable position.

At 9:45, I squat down, gluing my eyes to the door in case I need to shoot up.

I walk in a small circle until 10:15, shaking my legs out to get the blood flowing. I try to distract myself by thinking of home, but that only worsens my nerves. When I hold out a hand, it's still wobbly; my ears still ring and the corner of my vision still grays.

At 11:00, I start negotiating with myself. Alex isn't here. I can sit down and he won't even know. If I kneel, all it'll take is a quick roll back onto the balls of my feet and I'm up.

The second my knees hit the floor, the stairs creak and I jump upright. I remain still until 11:15. It's not him. Probably a guest. Dance music seeps up through the floorboards. Every song has the same beat and the same accompanying squeals and chatter.

Come midnight, I'm hugging my right knee to my chest with my eyes closed. Balanced, I breathe in and out. Slowly, I change feet, pulling my left leg against my stomach, holding it there while it tingles. I wriggle my toes inside my new, expensive leather shoes.

The door opens and my eyes follow. I stumble, almost falling over as Alex sets the black box on top of the little writing table. He only looks at me for half a second, jaw set, lips thin, face blanched. Before I can do something stupid, like apologize, he goes into the bathroom and closes the door behind him. I haven't done anything wrong. Never lied, followed all of Alex's rules. And yet the whole room seems to throb with my heartbeat.

7

ALEX

"So, who wants cake?" I say, as soon as my bedroom door closes behind Elisha. But no amount of dessert will help these people forget what just happened. Alexander Bishop's Docile refused Dociline. It'll be all over the media tomorrow—unless Mariah's willing to shut it down. She owns almost every media company in the United States. But that won't stop the endless feed of gossip. Most of my guests aren't like Mariah and Dutch. They don't care about my privacy.

The caterer's Dociles return with slices of dark chocolate cake, trimmed with edible gold leaf. Dragon fruit liqueur filling. I don't even want it, anymore, but I force a smile onto my face and cake into my mouth, just as my parents meander over with my friend Jess between them. Oh god, I can't even look at them. Maybe Jess will save me. She's known my parents almost as long as I have; she knows how they can be.

"Happy birthday, sweetie." Mom kisses my cheek, then passes me off to Jess, who embraces me and kisses the air beside my face. There are few people she likes to touch, but as her oldest friend, I'm one of those she's okay with.

"Sorry we didn't get here earlier," Mom says. "Your father stopped at the lab to pick something up and we found this one"—she points her thumb at Jess—"still working. Can you believe these two?" Mom laughs and shakes her head.

Dad stretches out a hand to shake mine, then pulls me into a tight hug, as if he didn't chastise me in front of the Board the last time we spoke. "Alex understands." He pats my back, then accepts cake from a passing Docile. "It's those Bishop genes."

I smile and rub his shoulder. Maybe he won't mention Elisha's refusal, after all. Maybe I'm—

"Got here in time for the show, though."

Oh no. No, no, no.

"That was something." Dad stuffs a bite of cake in his mouth, watching me expectantly while he chews.

That was *something,* all right. It hasn't even sunken in, yet. Elisha refused Dociline. Seventh Right. I even said it aloud in front of everyone, like I expected it. Of course, I know the Rights by heart; I work with hundreds of Dociles, every day. But this is different. This one is going to live in my house. *Forever.* I'll have to come up with rules—more rules. Ways to keep him in check. And what do I do with him while I'm at work?

"I don't remember seeing Elisha on the list we sent Charlene." Dad finishes his cake, leaving the implication hanging in the air.

Jess locks eyes with me, wondering what I'm going to say just as much as I am. She's my Head of Research for Formula 3.0, which means she didn't have to watch the train wreck that was supposed to be my presentation.

"He, uh . . ." I decide to tell the truth in the span of a single breath. I made a decision; now I need to own it. "He wasn't. None of them were quite what I was looking for."

"And what is it you were looking for?"

I angle my lips into a smile and the conversation into my favor. "An opportunity."

"Really." His eyebrows raise. "Are you going to bring him out in public?"

I scoff, my reaction genuine this time. "Of course." I hand my unfinished cake off to a passing Docile, who doesn't even look up. "Since you were *late,* you didn't get to meet him, earlier, but Elisha is well behaved, intelligent, and presentable." I flash him a confident smile. "I foresee no problems training him for public appearances. Besides, he'll be interesting to study alongside those injecting Formula 3.0. Just like you wanted, an opportunity to prove myself."

Dad nods his head, not pushing it further. I watch Jess' shoulders slump with relief and a light smile grace her lips.

"Well, we'll leave you kids alone, then, and go find the adults' table." He nods and leaves with my mother.

"Holy shit, Alex," Jess whispers.

I offer her my hand, which she contemplates before taking and following me into the bathroom. I close the door behind us and run my sweaty hands through my hair. In here, it's dark and quiet. Calming. "I can do this. Right?"

Jess stops shaking her head and puts on her most convincing face. "Totally!"

"Wow, you are a bad liar." I bite my thumbnail before remembering I just scolded Elisha for doing the same. I squeeze my hand into a fist to halt temptation. "I'll have to bring him to Preakness and at least one big party—Mariah's? She'll be cool about it, right?"

"Yeah, I'm sure she will."

"Really?"

"No, not really. Her parties are basically performance art. If you fuck up, it'll be everywhere."

"Dammit." I bite my thumbnail, again, then dig my nails into my palm as punishment. "Maybe I can take him to the lab. Put him up in a cell."

"That'll look good. Pawning your personal Docile off on work. Dutch told me about the Board meeting. I know this is because you broke up with Javier—which I don't blame you for!" she adds before I can defend myself. "You should get to decide who you partner with. But you've got to see this through. How long did you sign Elisha for?"

"Forever."

"Forever?" Jess' eyes widen. "I mean, yeah. You can—that's a long time, Alex."

Before I slip into self-doubt, again, I say, "No, I can do this. I already have a few rules in place. He follows them." I regurgitate the same lines I used on my parents, hoping to convince myself as much as Jess. "He's attractive and willing and I can do this. It was my decision to purchase Elisha's debt and I'm going to make this work." Somehow.

It's after midnight when the last of my guests leave and I'm forced to face the Docile waiting for me in my bedroom. With a deep breath, I go upstairs and walk right past a disheveled Elisha, into the bathroom. He's been standing for the past four hours; he'll last another four minutes.

Cold water erupts from the faucet when I hold my hands below it. I splash it over my face and run my hands through my hair. Elisha touched his hair. He doesn't know I've noticed yet, but I'll make sure he does. I'll have to discipline him for it.

Without Dociline.

The drug makes things easier for everyone. Certainly would've made tonight easier for me. I pinch the bridge of my nose, hoping to stifle the headache brewing behind my eyes. Alexander Bishop, heir to the Dociline legacy, surprised by some kid from Northern Maryland. Thank god I didn't let on when Elisha refused. To have been caught off guard would have been humiliating.

I can still do it, though. Elisha is intelligent, prone to submission, and if all else fails I'll simply threaten to revoke his monthly stipend. I'm glad I had my attorney look the contract over.

Okay, Alex, pull yourself together. I stare at my reflection, fix my hair, dry my face. I need to fuck him right away, establish that his body is wholly mine. I no longer get to enjoy Elisha's first time; it's now a job I have to do.

I open the door and cross to my closet. Elisha watches me peel my shirt off.

"Come here," I say.

He obeys, trying hard not to stare at me. I steady him, resting my hands on his waist. Little hairs rise under my touch as I unbutton his shirt and slide it off his shoulders.

"Up." I have to encourage him to raise his arms.

Elisha immediately crosses his arms in front of his bare chest. That's not what I paid for. If I have to train him, I'm doing it right, from the start.

"Don't." He opens back up for me with only a light touch. "Don't hide your body from me."

Without Dociline, he's shy, nervous. I need to build his confidence without building his ego. So, I pull him close and run my hand through his already-messed-up hair. "I enjoy looking at you," I say, our faces only inches apart. "Or you wouldn't be here."

I reach between our bodies and grasp his belt, undressing him so he knows I'm free to do so whenever I please. He watches the pants disappear into my hamper. No hiding, now.

While I unfasten my pants, Elisha fidgets with the underwear I picked for him. The thousand-dollar briefs frame his bulge so nicely, I almost don't want him to take them off. Almost. Maybe this won't be so difficult. Or, at least, it will be enjoyable at the same time.

I press our cocks together through the thin layers of fabric. We're both aroused. But even though I'd like to bend him over my bed and end this exhausting night with a hard fuck, I can't.

He watches my lips when I speak. "Always give when I kiss you."

He's not paying attention. This is only his second time kissing anyone. The first was effortless. Near perfect. His lips fumble against mine, now that he's thinking about it.

"Give when I kiss you," I say again.

"I don't know what that means," he confesses.

"Give—give in to me, give way."

I kiss him more forcefully this time, cupping his head with my hands, flicking my tongue inside his mouth. He relaxes, yielding to me. It's difficult for me to pull back first, but I have to. I dictate when kisses begin and end.

"Get on the bed."

The muscles in Elisha's face slacken as realization sinks in. He's not stupid. He knows what the bed means. This isn't a kissing lesson.

I can't expect him to memorize my tastes in one night, though. Tonight, I just need to mark him. I need him to wake up tomorrow and feel me all over him—in him. And I need him to think about it until the next time I touch him. If he's not going to inject Dociline, I need to make him look forward to it, like an on-med would.

Elisha sits on the edge of the mattress, legs together, hunched over. Not a pose I dream of coming home to. I move between his knees, spread his legs, and tilt him back onto the bed. He's rigid everywhere except where I want him.

"Relax." I prop myself over his supine form. "Look at me."

His eyes fight to remain on mine. When they settle, I dote on his lips and neck with chaste kisses and he melts under me.

"How does that feel?" I ask.

"Good," Elisha says.

His legs press against my sides, hands grip the sheets. Hopefully, he'll learn what to do with them, how I like to be touched. Hopefully, I'm a good teacher.

"And how about this?" I massage the growing bulge in his briefs.

His mouth gapes, eyelashes flutter. That's how it's done. Show him how good I can make him feel. How behaving himself will bring him pleasure.

"Elisha," I prod him to answer, struggling to enforce my own rules.

When he does it's with heavy breaths and a moan. Technically, an audible response.

"Lift your hips," I say.

He does without hesitation, but when I slide his briefs down, he jerks up and covers himself. I feel bad that I'll have to count it against him later, because the instinct is only human.

"Elisha," I remind him with a stern tone, but even as his hands draw back, he folds his knees up. This can't be how his training begins.

I pin his wrists to the mattress. "Don't make me restrain you."

That shoots the message home. Elisha relaxes his legs so I can finish removing his briefs. When I stand to remove my own, I allow myself a few moments to drink him in—and to let him do the same with me.

I know what my body looks like; I planned it, built it, maintain it. Elisha's body is an accident. Freckles pepper his shoulders and torso without pattern or symmetry. His right arm flexes thicker than his left, and his chest and abs need definition. I see the imperfections—can't help but see them—but they complement Elisha. I'm reminded why I wanted him.

My gaze lingers on the pout of his lips, the flush of his cheeks, the way the pink head of his cock pokes out from its foreskin. He's splayed out on my bed, knees half-bent, legs slightly spread, arms framing his face in surrender.

My hand drifts down to my erection. Elisha's eyes wander while I stroke myself to full length. He's supposed to be looking at me, but I don't call him on it. Who isn't nervous their first time? I'm sure my cock looks intimidating. Soon, he'll feel it inside him.

"Reach into the bottom drawer of my nightstand and retrieve the red bottle," I say.

It takes Elisha a second to realize I'm instructing him, but he complies, glancing at the label. He hands it to me like a prisoner handing his executioner the gun. If he doesn't learn to relax, this will hurt, and hurting him will not earn me his loyalty, only fear.

I kneel between his legs, again, and take his bare cock in hand. His eyes close, lips part. I surprise them with a kiss and he arches into my touch. When he's at full length, I slow my motions.

I trace one finger down his shaft, over his balls, and back to his little hole. It clenches when I brush over it. "Have you ever touched yourself here?"

"Kind of," Elisha says. "Not much—not deep."

I squirt a dollop of lube onto my fingers and circle the spot, again. Elisha looses a string of whimpers as he writhes beneath me. I distract him with a kiss, then press my middle finger inside him. He gasps. Panic crosses his face.

But I kiss him again, holding our mouths together as I wiggle my finger all the way in. He's no longer squirming away from, but against my knuckle. After a few slow movements, I ease another in. Elisha isn't alarmed, though momentary discomfort shows. I pause, an inch in, and wait for him to relax.

He breathes out a slow breath and I slip past the barrier. This time, I curl my fingers, like I'm beckoning him over. His hips spasm in response.

I can't help but smile and nibble on his ear. "Didn't know that was there, did you?"

"No—ohh . . ." His words dissipate into sounds.

I toy with him for another minute, stroking myself to the same rhythm, until I can't wait any longer. It's not enough watching him. We aren't in this bed together to get off separately. When I remove my fingers, Elisha's eyes open on me.

Sixth Right, I haven't forgotten—not that I'm in danger of impregnating him. "Grab the envelope out of the bottom drawer," I say.

Elisha stretches back, like a cat, and holds the envelope overhead, while I wipe my fingers clean.

"Read it," I say.

"'The Johns Hopkins Hospital.'"

It's sealed, still. "Go ahead, open it."

He does, unfolding the letter inside. His eyes scan back and forth.

"I know you tested negative for STIs at the ODR. It's your right to know that I'm negative, too."

Elisha folds the paper back up. He clutches it like a shield between us. But I pull it away between pinched fingers.

"What am I going to tell you?" I lower myself onto him and grind my hips slowly against his.

"Relax," he says.

"How are you feeling?"

"Scared."

"I'm not going to hurt you." My kisses calm Elisha like a glass of strong wine. "I'm going to give you a safeword; do you know what that is?"

"Um . . ."

"A word you say if I'm hurting you, during sex. And I don't mean if I'm spanking you." I slap the side of his ass to illustrate my point.

Elisha gasps.

"I don't want to damage you, but I can't always tell what you're feeling. That's what your safeword is for."

"Okay."

"The word's 'midnight.' Repeat it, so I know you remember."

"Midnight." Elisha says it like he means it. We haven't even started.

"Good." I ready the lube. "Now, hold out your hand."

He props himself up. I squirt a liberal amount onto his fingers.

"I want you to do it."

His eyes follow mine to my cock. "What do I . . ."

"Just take it like your own." I wait patiently while he figures an angle.

I've managed to quiet my own feelings, so far. But I let out a long breath and hum the pleasure his hand brings me. His grip isn't too tight, strokes not too fast. The concentration creased in his forehead and pursed in his lips is turning me on almost as much as his hand.

"That's enough," I say, as flustered as he is at this point. I give him a moist towel to clean off. He moves too slowly. I take it from him and toss it in the direction of my hamper. "Wrap your legs around me," I say.

Elisha lies down and bends his knees back. I hook my arms under them, lifting his hips and opening him up. He's unsettled. This is happening too quickly for Elisha, but I need to move this night along. It's only the first of thousands more.

I guide the head of my cock inside him. This should be the easy part. If he doesn't relax, I'll have to force my way in, and I really don't want to.

"Elisha," I murmur before sucking his bottom lip between my teeth.

He moans and waits eagerly for a real kiss. As soon as I treat him to one, he's mine. With a steady thrust, I sink into him—one inch, two, three. I take his cock in my hand when he cries out. Four, five.

Elisha's arms are suddenly around me. He holds on like I'm pulling him from rough water, like he's drowning. I kiss his forehead to ease the tension.

"Tell me how you feel," I say.

His eyes remain closed. "Weird. Full." If he were a lover, I'd have laughed at his word choice, but I can't do that. This is a lesson. I have to focus.

I give him another inch. He takes it silently. I want to fill him all the way, but I'm not sure he can handle it. Well, he has a safeword.

I finish it, settling all the way inside Elisha. This time he's loud. His voice cracks, but he doesn't say the word. My pelvis rests flush against his ass. His body contracts, tight around my cock. I suck in a quick breath and hold it. My self-control is slipping.

Elisha's fingers tangle in the base of my hair. His legs tremble around my waist. I leverage them back onto my shoulders, pull out, and push in. We both moan. I'm beyond ready to come, but I want him to, first. He needs to know I'll continue until I'm sated, even if he's finished.

I'm hard and fast with my thrusts and my hand. His limbs slip against me as a sheen of sweat coats us. My lips touch down on every freckle, then find his neck. I swirl my tongue over his pulse and latch on, sucking at the pliant skin.

Elisha's moans and cries blur together as pleasure consumes us. The harder he grips me, the closer I know he is. I hope. I can't hold on much longer.

His back arches, head tips back, eyes close, mouth widens. I bury myself in him, grinding against his sensitive hole. His nails dig into my neck. I massage the head of his cock.

Elisha comes, convulsing and screaming against me. I barely hold my orgasm back as he flexes around me. He presses his forehead against mine, and I wait until he comes down from the high. He wriggles, as if we're finished and he wants me to dismount, but I hold him in place.

He's done with me, but I'm not done with him.

8

ELISHA

I want Alex out of me. When he was touching and kissing me, I forgot the discomfort. But now the stretch and fullness feels like I'm sitting on a baseball bat.

Something changes in Alex when he starts thrusting again. He doesn't look at me, doesn't touch me. I might as well not be here.

His forehead scrunches up as his eyes screw shut. I realize, when Alex moans, this is the first time since we've met that he's not thinking of anyone else.

"You feel so good. So good," mumbles Alex. The man who only speaks in full, explicit instructions.

I wrap my arms and legs back around him. He did take his time with me. Time I'm sure Dociles like Opal didn't have, their Patrons too busy fucking to think about their "happy pills." Dutch probably plunged right in while she still had her skirt on.

Alex waited.

The part of me still high from orgasm wants to kiss him. I remind myself we are not lovers, that I shouldn't give more than required. My uncertain lips brush his neck. He shudders at my touch. Orgasm seizes his body, smashing it against mine. I try to relax—it hurts less when I do. Alex falls against me, panting, exhausted. I almost want to hold him.

We don't lie together. He pulls his softening cock carefully from me. I yelp in surprise at the pop on its way out. A thin string of come attaches us.

Alex reaches over me, getting something from the nightstand. I don't trust anything that comes out of there, after tonight. A shiny metal object fits in his hand.

"Bend your knees." He upends the bottle of lube and squirts a glob onto the object. He's going to put it inside me.

I clear my throat, stare at the ceiling, and pretend I'm at the doctor's office. I gasp when Alex pushes it past the tight ring of muscle. It's cold, but otherwise slips right into the space he's left empty. I can't help but squirm around it, like I'm wiggling into tight clothes.

My body swallows it. I shoot up in a panic, but Alex rests a reassuring hand on my shoulder.

"Lie back down," he says. "It's supposed to do that. There's a handle down here." He wiggles the thin strip of metal that now sticks out of me. "This is called an anal plug." Alex presses the pad of his finger against the base. "Do not try to remove it; you'll only hurt yourself. I've locked it for the night."

"I won't," I say, though my immediate instinct is to touch the protrusion.

"It shouldn't be uncomfortable." He holds out a hand, which I take, and helps me onto my feet. Then, like we're lovers again, he pulls me so close I can barely balance. "It should feel good." He looks almost hopeful, like *he's* trying to make *me* happy.

I clench around the plug and bask in the momentary pleasure that ripples through me. Alex watches for the reaction on my face. I force a smile and say, "It does." Which, I guess, is true.

Alex doesn't look like he believes me though. "Come on," he says, his voice not as commanding as earlier. Low, airy. Tired. I realize I've thought of Alex as superhuman—no rest, nourishment, or emotions required. "It's been a long day."

I'm not sure whether I like thinking of Alex as a whole person. What if he's not such a bad guy? Even if I want to, I can't possibly go a lifetime without getting to know him, without smiling at one of his comments or laughing at one of his jokes. Whether or not I want to, there will be a point in the future where I feel like I'm having a good time with him, even if only for a few minutes. Maybe I should've signed with someone it'd be easier to hate.

Inside the bathroom, Alex turns on all ten shower heads with a single touch. On the community farm, we have the opposite ratio of shower heads to people. And, like that, my irritation returns.

He points out soaps and shampoos. Alex has more products than the ODR. Good thing the bottles are labeled; I'll never remember them all. We don't talk while we wash. He does catch my eye every so often. I can't help it; his body is like nothing I've ever seen, and I can't just switch my libido off.

I rinse Alex's volcanic ash–infused conditioner from my hair, close my eyes, and let the water drip down my face. His arm wraps around the front of my body and he casually fondles my cock.

"Oh, and uh," he says, as if he's just remembered something.

I try not to pay attention, but between Alex and the plug, I'm aroused again and I don't want to be.

"You are not to touch yourself without my permission."

I brace myself against the shower wall as he picks up speed. "Okay," I breathe out, barely audible over the water pressure. My hips jerk forward on their own to meet Alex's rhythm.

Then, just when I've given in, he's gone. The water shuts down, leaving me hard and alone. My mouth hangs open as I stare at my erection. Can't touch my hair; can't touch my cock. Why do I even have hands?

Alex dries off with a black towel that looks like a whole sheep's worth of fluff. I barely stifle the words to ask for more—beg him to finish.

Beg him to finish? What the fuck is wrong with me? I can't think that. He just raped me.

Did he? I tricked my parents into signing their debt over to me. Bought a fake ID. Registered with the ODR. Even aspired to sign with a trillionaire. I chose Alex, knowing we would have sex. I signed a fucking consent form.

But what else could I have done? Let my family get arrested? Watch Dad sell my thirteen-year-old sister into this? She could easily have ended up with someone like Dutch, and then who could blame her for taking Dociline—for risking ending up like Mom?

No, this is better. The farm is paid off. They're eating well, maybe even making a surplus. Abby can save money for the University of Maryland.

"Elisha." Alex's voice ropes me back into my present. Back to his ten-head shower in his Baltimore City penthouse.

My dick's softened. Alex doesn't touch it anymore. He leads the way back into the bedroom and motions to the side of his bed.

"Do you remember how to open it?" he asks.

"Yes." I wave my hand by the corner, like Alex did, and out glides the trundle bed—my bed. It fits right inside Alex's bed, just like I fit right inside Alex's life.

"The alarm will go off at seven a.m.," he says. "Tomorrow, we'll go over your daily schedule and revisit today's mishaps."

"Okay," I say. We're both standing around my little bed, like he might read me a fairy tale and kiss me on the cheek.

"Get some sleep." Alex watches me lie down.

I feel like I'm settling into a grave—one with sheets as soft as clouds against my skin.

"City sounds," Alex says—not to me. I wouldn't know what that means.

I find out as the soft sounds of cars and conversation bleed through the room. A horn blares like it's a mile away, but it's only a recording. Between that and the plug, my senses are too overwhelmed to fall asleep. Instead, I stare at the ceiling, forcing myself not to glance at Alex's curled-up body. At the rise and fall of his chest, the damp tangle of his hair, and slight part of his lips. And I feel so, so alone.

9

ELISHA

If I slept, I can't remember. Birds twitter amidst Alex's city sounds. The room is warm, the sheets slippery soft. I've never been so comfortable and yet, as much as I shift, I can't forget the metal plug inside me.

I'm horny. Nothing special, just morning. But since I'm not allowed to touch myself, it takes over my whole brain.

A loud honk startles me. I sit up. Beside me, Alex is already rolling out of bed. He slept naked, too, I see, as he silences the alarm. I haven't even been here for twenty-four hours. Already time drags like the beginning of a long, humid day of work.

My face musters up some color when Alex reaches between my legs and unlocks the plug with his fingerprint. "Go use the bathroom, if you need. There's a new toothbrush in the cabinet for you. Clean the plug off and place it in the stainless-steel container beside the sink. It's a sterilizer. Any time we finish with a toy, place it there."

"Okay."

He doesn't follow me as I carry out his instructions. I'm glad. My face contorts as I remove the plug. I almost drop it; it's covered in Alex's come, from last night. It's like he's inside me all over again.

As I wash the fluids from my body, my stomach rolls. I barely make it to the toilet before I hurl. Not much comes up. All I've eaten in the past twenty-four hours is the two crab balls Alex fed me. I flush them down what I'm sure is a ten-thousand-dollar toilet. Can't believe it isn't made of gold.

Well—I open the cabinet and find a perfectly ordinary tooth-brush, identical to Alex's—I can believe it. If there were dia-monds and jewels and imported fabrics everywhere, it would be easier to hate this place. I'm probably the most expensive thing here.

The door opens without warning. "Almost finished?" Alex grabs his own toothbrush and joins me. I can't look in the mirror. The reflection of us brushing our teeth side by side, naked, is too ridiculous.

I spit. "Finished."

"Good." Alex rinses his mouth. "I need to measure your wrist." He pulls a tape measure out of a drawer full of pins and clips and cologne bottles.

"What for?"

Alex holds my left arm out like he's selecting a cut of meat, then wraps the tape measure comfortably around my wrist, above the bone. "Don't ask superfluous questions. If I want you to know something, I'll tell you."

"Sorry, but what does 'superfluous' mean?"

"Unnecessary."

"Okay." Alex and I have different ideas about what's necessary.

"File that rule under 'don't speak unless spoken to' and 'sup-press your curiosity.'" Alex speaks the measurement out loud, though it doesn't appear to be for my benefit. "Since you've de-clined Dociline—"

Refused, I correct him in my head. I *refused* Dociline.

"—we'll be having a discussion about the rules, later."

I doubt Alex means "discussion," but I don't fight him on it, since I've already fucked up by asking him a "superfluous" question.

"I'll also be providing you a full schedule." Alex acts differ-ently, this morning. He moves with intention and sounds surer of himself. "Monday, Wednesday, Friday, you'll work with a personal trainer in the gym downstairs from six a.m. to seven a.m. Tuesday, Thursday, Saturday, you'll go for a run during the same hour. I'm not going with you—I have an errand to run—but I want to show you your route, today."

"Okay." I haven't exercised for its own sake in years. The act feels indulgent.

"I laid clothes out for you. Get dressed, make your bed, and tuck it back into place."

I don't even have time to respond. Alex goes through the rest of his morning routine completely oblivious to my presence. We dress side by side as if we're strangers in one of those boutique dressing rooms.

He watches me make my bed, then fixes a corner, and shows me how he prefers it. I try again on his bed with only a wrinkle or two at fault.

"Good." He examines my work while I fix it. "You'll make them both every morning, yours before you work out, mine after you return."

I've been making beds for years; this is the easy stuff. "Okay."

"Ready to go?"

"Yes."

I follow him to the elevator and we ride silently down to the lobby. My neon running shoes clash with the preppy colors that decorate the building. Alex complements it in jade-green corduroy pants and a thick wool cardigan that matches the gray horses embroidered on the pants. Even after last night, I still can't believe trillionaires really wear this stuff on a daily basis.

"Morning, Dr. Bishop!" The doorman waves.

"Morning, Tom." Alex smiles and stops.

I do the same, minus the smile.

"How's the family?"

I fail to hide my surprise. Alex cares about his doorman's family? Has to be an act. Trillionaires don't care about anyone beneath them. Not debtors and not doormen.

"Good!" says Tom. "Wendy's graduating this spring. Looks like she's going to pull a four-point-oh."

"Congratulations." Alex pats him on the back. "Has she applied to the University of Maryland?"

"Yes, but . . ." Tom wavers despite his smile. "We'll see."

He can't afford it. Not all the folks who work in the city are rich;

trillionaires need people to drive them and groom them and sell them overpriced clothes

"We'll talk." Alex motions between the two of them. "I'm heading out for a bit."

"Yes, I see." For the first time, Tom looks at me—at my eyes, like there's a person inside this body. "Who's this?"

"Introduce yourself," Alex says, as if I'm six and need manners handed to me. I would have, immediately, if I thought I were allowed to speak.

"I'm Elisha." Tom takes my hand when I extend it. "Nice to meet you."

"You too, young man," Tom says, though he can't be older than fifty. Lines barely crease his dark brown skin and his hair is only beginning to recede.

"Elisha is my new Docile." Alex clears the confusion on the doorman's face.

"Oh. You know, I couldn't tell. He's very natural," Tom says, suddenly forgetting I'm standing in front of him. Just a second ago we shook hands like equals.

"Thank you," Alex says.

I can't decide whose comment embarrasses me more.

"He doesn't have that look." Tom motions to his own face. "That plastic look."

Alex clears his throat. His smile falters. "Elisha's not on Dociline."

"He's not, huh." Tom sounds intrigued. "Do you plan to go on Dociline, Elisha?"

"No, sir."

"Call me Tom."

I look to Alex for approval. He nods.

"No, Tom. I don't plan to take Dociline."

"Must be a short term, then."

"No," I say.

"Elisha and I signed a life term contract," Alex adds, because I can't bring myself to say the words.

"Interesting." He pauses. "Well, I guess I'll be seeing you around then, Elisha. Dr. Bishop." Tom nods and returns to his desk. "Enjoy your morning."

"Thanks, you too," says Alex.

Tom nods when I pass. His black eyes draw me in like a magnet. Whether that's good or bad, I don't have time to worry. I shiver, shaking off my unease, and follow Alex across the street toward the pier.

"Stretch, first," he says. "Then you'll follow this route around the harbor. Look." He points at the painted path along the road, flagged by signs with stick figures walking or riding bikes.

"And you want me to go alone?" I confirm, suspicious of his intentions.

"Yes."

"Every time?"

"Are you planning to run away?" he asks to make a point.

"No."

"Then yes." Alex squares with me. "Every time." We hold silent eye contact for a moment before he continues, as if it had never come up. "I want you active the entire hour, but I don't expect you'll be able to run for that long, at first. Once you tire, walk. If you feel like you can resume, do. I've linked your microchip to a program that will track your progress, so you can check when you get home."

"Okay."

"I'll see you back in an hour." Alex consults his watch, then walks back toward his building. I watch as he chats with Tom the doorman, again, before getting into a black car.

For several minutes, I stand absolutely still. It feels worse being trusted than being forced. That this trillionaire knows I have no other choice, that my family so desperately needs his one thousand dollars per month that I will do anything he tells me. That I won't fight. That I'll take his friends' lewd comments, let Alex do whatever he wants to my body, run laps around the harbor, and go back to him for more, every time, without restraints or guards or locks.

Because, inside, I'm churning with anger and fear and want. But outside? I'm still. Trustworthy. Docile.

I could run, but I choose not to. I choose to obey the trillionaire who could probably buy my entire community out of debt with a month of his salary. I choose to be complicit in the system that fucked my family into three million dollars of debt and my mother into a permanent docile state.

I stretch against one of the path signs while city folks stroll past in wool sweaters, embroidered pants, feather-stuffed vests, and colorful scarves that circle their necks like collars. When I run, it's like I'm in a zoo, though whether I'm the attraction or visitor I'm undecided.

The path goes against traffic, winding around a long stretch of shops and restaurants along the water. A barge leaving the harbor boasts a glass-enclosed tennis court along the roof, in which two older men hit a glowing green ball back and forth. One whacks it past the glass and the ball bursts into hundreds of little pieces.

"Watch where you're going!" Someone bumps me—or I bump her.

"Sorry," I say, too late, only to bump into someone else. A man with shiny black hair, whose movements are as smooth as his voice.

"May I help you?" he asks. He repeats his questions in two other languages before I notice the badge on his uniform that reads:

DOWNTOWN PARTNERSHIP DOCILE.
Hello, my name is Antonio! Ask me for assistance.
I speak English. Yo hablo español. Je parle français.

"I'm fine." I back away slowly, then pick up speed before turning around. They're everywhere, in the city. And people walk past them without thinking twice. Not me.

My feet beat against the stone path in sync with my heart. I'm only vaguely aware of others joining mine, of labored breath besides me, of human warmth.

"Don't slow down. Keep running," says a medium-pitched voice to my left with a singsong quality. I glimpse a tall Black woman wearing a baby-blue tracksuit jogging beside me, her long box braids fastened in a knot on top of her head, before returning my eyes to the path.

"It's okay. My name's Eugenia. I'm with Empower Maryland," she says.

My pace quickens with my heart. Empower Maryland barely shows itself in my community. I don't like that she's following me. "My Patron is tracking me, just so you know."

"That's why you're going to keep moving," she says. "I'm not here to hurt you; I'm your ally. I just wanted to introduce myself and let you know Empower Maryland will help you, if you want us to."

I return my eyes to the road. I don't trust her, regardless of whether she calls herself my "ally." What does that even mean? I'm stuck with Alex until I die. "How can you possibly help me?"

"Sorry, I didn't realize you were enjoying debt slavery. Guess your mother's fine as she is, too."

I stop. She isn't supposed to know about my family without permission—no one is. Third Right.

She only makes it a few paces before realizing she's lost me. Narrowing her eyes, she says, "Aren't you supposed to keep moving?"

I force my feet in front of each other. Even when I'm alone, Alex is with me. "How do you know about my family?"

"One of our contacts at the ODR tipped us off that a new Docile was planning to refuse Dociline. I didn't believe her, at first, but . . ."

Carol? She wouldn't have. She's my caseworker. I trusted her.

"Listen," she says, "no pressure. But we're here if you need us." I glimpse a scarred-over "US" branded on her wrist before she stuffs her hands into her pockets. A group of people running the other direction tangle between us, bumping shoulders and elbows, until I can no longer keep track of Eugenia. Until she's only a flash of baby blue in the dispersing crowd.

/ / /

Alex isn't home when I return. I stand sweaty and parched in the entranceway, still thinking about Downtown Partnership Dociles and my own trustworthiness. About Empower Maryland's offer and invasion of my privacy. About how I want a drink but don't know if I'm allowed to get one.

I let it all go with one deep breath. I live here now; I shouldn't feel like I'm trespassing. Alex sent me for a run; he can't intend to punish me for helping myself to a glass of water. I peel off my running shoes and socks, place them neatly along the wall, and tiptoe into the kitchen.

I can't remember which cabinet has cups in it—or even which parts of the wall *are* cabinets. Everything is seamless and identical. I notice a small indentation at shoulder height, then another a few feet down, and another. Now I remember.

I fit my index finger into the groove and slide it left. The cabinet door slides open, mimicking my motion. Dishes. I try two more before I find the cups, select the plainest-looking one, and close the cabinet behind me.

Even the tap water here tastes better.

I sip my water while I wander through the airy living room. I glide my fingers along the dark wood of a grand piano, daring to touch the expensive instrument only in Alex's absence. I still feel like I've broken in. Best to shower and clean up before Alex gets home. That's probably what he expects of me without having specified.

It's not until I'm washed and dripping on the bathroom rug that I realize I don't know what to wear or where Alex keeps my clothes. And I do not want to be naked when he gets home. Don't want to put any ideas in his head.

I shiver at the memory of his touch, close my eyes, and feel his lips against mine, his heavy breaths, and warm tongue. A moan vibrates in my chest and, embarrassed at my own reaction, I clear my throat. Don't become aroused. Don't touch yourself—don't want to touch yourself, Elisha.

Downstairs, the elevator dings. And I'm still naked. *Fuck.*

I grab my towel and wrap it around my waist. What should I be doing? I should be doing something, rather than wandering around the house like it's a fucking spa.

I hear Alex's feet pound up the stairs, watch the bedroom door swing open, and see him stop in front of me. Surprised and yet trying not to look surprised.

"I-I took a shower," I say, gesturing to the bathroom as if Alex doesn't know where his own shower is.

"I can see that." His eyes dart around the room, landing on my half-empty glass of water.

"And I don't know where my clothes are."

"That's okay; don't bother. We have something to take care of, first." Alex sets a white paper bag down on the writing table, then removes a dark wooden box with a gold hinge. It creaks open in his hands and I do my best not to crane my neck to see what's inside.

I'm still staring at the ceiling, minding my own business, when Alex says, "Hold out your left arm."

When I do, I see why he measured my wrist, this morning, and why he wouldn't tell me what it was for. The cuff is almost two inches wide and pinkish gold with a glimmering oily finish. I can't find a clasp, but I do notice a pull chain that disappears into the band and ends with an O-shaped ring. It's almost clear with the exception of a few cloudy spots.

Alex's fingers brush the fading scar on my wrist—the marker that it's been over a decade since the state took my mother away and branded the rest of us debtors. And this trillionaire—this man whose family invented Dociline—is going to cover it up with jewelry.

"I was seven." I blurt the words out before I can consider the rules. He can't just ignore it. Pretend he wasn't part of this. "The cops took my mother. Left me and my dad with these."

Alex doesn't look at me. He adjusts the cuff so that it completely covers the scar. "Rule number two."

"Don't speak unless spoken to," I finish.

"This is expensive," Alex says, as if I didn't just share a traumatic childhood experience. He fastens it and then runs his fingers around the edges, checking the fit. "It's made from rose gold, opal"—he hooks a finger through the chain and pulls out six inches of length—"and diamond. It will not rust but requires daily cleaning not only to maintain its shine but also to keep your skin healthy. It cannot be removed by either of us, so don't try. Do you understand?"

"Yes."

"Good. Now, you've broken three rules since you arrived. Know that beyond disciplinary measures for minor infractions, our contract stipulates that I can revoke the thousand-dollars-per-month stipend I'm currently sending your family."

Alex's newfound confidence slices cold through me. Yesterday, it sounded like he was making the rules up on the spot. This morning, he's prepared and I am not.

I muster up a whispered, "Yes, Alex." It's easy to imagine defiance outside, when I'm alone, when allies present themselves. Here, I'm alone and, frankly, powerless. But I cannot forget that he owns my debt; I cannot relax.

Relax and I might as well inject Dociline.

"Can you name your infractions?" Alex holds up three fingers.

"Um." Think, Elisha, think. I don't want to think. I can't. My fingertips are like ice. I'm failing this quiz. What if he adds to my punishment or takes the stipend away or—

Alex must see me struggling, because he gives me a hint. "What rule did you just quote me?"

"Right." I press my fingers to my forehead and squeeze my eyes shut. "Rule number two." I just broke that one, too. How stupid must I look?

"Correct." Alex puts one of his fingers down. "What else did I tell you yesterday, before my party?"

This one I know. I knew the second I broke it. "You told me not to touch my hair and I did when I went upstairs."

Another finger down. One left. And I have no clue what it is.

"The third I don't expect you remember. You were preoccupied, but it's still important that you learn from your mistakes."

"What is it?" I ask.

"Last night, I told you not to cover or hide your body from me. You did so as soon as I removed your briefs."

"Sorry," I mumble.

"Like I said, I understand. But—"

I huff a silent laugh.

Alex stops. His composure falters. "Excuse me?"

"Nothing, sorry." I purse my lips to keep myself quiet.

"No, say it. Say what you're thinking." He crosses his arms.

Do I tell him? Rule number one, always answer Alex honestly. He wants to know or he wouldn't have asked. I'm going to say it. Once I start, I won't be able to hold myself back and then who knows what kind of trouble I'll get into.

"Well?"

"You said you understand, but you don't." The words tumble out. "Yes, I hid my body from you. You're a stranger—I know we signed a contract, that I picked you as much as you picked me. But you'll never understand what it's like to go hungry or freeze through a winter. To be so far in debt that the cops come to drag your family off to debtors' prison. That you'll do anything to keep them safe and together, including sell yourself to a stranger who expects you to have sex with him the first night you're together."

I'm shaking. I clasp my hands to stop them and my gaze falters for the first time. Heat rises in the corners of my eyes, but I can't let myself cry. I can't lose it in front of this trillionaire.

"I've never done that before," I confess. "I've never been naked with another person, never let them touch me. It's even worse that I didn't hate it. I want to hate you."

"Do you?" Alex interrupts me. "Hate me."

"Yes—and no."

He nods, eyes fixed on the floor as if he's reconsidering my fate. I imagine, for a moment, that he might have a change of heart, might at least see where I'm coming from, even if he doesn't understand fully. Finally, he says, "For speaking out of turn—"

"But you asked me to—"

Alex raises his voice. "For speaking out of turn and for continuing to argue with me, I'm adding another infraction to this disciplinary session. Come with me. And leave the towel."

I grit my teeth to stop myself arguing further. He fucking asked. He asked, but he doesn't want to hear the answer. Wants to pay for my company but doesn't want to see me too closely.

Alex leads me downstairs into the kitchen, where more shopping bags rest. He reaches into one and removes a tray and a bag of rice. "You are being punished for your outburst, not for honestly answering my question." Then he adds, "I'm not unfair," to make himself feel better.

I watch, still naked, as Alex sets the tray on the floor and pries open the rice.

Is he—he's going to waste—

My mouth forms a silent O when Alex pours a thin layer of uncooked rice onto the metal tray. One of our neighbors used to do something like this, but with sand and little rocks from the shore—never with *food*.

"Hands behind your back."

I clasp them behind me.

Alex wraps the chain from my cuff around my right wrist. "I hope this will only be a temporary measure, until you're not tempted to relieve the pressure with your hands." A lock clicks, securing them.

Alex supports me as I step into place. Slowly, I kneel down on the tray. Rice digs into my stretched skin, making room where there isn't any. When Alex lets go, I groan and readjust. The movement only causes the little grains to burrow farther into my knees. I pull at my wrists, desperate for something to lean on.

Alex touches my back. "The less you move, the less painful it should be. I'll be back in forty minutes, ten for each infraction. I expect to find you in this exact position."

"Yes, Alex." My words make me nauseous, unless that's the pain. I don't turn to watch him leave. I can't move. Every shift burns and stings.

I can do this. It's only forty minutes. I try not to think about it. Each grain lodges in a different nerve, grinds against my bones.

I strain my arms against the chain, desperate. I'll do anything for relief. My jaw aches, but I can't unclench my teeth. The rice grates my whole body. My arms and chest tingle with pain.

I throw my head back to stop the forming tears. Another whimper escapes me. I change positions without thinking and new grains make their homes in my knees. My body must have swallowed them all up by now. But I can do this. I can.

A few grains of rice won't break me.

ALEX

I've read the same sentence a hundred times, and probably only the first few words. Fifteen minutes in, Elisha starts breathing heavily. The chain clinks against the cuff when he tries to break free. He'll never learn if he doesn't understand consequences, I remind myself, then force my eyes back onto the literature tablet.

He forced me to do this when he refused Dociline, to institute rules and disciplines, to put that cuff on him. I barely slept last night for wondering if Elisha was going to attack me in my sleep or wreck the house or run away—all of which would betray my inability to manage. My father's disappointed voice, Dutch and Mariah's patronizing *it's not your fault*—they haunt me. It would be my fault if I failed. I have to prove to them that I can handle a Docile, handle being a Bishop. Represent my family legacy. Own it.

Thirty minutes in, Elisha's breaths have turned to whimpers. Ten minutes for each infraction. It won't kill him. My grandmother used to tell me I got off easy, that her mother made her kneel on rice when she misbehaved, and that was how she learned discipline. If it set her right enough to found Bishop Laboratories and invent a world-changing drug, then it's good enough for Elisha.

Right?

Ten minutes left. I glance into the kitchen, where there are no clocks. Even from the living room, I can see beads of sweat condensing at the nape of Elisha's neck, sliding like tears between his shoulder blades. I wonder if it hurts as much as it looks like it does or if he's being dramatic. If it was awful, my grandmother would never have recommended it to my father.

Maybe it should hurt. I have no other way to control him, without Dociline. If he doesn't want to kneel on rice for forty minutes, he should break fewer rules. And yet I find myself back at the beginning of the chapter I've been trying to read casually, as if Elisha isn't making me anxious. Maybe ten minutes per infraction is too long. Maybe I should shorten it to five minutes. Tell him it was so long this first time to make a point. Or will that make me look weak?

With three minutes remaining, I force myself to walk slowly into the kitchen and stand before him. "Pay attention," I say.

Elisha rights his head and opens his eyes, red and watery, to meet mine. "Yes, Alex," he mumbles.

I clear my throat to hide my shock. This can't be what my grandmother experienced; she would never have recommended the pain I see on Elisha's face. Hold yourself together, Alex.

I close my eyes momentarily to refocus and remember the punishments I came up with, last night, rather than sleeping. "There are three disciplines I'll utilize. The first is this, kneeling on uncooked rice for a set period of time." I refrain from citing the ten-minutes-per-infraction rule, allowing myself to adjust in the future. "The second is writing lines, such as 'I will not talk back,' a hundred times. The third is confinement." As soon as I say it, I wonder whether, once again, I've gone too far. "I'm having a small cubby installed in my bedroom closet. You'll remain in there for short periods of time to reflect on the rules." No, it should be fine. Moderation is the key to all things.

Elisha stares at me, unmoving. Phantom pain sears through my knees.

"Repeat them." I glance at my watch so I don't have to look at him. "And then your time is up."

He speaks between ragged breaths. "One: kneeling on rice. Two: writing a number of assigned lines. Three: isolation for a short period of time in a cubby."

"Very good." I reach back and unlock his wrists, then extend a hand to help him up, but Elisha throws both arms around me. I almost drop him, unprepared for his full weight. I want to carry him, but I shouldn't. We're not in this together. This is discipline. I am not rescuing him.

"Walk with me to the bath," I say.

His feet barely touch the floor. Grains of rice fall from his knees while we walk.

"Get in." But he barely needs the prompt.

Elisha reclines. Rice plugs at least half of the indentations in his knees. The empty ones run deep and red. I flick my finger against one of the embedded grains. Elisha gasps and grabs my hand. My instinct is to apologize, but I can't. I'm a Bishop; I'm in control.

"Let go," I say. This is only his first discipline. He can't learn that he'll be coddled afterwards. But that doesn't mean I won't care for him. His health is my responsibility, legally. Not to mention I've got him for life. I can't keep losing sleep, worrying Elisha will stab me with a kitchen knife or rob me and run.

"You should probably soak them." I plug the drain, then turn on the hot water.

A little cry slips from his throat as he straightens his legs and leans his head on the porcelain rim. He's holding back. Holding on to his pride. He doesn't need it, here. The sooner he realizes that—the sooner he relaxes and falls into place—the happier we'll both be.

I cannot stay here and coddle him. I swallow and push myself to my feet. "When you're finished, dry off and meet me in my room."

"Okay," he says.

I close the door behind me and listen. A small splash breaks the silence. Labored breathing and quiet groans follow. I need a distraction. Normally, Saturdays bore me. If Elisha weren't here, I'd pop down to the lab for a few hours. I'm not used to babysitting—and that's what this is, for the time being.

I return to my mystery novel—something I can lose myself in for a while—but glance at the bathroom door every few paragraphs. It's mostly quiet, now. Twenty pages in, the door opens.

Elisha stands with the same towel from earlier wrapped around his waist. Below the hem, dimples mark his knees. I stop reading and watch while he smooths the sides of his hair down—any excuse to busy himself and not acknowledge that he's standing naked in front of me.

"You can put on a pair of briefs and a tee shirt," I say. "Your clothes are in the drawers on the other side of my bed."

Relief grips Elisha as he searches for the prescribed clothing. I didn't buy him any underwear I wouldn't want to watch him walk around in; if he's looking for boxers, he won't find them.

Elisha settles on red boxer briefs that cover a few inches of his thighs, and a white, V-neck tee shirt. He looks cute, like a guy I would've flirted with during undergrad. Suddenly, he doesn't feel like such a chore.

Without warning, I stand and kiss him. Elisha tries not to look flustered when I end it.

"Downstairs." I nudge him with a hand to the ass and he moves quickly, still not used to my touch. Hopefully, he will be soon.

"Have a seat." I gesture to the breakfast bar and tap its surface to bring forward the new rules I brainstormed while he was running. The original four remain, followed by:

5. Tell me immediately if you feel ill or injured. I'm legally obligated to care for your health.
6. Do not ask superfluous questions. I will always give explicit instructions. If I don't tell you something, you don't need to know it in order to complete a task.
7. Keep yourself groomed. Nails, hair, skin, clothing. You should always appear aesthetically pleasing, not only in public, but in private, as well.

Elisha's eyes follow when I reach back into the shopping bags from my morning errands. His body relaxes when I pull out a note-book rather than another bag of rice. I set down the leather-bound journal and a pen in front of him. "Write these down—and any others I give in passing. The rules are a living document that I can edit at any time. Don't try and debate them."

"Yes, Alex."

"Remember them. Live them." I smile, satisfied with the authority in my words. I'm getting better at this. And won't it impress my parents and the Board when I'm able to show off a presentable and compliant Docile that I trained from scratch?

When dinnertime finally rolls around, Elisha sets our places at opposite ends of the table. I put two fingers against one of the black ceramic dishes and slide it down toward the other.

"Sit." I gesture to a chair and Elisha takes it.

He waits, either for my instruction or for my approval. He's made roasted potatoes and chicken breast. The preparation appears amateur at best. I slice easily into the juicy chicken and taste a bite. Elisha watches. Chefs have watched my first bite, before, but I've never had such a rapt audience.

"Not bad," I say, before trying the potatoes. "Could use a little more seasoning. But they're cooked well."

"We don't have the same spices back home. I wasn't sure what to use." Not the response I wanted, but at least it was devoid of attitude. Well, mostly.

"You'll learn," I say. "I scheduled a chef for your afternoon lesson on Monday. Eat."

He tries to match my pace, but I can tell he's hungry even after he cleans his plate.

"You're allowed to have seconds. I'm not trying to starve you." I allow a slight smile.

"Thank you. Do you want some more, too?"

"No, but I appreciate you offering." He was just being polite, but I'm not; I mean it. I like when he picks up on acceptable behavior. Hopefully, we'll reach a point where I barely need to instruct him.

"So," I say, "did you enjoy the harbor, this morning?"

"Yes," Elisha says between bites. "I've always liked the water."

"Do you swim?"

"I can stay afloat."

"I'll enroll you in lessons."

"I'd like that." Elisha fiddles with his last potato, picking at the skin with his fork.

He's stalling. It's nearly time to retire, and he knows what that means.

"If you're finished, you can clear the plates and put the dishes in the sanitizer. It's under the coffeemaker." I point so he can find the camouflaged appliance.

Elisha takes both our plates and puts them away. When he finishes, he remains standing. "Do you want anything else?"

"Nothing from the kitchen. Why don't you head upstairs and wait for me on the bed."

His body is heavy when he walks. His emotions cannot rule his actions; he needs to learn that. When he's distracted, I'm the one who has to deal with it.

I give him a few minutes—enough to unwind, not enough to become nervous—then walk upstairs to my room. Elisha dents the otherwise smooth comforter, curled up on his side. His eyes lock on me when I close the door.

I take off my shoes, socks, and pants until we're in equal stages of undress. Elisha watches, unmoving. I recline beside him and do the same. I never really look at people—not even lovers—it's too awkward, too intimate, vulnerable. But I like looking at him, studying where the tension builds in his body. His shoulders and lips. Calves. Always so guarded.

This would've been easier for him if he'd just taken the drug instead of carrying his pride around. Now I want to unlock him.

"Why did you refuse Dociline?" I'm not even sure it's the right time to ask, after his earlier outburst.

"The side effects."

Surprising. I expected some ideological objection, some kind of martyrdom. But a medical decision? I can't help asking, despite how it may reflect on me. "What side effects?"

"Are you joking?" Elisha narrows his eyes at me like I've just said the Earth is flat. "Didn't your family invent it?"

I feel the warmth of embarrassment on my face, but I cannot allow him the upper hand on this. "What did I say about talking to me like that?"

Elisha's gaze falters. "Sorry." He sounds like he means it, so I go easy on him.

"Lines, tomorrow."

"Fine." He doesn't fight it, this time.

"Continue."

"Dociline doesn't always leave your system when you stop injecting. Maybe it does for short-term Dociles." He picks at a non-existent thread on the sheets with intense focus. "But not after a decade. It holds on to some people and doesn't let go. They keep doing what they're told. They're empty inside. I didn't want to turn into one of them—a drone."

I roll my eyes. The number of times I've heard that goddamn word shouted by Empower Marylanders. Dociline doesn't turn people into drones. It's designed to exit the body within two weeks of the final dose. "No," I say.

But Elisha plows on. "A lifetime on Dociline is mental suicide."

"That's a lie."

His face tenses, brows furrow, while he stares at me, incredulous. "No, it's not. Rule number one, I'm telling you the tr—"

"If you followed all my rules perfectly, that might mean something." I feel my jaw tense, teeth grind. I take a breath to relax myself. How dare he. As if refusing my family's drug wasn't enough, now he's slandering me.

"If you don't believe me, ask my mother. That is, if you can get her to answer you."

"That's enough!" My voice fills the room. Its silent echo laps against the walls. I can hear myself shouting at him over and over.

But he doesn't fight. He opens and closes his mouth like a suffocating fish.

"Additional lines, tomorrow. Sleep, now."

Elisha slinks down to his trundle. I remove a small lock from the nightstand, reach down, and unfurl the chain from his cuff. He doesn't resist when I lock it to a rung on the bed. I dismiss plans for sex. How can I touch him after what he said—a direct affront on my family, my work? It's within his rights to decline Dociline, but he has no right to spread lies and make false accusations.

I clench my fists beneath the covers, then unravel them, releasing my anger where Elisha cannot see. Dociline works. Dociline helps debtors make better lives for themselves. In all my years at the lab, I've never once seen the drug affect a person after their dosage wore off.

Then again, I've only been working there ten years. Bishop Labs never studied the effect of Dociline over a life term because, well, we would have died before the study concluded, and the Office of Debt Resolution was eager to get their hands on the drug and we were similarly eager to help.

I feel blasphemous even thinking we might've been *too* eager. That Elisha might not be making this story up. For the second night in a row, I lose sleep because of Elisha.

11

ELISHA

The next morning, we shower and dress in near silence. My arm aches with stiffness from being cuffed to the trundle all night, and I'm itching with anger. Alex practically shoved me over the side of the bed when I didn't answer his questions about Dociline the way he wanted me to. I make a note to weigh the truth against its consequences, from now on.

He dresses me in clothes I've only seen trillionaires wear. A baby-pink button-down shirt, silk mustard scarf, pale khaki pants with a brown belt, and a matching pair of soft leather shoes. Alex hands me a textured gray-brown blazer with patches on the elbows—tweed, he calls it—and the same notebook I copied the rules down in.

We are clearly going out—someplace nice, at that—but I don't dare ask where. We pass Tom at the front desk, then cross the street and walk along the harbor path that I ran yesterday. Despite the cold, city dwellers walk along the water with brown paper shopping bags swinging from their arms. Others dine on enclosed balconies that overlook the harbor. While I look around, Alex looks only ahead.

We don't go far. I'm surprised when we enter the Science Center building and even more surprised when Alex leads me through a door marked "Bishop Laboratories: Staff Only." The hallway on the other side is long and beige. A stocky white woman in a black security uniform nods at Alex when he passes; her eyes linger on me while he goes through multiple security scanners and enters half a dozen codes. Finally, a door swings open and we leave the hallway behind.

The sight of our new surroundings stops me. I feel as if I've stepped through a gateway into another world. The room is a giant hollow cylinder. There must be thousands of rooms. A tall railing encircles each floor—I immediately grab on to the one nearest me, imagining what it would be like to fall over the edge. My stomach drops, eyes squeeze shut.

I feel the warm weight of Alex's hand on my shoulder. "You okay?"

I nod. "Yeah."

"Take a few deep breaths, if you need to." He casually glances over the railing, down dozens of floors. "We call this the Silo. Magnificent, isn't it?"

"Mm-hm," I manage, slowly opening my eyes again. The ceiling is only a few floors above us, a wide circular stopper made of glass so clean and clear I almost don't notice it.

Alex leans forward on the railing beside me. "Bulletproof, acid-proof, hacker-proof." He smiles. "Everything-proof."

"Good to know," I say between the recommended deep breaths.

Alex chuckles, sliding his arm around my waist. He pulls me away from the safety of the railing and toward a glass box. With a swipe of his hands, a door slides open for us and we board. We're in an elevator. A clear elevator that is about to drop a hundred floors—*oh god*.

"Lower lab," Alex says.

My stomach flops again.

We drop.

I grab on to Alex, digging my fingers into the wool of his coat. The fall pulls a gasp from my lungs. Terror ripples through my limbs. I close my eyes.

"I didn't realize you were afraid of heights." I can hear Alex's amusement.

"Neither did I." When I peek, we're already slowing to a stop. "I don't think it's heights. Just falling from them."

"Well, we have a safety system installed that will catch any object that drops more than two floors. So, rest assured."

I am only slightly assured. When the doors open, I'm the first one out, glad to be safely on the bottom floor of this place. From here, the glass ceiling is a small sky-blue disc. We must be a mile deep, if not more. It doesn't hit me until then: Bishop Labs is empty. Mostly.

"Where . . ." I trail off, realizing I'm about to speak out of turn. I haven't forgotten I'm still in trouble for that.

But Alex says, "Please, feel free to ask questions. I brought you here to demystify Dociline. When you've only heard lies and rumors, you're bound to believe them; I understand that."

I bite my lip to stop myself from mouthing off. When the urge passes, I ask my original question. "Where is everyone?"

"It's Sunday." Alex says, as if that answers my question. When I continue staring blankly at him, waiting for further explanation, he says, "No one's required to work on the weekend."

Right. People in the city can afford not to work on the weekends. I nod and fold my arms behind my back. The magnitude of Bishop Laboratories is even clearer from the bottom floor. Rows of glass-doored rooms line each floor and, if I position myself properly, I can see inside some of them. I can see—"There are people." I turn. "Hundreds of them."

"Thousands," Alex says. "They're Dociles. Like you, they all interviewed at the ODR, negotiated, and signed contracts. Though their contracts are with Bishop Laboratories, the company. Not me, individually."

"And who are the people in scrubs?" I point at a woman walking along a floor above us. She glances into the Dociles' rooms, as she passes, tapping her tablet.

"Caretakers. We don't need a full staff on the weekends, but for those who want flexible hours, the opportunity exists. Since most of our subjects are on-meds, we don't even really need caretakers. On-meds follow their prescribed routines without prompting or monitoring. But, for safety reasons, we employ caretakers twenty-four hours per day, every day of the year."

"Most? There are off-meds here?" I've never heard of anyone else refusing Dociline.

"Well, yes," Alex says, as if the answer is obvious. "We need a control group."

I don't know what that is, so I ask, "What do you do to *them*?"

"We don't 'do' anything to them." He wanders out across the workroom floor, between glass tables and panels with softly glowing lights. "They take a variety of enrichment classes—practice crafts, read, exercise—and participate in periodic tests to act as a comparison point for those on various Dociline formulas. All painless, I promise."

A door slides opens across the way, prompting both Alex and me to glance over. I don't like that he's caught by surprise. Despite the bright colors and open, airy feel, this is still Bishop Laboratories. The drugs made here still change people. Still hurt them.

A light-skinned Black woman in a yellow blouse and purple knee-length skirt walks toward us. She tucks her stylus into the pocket of her unbuttoned lab coat and waves casually at Alex. "What are you doing here?" she asks, sitting on one of the workstation tables. "And who's— Wait. Is this . . ." She smiles at me. "Elisha?"

"Yes, ma'am," I say.

"Oh." She waves my comment off. "You can call me Jess."

"Dr. Pearl," Alex interjects.

"Jess," she reasserts.

"Fine," he says. "This is Dr. Jessica 'Jess' Pearl. Bishop Labs' Head of Research."

I've yet to see anyone overrule Alex. They must be close. Already I like her better than Alex's other friends from his birthday party, Dutch and Mariah. She doesn't seem to take herself too seriously, and yet she must know what she's doing if she's Head of Research. I don't know how I feel about that. I dislike this place on principle, but it's harder to dislike the people involved when they're kind.

Jess nods her head in my direction, forgoing a handshake. "Nice to meet you, Elisha."

"You too." I return her nod with a smile. Why does she have to be so nice?

"Did you get the Board's memo about our latest trial?" Jess asks Alex.

"Yeah, let's"—he glances between me and Jess—"continue that conversation in a few minutes. Elisha has something to take care of, first."

"You're the boss." Jess hops up and repositions herself in an actual chair, at one of the workstations.

Alex gestures to another elevator, and I'm already nervous about the ride. At least up is better than down. Inside, he types a passcode into a panel, then says, "Lower lab three." We rise so quickly, I have to steady myself on the railing. Alex doesn't. He steps off and I follow.

The third floor is not an open-air walkway, like the others. The same glass that makes up the doors and tables and panels walls-off this floor like a glass doughnut. Portions of the panels light up as Alex passes them, sensing his presence.

"Is this your office?" I ask, hoping the invitation to ask questions still stands.

"Yes." Alex pushes through another glass door to a small room with a single workstation. "Have a seat and take out your notebook."

I remove my blazer and scarf, laying them over the back of the chair, roll up my sleeves, then do as I'm told.

Alex fastens the ring of my cuff to the table leg and says, "I promised you lines, today. I want you to write 'I will control my attitude' one hundred times to impress that yesterday's tantrum was unacceptable and will not happen again. Then, another hundred times, you will write 'I will not lie to Alex' as punishment for your slanderous remarks about Dociline, last night."

I clench my teeth to keep from arguing. All I'll earn are more lines. He doesn't care about the truth, anyway. So I say, "Okay," and begin.

Alex touches the walls on either side of me and they fog up, acting like blinders on a horse. When he leaves, I am left overlooking Bishop Laboratories. Even though I know they aren't really aware, I feel the deadened eyes of every Docile on me. The weight of their previous lives. The judgment of the off-meds. Dociline pumps like blood through the veins of this place. This "Silo," where Alex stores people rather than grains.

It's hard to ignore the cuff while I write. The first few sentences rekindle my anger from last night. I was justified. Alex will never be in my position. He's probably never skipped a meal, much less felt hunger or desperation. He doesn't feel the burden of keeping his family out of prison. Of choosing between a doctor's appointment and another year's worth of debt to sell off.

I will control my attitude. If these sentences are supposed to help me reflect or some bullshit, they're not working. Halfway through, I stop seeing words and start seeing letters. They lose meaning as I focus on my handwriting.

I will not lie to Alex. I will not tell him about my mother's biannual visits home, and how I watched her change. Won't tell Alex how his drug bent her slowly over a decade. How her voice lost its edge, then personality, then humanity, until she spoke like the automated service that calls to tell you your bills are past due, before your father flings a cell phone he can't afford to replace into the reservoir.

I'm almost finished when I hear the glass door open, again. Alex walks over—I don't look up, but I can hear him breathing, feel the heat of the authority he wears, especially here.

"How many left?" He's removed his coat to reveal a casual knit sweater pushed up over the rolled sleeves of his pastel yellow shirt. When he leans over to check my progress, my eyes linger on the line of his forearm and curve of his fingers.

I blink, refocusing on my work. "Seven."

"Good. When you finish, I want you to start a new page and write three things that relax you." Alex leaves, this time through a door on the opposite side.

Three things that relax me. After I finish my lines, I number the next blank page. How honest does he want me to be? I look at the honeycomb of cells in the Silo, full of Dociles who probably haven't been home in years. Who haven't been outside. Whose only window is the sky-blue disc a mile up. I write:

1. Being alone.
2. The outdoors.

I bite the top of my pen. Being alone outside sounds like heaven, right now. No schedule but the sun's, no one to please, no city sounds. Just my back against the cool grass and—

3. Stars.

I glance up at the glass ceiling. Do they even have stars, here?

I gasp when I realize Alex is leaning against the doorjamb, watching me finish.

"What?" I look at my notebook, then back at him. "Have I done something wrong?"

"No," Alex says. "Nothing, I just . . ."

He smiles, and I smile back.

I don't know why. It's a reaction, like when someone vomits and it makes you vomit, too. I have smile-vomit, and I wish it would stop, because I'm supposed to be angry with Alex and his stupid ego.

He walks over without hesitation and unfastens my cuff from the workstation. My smile falters; the pen falls from my hand. Before I can stand, Alex pulls me to my feet and holds me close.

Don't look at him, I think. Stare forward. At the strong curve of his neck and line of his jaw, and lips—they press against mine and I tighten my grip on Alex's sleeve. My hips grind up against his. I can't stop them—can't stop myself from holding on to Alex as his strong mouth captures mine.

He pulls away, leaving me wanting more.

I shouldn't want this. I don't. Especially not *here,* in the heart of Bishop Laboratories.

His mouth moves to my ear, leaving a trail of hot breath on my cheek. "Come with me." I've never had one, but it feels like the kind of thing you say to a lover—the words are heavy with want. And I want him back.

I let him pull me through the unknown door, past its fogged walls, beyond my blinders, and into the smallest room yet. Here, all the walls are fogged and the lights that line them dimmed. In the corner stands a modest bed fitted with white sheets. Navy-blue letters monogram the pillowcases and comforter: "ABIII."

"You have a bedroom in your office?" I ask.

Alex shrugs while he unbuttons my shirt and slides it off my shoulders. "I used to work a lot of late nights, before I signed you."

"And, what"—I struggle for words while he works my khakis off—"what about n-now?"

Suddenly, I am naked and cold. Alex threads his fingers through mine, our legs tangle, and we topple onto the bed. He leads, of course, and I don't stop him, the soft cotton of his pants sliding across my bare legs, warm ribbing of his sweater on my chest. Sure hand kneading my ass.

He bites my lip, his mouth so close to mine. Not asking, only taking. But I miss the pain when it subsides, a dull throb in its place. Alex buries his nose and tongue in the ticklish nook of my neck, making me squirm and twist both toward and away from the wet heat.

Cool air blankets me when Alex slides south, leaving me half-hard and alone. I wait—afraid he'll stop if I so much as breathe, and I'll turn back into one of his decorations. With a twist, Alex rolls me onto my stomach. Suddenly, I'm nervous, my throat already thick, head light. Am I ready for him to fuck me, again?

His hands slide up the backs of my thighs.

Does it matter?

Fingers dig into the mounds of my ass, spreading me wide.

I'm not sure, I—

"Oh god," I moan when Alex swipes his tongue across my exposed entrance; cool breath sends chills up my spine. His tongue swirls around my hole, again, and I surrender any control I might've had.

Moans pour from my lips as Alex probes me with his tongue. I anchor myself with handfuls of sheets as if I might rise off the bed. I want to come, for Alex to finish me. But instead of taking my cock, he pushes a slick finger inside me, brushing it against that nameless spot that feels like bliss. I call out his name, breaking the silence. Wondering too late if this room is soundproof or whether the Dociles who line the Silo can hear my shameless cries of submission.

Alex adds a second finger and strokes deep in me, touching every nerve ending. "I like hearing my name on your lips," he says.

I writhe against his knuckle, while he twists and strokes inside me, then kisses the curve of my ass. I want to feel his lips on my cock, but it's trapped between my stomach and the sheets. I raise onto my knees, begging for his hand. Instead, fingers pinch and roll my left nipple. Somehow, the pain adds to the pleasure inside me.

"Do you like that?" Alex asks, holding my body against his. His sweater against the sweat of my back, cock hard against me through layers of clothes.

I release the breath I've been holding. "Yes."

"Then tell me. Let me hear you."

"Please, Alex." If he wants to hear his name, I'll give it to him. I'd shout it from the top floor of the Silo, let it echo off the cells. "—feels so good." I can play my part; I can—

"Are you going to be a good boy, from now on?" His words stop me cold, cause my body to tense, but Alex eases his fingers slowly into my ass again, drawing deep moans from my throat.

"Yes!" I cry.

The pad of his thumb slowly strokes the head of my cock. Sharp breaths force their way out of my lungs. I'm so close. "Yes, what?"

"Yes, I'll . . ." I can't say that.

Alex coos in my ear. "Elisha?" He bites the lobe, sucking it between his teeth.

I arch against him, strain for his touch. I need it. I need him. But

I can't say this. Can't say I'll be a good boy, can't become his obedient little fucktoy. That's what I am, though. I'm playing into his rules right now.

"Elisha."

His fingers wiggle inside me. Body hugs mine. Tongue flicks my swollen ear. Voice—"Say you'll be my good boy."

I want to. It would be so much easier, if I could just relax. Just give in. Just come. Just say it. Just—

I mouth the words, testing their feel. Blood rises in my cheeks; they're almost as hot as the need between my thighs. Alex smiles against the back of my neck. Smiles while he kisses and sucks and nips, leaving little marks behind. His marks. I'm already his. Why put myself through this any longer?

"I'll be your good boy," I say. "I'll behave—be your good boy, Alex, I'll be, please let me . . ."

He lingers on the spot inside me. The thumb that drags slowly across my cock might as well drag my entire world.

". . . come."

Alex clings to me as my body spasms. Colors swirl behind my eyelids. My body clenches around his fingers. Warm come hits my chest. I collapse onto the bed and bury my face in pillowcases monogrammed with his initials, waiting for my breath and heart to slow.

I came.

I said it.

"You're beautiful." Alex nudges me onto my side. He lies facing me, clothes and hair only slightly askew. "Did you know that?"

What do I say now? I don't feel beautiful. I feel raw and exposed. "No," I whisper because he's so close and "yes" would be a lie.

Alex kisses my nose—my *nose*—then disappears for a minute, but I'm too tired to see where he's gone. He'd tell me not to show my curiosity, anyway. When he returns, I sit up—a defensive position. Alex climbs onto the bed, his breath smelling of spearmint and lemon. Come still stains the sheets and my chest. I shiver when he traces a hand over my thigh, up my torso, slides a finger through a stripe of come. He moves it toward my mouth.

I wet my lips and wrap them around the offering. Alex caresses my hair with his other hand as he slides his finger slowly in and then out of my mouth. I swallow, my throat sticky with my own seed. I did exactly what he wanted without a word between us. Not because I thought I had to, but because I wanted to.

For the rest of the day, I'm overly aware of how close we stand and how he touches me. He kisses my head when we take the elevator back to the top of the Silo, rests his hand on my waist as we walk home, holds my hips while I cook us dinner.

Tonight, Alex doesn't lock my cuff to the bed frame.

12

ELISHA

Alex is still in bed when I return, hungry and breathless, from my scheduled 6:00 a.m. workout. My personal trainer, Rita, has far too much energy. I head straight for the shower, even though my legs are so sore they barely hold me upright. Hot water soothes them.

The glass door slides open behind me. A gust of cool air disturbs the steam. Alex wets his hair under one of the other nine shower heads, then lathers up.

He catches me watching him. "How was your workout?"

"Fine," I manage to say. "Hard." I wonder if my body will ever look like Alex's, warm skin stretched over tight muscle.

"You'll get used to it."

I finish before he does and dress before he can watch me do so. Breakfast is scrambled eggs, turkey bacon—a meat I did not know existed—and coffee with a fake sweetener. Rita says I need foods that are high in protein and low in sugar. Alex nibbles his between checking his email, watching the news, and getting dressed.

"This morning, the California Legislature approved the use of Dociline in association with their own Debt Solution Office, which has struggled for years to siphon off the trillions in debt—"

"—today, as the European Parliament discusses the implications of Dociline in their respective countries. We asked citizens in Ireland what they thought of the drug and the response was overwhelmingly 'too American.'"

Alex taps his fingers to one another in different patterns, changing channels on the living room wall to bring up his messages. As he walks back upstairs for shoes, the images follow on the wall beside him into the bedroom. I put the empty plate in the sanitizer when he finishes, eyeing its insides with skepticism.

"I'll see you after work." Alex tilts my chin up and kisses me. He pulls only an inch back. "Have fun in school."

He smiles as he leaves. I blink rapidly as if he's an apparition I can unsee. But when I lick my lips, I still taste him and the sweetness of the gesture. It's nice. I wish it weren't.

I happily forget about Alex when the humanities tutor arrives. Sharon isn't like any teacher I ever had in school. She has degrees from universities in three different states and can actually read the ancient language carved onto all the city buildings.

"Latin," she explains, at the end of our lessons. "The dominant language of the Roman Empire. Do you know what other Roman tradition exists within our modern government?"

"No." I ready my pen. She offered me a tablet, but I'm not fast enough with them yet.

"Nexum, the system by which citizens can pay off their debts with personal servitude." She smiles.

I hate the Roman Empire.

After she leaves, I fix myself a chicken sandwich. I wander into the living room, chewing the dense, Rita-prescribed protein bread, wondering how I'm going to fill my lunch hour. Alex explained how to watch television, but now that I'm alone, I can't remember.

The elevator dings. I look between it and the clock. The cooking tutor isn't supposed to arrive until 1:00 p.m. It's barely past noon.

A short white guy with glasses and a chef's coat steps off the elevator. I set my sandwich back on its plate, then scramble to my feet, hoping he won't judge me harshly for not having cooked lunch.

"My name's Roger." He glances at the clock on the wall, then back at me. "Didn't mean to surprise you, but I wanted to get here early—I'll still need to teach you how to cook, since the Third will inevitably check your progress."

His words come so fast, I can't process them. "I'm sorry, who's the Third, Alex?"

"Yes. All the Bishops who've had their hands in Dociline are named the same thing—as if it weren't already clear how much they love themselves. So, we call them the First, the Second, and the Third, for clarity. That, and none of us particularly like the taste of their names in our mouths."

I take a step back. This man is not my cooking tutor. "Who's 'us'?"

"Empower Maryland." He says it as if I should know, already. "Eugenia said she slipped you my business card, while you were running. I wanted to check on you. Make sure—"

"Business card?" I don't remember her slipping anything—I pat my pockets instinctively, despite it being a different pair of pants.

"We can't transfer e-information—too easily traceable," Roger says, though I barely hear his words for the ringing in my ears. "None of these trillionaires expect paper, anymore."

"I don't have it," I say to myself as realization sets in. Somewhere, in my laundry, there is an Empower Maryland card. I'm sure I'm not supposed to be talking to them. Alex won't be happy if he—my stomach lurches—*when* he . . . I close my eyes and lean against the nearest wall as panic sets in.

"Are you okay?" Roger puts his hand on my shoulder. "The card doesn't really matter, anymore. I can—"

"It does matter." I'm still wobbly when I face him. "If Alex finds that, I'm the one who'll be punished, not you."

Roger opens his mouth and glances upward in thought, but fails to respond. I push past him on my way up to Alex's room, slide open his closet door, and knock over the hamper. I rifle through the mountain of dirty laundry for the gym shorts I wore that day, but grab only fistfuls of briefs and button-down shirts.

They're not here. The card's not here.

There aren't laundry machines in the house and Alex hasn't

asked me to wash any clothes. He must send it out. I wipe oil from my forehead, right the hamper, and toss the clothes back in. Maybe the laundry service will throw out the card. Or it'll get ruined in the wash. Either way, it's out of my hands.

"Elisha," I hear behind me.

I don't turn around; I'm still trying not to pass out. "Leave me alone."

I hear the soft creak of Roger's weight on Alex's bed and wonder whether he'll notice the dent. "I thought you might like to know," he says, "we've sent a team to help your community. They're building a schoolhouse and training a few folks to be teachers, so the kids don't have to walk miles to school. They're bringing unbranded winter clothing and helping build fireplaces for those who need the extra heat. An attorney from our legal clinic is also donating her time to assist folks with divorce or marriage petitions where financially advantageous, drafting or updating of wills, and fending off any particularly obnoxious debt collectors. No strings attached."

I should be grateful, but all I can manage is a flat, "Okay."

"I'm serious. We wouldn't do it if we didn't believe that all people should be free from debt slavery and the tyranny of the rich." Roger stares at me.

I know what he's implying. "Not all people can afford to stand by their principles."

"And that's why we're offering to help you."

"As long as I risk everything."

"Elisha, you've presented us with an opportunity we'd be hard pressed to duplicate. You live with the man developing the next Dociline formula, and you're off-med."

"You mean I'm not a drone."

"Yeah, and you have access to the Third's person, house, social circle—"

"I guess I have access to his space, but I can't—"

"Not only his space, but his computer system, maybe even his bank accounts and laboratory, someday."

I do not tell him I've already been to the lab. That I had sex with Alex there. I feel both ashamed and aroused thinking about it.

"But even better," Roger continues, oblivious, "you're clearly smart. I can feel the fire inside you."

"I won't hurt him, if that's what you're thinking," I say. "I'm not that kind of person."

"Oh god, we wouldn't ask you to do *that.*" Roger looks offended. "Just take notes—mental notes. The more information you can get us about Formula 3.0, the trillionaires' social and political plans, places they frequent, anything that excites or angers them, and so on, the better we'll be able to effect real change."

"Effect real change" sounds like a campaign slogan. No organization needs to know Alex's whereabouts unless they're planning to hurt him. And what if something happens to him? What happens to me, and what if the cops think I've done it? Alex's off-med Docile would be an obvious suspect. I'd go to jail—and so would my family, when my contract with Alex was voided.

This is too much. I can't do this. "Come on. We have a lesson to get through." I stand and lead Roger down to the kitchen, where his supplies still rest on the kitchen counter.

He looks like he wants to carry the conversation further. Get me to commit. But Empower Maryland could ruin me and my family, and I'm not sure they realize that. Or care.

Dinner is almost ready when Alex gets home. His head turns immediately to the kitchen, nose in the air. "Smells good in here." He hangs his coat up, then joins me. "What's for dinner?"

I recite the recipe exactly as Roger taught me. "Lamb chops with a balsamic reduction and roasted butternut squash."

Alex tastes the thickening sauce and nods. Took me three tries to get it right. He heads upstairs without telling me why. I don't ask. He's probably going to change clothes or shower—something trivial. But since I'm not allowed to ask superfluous questions, I can't help but wonder.

I plate the lamb, hoping its insides are still pink. When I over-cooked my test chop, Roger threw the whole thing in the bin, still hot. I almost reached into the composter after it, but he wrapped a hand around my wrist and held my eyes. Just as with the uncooked rice, wasting food is part of the game, now.

When the sauce is finished, I set it on a trivet between the two prepared table places, then join Alex. I salivate watching him take the first bite.

"Good flavor," he says. "Could be a bit rarer, but you're close."

"Thank you," I say, releasing my held breath.

With a tap, Alex brings up a document on the dining room table. He reads while he eats, ignoring me. I eat at Alex's pace, despite my hunger. After we both finish, I clear the plates. Alex touches an electronic document; then, with a few taps of his fingers, e-paper materializes between his fingers.

"Would you like a drink?" I ask. Roger gave me a quick rundown of the bar, though not enough to mix cocktails like Alex served at his birthday party.

He doesn't answer right away. I don't move, fixed in his gaze. "Yes," he says. "Pour us each a glass of the Cabernet Sauvignon and meet me upstairs."

He reads while he walks.

I take my time, holding the bottle steady, unscrewing the cork, and selecting the right glasses. Now that I've started lessons, I feel pressured to do everything right. Roger said he'd be checking my progress.

I walk slowly up the stairs, holding a stem in each hand. Roger assured me I'll be able to pair wine with food in a month. I nudge the door open with my elbow. Dim lights halo the headboard. Alex reads in bed.

Naked.

I stare into the dark red liquid as I approach. Alex turns down the covers beside him and takes one of the glasses from me. He wants me to lie with him. Cuddle. I work up the nerve to join him, but he shakes his head.

"Clothes." Alex sips his wine.

I undress with as little performance as possible, putting my clothes in the hamper. Being naked with Alex isn't as hard now as it was the first time, but it still takes effort to keep my hands by my sides and relax my muscles. I ease my own tension by keeping mobile: rolling my shoulders, rubbing my hands over my forearms, flexing my fingers.

"That's better." Alex's smile is soft and warm as he welcomes me into the bed beside him.

He raises his right arm, inviting me to lie with him. I can do that. I've already let him pleasure me, called myself his good boy, licked my own come from his fingers. This is nothing. This is easy— enjoyable, even, if I try hard enough. I slip under the covers beside Alex and rest against him. It feels kind of nice.

He hands my glass back to me, then takes another sip from his. I bring mine slowly to my lips, very aware that the sheets are cream colored and my wine is blood red. Alex continues to read, occasionally rubbing my side, kissing my head, drinking his wine. I gulp the dry alcohol down until the flavor doesn't make me wince.

His hand appears out of nowhere to steal my empty glass. When Alex angles my neck back and kisses me, I notice the buzz in my head and hum below my skin. He tastes like wine, and I want another drink.

By now, I can guess how Alex wants my mouth and tongue. The more the alcohol settles into my system, the more I give in. I remember how he felt against me—on me, in me. I want him and I don't even hate myself for it. I'm sure I will, later.

"Alex." I moan and nuzzle against him. My cock slides against his. He likes when I say his name. "Please, Alex."

"No, no, no."

No? No. *Yes.* Definitely yes. I've behaved the way he likes; what more does he want?

Alex props his pillows up against the headboard and scoots back against them. "I assume, from previous conversations, that you've never given head before."

"I don't think so." I don't even know what that means.

"Get between my legs. Hands and knees."

I grip the sheets so my heartbeat won't knock me over. Warmth crept over my skin while I wasn't paying attention.

"Lick your lips."

I do, cooling them with my saliva.

Alex's hand moves to his cock. His hips inch slowly up to meet his strokes. A low moan rumbles in his throat. "If you forget everything else, remember this."

I look up at him, waiting, not even breathing.

"Swallow."

"Swallow," I repeat.

"Always, unless I say otherwise." Alex threads his free hand through my hair.

He continues to pump his cock without my help, which is perfectly fine with me. I can handle being the hole he fucks. I can lie beneath him and call out his name while he comes inside me—right now I even want to.

I don't know if I can suck him—give head, whatever these trillionaires call it.

"Go on." His voice is breathy. "Watch your teeth."

He guides my mouth down onto his cock and I have no choice but to open wide. I close my lips around the head. My tongue brushes the sensitive skin. Alex juts up, suddenly. I choke and pull back, but he keeps me close.

"Take your time."

I wet my lips again. Putting my mouth on Alex's cock isn't as repulsive as it should be, especially not with him gently fingering my hair and smoothing his fingers down the back of my neck. The sensitive skin is smooth, almost soft, despite its rigid core. I move my tongue deliberately against the head—I can't fit much more inside me.

Soon, his fingers press against my neck, urging me deeper. I breathe slowly through my nose and inch down the shaft until I gag. Saliva wells in my mouth, drips down Alex's cock, and slides between his fingers as he works himself.

I strain against his grip, but Alex holds me in place. When I glance up, he's not even looking at me. His eyes are closed, lips slightly parted, chest heaving with heavy breaths. I'm not with him anymore; I'm not a person. I'm a wet hole.

"That's good," he whispers, while I do my best. "Just like that."

My jaw is sore when Alex moans and bucks his hips up, ramming his cock down my throat. I gag, but he holds me still as come fills my mouth. I can't breathe. I try to swallow, but it coats my dry throat. Alex's grip finally softens as his cock does. I pull back with a mouthful of come and catch his eye.

Swallow.

I force it down and wipe the tears from my eyes. They're a physical reaction to gagging, nothing more.

Alex releases a post-orgasmic sigh. "Good boy." He pets my hair and fluffs his pillows. "Get the rest of it and then you can go brush your teeth."

The rest of it. I resign myself to licking him clean. He shudders, still sensitive, then dries himself with a tissue. I take my cue to leave.

No amount of brushing can remove the taste from my mouth. I sip mouthwash right from the bottle. The alcohol burns my throat. I have to go out there and smile and kiss him like I enjoyed myself.

I enjoyed myself when Alex licked my hole. The memory sends a quick jolt of pleasure to my groin. I breathe deep and reassure myself: I knew when I signed the contract that he'd use me like this. I knew, and I still signed.

"It's okay," I whisper, safe behind the closed bathroom door. "It's okay to hate yourself and it's okay to enjoy yourself. Sometimes."

Alex seemed to like giving me an orgasm. He didn't take anything in return when he easily could've. I stare at my face in the mirror. It looks the same as always, but I know where those lips have been, what that tongue has done.

Alex liked it, though. Maybe that's enough. It might have to be.

13

ALEX

The first two months with Elisha are the longest of my life. Preakness is still a few months away, but the invitation to Mariah's annual costume party arrived, this morning, with a personalized message attached:

Dear Alex, it says. *If you've worked as hard with Elisha as you have on Formula 3.0, I hope my party will provide an opportunity to show him off. I've already arranged journalists and photographers for the event, eager to spotlight your success. All my love, Mariah.*

Only one month until Elisha is put to the test in front of uppercrust Baltimore—the families whose roots run deep through this city, who are shareholders at Bishop Laboratories, political officials, moguls and entrepreneurs in their fields. He's still unpredictable. As my Docile, his behavior does not reflect on him; it reflects on me. My ability to manage. To steer and represent Bishop Labs.

I set the invitation aside, on my desk, bring up my digital calendar, and enter the details so I won't forget. Why Mariah insists on mailing paper invitations I'll never understand.

With my letter opener, I slice open the seal on my other piece of mail: a small rigid envelope with two tiny plastic bags, a business card, and a note inside.

Dear Dr. Bishop, it reads. *The three enclosed items were found in our laundry facilities and inadvertently returned to another customer. We send them along, now, with our deepest apologies for the error and delay. Please consider your next service complimentary. All our best, Sisson Street Suds.*

I toss the packing paper and note, then overturn the first tiny plastic bag. The white-gold tie clip from my grandmother falls into my palm. I squeeze my fist around it, relieved it made its way back to me and horrified that I let something so precious slip away.

I take it, along with the rest, into my bedroom, and pull open the top drawer of my dresser. It's shallow with black suede inset and shaped to display jewelry and accessories for ease of selection. I place the tie clip with the others; the engraved *Legatum nostrum futurum est* catches the light. The other plastic bag contains a set of monogrammed cuff links, which are replaceable, but that doesn't mean I'm not glad to have them back. I set them in their place, then pick up the business card.

I flip the blank white side over to reveal text:

R. WARD—OUTREACH
EMPOWER MARYLAND
Baltimore City Division at
Clipper Mill, Woodberry
E. Halliday—Director

I purse my lips, pinch the card hard between my fingers. When I was in third grade, Empower Marylanders bashed in the window of the car that drove me home from school with a baseball bat. In sixth grade, they protested my first school dance so violently, the administration had to call the police. For decades, they have threatened my family, vandalized our property, slandered our name.

Our publicist calls Empower Maryland a "misguided anarchist organization that masquerades as a nonprofit and has nothing better to do besides protest Bishop Laboratories." I find that description generous. As far as I'm concerned, Empower Marylanders are terrorists.

They want to dismantle Bishop Laboratories. Imprison my family. They won't stop until everything we've worked for has been destroyed, which is ridiculous, because we've done nothing but help debtors. Baltimore would still be drowning in debt if it weren't for my grandmother. We cleaned this city up. I just spent three fucking million dollars—not to mention an additional twelve thousand per year—to support the poor. Every time one of us "trillionaires" signs another Docile, we help clear debt. And every debtor in one of our homes is another that doesn't go to prison.

This business card is not mine.

"Elisha!" I shout.

I hear his bare feet hit the hardwood and trudge up the stairs. He peeks over the threshold. "Yes, Alex?"

"Here. Now." I do not disguise the edge in my voice.

Elisha walks as if upstream, slowly and with effort. He knows what's coming. This is his. I can fucking smell the guilt on him.

"Where did you get this?" I hold up the card.

He glances at it for only a second before his face falls.

"Look at me." I am not letting him off easy for this. "Where did you get this?"

"I didn't know—"

"For every lie you tell me, you will earn another fifteen minutes in the cubby. For every hesitation or indirect answer, another five. You begin at sixty minutes."

"I didn't know she gave it to—"

"Sixty-five minutes."

Distress lines his face. "I'm not lying; I didn't know she gave it to me!"

"Who is she?"

"Her name was Eugenia. I don't know her last name."

"It's Halliday." I flip the card so he can see the text. "Where did you meet her?"

"On my run."

"When?"

"The first time you showed me the route."

"Was there anyone else? Who is R. Ward?"

"It's—" He struggles to force the word out.

"Seventy minutes."

"—Roger. He's also my cooking tutor."

"Consider him fired. Why did they give you this?"

"I told you, I didn't know. Eugenia slipped it into my pocket; I never saw it before it went to the cleaners."

By now, I think he's telling the truth without reserve, and Empower Maryland is the type to do something like that.

"Did they say anything?"

"Yes."

"What?"

"That they would help me if I wanted it."

"Anything else?"

"They mentioned my mother. I can't remember their exact words, but they implied they could help her, too."

Right. His mother who allegedly suffers from side effects of Dociline. Another lie. If she is sick, she was probably that way to begin with. I could send a doctor to check on her. Prove that it wasn't Dociline. Maybe even treat her, as a gesture of goodwill.

No, what am I thinking? This is a business relationship; I owe his family nothing outside of our contract. His mother is not my responsibility.

"This is the first you've seen this business card?" I confirm.

"Yes."

"And you haven't contacted Roger Ward or Eugenia Halliday?"

"No!" Elisha's eyes meet mine, voice fills with desperation. "I don't even know where Clipper Mill is—they found me."

I flip the card between my fingers several times while I center myself. Elisha's punishments must suit the infraction, not my anger.

"Please believe—"

"Be quiet."

He presses his lips together as if they might burst apart of their own free will.

"You are forbidden to have any contact with anyone from Empower Maryland, again. If they approach you, you are to tell them such as many times as they need to hear it. If they continue, you can refer them to me, personally. And if they approach, you are to tell me immediately. Do you understand?"

"Yes, Alex."

"Good. They do not have your interests at heart. They care only about themselves and their deluded cause."

"Yes, Alex," Elisha whispers.

"Now, undress."

I disappear into the bathroom and fill the cup beside the sink with cold water. Confinement is a harsh punishment; I need to be careful administering it.

When I return, he's standing naked, hands clasped behind his back. He drops his head when I look at him. Elisha's breathing is loud and ragged against the silence.

For a moment, I worry. What if he's not ready for this? What if he has a panic attack, and I have to pull him out? I'd waste weeks of training

The look he gives begs me not to. I see the offer on the quiver of his lips. He'd take a thousand lines or an hour of rice. Two hours, even. But he knows that bargaining is as bad as back-talking.

"Though the cubby is soundproof, I'm giving you this." I press a quarter-sized button into his hand. "If you press it, a buzzer will play over the sound system. You are only to press it for emergencies. Understand?"

"Yes." The button disappears in his trembling, sweaty fist.

I thrust the cold water into his other hand. "And drink this first. The whole thing."

He presses the glass to his lips and drinks it down without stopping to breathe. Then he gasps and hands it back.

I set the empty glass on the nightstand, then pull open the closet, freshly filled and organized by the laundry Docile. The thin edges of a trapdoor show in the middle of the walkway. I press my index finger against the lock, then lift the top to reveal a small crawl space.

"Get in."

Elisha's knuckles whiten as he grips the edges and lowers himself down. His knees bang against the hard tile.

"Let go." I prod his fingers off the ledge.

When he's all the way in, I begin to close the hatch.

"Alex?" His voice comes quietly from the dark.

"What?" I lift the hatch a few inches. Elisha's eyes catch the light. The hope is gone from them.

"What if I have to pee?"

I can't look at him when I answer. His question exposes the reality of what I'm making him do. It's different looking at an empty crawl space, knowing there's an emergency buzzer and a vent, and that the company who installed it has installed dozens of these around Baltimore without a single complaint. Who would complain? Not the Dociles.

I swallow hard. "There's a drain in the floor."

With that, I shut the hatch. My fingerprint locks it. Once again, the hardwood blends with the rest of my closet floor. You'd never know a person was inches below. I set a timer with a touch of my fingers and do my best to forget.

I take my time drawing a bath, draping a towel over the warmer. I tap the wall and then my fingers together. Dim lights, no bigger than fireflies, dot the bathtub walls. The overhead fades to black. I sink below the hot water, burning my face. Cool air kisses my skin when I surface. It's too quiet. All I hear is Elisha pleading with me, begging I go easy on him.

Seventy minutes is too long, isn't it? It's not like he'll know how long it's been, if I take him out early. "City sounds," I say, louder than necessary. Conversation and cars creep up around me. But in my mind, Elisha drowns them out.

During the week that passes, the spark snuffs out of Elisha, out of our conversations and our touch, and I hope that doesn't means I broke him. I need to do something to revive him—and not only because Mariah's party looms around the corner, but also to show him I'm not upset. That a punishment only lasts as long as its timer.

Elisha returns from his morning run red-faced and sweating. He almost doesn't notice me sitting at the island in the kitchen. I motion him over and he complies. "You're getting fast." I rub the small of his back; it's damp and hot against my hand—unpleasant—but I don't want Elisha to know, so I pull him closer. We look over his running times. "Really fast, actually." I am genuinely surprised. "Faster than me."

He shrugs, not as impressed as I am. "I like running."

The idea that Elisha could enjoy an assigned activity, like a hobby, completely evaded me. And, now, I know how to fix this. With a few taps on the tabletop, I bring up one of the basic diagnostics we use on the Dociles at work. "Would you like to take a creativity test?"

Elisha leans over the counter, afraid to touch it now that it's alight with documents and menus. "You're asking me?"

"Yes. All our Dociles at the lab consent to testing in their contracts. It wasn't in yours, so . . . I'm asking, now."

"You won't"—he looks sternly at me—"inject me with Dociline?"

"Absolutely not." I hand him my stylus.

I slide the test window in front of him. Each question prompts the subject to describe how a different work of art makes them feel. First, a physical replica of van Gogh's *Starry Night* materializes— paint, brushstrokes, and all.

"Can I touch it?"

"Please," I say. Most Dociles do so without asking.

Elisha traces the wind with his fingertips, circles the stars. He's never looked at me the way he looks at blue swirls of a painted sky.

"What do you think of it?" I ask, while he writes.

"It reminds me of home," he says, without looking up.

When I hold my palm open beneath the painting and its gilded frame, the paint and precious metal dissolve back into meaningless particles and return to whence they came.

Elisha is still working when I ask, "Would you like another piece? Perhaps music, this time." I select Franz Liszt's "Liebesträum no. 3," a favorite.

"Sure."

Warm notes dance throughout the room. Up they twirl and tiptoe like a ballerina's bourrée en couru. Elisha closes his eyes while the piano diminuendos. Only when he bends down to write again do I catch the hint of a smile—not meant for me. It overflows from inside him.

"And this one?"

Elisha closes his eyes for more than a minute before answering. "I imagine this is what love sounds like." His forehead creases. "It sort of hurts, doesn't it?"

I take a breath and hold it. The knot in my chest feels as fresh as the day it was tied. "Yeah, I guess it does. 'Oh lieb, solang du lieben kannst.'"

"Are those the lyrics?" Elisha asks.

"No, it's a German poem that inspired the composer."

"But you know the poem."

By heart. "'Er aber sieht und hört dich nicht, kommt nicht, daß du ihn froh umfängst; der Mund, der oft dich küßte spricht nie wieder: Ich vergab dir längst.'"

"What does that mean?"

I draw in a breath and close my eyes. "'Yet he sees and hears you not, you cannot comfort him again; the lips which kissed you often speak, not again: I forgave you long ago.'"

I remember reading the poem as a boy and asking my tutor why anyone would write such a horrible thing. She replied, in German of course, that love was horrible and struck down even the best of us.

They don't make love like that, anymore. Now it's all bank accounts and subpoenas and Genea-Economic records. There's no ache. Breaking up with Javier didn't *hurt*.

"Alex?" Elisha asks as if for the second or third time.

"Hm?"

"Are you okay?"

"Yeah, I uh . . ." I study Elisha. He looks alive, again. "You'll take German," I say. "And piano. I'll arrange for tutors, next week. How would you like that?"

"A lot, actually," he says, and I kiss him for it. If no one else, Elisha is real. And I have to take care that he remains that way.

14

ELISHA

Alex stretches his hand toward me through flashes of light. I fumble for his fingers, squeezing harder than I should when I find them. He pulls me from the limousine—a car designed much longer than two people could ever need—and onto marble pavement.

I'm thankful he picked the tie-on sandals for my costume. Those shoes with the spiky heels would've sent me flying to my death in front of all these people. It's hard enough to balance with giant feathered wings fixed to my back.

"Dr. Bishop!"

"Over here, Dr. Bishop!"

"Dr. Bishop, is that your new Docile? Can we get a picture?"

Alex stops and the flashes flare around us. I shield my eyes.

Their laughter deafens me. "Don't you ever let him outside, Dr. Bishop?"

Alex's smile blocks the light. He's all I can see.

"This is Elisha."

"How long have you had him?"

"Three months."

"Turn around for us, hon!"

Alex grabs my shoulder to stop my guessing whether I should listen to these people.

"Aw, come on, Bishop. Just a spin. Let's see the goods."

I lean into Alex, not sure if I can stand much more of this. Even though he warned me, I didn't expect such a fuss.

"Fine." Alex raises my hand over my head. "Go ahead, Elisha. Give me a quick spin."

My skin is hot against the early spring air. The only real clothes I'm wearing are a pair of thick, white briefs, embroidered with threads of real gold and studded with diamonds. I'm afraid to walk in them. But I promised Alex I'd behave. I'm doing this for him, not the tabloids.

No, wrong, this is for my family.

I raise up onto my toes, turning while Alex guides me.

"Good boy," he says—loud enough that only I can hear—then kisses my neck.

The first notes of shame play across my face. *Good boy.* It's one thing when he calls me that in private—and even alone, the pet name embarrasses me. It means I'm giving in. And in front of these cameras? Everyone can see what I've become. Thankfully, my family doesn't get the tabloids out that far.

"Dr. Bishop!" A man lunges forward, thrusting a small electronic device into Alex's face. "Are the rumors true? Did Elisha refuse Dociline?"

The crowd falls silent.

Alex looks me over, from the diamond-dust halo projected over my head to my polished toenails. "Elisha declined Dociline," he says—to me. Not with anger or regret. With a smile. With pride. "As is his right."

Another journalist steps forward. "Dr. Bishop, Keesha Owens with *The Baltimore Sun*." Alex gives this one his full attention. "First, may I compliment you on how well-behaved and presentable Elisha looks."

Alex smiles, proudly. "Thank you."

A small part of me wants to disprove the compliment. To disobey. I'm the one doing all the work, not him. I'm the one who exercises six days a week and has changed his entire diet. Who's suppressed his curiosity, his instincts, his identity. Who's become a *good boy*.

I'm glad when Owens continues and the moment slips away. When I remember that it wouldn't be strong of me to get myself punished, to get on Alex's bad side, to make him revoke the stipend he's sending my family. It would be stupid.

"What's it been like working with an off-med so extensively, and has the experience influenced your work at Bishop Laboratories with regards to leadership or the forthcoming Formula 3.0?"

"It's been enlightening!" Alex and Owens both laugh. They sound fake.

"I bet," she says.

Alex slides a hand around my waist, pulling me against him. "Truly, though, the experience has allowed me to think outside the box, as they say. I'm hoping to bring a fresh point of view to Formula 3.0 based on the insights working with Elisha has provided me."

When he rubs his hand over my body without any overt sexual agenda, I become aware of mine resting over his ribs, fingering his red polka-dot button-down. It strikes me that our motions mimic actual affection.

Owens smiles, clearly satisfied with Alex's answer. "I've never known a Bishop to back down from opportunity. And you seem to be handling this one expertly."

"Thank you," he says.

"And thank you for your time."

Owens steps back, but before we can pass, a recording device thrusts forward. I recoil, surprised by the intrusion, and Alex holds up his palm to stop them.

"Dr. Bishop, do you think that Elisha's refusal of Dociline reflects the drug's decline?"

"No," he answers without looking the reporter in the eye.

"Do you know why he refused?"

Alex moves on, ignoring them.

"Dr. Bishop!" they shout. "What about the rumors that—"

"I don't respond to rumors." Alex stops to face the reporter. "What outlet do you work for?"

"Chadwick Bell, for the *City Paper:* can you comment on the rumored side effects of—" He speaks so fast I can barely understand him.

Alex closes his hand over Chadwick's and angles the device toward his mouth. "Come back when you have some facts. Until then, *City Paper*"—he looks Chadwick up and down—"show some integrity."

Questions and comments fly amidst the camera lights. Alex steers me up the stairs into Mariah's building, declining further pictures. Another limousine pulls up behind us and we're soon forgotten.

A woman in a crisp black suit stops us in the entryway, then consults a tablet. "Dr. Alexander Bishop the Third?"

"Yes," Alex says. "That's me."

"Your Docile is off-med?"

"Yes."

The woman taps the tablet. "Ms. VanBuren requests that all off-meds be leashed, inside her home. At least until she's sure they're sufficiently well behaved."

Alex purses his lips only for a second before smiling again. "Understood."

"Thank you, Dr. Bishop. You can pick up a courtesy leash at the coat check."

We follow the line of guests to a closet as large as my house, where Dociles exchange coats and bags for tickets. Alex hands over his blazer and receives both a ticket and a long chain that matches my cuff.

Alex sighs while he slides the chain through the O-shaped end, creating a loop. "You don't need this," he mumbles, slipping the loop over my head. The chain is shockingly cool against my skin. "Don't act like you do."

"I won't." I hold my chin up while he adjusts the chain. A tug signals he's finished and I follow, no longer able to dally or hesitate. I should be embarrassed, but when I remember I'm mostly naked in a stranger's house, the chain feels more like a security blanket than a leash. Alex, on the other hand, fiddles nervously with the chain, unsure how to hold it.

The ceiling arches high above us, as we make our way past the foyer. The only light shines from tiny stars patterned across the ceiling and floor in real constellations. White silk cushions shaped like clouds—big as king-sized beds—sit around the room.

Trillionaires lounge on them, wearing expensive suits and dresses in white or red to go with the heaven and hell theme. All the Dociles on this floor are painted in white and gold swirls, like clouds wrapped around their skin. Fruit, golden sauces, and white liquor are laid out on every table. The scent of sex and sugary fruit wafts from a recessed pit, padded entirely with pillows, where an orgy of Dociles moan and writhe against one another. This must be Mariah's version of heaven. I clench tightly around the anal plug, grateful for its presence.

"Alex!" I recognize the woman who waves from our visit to Bishop Labs—Jess, Alex's Head of Research. "Thank god you're here." She walks over and nods hello, dressed in theme with a silver halo and a white strapless dress that ends in cute lace trim. "Hey, Elisha."

"Good to see you." It feels odd acting as casual with her as she does with me. Jess is not my friend. She makes Dociline.

"Keep me company?" she asks Alex. "Mariah's holding court downstairs and you know how much I love Dociles trying to get up my skirt."

I sympathize with her, since I feel that way about trillionaires, but then Alex says, "Same."

I'm so surprised, I don't notice he's begun to walk downstairs with Jess until the leash pulls tight around my throat. Alex swats my hands away when I reach up to loosen it. "Don't touch it." His fingers linger around my neck while he fixes the chain. "You're not supposed to need it, remember?"

"I remember." I nod for extra assurance.

"Good." He grips the leather handle in his fist as we near the bottom of the steps and step into what might as well be hell.

Flames rise up from the bronze vases, glittering unnaturally. When Alex swipes his fingers through them, I gasp before realizing he's unharmed. Despite my shock, I manage to keep slack in the chain that joins us.

"You've really outdone yourself," Alex says loudly enough that Mariah and Dutch look up from their conversation.

"Bishop!" Dutch hops up and grabs Alex's hand for a hard shake. "I see you brought the Docile out of hiding. All trained up?"

"Absolutely." Alex looks at me as if to say, *Right?*

"Good." He nudges Alex. "I'm getting a little bored with all these preprogrammed blow jobs from the on-meds, you know? I could use a real live cocksucker." His laugh billows over the thumping bass.

Mariah kisses Alex's cheek, then turns to inspect me. Her eyes linger on the halo of diamond dust that hovers over a thin brown headband disguised by my hair. She smooths her hand over my feathered wings—I did not ask if they were real, and I hope no one does because I don't want to find out—then slides her fingers down my side, stopping to squeeze the ridge of muscle developing.

"You're doing well," she says—again, to Alex, not me. I squeeze my fingers together behind my back when she eyes my crotch, but she doesn't touch me any further. "I'll put in a good word for you with the Board," she says.

"Appreciated." Alex tugs on my leash and I follow the group of trillionaires to their seats.

Not seconds after they grace the couch, Dociles descend between their legs, unbuttoning pants, diving up skirts. My eyes widen, but the trillionaires don't even seem to notice. They take drinks layered in red and orange that stain their lips, thrusting their hips up occasionally to meet a waiting mouth.

I hope I've blended into the couch. That no one will notice I'm sitting here beside Alex. He remembers me. He fondles my hair and rubs my neck, all the while laughing, discussing technology I've never used and businesses I've never heard of.

"Hey, Bishop," Dutch says. "Let me do you one. I brought Opal and Onyx with me. You deserve not to think about the Docile bobbing on your junk, after three months of work."

"You know I like a challenge," says Alex.

Is that how he sees me, as a challenge? He didn't decide I wouldn't take Dociline; I did. I refused him. I grind my teeth to keep the words inside.

"I also know you like pretty boys. Onyx!" Dutch snaps his fingers and a lithe Black guy, probably around my age, crawls over. Come frames his smile. "That's my good boy."

"Don't be rude, Dutch," Mariah says, a Docile already buried up her skirt. "Aren't you going to offer Opal to Jess?"

Jess looks at us through her tilted wine glass. "Hm?"

"Oh, uh." Dutch looks thrown. "I think she's occupied."

I've never heard Dutch fumble his words, before.

Mariah watches Jess chug the rest of her drink.

"Yeah, I'm going to go freshen up and check out the desserts, upstairs." Jess stands carefully in her heels, hands her glass to a serving Docile, and hurries off.

A slap turns my and everyone else's heads. "You like that?" Onyx leans into Dutch's hand for another and Dutch indulges him. "Go help Bishop relax."

Is he what Alex wants? An eager on-med? I want to hate Onyx for giving in and becoming *this* and liking it. And Alex for liking him. But Onyx isn't a real person anymore. Whoever he was before disappeared along with his name.

"Elisha." Alex tugs on my leash.

"Yes?"

Alex nods at Dutch. "Return the favor." It doesn't matter that I've refused Dociline. To these trillionaires, we're all the same. I might as well be Onyx.

Any hesitation will only hurt me later, so I crawl over between Dutch's legs. He's already unbuckling his belt. I sneak a glance at Alex, who leans back, arms folded behind his head while the other Docile swallows his entire length. I still can't deep throat, as Alex calls it.

"I've never been sucked by an angel, before." Dutch smiles down at me. "Come on, wild thing."

Wild thing. *Wilder.* I almost forgot my surname.

Dutch grabs the back of my head and guides my open mouth around his cock. "Oh yeah. Fuck."

I close my eyes, pretend he's Alex. That we're in bed and the sounds around me—conversation, slurps, and moans—are a soundtrack, like city sounds.

Hell sounds.

When he's close, Dutch wrenches my head back. "Here it comes— ohh yeah, wear it."

I'm staring down his cock like the barrel of a gun when revulsion overcomes me. He's going to come on my face. Even Alex doesn't do that. I squeeze my eyes and mouth shut and jerk back against Dutch's grip before he comes. Warmth splatters against my chest. When I dare look, most of it's on the floor.

Everyone stares—Mariah cringing, Dutch like I've spat on him, Alex blank. His green eyes gloss over with indifference, jaw clenches. I can only look at the mess on the polished hardwood; my whole body flushes with heat; a buzz settles into my ears; gray clouds my vision.

What have I done?

"You said your off-med was perfectly trained, Alex," Mariah murmurs from somewhere behind me.

"I thought he was." Alex's voice and footsteps near me. "He'll be punished for this. Severely."

I can't move—can barely breathe. I've ruined everything. He'll have me kneel on the rice for hours, write a novel's worth of words, spend the night alone in that cubby. Already my knees hurt and my legs cramp up. What if he revokes my family's stipend?

"Really, Alex." I feel Mariah's soft hand stroke my hair and it takes all my strength not to recoil from that as well. "There's no reason we can't settle this now. Dutch?"

I still can't look at them. Only the floor—at the mess—while I count my heartbeats.

"Yeah." Dutch clears his throat. "No reason Elisha can't finish the job." I hear his clothes and body shift as he leans forward. When he speaks, his voice is close. "Clean it up, Docile."

I don't look to Alex for confirmation; I can feel his eyes on me, the heat of his anger. I deserve this. Slowly, I move onto my hands and knees, then bend down so that my face is inches from the thin white lines.

I can do this. These people don't matter. I don't have to live with them. I have to live with Alex. He matters. My family matters.

Eyes closed, I draw my tongue across the hardwood. I swallow my revulsion along with the come. The chemical taste of floor polish burns my mouth. When I finish, I remain on all fours, eyes fixed on the floor, praying I've redeemed myself.

"That was almost hotter than seeing him wear it." Dutch snickers and I hear the couch shift as he relaxes back, satisfied. "You should have Elisha clean all your floors with his tongue, Bishop."

"Thank you for the suggestion," Alex says, "but I'll deal with him in my own way."

"Here you go, sweetie." Mariah tilts my head back. "Wash down Dutch's nasty spunk, then go play in the pit with the other Dociles while the adults talk." She presses a glass to my lips and I drink whatever it is—bitter, orangey, and dry. But she's right; it does taste better.

She removes the chain from my neck—though I don't feel like I've earned the freedom—and nudges me toward the cushioned pit between the couches. Around me, Dociles touch and kiss and suck each other. But they're all on-meds. I'm not, and I don't know what I'm supposed to do.

Dutch's Docile, Onyx, smiles and runs a hand through my hair. I try to see through the Dociline. There's a person in there, somewhere, and I'm as bad as the trillionaires if I have sex with him.

Onyx captures my lips before I can consider doing the same. There's no hesitation when he presses his body against mine, and he doesn't feel like a robot when he pulls me onto the cushions.

He kisses down my jawline. I tilt my head back, exposing my throat. I glimpse Alex, upside down, watching. Dutch points and whispers, a twisted smile on his lips, Opal in his lap.

I can't care anymore. It's too hard, and my world is too plush. Too warm. Too smooth. Vibrating with pleasure.

"Look at him!"

"He likes it."

Our cocks slide against each other until Onyx takes them in

hand. He moans and whimpers against me. Soon enough, similar sounds spill from my lips. My fingernails dig into the smooth skin of his ass, pulling him against me. My kiss falters; his lip catches between my teeth.

Alex's inverted figure blurs. The room tilts around me. Their laughter echoes. I welcome the refuge of whatever chemical is working itself through my blood.

Onyx dives into my neck, sucking and nibbling on the sensitive flesh. He rubs the heads of our cocks between nimble fingers, sending me over the edge. I feel the sound in my throat but can't distinguish my moans from the others.

When I blink, the room smears. My lips move. Darkness comes.

15

ALEX

"What did you give my Docile, Mariah?" I'm sure there was more than alcohol in that cocktail, but there's no nice way to ask. Just because I'm socially obliged to share Elisha at events like this doesn't mean I'm not still his Patron. I'm still responsible for his health. I still care.

"I didn't give him anything I wouldn't take myself," she says.

"You didn't need to give him *anything*."

Mariah lowers her voice. "He was having a panic attack, Alex, and you were making a scene. I'm trying to help you."

I close my eyes while I take a deep breath. "You're right, thanks."

Elisha wasn't prepared for this—neither of us was. For the pressure. I feel it crushing my chest into rubble. Mariah and Dutch live for the social circuit. I can shake hands and bullshit with the best of them—I am a Bishop—but no one can know I'd rather have spent tonight at home with Elisha than letting every Docile within a mile of Baltimore City put their mouth on my dick.

Elisha's motions grow sluggish while Onyx kisses softly down his neck. They look like lovers and, for a fleeting moment, jealousy passes through me.

"Alex," Elisha mumbles, eyes half-closed.

"It's okay," I say with my best smile. "Just relax." I doubt he can even hear me.

Elisha's eyelashes flutter as he tries to stay awake. "Please, Alex . . ."

"Let him rest." Mariah pulls me toward the stairs. "Shall we move along?" The others follow at her suggestion. She is, after all, the hostess, and we don't dare insult her. "I've scheduled acrobats on the third level of heaven."

"I shouldn't leave him there." I gesture to Elisha sprawled out in the cushioned pit, Onyx curled up beside him.

"I'll have a Docile move him into a crate for safekeeping." Mariah snaps her fingers and a man scoops him up.

"Thank you." I sigh with relief when Elisha stirs in the Docile's arms. He mumbles and whispers incoherently. Has he always been so small, or does he only look it now?

"He's not going anywhere, man." Dutch lowers his voice. "I know you have a soft spot for your lab rats, but you don't want the paparazzi to caption your picture with 'Alexander Bishop leaves social event of the year to cuddle with his Docile,' do you?"

It would be foolish of me to ignore public relations advice from Dutch. Everyone thinks he's some rich asshole—hell, he often fools me. They'd never guess he spent his childhood in Bishop Laboratories, that we met while he was an on-med and continued to be friends after he detoxed. Dad let him stay and work around the lab after his contract was up, and before long we were heading off to university together. Dutch built himself from scratch—learned how to present as a person of class rather than a debtor. That's why I always listen to him.

I throw an arm around his shoulder and smile wide. "Who said anything about leaving?" I can have fun. For one night, I can stop worrying about Elisha.

By 3:00 a.m., guests are sneaking into unclaimed rooms with one another, finally leaving their Dociles to rest. I glimpse the microchip app on my phone; Elisha's vitals are still normal, but I'm anxious to check on him in person.

Dutch doesn't look back as he disappears into the elevator with William Barth's daughter, Linda, heiress to the construction throne. Her father would shit himself if he knew she was even here. Thinks hard work puts him above the social circuit.

I make sure no one's watching me, then approach a nearby Docile. They don't need supervision, here. They wash up in focused silenced—never speaking unless spoken to—and situate themselves in bunk beds that recess into the walls like slabs at the morgue. They even lock themselves in.

"Excuse me."

She perks up. "How may I help you, sir?"

"Show me where the Docile crates are."

"Of course, sir. Right this way."

I hesitate before following her up a back stairwell. Though it's probably the fastest route she knows, a guest would never use this entrance. As long as I go forward with confidence, no one will question me. And if they do? I'm simply picking up my Docile. Like a checked coat. I fidget with the numbered ticket in my pocket. Elisha isn't a coat. He should've been with me.

"I'm looking for a specific Docile," I say, when we arrive. "His name's Elisha."

All our studies show that on-meds are as observant as off-meds, though any memories made while on Dociline fade when it leaves their bodies.

"He's in that crate." She points to a waist-high bunk. Gold gladiator sandals press against the platinum bars.

I bend down and unlatch the crate door. "You can go," I say to the helpful Docile, and she joins the others readying for bed.

"Elisha." I massage his calves, hoping that will wake him. I couldn't fit inside if I tried. The bunks are only wide enough to accommodate one person, so the Dociles don't try and share. They won't fuck each other unless directed, but the precaution doesn't hurt.

Elisha stirs under my touch. "Wake up. It's time to go home."

"Home." He bangs his head on the ceiling when he tries to sit up. "Ow." He rubs the spot and lies back down, crushing his already-mangled wings.

"Come on." I don't have time for this. Not that any other guest would wander in here, but they could. I'm still not sure how we're going to leave unnoticed. This is why most of Mariah's guests spend the night. There are few spaces where people of class can interact without the paparazzi following us.

I grip under Elisha's knees and drag him out. He can't weigh more than a hundred and fifty pounds, but his limp weight fights me.

With a few taps of my fingers, I dial my building. "Tom, it's Alex Bishop." I hoist Elisha into my arms.

"How are you, sir?" His voice is crisp in my ear.

"Okay, but I need a car to pick me up from Mariah's house. Fast as you can."

"Right away, Dr. Bishop."

"Tom?"

"Yes, sir?"

"Send it around the back. Have them call as soon as they arrive."

"Should be five minutes, sir."

"Thank you. End call."

Elisha tries to roll over in my arms. Instead, his feathers smack me in the face. He slides from my grip just as I find a cushion. A thread of diamonds unravels from his underwear. I pull the broken wings off his shoulders and abandon them.

"I want to go home," he says, looking at me through slitted eyes.

"We are. Can you stand up?"

With my help, he manages his own two feet, but quickly leans all his weight against me. I'm practically carrying him—down the back stairs and out through Mariah's kitchen, where Dociles clean up after the chefs. My phone rings just as we make it outside. I don't bother answering. The driver helps me maneuver Elisha into the back seat.

When we arrive at my building, Tom joins us, extracting Elisha from the car like the jaws of life.

"Am I home?" he mutters, clinging to me.

"Just up the elevator and then we'll get you into bed."

I refuse further help from Tom and the driver, propping Elisha against the elevator wall as we ride up, alone.

"No." He slumps in the corner, head lolling back against the wall. He hasn't refused anything since Dociline. Not even while we were fighting.

"Elisha," I warn him. "Don't talk to me like that."

The doors open and Elisha stumbles into my living room.

"This isn't home." He catches himself on the side of the couch. "You said I was going home."

Oh. Just fucking great. Whatever Mariah gave him comes with a side of nostalgia. Dociline would have prevented this whole episode, including my friends' curiosity and Elisha's reaction to Dutch and whatever Mariah gave him afterwards and—*everything*.

"We are home," I say.

He pokes my chest. "This is your home."

I restrain his hands with one of mine. He's going to hurt himself. "That's enough," I say.

"This is *not* my home." Elisha's speech slurs as he attempts to gesture at the grand piano. "Look at this place."

I'm not having this conversation. "Do you want to go to bed? Come on, let's get into bed."

But he fights me, trying his hardest to pry my hands off of him. He'd run for it, if he could stand up. "Let me go."

"Elisha. Stop."

He shakes his head. "I'm going to be sick."

That's where he's trying to go: the bathroom. I release Elisha in time for him to throw up on my two-hundred-thousand-dollar love seat.

I sigh and put an arm around him. "Let's get you to the bathroom." This time, we make it.

I wet a washcloth and press it to his forehead while he hugs the toilet bowl. Hundreds of dollars' worth of liquor mingle in the water.

"That's it." I rub my hand over his back. "Get it all out."

After an hour, he raises his head from the toilet. Tears shine in his reddened eyes. I strip what's left of his costume and help him into the bath. He'll need to see a doctor. Just in case.

"I'm sorry I puked on your couch," he says, once he's clean and wrapped in a towel.

"Don't worry; you can clean it up tomorrow."

He bows his head.

"I'm—" I scratch the back of my neck and pretend to study the ceiling. What was I thinking? "That was a terrible joke." The only reason I continue to ramble is because he probably won't remember tonight. "You don't have to clean it up. It's a piece of furniture. If the cleaner can't handle it, I'll buy a new one."

Elisha squeezes my hand, incapable of more words. I don't have the heart to move him when he collapses onto my bed. I should. I don't want him to pick up the habit of sleeping with me. That would be scandalous: a Docile sleeping in his Patron's bed.

This isn't his fault, though. I want to blame Mariah, but it's probably mine. What if Dad and the Board are right? How am I supposed to develop the next Dociline formula—which will affect millions of lives—when I can't even manage one Docile?

I sit the trash can beside Elisha on the floor. My bed feels so small with him in it—beside me, not under me or between my legs. I can't remember the last time I slept next to someone. Where do I put my feet? My arms? Elisha probably doesn't even know where he is. My hand drifts to his hair, still damp from the shower. He curls against me. I raise my arms, suddenly afraid to touch him.

No one's here. No one's watching. I put an arm around his back and hold him. He falls asleep long before I do.

The next morning, I wake up Elisha to discipline him. I have to do it first thing—as close to the offense as possible, so he'll feel direct consequences. He insulted Bishop Laboratories' Chief Financial Officer. One of Mariah's guests. My friend.

I can't coddle him. Not when my future is on the line.

"Wake up." When I nudge him, he doesn't move. "Elisha." I roll him over.

He blinks up at me and presses his fingers against his forehead. "Mmmm."

I suppose that's an audible response. "Let's go. You have—"

He grabs the bucket I left beside the bed and retches.

"—lines," I mutter. I sigh and rub a hand over his back, slick with a thin layer of sweat. Maybe now's not the time. What's the point if he's too sick to pay attention, anyway?

Instead, I call a doctor. She tells me he's dehydrated, so I wait downstairs, mostly tapping my stylus against the SmartTable, while she gives Elisha intravenous fluids.

"He'll be fine," she says while she packs up. "Just let him rest."

"Thank you." I see her out.

For the rest of the day, I work from home, summoning city sounds to keep me company amidst the sickly silence. When I open my email, the first thing I see is a flagged forward from Dutch: the ODR's accepted our proposal for renovation. We won the contract. We *won*. Bishop Labs has worked alongside the ODR almost since its inception. This contract is the culmination of a hundred-year partnership. The better our ODR functions, the more integral it will become in Maryland, and the more eagerly other states will follow. I'd like to see Dociline in other countries, during my tenure. I could be the Bishop who rid the world of debt.

I hop up with a smile and make it to the stairs before remembering Elisha's in no state to appreciate the news. Damn. With a sigh, I call Dutch, instead, to discuss details.

Around 7:00 p.m., I hear the shower turn on. Half an hour later, I hear the bedroom door open and scramble to look absorbed in my work. I've been working all day—or, at least, trying. With a few swipes, I dismiss physical documents to their digital forms and organize them into stacks.

"Alex?"

"Yes?" I look over my shoulder to see Elisha hugging his arms to his chest. If he's cold, the underwear and tee shirt he's wearing won't help.

"I wanted to make some dinner, if that's okay." He closes his eyes and holds his breath for a moment, then returns to the world. "Maybe just some toast."

"Of course," I say. "You can always feed yourself if you're hungry."

"Thank you." Elisha uncurls as he heads to the pantry. Slowly, he removes two slices of bread and puts them in the toaster oven. When he finishes, he leans against the counter as if he's using it to hold himself up.

"Sit down." I stand. "I'll finish this. The doctor said you need to rest."

"I can—"

"Don't argue with me or you'll write lines for dessert."

"Oh." Elisha considers how to end his thought. "Kay." He sits at the table beside my workstation and waits with his hands clasped in his lap, while I remove the toast and butter it. Haven't done this for anyone ever—buttered their toast. Feels like a thing you'd do for a child or for a—for a lover.

"Here." I set the plate down harder than intended. "Let me know if you're hungry for something more substantial, later."

"Thanks. I will."

I settle back in beside him and evaluate the documents stacked on my screen. What was I working on? I ignore the soft crunch of toast and select whatever's on top, determined to at least look busy.

That night, Elisha returns to his trundle bed. I sleep facing the opposite direction, so I won't be tempted to check on him every five minutes. Instead, I stare at the wall until my eyes grow too heavy to keep open.

Screams startle me awake. I clutch at the sheets in the dark, reminding myself I'm safe in my own bed. Then the screams turn to gasps. And they're coming from Elisha.

I lean over. "What's wrong?"

He sits up, hands pressed to his forehead while he tries to regain his breath. "I don't—I'm sorry, I . . . Just a nightmare. I don't usually get them; it won't happen a—"

"Stop that. You can't predict when you'll have a nightmare." Though I hope Elisha's right. That he won't scream us both awake every night. Maybe I can help him through whatever this is. "Do you remember what it was about?"

"Um." He either hesitates or tries to remember, and I'm worried it's the former.

"If you don't tell me the truth, I can't help you."

Elisha continues to stare at his lap. "I was at a party. Alone. Everyone was—" He whispers, "I don't want to say it out loud."

"It's okay. Why don't you . . ." I glance around the room as if it will provide a solution. It won't. I'm the only one who can fix this. The more comfortable Elisha feels with me, the more he'll relax, the fewer nightmares he'll have. I hope. "Come up onto the bed with me."

"Are you sure?"

"I'm always sure." I throw back the covers.

Elisha tucks the trundle away and joins me, lying so close to the edge, I worry he'll fall off. That won't do. I loop my arm around his waist and drag him across the king-sized mattress until our bodies are flush against each other.

"There," I say. "Is that better?"

"Yes."

"Good." I flop back down onto my pillow.

Elisha reclines, his body stiff. He stares at the ceiling while I stare at him.

"I would never abandon you at one of those parties." Some norms are beyond my control, but I'd never lose track of him. Never let anyone break him. Mariah and Dutch have already come closer than I'd like.

"Thank you." Finally, Elisha closes his eyes.

And I close mine.

I wake up aroused and excuse myself to the bathroom before Elisha notices or thinks it's his job to handle. Not that I wouldn't appreciate a hand, but he's still having nightmares from his last sexual encounter. I want him to take refuge in me. View me as his protector—I am. I'm the only one he needs to please, the only one who cares.

When I return, he's waiting to shower—a step in the right direction. And after that he takes even more steps, like real clothes and breakfast.

"How're you feeling, today?" I ask, cutting the spinach and egg white omelet he slides onto my plate. "You look better."

"I feel better," he says.

"Good."

I watch while Elisha stirs his own eggs, wondering when I should say something about his infraction. Now is the right time. He's better; the incident is relatively recent. I draw a breath to form the words, *After you eat, we need to discuss your punishment.* But while I'm holding it, I decide "discuss" is the wrong word, because it's not up for discussion. It's happening.

Elisha walks over with the pan and slides his omelet onto the plate beside mine. Stagnant air burns in my lungs until I'm forced to release it—slowly, and only once Elisha turns his back. I stuff a forkful of egg whites into my mouth to quell any urge to speak. Elisha joins me and does the same.

Afterwards, we go for a walk along his usual morning route. A cool April breeze wafts over the harbor, blowing his chestnut hair over his eyes; it needs a trim, but in this moment, I don't mind it. Relaxed, casual, paired with his navy cable-knit sweater, the sleeves pushed up around his elbows, his hands tucked in the pockets of khaki shorts that only half-cover his thighs.

I want to run my hands over his legs, from the ankles up. Want to recline him on the next bench we pass, toss aside his boat shoes, smooth my palms over the wispy hairs on his legs. Kiss the undersides of his knees, which would probably tickle, and he'd giggle or moan and melt into the bench, under my touch.

When we get home, I do exactly that. I can't resist and I don't have to, so why bother? Elisha arches back onto the couch. His breath stutters out between airy laughs and whimpers when I dart my tongue out into the crease behind his knee. Eventually, when I tire of sucking and probing at the sensitive spot, I kiss the rest of the way up his thigh, stopping at the hem of his shorts.

He props himself up on his elbows. I balance over him on mine. I shouldn't be doing this. I should punish him for pulling away from Dutch before it's too late.

But then I kiss him because his flushed lips part and he glimpses mine long enough for me to know that he wants them and I want him and, since he's mine, I can have him whenever I want.

I forgot to punish him, again.

The thought wakes me up and keeps me that way. It's been three days; it's too late. He probably doesn't even remember Mariah's, and he's finally relaxing, so what's the point? Punishment enforces training, but he's doing so well without it. It could actually set him back.

I push the thought away and go back to sleep.

The bed shakes me awake.

In the trundle, Elisha gasps like someone's holding him under-water. He wipes the sweat from his forehead, slicking back damp hair with tense fingers.

What do I say? *Are you okay?* Of course he's not okay. He's still having nightmares. "Elisha, you're safe." I reach down and rub his shoulder. "You're with me."

"Sorry," he whispers.

"Don't be sorry," I say, throwing back the covers. "Come here."

He doesn't hesitate.

When I finally wake up, I'm alone. The bedroom door hangs ajar; natural light filters in from the downstairs windows.

I roll out of bed and check the bathroom. "Elisha?" I call, when I can't find him. The trundle's still tucked away, downstairs lights still off. I hurry down the steps and peek into the den and the kitchen. He didn't leave. Wouldn't have left. Where would he—

"Oh, hi." Elisha stands sweaty and shirtless, in the foyer. "I went for my morning run. Hope that's okay."

"Yes." I force myself to end the sentence, so I won't ramble, and recompose my thoughts. "As long as you're feeling better, you can pick up your regular schedule. I don't have your tutors lined up for today, though. You'll have to wait until tomorrow."

"Okay." He walks at a useless angle, trajectory somewhere between me and the stairs, eyes everywhere and nowhere. "Um, Alex?"

"Yes?"

"Thanks for taking care of me. I think." He scratches the back of his head and walks toward the stairs.

He *thinks*? Oh. He isn't sure whether I'm caring for him or if I'm going through the required motions. He can't decide if he's supposed to thank me. I make it easy for him. "Just upholding my end of the contract," I say. "Second Right."

"Well, thanks, anyway." Elisha leaves before I can bring myself to mention his punishment.

It's been too long, anyway. To be effective, discipline must be administered as soon as possible. And besides, he's learned his lesson. He even atoned in the moment. The point of training Elisha is so that he'll become eager and obedient like an on-med would. Right now he's closer than he's ever been. Punishing him would set him back.

I can overlook it. Just this once.

16

ELISHA

As spring gathers speed, I run more than Alex prescribes. Between the rhythm of my feet and the warm breeze from the harbor, it almost feels like home—like freedom. Like I'm okay right where I am. Alex doesn't mind when I go, so long as I ask. He extends his trust, and I'm happy to earn it.

I finish, sweaty and panting, high from the rush of endorphins and the tingling in my toes. Tom holds the front door, ushering me into the building. "Good to see you again, Elisha."

"You too."

"Do you mind if I, uh . . ." He walks beside me, like we're going to the same place. Even waits with me for the elevator. "Do you mind if I join you?"

"No," I say, assuming he must be riding up to visit another tenant.

"Penthouse," I say, once we're inside. Tom does not request another floor. We stand side by side in silence while the elevator rises. My heart beats faster than it should

Then, with a swipe of his hand, Tom stops the elevator. "Forgive me for going about it like this, but I wanted to reach out to you."

"What do you mean?"

"Elisha, I work with Empower Maryland."

Oh god. "No."

"I wanted to—"

"I can't talk to you."

"—let you know that I'm always here if you need me."

"For what?" I don't mean to shout it. "What can you possibly do for me? The last time your organization tried to help me, I was locked in a cubby for an hour."

Tom presses his palms together as if in prayer. "I'm sorry. Eugenia and Roger don't know Alex like I do. I asked them to let me reach out to you, first, but—"

"If you want to help me, you can leave me alone." I stand in front of the closed doors. This conversation is over. It has to be. Alex seems to know everything, and if he finds out about this? I can't face him that angry, again. Can't live with the regret and fear and shame, in the dark of the cubby for seventy minutes. Already my heart feels like it's going to explode and my hands vibrate at my sides. I clasp my fingers to still them.

"Look." Tom holds up his hands to show he means no harm. "I'm risking my position telling you this, but I'm extending my trust and hope you'll do the same."

"Then don't tell me." I squeeze my eyes shut. The last thing I need is more information to hide from Alex. I don't know if I can lie to him.

Tom swipes at the sensor and the elevator moves, again. "I know you've been to the lab with Alex and, if I know him like I think I do, he'll take you again. He wants to trust you—it's easier for him if he can. And the more he trusts you, the more likely he is to give you access to places and information that we could only dream of."

"I'm not stealing information for you—I'm not even supposed to be talking to you. I'm supposed to tell Alex if anyone from Empower Maryland contacts me."

A soft tone signals our arrival.

"Are you going to?"

Already the dread of living with this secret—of seeing Tom every day and knowing that he works against Alex while smiling to his face—presses slowly on me. Another rock on the pile. And yet, if I tell him? He'll be angry. It won't matter that I'm doing what he told me; he never believes me when the truth is hard. When his inventions don't work like he thinks or his loyal doorman is keeping secrets.

"Probably not." Relief comes when I step onto the familiar hardwood. Even more so when Tom doesn't follow.

"Thank you," he says. "Remember that I'm always here if you want to talk—about anything. And if the worst happens—whatever that means to you—know that I can get you out of here. Take you somewhere safe."

"I'm good, thanks."

Tom nods and the doors close.

That was the right answer. Saying anything else—thinking anything else—while standing in Alex's house feels wrong. Besides, I don't know these people. If they were willing to intercept me on a run, to follow me into an elevator, to violate Third Right, then who's to say I'm any safer with them? At least with Alex I know what I'm getting. At least I'm with someone who cares for me.

17

ALEX

Elisha stands naked and damp, looking over the clothes I've laid out on the bed: two navy seersucker suits, crisp pink button-downs, plaid pastel bow ties, matching pocket squares and socks, rose-gold cuff links, and brown belts with matching hardware. All the makings of Preakness fashion.

"Are we going somewhere?" Realization settles on his face when he looks at me. He immediately stares at the floor. "I shouldn't have asked. Alex, I'm—"

"Shhh." I smooth a hand down his bare back, absorbing leftover water droplets from his shower. Training him without Dociline has not been easy, but after four months of mistakes and consequences, he rarely misbehaves. Asking questions has been one of the hardest aspects of Elisha to train away. He's human. He wants to know what's going on and why. And he is allowed to be curious—it's good for his education—I just don't want to hear it.

"We're on a schedule," I say. "You don't have time to write lines, so you'll kneel on the rice until I'm ready to leave. Understood?"

"Yes, Alex."

"I trust you to carry it out, yourself, while I get ready; do it in here."

"Okay." He leaves while I peel off my clothes and toss them into the hamper.

Elisha's wet footprints still soak the bathroom rug. I lean in and turn the water on, testing the temperature while his feet pound back up the stairs. I watch through the partially open door while Elisha sets the old silver serving tray on the hardwood and uses the scoop to pour a thin layer of uncooked rice over its surface. When he reseals the rice bag, I step into the shower.

Disciplines are easier, now. Elisha no longer talks back or carries the effects with him. He acknowledges his mistakes and atones for them without a fight. But that doesn't mean I watch. They're a time when Elisha can reflect, and I don't want him nervous, thinking about how he should be reacting. And they're too intimate.

I finish, dry, and dress. Elisha kneels at the foot of the bed. Silent, still, eyes closed. He holds his hands behind his back—no longer requiring the restraint of his cuff. His fingers are the only part of him that moves, tightening and loosening their grip on one another.

"Time's up," I say.

I hold out both hands to Elisha and he takes them, leveraging his weight against mine to rise. He doesn't cry or whine about it, simply makes his way into the bathroom to remove the remaining grains with a hot towel.

When he returns, I help him dress—the finer points—fixing his bow tie, introducing him to cuff links, showing him how to fold a pocket square so that it looks put together, yet casual. As I fasten his lapel pin, I can't help feeling like I'm taking him to prom.

I don't regret choosing a Docile over one of the Board's pre-approved marriage partners. Elisha, despite earlier hiccups, is blossoming into a perfect companion. Well behaved, educated. Refined and attractive. Capable from the kitchen to the bedroom. And I cannot wait to show him off to the Board, at the races.

Preakness Village occupies an exclusive section of Pimlico Race Course—too close to the Infield for my liking. InfieldFest is like Halloween for people of limited means. They put on their brightest formal wear, then ruin any semblance of class by drinking cheap beer until they pass out on the dirt. Their mascot is a shirtless man dressed as a centaur and inaccurately named Brewni-corn. Kill me.

Our car pulls up to a private entrance, void of cameras, record-ing devices, and Brewnicorns. Too many paparazzi want to ask me how the ODR renovations are going, instead of reading our press releases or going to see the progress themselves. I tell as much to Chadwick Bell, who manages to sneak past security, dressed as a jockey, and ask whether Bishop Labs is *too* involved with local government. No, we're the right amount involved. The same day Dutch emailed me the news, we mobilized all of our resources to complete the structural upgrades within a month. There's no time-line money can't buy.

I smooth down my suit jacket and join my parents at the edge of the stables. "Good to see you both."

Mom leaves her horse to its jockey so she can greet me. "Visiting your mother before your friends? What did I do to deserve such a wonderful son? Come here; let me hug you."

She makes good on her promise, then passes me to Dad, who shakes my hand firmly before patting me on the back. "Long time no see." He smiles at his own joke. Dad still makes it into the lab once a week. We Bishops do not easily give up control.

"And who is this?" Mom walks toward Elisha, arms outstretched.

His eyes widen, body stiffens. She's going to hug him and he has no idea how to react. There she goes. Oh god.

"I don't recall the lawyers sending over anyone's GenEcs," she says, her arms already around Elisha, who holds his stiffly at his sides.

I cover my laugh by clearing my throat.

Thanks to the Next of Kin laws, legal marriage is complicated for people of means. If we—or, more often, our parents—are inter-ested in proposing legal marriage, the first step is for everyone's lawyers to subpoena each family's Genea-Economic records. A dozen people have to say yes to my future partner before I can. And that's why most of us indulge in Dociles and casual dating, instead. That's also why my mother is confused to see me arrive with a man she doesn't recognize. To be fair, Elisha is nothing like he was four months ago.

"Mom, that's Elisha. My Docile." I wink at her. "Remember?"

"Oh!" Mom makes a *whoopsie!* face and clasps her hands, suddenly. "He looks nice." She speaks to me, now, rather than Elisha. "You've done a good job, though he isn't dressed for the . . ." She pauses. ". . . *occasion.*"

While the real horses are warming up, Patrons send their Dociles onto the track dressed in tails and ears and ridiculous tack-inspired costumes, and place unregulated bets that usually end in an exchange of obscene sums of money, Dociles, or their services.

So, no. I did not dress up Elisha, who is a human being, in a pony costume, so that I could bet his mouth for someone else's. I get enough of that, already.

"Elisha will be joining me in the chalet," I say. "I hope you both will, too."

"Of course," Dad says. "Wouldn't miss the chance to celebrate my son's big success with the ODR." He squeezes my shoulder. "And it looks like you've trained your Docile up well. The Board is impressed, despite your initial setback."

"What setback?"

"When he refused Dociline, of course."

"Right." It's become such a part of my life, I don't really think of it as a setback, anymore. It's odd realizing that others still do.

"Anyway, just wanted to let you know we'd be happy to see what you've been working on for Formula 3.0."

"Actually, I wanted to talk to you about that." I lower my voice. "Did the Board get my memo on Formula 3.0.8? I think it's too similar to version 3.0.7. My goal is more creativity and development for on-meds. Version 3.0.7 takes so much control from the test subjects, I'm worried they won't know to breathe on their own."

"That's why we're no longer focusing on version 3.0.7," Dad says, as if we've been on the same page the whole time and this is a moot issue.

"Okay." I don't ask why we're still testing 3.0.7. "I'll send along a memo detailing my progress with version 3.0.8."

"Sounds good, Son." Dad squeezes my shoulder and says, "Your mother and I will be over in time for lunch." He waves us off with a reassuring smile on his face.

Inside the chalet, Elisha and I sit together with friends and co-workers from Bishop Labs and the ODR alike, at a wide, round table covered in black and yellow paisley linens. Old Bay–seasoned scones, rich coffee, and carafes of juices and champagne sit in the center of each table; Dociles with serving trays weave nimbly between them, offering more substantial food and drink to those who are ready.

The clopping of heavy metal draws my eyes from the race program, which droops in my limp fingers when Mariah approaches with reins in hand. Behind her, a Docile steps nimbly in black thigh-high boots that end in hoofed feet. A sleek horsehair tail sprouts behind her. Elaborate braids gather hair in a row down her head and neck.

Beside me, Elisha shifts in his seersucker suit and tightens his bow tie.

"Alex," he whispers.

I shake my head. "Not now."

The girl steps high and balanced, despite having her hands bound to her back with leather straps. The green and turquoise plumes that tower up from her head harness match the tiny floral pattern of Mariah's dress.

"I hope you don't mind me showing off my new Docile." Mariah fastens the girl's reins to a pillar along the edge of the chalet.

Dutch stands, setting down his mimosa. "Mariah, darling, she is exquisite. May I?"

"Of course."

"Damn." He traces his hands up the Docile's thighs, stopping before he can reach the leather straps that cover her crotch. "If I weren't planning to eat . . ."

I clear my throat, reminding him there's a standard of decorum in the company chalet.

"Yeah, yeah." He takes Mariah's hand, instead, and accompanies her to the table, holding her seat out before taking his own.

"So, how're all my lovelies"—Mariah stops when her eyes land on Elisha—"doing." It ceases to be a question. "Alex, your Docile is sitting at the table," she says through a tightening smile.

"We don't all have platinum horseshoes laying around." I wink. "Besides, seersucker flatters Elisha."

"Really? I think 'cocksucker' suits him better."

The word hits me like a slap to the face. "What are you doing?" I look around to make sure none of the senior Board members are nearby, then lean across the table. "I'm trying to make a good impression."

Skepticism crosses her face. "Well, you're embarrassing yourself."

"No, I'm not." Dad heard me tell Mom Elisha was accompanying me to the chalet. He said he and the Board were impressed. I'm doing well and Mariah is wrong.

"Hope you don't mind us crashing the kids' table." We both turn to see my parents ascend the stairs to the chalet. "It was the only way we could escape the ODR folks. Don't get me wrong, they're nice, but . . ." Dad searches for an acceptable word.

"Excited?" I offer.

"That's it." He chuckles and sits beside my mother.

"I found my Patron Liaison, Charlene Williams, exceedingly professional, if you're headhunting."

Dad waves his hand. "Later, later. For some reason, everyone thinks I want to talk business when what I really want to do is eat."

I shoot Mariah a look. *See? Everything is fine.*

Catering Dociles serve us a salad of mixed greens with seared scallops, a squeeze of fresh lemon juice, and truffle salt. Elisha examines the many forks laid before him, then remembers to use the outermost one. Every now and again, while the rest of us discuss the contract or the forthcoming races, I catch Elisha staring at Mariah's pony Docile.

"Pardon me, would you like a refill, sir?" a catering Docile asks, distracting him. Her smile is warm and gentle, like a stock photo of customer service.

"Um, no thank you." Elisha doesn't meet her eyes, unsure how to interact with her. She's not like Dutch's Dociles, convincing him of their lifelikeness with warm bodies and mouths. "I'm fine."

"Okay. Thank you, sir. Have a lovely day and good luck in the races." She turns to me and repeats her script: "Pardon me, would you like a refill, sir?"

"Yes." Unlike Elisha, I do not thank her. Courtesies are wasted on Dociles—they won't remember. And the one Docile they wouldn't be wasted on doesn't need to be thanked for doing what he is already supposed to. We do not thank Dociles. They, however, do so profusely. Manners are always taught first.

"Thank you, sir," she says while topping off my champagne. "Have a lovely day and good luck in the races." She moves on to my mother and begins her spiel again, passing out of my mind.

As lunch ends, friends and coworkers head for the track in small groups, wagering on Dociles and horses alike. All except for Elisha, who is still staring at Mariah's Docile. I snap my fingers to get his attention and he blinks like I've just flashed a camera in his face.

"Sorry," he says. "I've been distracted."

I catch myself before I can apologize for making him sit through hours of conversation far over his head. Talking about him like he's not even there—it's less awkward when they're on-meds. Elisha might care, but he suppresses most of it. If anything, it shows how well his training is coming along.

"Distracted with what?" I ask.

His eyes have already roved back to the pony Docile. "Her," he says. "Dylan."

"Dylan?" Mariah would never name a Docile "Dylan." She's probably called something stupid, like "Fluffy." Elisha must—

Oh god.

"She lives in my community. Lived, I guess. Our parents are— We're friends." Elisha speaks in a monotone, unable to look away from his—I can barely bring myself to use the word—*friend.*

Third Right exists to protect me from this. No Patron should see their Docile as a whole person who existed before their term. I can't even look at him; I bury my face in my hands, grateful that everyone has left.

"I didn't know she was considering selling her debt. We don't share the same genes, but we're still family. Her parents picked up the slack when my mom left for her term. Dad was having a hard time alone, but Nora and Riley—well, until he took his own life—"

"Enough." I press my fingertips to my forehead. This is too much history; I'm too close. "Enough of this." But when I look up, Elisha's eyes are pink and watery. They meet mine for the first time.

"Okay." He folds his hands carefully in his lap.

"She's fine," I say. "She's on Dociline. She doesn't even know what's happening to her."

"Okay," he whispers.

Dammit. "What? What're you thinking?"

He fidgets with his cuff in silence.

"Dociline hurts people—I know you don't believe me. But if she's on it for more than a few years, it could— She'll go home like my mother, like a Docile, still."

"I can't make Mariah detox your"—I force out the word—"*friend* any more than I can force your friend to refuse it. If she's on Dociline, it's because she asked for it."

"I don't know why she would when she's seen what it did to my mom. Maybe she thinks a short term will . . ."

Too much, too much. This is too much. Too much debtor drama that I shouldn't have to deal with. I need to shut this down, now. I could leave Elisha home whenever I go to Mariah's—but what if she brings Dylan around to my house, or Dutch's? Or Bishop Labs? Or anywhere? She's a friend and a shareholder; I can't avoid our Dociles crossing paths forever and if I tell her why it'll be my fault all over again and—

I could fix this. Offer to buy Dylan.

No, Mariah thinks I can barely handle one Docile, much less two.

"Hey, man." Dutch pops his head in. "We're all heading over to watch the Docile races. You coming? Folks have started betting."

His Docile, Opal, untethers Dylan, whose name I am trying to forget, and leads her away to the track.

"Yeah, I'll meet you there."

"If you say so." He disappears.

And, like that, I have the answer. I block Elisha's path with my arm. He doesn't require further force, simply stops and looks to me for instructions. I'm already doing the math in my head.

"You run a fast mile."

"I don't know what's average, but I suppose—"

"That wasn't a question."

"Sorry."

"You'll compete."

"In what?"

"The Docile races."

"Okay." *And?* hangs between his lips like a cigarette, but he doesn't dare ask what that means.

I lower my voice—not that anyone's listening. I'm terrified that someone important will see through the perfection I've promised them, that my Docile is causing yet another problem, and that I am by all appearances doing him a favor. "It's customary for Patrons to wager on their Dociles." How to word this . . . "If Dylan is going to cause problems, I am willing to wager for her contract."

Elisha's lips part, eyes widen. Now he understands.

"But you have to win. If you don't, I'm the one who will suffer the embarrassment. Not you. Do you understand?"

"Yes."

"Good." I didn't bring anything for him to wear. He can't run in a seersucker suit; he'll be laughed off the track. "Follow me."

Elisha's stupor gives me a head start and he's forced to jog to catch up as I stride across Preakness Village to the Docile stables. Good. He'll need to warm up.

Dammit, this is a terrible idea. I'd have hired him a coach if I wanted him to race—to win. I wouldn't have fed him a large meal. Would have deposited him in the stable with the other Dociles. But if I don't do this, Elisha's *friend* will cause complications, for both him and me.

This is why Dociline exists. This is why Dociline exists. This is why Dociline exists: so a debtor's problems don't become my problems.

The Docile stables are right beside the horse stables. They *smell* like the horse stables, but never mind that. "Dutch!" I dare not call his name too loud, lest I attract attention. There's nothing scandalous about entering my Docile in the races, but after declaring I wouldn't, well, it needs to be a surprise. And he needs to win.

"Bishop, what're you doing over here?" He ties off an intricate braid in Opal's bleach-white hair. She, unlike Mariah's pony Dociles, is at least wearing some kind of sports leggings and bra with a gray and white dapple pattern under her white leather tack.

I hold a finger to my lips.

"I didn't realize this was a secret rendezvous." Dutch looks around, mocking me.

"It's not." I look around in earnest. "But, um . . . Are you racing Opal and Onyx?"

"I was planning on it. Why?"

"You didn't wager them, did you?"

"I'd never bet my babies." He slaps Opal's thigh, then grins. "Only money."

"How much?"

"Five hundred thousand on Opal, four on Onyx." When I don't humor him, he volunteers, "She's fucking fast."

"I'll give you four for Onyx's tack."

"Why? Are you—you're—but you said—"

"I know what I said and that's why we're"—I give in—"having a secret rendezvous. Look, I'll tell you about it later. I need to bet against Mariah, and Elisha's all I have to offer. He's fast; he can win."

"Well, if you think he's going to beat Onyx and Opal, I'm going to be out nine hundred thousand."

"Do I not pay you enough?" I chuckle.

For a moment, desperation tenses Dutch's face. Sometimes I forget he's new money. That he knew debt. That any hoarding tendencies stem from previous financial insecurities.

But he covers it with a smug grin and curled upper lip. "I'll accept it as a bonus."

I join him in leaving discomfort in the dust of humor. "You drive a hard bargain. I'll have my accountant send it tonight."

"Deal." Dutch relaxes back into his usual smile and runs a hand through his already-full hair. He whistles and Onyx appears. "Prep Elisha for the race—and don't forget to warm him up, you know, stretches, whatever you do. Keep it quiet."

Onyx nods his head, unfurls the diamond chain on Elisha's cuff, and leads him off. Elisha looks over his shoulder, but the second he catches my eye, I look away.

If he wants to help his friend, he needs to do his part.

I pinch the bridge of my nose as if that will squeeze the tension right out of my face. It doesn't. Maybe I need a drink. Yeah, that'll do. A drink.

I head toward the finish line, lift an unidentified cocktail from a catering Docile along my way, down it in one long gulp, and set the empty glass on another Docile's tray. Lavender and cucumber sting my mouth when I approach Mariah. She stands alone along the perimeter fence, swirling a glass of red wine.

"Where's your other half?" she says, still gazing at the track.

"Other half?"

"Elisha."

"There it is," I say.

"I'm not trying to be witty, just calling it like I see it. And I'm not the only one."

"Whatever you say." She has no idea what she's talking about. I've worked hard—on top of my already-busy career and social calendar—to train Elisha from scratch. I'm breaking new ground. If she can't handle it, that's her fault.

"I'm trying to help, Alex." She presses a hand to her forehead. "You know I want what's best for you and Bishop Labs, and that's why—"

"Elisha's racing." I give first, so that she'll see I'm not fighting her. "He's in the stables, getting ready."

Her eyebrows hit her bangs. "Really?"

"Yeah. I, uh, decided to show off all my hard work, after all."

"And you're here to wager."

"What fun is showing off if I don't win anything?"

"Well, I want something." A breeze catches Mariah's hair. She fondles the riding crop in her belt, lovingly, the fight gone from her face.

"What's that?"

"I want you to subpoena Javier's GenEcs." When Mariah finally looks at me, she's tucking her hair back to reveal rosy cheeks. "I'm serious, Alex. Breaking up with him was a mistake. You *liked* him, for fuck's sake, and why shouldn't you have? So he didn't make you vomit your heart up, but he's smart and cute and likeable, and new money isn't old money, but it's better than no money."

"No. I can't *un*-break up with him—even if I wanted to. Imagine how that'd look."

"It'll look great! People love reunions. We'll do a television special on your engagement. We'll—"

"If a television special is part of the wager, deal's off." There is literally nothing I want less than camera operators following me around in a relationship I already have to work to maintain.

Mariah holds up her free hand. "Not part of the deal. Just something to think about."

My heart is beating faster than it should. GenEcs aren't a commitment, but they are intent. If I requested Javier's GenEcs, he'd expect me to propose pending a favorable comparison to my own. And rejecting him a second time feels unnecessarily cruel.

Mariah slides her arm around my waist; our hips bump and she rests her head on my shoulder. "I want what's best for you, Alex."

I sigh and hold on to her. "I know."

"If I were a man, I'd subpoena your GenEcs so hard."

I snort.

Mariah smiles. "Our test-tube babies would be beautiful."

"Test-tube babies? That's not very romantic."

"Yeah, I can't take nine months off to be pregnant." She makes a face. "Also? Who said anything about romance?" Her tone isn't rude or disgusted, just matter-of-fact.

I doubt Mariah remembers, but we've discussed marriage before. It was the day before high school graduation, and we were lying in one of the sand traps of the old Eldridge Club, our Poplar Hill Prep uniforms wrinkled and untucked.

"Have your parents subpoenaed anyone, yet?" she asked. That only ever meant one thing.

I shook my head. "Yours?"

"I overheard them talking about it. I don't really want to marry anyone, though, I don't think. Maybe a friend. If I have to."

"I think we have to." My laugh faded and a peaceful silence warmed us.

"I'd marry you." Mariah looked at me. "As friends."

I remember the burning blush on my cheeks while I fumbled for a response. I ended up laughing because I couldn't think of what to say. The idea wasn't bad. It was practical, but awkward, eighteen-year-old-Alex was still holding on to the idea that he'd marry someone for money *and* love. That he wouldn't have to settle for a friend or a financial ally, like others did. Thirty-year-old Alex hasn't quite grown out of that.

The Dociles emerge from the stables, steered into place by jockeys with riding crops. I am suddenly aware of my pulse rippling out in waves to my fingertips where they grip the fence. While I'd rather him in nothing but briefs and a tee shirt at home, the thought of Elisha dressed like Mariah's pony Docile isn't unappealing.

"All you want is for me to *look* at Javier's GenEcs?" I lean on the fence, again, and squint at the different Dociles, trying to discern them in their tack.

Mariah joins me. "Not even you, your lawyers. It's that easy."

"And if I win?"

Mariah shrugs. "Whatever." She can afford to give me whatever I might ask.

I almost forget why I'm making this wager. This wasn't supposed to be about me. Yet again, Elisha's problems have become mine. "Your pony Docile," I say.

Mariah allows surprise to show on her face. "Chesapeake?"

I stop myself from saying, *Dylan,* and instead say, "The one you brought today, yes."

"I didn't think you were into girls, Alex."

"She's not for me." I can spin this truth into a lie; I've done it before. "I need to round out Elisha's education."

"Fine." She extends a hand. "If Elisha wins, you get Chesapeake. If he loses—even second place—you subpoena Javier's GenEcs on Monday."

I know before I shake her hand that I might not be able to get myself out of this one. My parents will find out, then the Board—and I can't disappoint them twice. I don't want to commit to Javier, but I've already committed to Elisha. I shake Mariah's hand.

"Deal."

18

ELISHA

I can do this.

I can do this for Dylan.

Onyx moves with determination, sliding straps around my naked limbs and torso, tightening, fastening. The leather is brown
and soft. Worn. If I close my eyes it doesn't feel unlike the seersucker suit's layers, buttoned, zipped, and tucked. Packaging my
body in navy-blue stripes, pink cotton, leather shoes.

None of these other horses—*Dociles.* I forget only because
they're all dressed like horses and we're in a stable; the scents of
hay, leather, and shit hang thick in the air. It's hard not to think
of the others as horses—or would they prefer "ponies"? They're all
slender, muscular, groomed. They're racehorses. They've trained
and I haven't.

Because I'm doing this for Dylan. My motivation is all that separates me from the others.

"Open your mouth." Onyx's face is relaxed, lips curved into a
light smile. His hair is pulled back in one thick braid from forehead
to neck. Everyone's is.

I wonder if he'll braid mine, too.

My mouth hangs open while he cinches and buckles at the top
of my head and back of my neck. Onyx threads silky rope back and
forth between the metal O-rings that press cold against my cheeks.
When he's finished, I reflexively try to close my mouth. The rope
braid is pliable but thick, and while I can force my teeth together,
it's easier to let the bit do its job.

When Onyx points me toward a mirror, I freeze. Warm chestnut leather collars my neck, trails down my back and chest, looping and crisscrossing. It ends in a V between my legs, supporting and covering my crotch.

Onyx rubs his fingers through my hair, messing it up between the harness straps. I feel like one of the Roman gladiators my humanities tutor described. Battle ready.

I follow willingly when Onyx loops a finger through my cuff and leads me and Opal out of the stables and into the sunlight.

I stop, raise my hand to my eyes so I can see the crowd: a patchwork of colorful dresses and hats and suits, shiny bows and belts and jewelry. They tower above me in the stadiums and grip the railing surrounding the track. A pleasurable and terrifying sensation sneaks up on me, starting at the back of my neck and spreading into my limbs. Like light slicing through my muscle and settling into my nerves.

I cannot move.

"He needs blinders," says a familiar voice, but I cannot look away from the crowds. "To keep him focused. I'll do it."

Thick hands tug at the straps on my head, forcing my face forward. They fit fat leather pads alongside my temples, blocking the sun's glare until all I can see is Dutch's face opposite mine. Like the light at the end of a tunnel I never want to reach.

I jolt in his grip, curl my fingers into my palms until my nails dig into softening calluses.

"Don't." Dutch looks directly into my eyes such that the chilling light returns to my body. "You can't. Not after last time." He pats my cheek, sighs, then loops his finger through a strap on my chest. "Now come on. I hear you're going to win this thing. Opal, that means you have to stay behind him, got it?"

I can't see her response, only Dutch's concern.

You can't. Not after last time. What does that mean?

"Bishop's paying me nine hundred to make sure you win, Elisha." He pauses. "That's nine hundred *thousand,* by the way."

I am too stunned to do anything but follow.

Unable to see the crowds, I stare at Dutch's back—a blue-green blazer that Alex calls seafoam. The colors ahead are muted, brown and black leather, the occasional white, wrapped and buckled around mostly naked bodies, like gifts.

The Dociles stretch in place without interaction, then line up. I can do this. I can win. Alex thinks I'm fast, and he's seen this race before. He monitors the times on my morning runs. He knows I can win.

I can do this.

I can do this for Dylan.

Dutch leads me into the starting gate beside Opal, slaps my ass, then closes the door. I stretch my jaw and swallow the spit that threatens to fly from my mouth in the wind, then position myself. Knees bent low, hands in the dirt.

A woman in a hot-pink blazer and navy blouse walks past my gate, a whistle between her lips, checkered flag in her hand. The crowd silences, Dociles beside me stop shuffling. I hold my breath.

A high-pitched whistle pierces the air, followed by the springing of a dozen gates. I don't wait, don't look to see if those beside me have started. As a hundred thousand screams erupt around us, I run.

The dirt that flies up in clouds around me sticks to my parted lips and clogs up my nose. All I have to do is run. It's only half a lap. Alex waits at the end. Alex and Dylan.

My bare feet sink into the soft earth with every step. Not one is easy, but I push harder than I ever have, picture Mariah holding my closest friend—my family—on a fucking leash.

A shoulder bumps mine. Dirt hits my calves as the others pound forward. I ignore the rub of stiff leather against my skin, the grit sticking to my sweat and working its way between my joints. The burn in my thighs propels me forward until I can no longer hear the labored breathing of Dociles beside me.

I can see the finish line. There are no crowds in my narrow view. Nothing but a chalk-white line, heavy breathing, and dirt. I'm going to fall if I run any faster. That's okay. I can fall over the line. I can do this. I can win.

Run, Elisha.

Run.

I don't stop when I cross the white line. The speed runs its course through my body, until I can think about my legs without tripping over them. I can't see any other Dociles and I don't want to. The silence breaks. Folks cheer. I grab at the leather blinders that limit my vision. I can't even tell how I did without help.

A body stops mine. A soothing voice says, "Calm down." The hands that cover mine belong to Alex, this time, not Dutch. His face appears on the other end of the tunnel and he's smiling. "It's okay. You did it. You won."

He hooks fingers under the braided rope that gags me, leverages it onto my chin, and kisses my lips. My eyes close like the first time he kissed me and I lean into him, holding on so I don't fall over with exhaustion.

"Good boy." Alex releases the rope and it slides back into place between my lips. I could take it off, myself, but I think that's the type of thing Dutch meant when he said *not after last time.* I can't step out of line because I've already embarrassed Alex, once.

It's okay. The leather and rope are soft and comforting, holding me tight. Besides, I did it. I won.

"Congratulations," I hear Mariah say before she steps into view.

"Thank you," Alex says. He rubs his hand over the back of my neck.

"An admirable performance," says a new voice, medium pitch, clear. "Your Docile is quite fast." I have to move my whole head to see who's speaking. Beside Mariah stands a petite Latino man in baby-blue slacks and a red suit jacket. His dark brown eyes flit between Alex's and the ground, like he's nervous.

"That he is," Alex says. "I didn't know you were going to be here, or I would've made a point to say hello."

"Luckily, I found Javier over by the stables," Mariah says, a gleam in her eye. "Care to join us for a drink? We have a chalet."

"Ooh, of course." Javier's smile is warm. "As long as Alex doesn't mind."

The tension on Alex's face breaks. "Not at all. You'll be my guest."

Leather stings my thigh, turning my head. A tall woman dressed like a jockey, with a rough, high-pitched voice, clicks her tongue and says, "Let's get you cleaned up."

I look to Alex for direction, see him take his hand from me and wipe the dirt off on a moist towel that he hands back to a passing Docile. He ignores me, engaged with Mariah and Javier.

The jockey clucks again and swats her crop against my thigh. "Come on, pony."

I stumble away from her crop. Alex catches my eyes and nods, less to me and more to the jockey. She strikes me again and I pick up the pace, heading toward the stable.

Every time I look over my shoulder to find Alex, I feel the crop's sting. Eventually, I stop peeking, though it takes all my willpower to face forward and go through the motions. To accept the jockey's direction and the crop's feedback. That my only job right now is to be wound down and cleaned up so I can be returned to Alex.

Deep breaths.

I accept my narrowed world and focus on the stables, growing larger as we near them. Jockeys lead Dociles in and horses out. All I have to do is follow their orders.

It's simple.

Relax.

"That's a good boy." The jockey smooths her hand through my hair. "Into the last stall."

I go without the crop's reminder. The stone floor beneath my feet is wet and cool against the warmth of May. She moves silently and rhythmically, loosening and removing the straps of my harness. I feel the warmth of blood flowing again, my circulation unrestricted.

The stall door clangs shut.

"You've looked better," the jockey says. She removes my head harness and the silk rope from between my teeth.

I blink, the room bigger without blinders. She tosses my tack onto the ground. My eyes widen and I see her fully for the first time, as she removes her helmet.

"Eu—" I cough, my mouth still dry and dusty.

She cracks the top off a plastic water bottle and thrusts it into my hands.

I drink half the bottle. "Eugenia," I say, mouth wet and dripping. "What are you doing here?"

"Checking on you."

"I'm fine," I say.

"You're dressed like a horse."

"It's—it's really not all that bad." I hug my arms against my chest and shrug, already missing the snug feeling. Suit or harness, it makes no difference. Besides, I was happy to win for Alex.

Or for Dylan. Both? The memory of his pride warms me from the inside out.

Eugenia snaps her fingers so close to my face that I recoil. "Wake up, Elisha. You're turning into one of them."

"I'm—No. I'm not." I back away from her, eyeing the clasp on the door.

"Okay, what can you tell us about Bishop Labs' new contract with the ODR?" She stalks forward, closing in on me.

"I don't know anything secret." It's the truth. That's not my business.

She corners me. "Bullshit. You live with him. He brings you to work."

"Not all the time, and I . . ." Where's Alex? I peer over my shoulder through the iron bars. Pony Dociles and their jockeys mill around, undressing, cleaning. Would any of them help if I called? Would they believe me?

Alex would believe me. He believes me. He's the only one.

"Come on, Elisha. Help us help you." She's so close, the brim of her helmet bumps into my forehead. "Help us help your family."

"They're fine, please. I don't need help. I need to clean up, get back to Alex."

"You're going home soon, right?"

"I don't think so. The horse race hasn't even—"

"No, Elisha, not the Third's home, *your* home. Where your parents and sister and the Falstaffs live."

"Oh, I . . ." When did I start thinking of Alex's as home? "I guess it's almost been six months."

Eugenia leans back and sighs. "I'm too late."

"What do you mean?"

"Nothing, Elisha." She throws a sopping-wet sponge at me. I barely catch it. "Clean yourself up. Get back to your master." She flings the stall door open and leaves. The latch clangs shut behind her.

"He's not my master," I whisper. Drops of water clear paths down my dusty chest and dampen the downy hairs on my thighs.

I don't move—can't move. I'm doing what I'm supposed to. What Alex wants me to do. I close my eyes and allow the calm to reverberate through me.

I'm exactly where Alex wants me.

Doing what I'm supposed to. I don't have to worry about anything—not Eugenia or Empower Maryland or my family, who are out of debt and living on my stipend—only what I'm supposed to do. Right now, I'm supposed to clean up for Alex.

I drag the still-heavy sponge down my left arm and wring out the dirty water over a drain. Wet the sponge, wipe myself clean. First my left arm, then my right. My face, shoulders, and chest. Back, legs, genitals. I bend over the bucket to wash beneath my fingernails and sit on a towel to clean my feet.

When I'm dry, I find my clothes in one of the cubbies and pull them on. Each article brings me one step closer to safety—to Alex. The socks and underwear cling, soft and comforting. Pants and button-down perfectly tailor to my body. The brown leather belt and bow tie fasten me in like tack. I shrug on my blazer, button it, and smooth the fabric over my shirt.

When I breathe in, my body pushes the suit's limits and I relish the pleasurable tightness. "Okay," I whisper. "Everything is okay."

I open the stall door and wind carefully around the jockeys directing Dociles with crops and leads, in and out of leather, under hoses. I leave the stables, alone.

/ / /

Tom tips his hat when he opens our car door. "Good evening, Dr. Bishop. Elisha." His knowing smile is for me.

I feel gross, again. Like I need another sponge to wipe away the dirt he has on me, even though my skin and suit are immaculate. Clean, ironed, pressed.

"Evening, Tom," Alex says.

"You received a delivery, sir." Tom holds out a black box tied with a black silk ribbon.

Alex takes it. "Thank you."

"My pleasure. Any luck at Preakness?"

"Yes, actually." He smiles and rubs my back. I lean into his touch, eager for his protection. Tom won't bother me while I'm with Alex. "Elisha's quite fast."

"You participated in the Docile races?" Tom asks me.

"Yes," I mumble, avoiding his eyes. Why does Tom make me feel bad about it, when Alex makes me feel accomplished, empowered, and safe?

"Put some more money in Dr. Bishop's pocket?"

I don't know how to answer—don't even think it's Tom's business. Why he thinks he's entitled to our personal lives.

But Alex doesn't seem to mind. "Ah, that would be the horses. Or perhaps my mother, since they're her horses and I'm obliged to bet handsomely on them."

"Isn't that how parents are." Tom unlocks the front door for us, then resumes his station behind the front desk. "I try not to guilt my girl too much, but I can't help that she loves her dear old dad."

Quiet settles like snow.

"Elisha, why don't you go on ahead. I'll meet you upstairs." Alex kisses my forehead and nudges me into the elevator.

I go, looking over my shoulder the whole way, watching Alex approach Tom's desk, straining to hear their conversation through the doors even after they've closed. I stare straight ahead at the glossy black doors, pulling the diamond chain in and out of my cuff. If I concentrate, I feel the rhythm of the links as they unwrap within the bracelet and break its surface.

I should tell Alex what happened. About the Empower Mary-landers. I don't want Roger showing up without warning. Don't want to pass Tom every time I go out for a run or fear being stopped by Eugenia on the street. They've already gotten me in trouble once and know more about me than even Alex does.

Will he be angry? He might. But then again, he might be glad. It might be worth it. Because Alex might be the only one who cares about me, anymore.

19

ALEX

Today was good. As I watch Elisha get into the elevator, I feel the familiar glow of pride return, not only in his progress, but in my work. Not only did I earn Dad's approval, but he's going to recommend my Formula 3.0 plan to the Board. All without having to subpoena Javier's GenEcs. Though I appreciate Mariah's concern, I'm doing well on my own. And I want to pay it forward.

I mosey back over to the front desk. Tom minds his own business until I'm so close it would be rude to ignore me any longer. "You never told me if your daughter was accepted to the University of Maryland."

"I . . ." Tom pokes at the desktop, flicking through a menu of documents he has no intention of accessing. "I didn't want to bother you."

"So, she was?" I open a new window on the desktop and log into my bank account.

Tom averts his eyes, backing politely away from information a doorman shouldn't know about his residents.

"Well, yes."

I open a separate window, the University of Maryland tuition page. "Dr. Bishop."

I ignore him, quickly calculating the cost of four years' tuition, room and board, books, and living expenses. I sign the virtual check, then tap my fingers to one another. The thin slip of paper materializes in my hand.

"Dr. Bishop, please—"

"This should cover it."

"I can't accept this."

"Why not?"

We stare at each other, two men made from the same stuff: skin, bone, guts. No one's here. No photographers. No Dutch to remind me of my image, no Mariah to criticize my behavior.

"I can't repay you."

I crook my finger.

Tom leans across the table.

I point at the amount on the check. "I bet more than this on a horse this afternoon. I can afford to invest the same in a person." I fold the check and stick it in Tom's breast pocket. "If you want to repay me, send her my way after graduation. Bishop Laboratories could use a mind like hers."

"She does want to major in biology." Tom smiles.

"I know." I touch my temple. "You've told me."

"You remember too well, Dr. Bishop."

I tuck my free hand in my pocket, wink, and back toward the elevator. "I trust you'll log me out and close up—"

"Oh, absolutely, sir." Tom jabs at the screen and wipes his forehead. "Taken care of. Thank you, I can't—"

I hold up my hand to silence his gratitude before he can bumble on for too long. I step into the waiting elevator; its doors separate us. I do want people like Tom and his daughter to succeed. Want them to work hard, do well, contribute. Find their places.

Upstairs, I find Elisha waiting by the island in the kitchen. He looks up when I enter, face tenses as I approach. Something is wrong and I don't know what and I hate not knowing.

"Why don't you go upstairs and get undressed. Shower."

Elisha nods before saying, "Okay," and slipping away.

I wait. Close my eyes and listen to the gentle pad of oxfords across the hardwood. Slide of his palm over the banister. Creak of the bedroom door and footsteps overhead. Even when the sounds stop, I imagine him sliding his blazer over his broadened shoulders and down his arms. His fingers manipulating shirt and slacks buttons out of their holes, loosening leather laces. The satisfying crumple of worn cotton in the hamper.

I listen to the shower spurt to life, the thud of Elisha's bare feet on the tile, and metallic slide when he closes its door.

Only then do I wander into my office, sit the black box on my desk, and pull the end of the ribbon until it unravels. Inside, a card reads: *Didn't realize how much I missed you. If you ever want to reconnect, please don't hesitate to call. Yours, Javier.* Beneath it, a phone headset embedded in a slim sticker—a piece of technology both fun and redundant that I have no present use for, much like Javier.

I set it in one of my desk drawers, then mimic Elisha's motions, undress, toss my clothes on top of his—crumpled, as I'd imagined—and make my way into the shower. Elisha doesn't startle. His eyes meet mine only for a moment before he tilts his head back and rinses the conditioner from his hair.

I want to kiss him from throat to navel. Want to hold him against the wall and suck him dry while he calls out my name.

I can't do that—can't go down on my Docile. Patrons don't do that. I wasn't really considering it, anyway. My face warms from the steam heat.

I clear my throat. "Finished?"

"Yes." Elisha wipes the excess water from his face and slides past me.

Our bodies brush. I ignore it, rubbing my hand down my chest to the base of my mostly limp cock, as if holding it down will erase the feeling. Through the fogged glass, I watch him wipe down his body and dry his hair. It'll stick out until he fixes it.

Already I can feel my hands in his hair, watch the contented smile settle onto his face. I stroke lazily between my legs, imagining Elisha's mouth on me. God, I want him. I want him in the shower, skin hot and wet. I want him slippery and wrapped in a fluffy cotton towel. I want to push it down his hips, push him onto the bed. And I'm not sure I'm supposed to want that. I'm not sure

I care about what I'm *supposed* to be, anymore. What my grandmother *was* and my father *was*. I care about what I *am* and what my legacy *will be.*

I finish washing, then shut the water off and grab a towel from the warmer. Through the cracked door, I watch Elisha smooth his hair into place, in the mirror. He knows how I like it—how I like him. He is blossoming into the perfect Docile companion. Imagine if Dociline could turn an off-med into him, without the training. A revolution in the field.

I toss my towel into the hamper, covering our Preakness outfits. Elisha's face is still tense, in the mirror. He's not like on-meds; he requires additional care. "I want to make sure you're okay," I say. "I'm responsible for your mind, as well as your body. Tell me what you're thinking."

I decide not to be opaque about my intentions. He's had a long day. We're both tired. And he deserves an emotional reward for his hard work.

"About what?" he asks.

"About everything. Talk to me for a few minutes."

"Okay. . . ."

Elisha opens his mouth, then closes it. He stands like a Greek statue: youthful, slender, muscled, with a twinge of innocence. I only know he's real from the way he fidgets with his cuff, pulling the chain out and in. Normally, by now I would have reminded him to answer aloud, mentioned the rules or, more likely, the consequences.

But I wait.

Elisha bites his lip and scratches his head, upsetting his hair. "I'm still processing today." He looks at his feet while he talks. I don't want him to feel inhibited around me. I want to know how he feels. "Seeing Dylan when I didn't expect to. Wondering whether I'm too late—if she's already—if the Dociline . . ."

Elisha begins to pull his trundle bed out from under mine, but I stop him. "Put that away." We push it back into place, together, and I pull him onto mine. "Just lie with me."

Elisha tucks himself inside my arms and takes a deep breath. I stroke his hair and massage his lower back, the skin warm.

"Dylan's fine, I promise you. Dociline works. You'll see."

"Yeah." He doesn't sound convinced.

After several minutes, I disturb the silence. "Are you happy?" I hold my breath, waiting for him to say yes. *Hoping* for him to say yes.

"Most of the time. I'm happy when I'm here, with you. And I like going to the lab and traveling around the city."

"But?"

"But social events are stressful. I'm afraid of messing up again and disappointing you in front of everyone."

"Want to know a secret?" I press my forehead against Elisha's and whisper, "I don't like social events, either. You only have one person to worry about disappointing. I have millions."

Horror creeps over his face. "I'm so sorry."

"Don't be." I close my eyes and tighten my hold on Elisha. "Don't ever feel sorry for me."

He buries his face in my neck, breathing in my scent.

"Is there anything else you want to tell me, before I fall asleep?" I ask.

A moment passes—long enough for Elisha to consider my question. A little too long.

"No," he says. "Nothing." He begins to pry himself from my grip, but I stop him.

"Stay here," I mumble. "Just for tonight."

20

ELISHA

Alex doesn't tell me why we're at the lab. Not that he usually does, but he looks happier at work today than he has in a while. I don't try to guess—it doesn't matter. As long as he's happy, so am I.

I still hold the railing inside the elevator when we ride it down. Alex rubs a hand down my back to calm the butterflies in my stomach. We stop on a floor I've never visited, not that any floor looks that different. The door slides open and Alex leads us down the catwalk, which is empty except for a caretaker and a line of Dociles who trail behind her.

"I have something to show you." A smile tugs at Alex's lips. He knows I won't ask what. He's teasing, which I think he enjoys—and I enjoy, too. It feels nice that he's excited to show me something, regardless of what it is.

I let the glow of contentment fill me and say, "Okay."

Ahead of us, the caretaker signals to the line behind her and they stop. She and Alex acknowledge each other with a nod when we pass, but I can't take my eyes off the Dociles. They stand facing forward, smiling, with their arms dangling by their sides. Dressed in Bishop Laboratories branded athletic wear, they look like a neat row of mannequins. I'm wondering what would happen if I nudged one, when Alex looks over his shoulder and I realize I'm lagging.

He waits, unbothered, while I catch up, then points at a room obscured by fogged glass. "Go on," he says, standing to the side.

Tentatively, I open the door.

"Elisha!" Dylan launches herself at me for a hug. "I didn't think I'd see you again."

I wrap my arms around her, rub my fingers over the clean blue scrubs she wears. No more pony gear. "You smell nice," I say, breathing in the coconut scent of her hair, no longer braided for Preakness. It's shorter, shaved close to her head, and tickles my cheek where she rests her head on my shoulder.

"Thanks, I guess." She steps back and looks me over. "All in one piece, I see."

"Yes, thanks."

Dylan continues to stare. Did I say something wrong?

"Elisha, sit down." Alex taps the back of a chair before taking the one next to it.

I do as he says, eager to help him get Dylan situated. She, however, does not move to join us. I look between them, growing anxious that she won't cooperate. Does she know Alex is helping her?

"Dylan." Alex gestures to the third chair. "We do have business to handle."

She sits, but my relief turns to discomfort as she continues to stare at me. Why is she looking at me like that? Like if she looks hard enough, she can see through my skin. It itches. I shift in my seat, scratch the goose bumps that rise on my arms.

"Stop fidgeting," Alex says without looking up from the Smart-Table.

I sit on my hands, so I won't be tempted. My eyes meet Dylan's before dropping to the tabletop again, unable to face her judgment.

"Let's go over your contract." Alex finishes typing and rotates the document with his finger so Dylan can see it. "Technically, your debt's been purchased by Bishop Laboratories, care of me, Alexander Bishop the Third. You'll live here for the duration of your term—which I convinced our contracts division to negotiate down to three years since you're coming to us secondhand—in a single room, no roommate. All your needs will be provided for by a caretaker. A variety of activities are available here, from athletics to arts, academics, and so on. All we require is that you complete our tests on a regular basis. A schedule will populate on the inside of your door every morning. If you need anything, feel free to ask one of the on-duty caretakers."

"Can I see that?"

"Of course." Alex slides it toward her with the touch of a finger.

"No, I mean, can I hold it?" She talks to him like Jess does, like they're equals.

Alex taps several fingers together and the contract materializes between his fingers. Dylan takes the document as if it might fall apart. She reads, slowly, underlining the words with her finger as she goes.

Finally, she sets it down. "What's the catch?"

"No catch."

"Mariah told me you wanted me to 'round out Elisha's education,' and now you're saying I'm free to live out my term in what is basically a luxury prison. Why?"

"Doesn't matter."

"Does to me."

Alex shrugs. "I have no more obligation to explain my decision to purchase your debt than you do for selling it."

"I don't think it's a mystery that I sold my debt because the alternative is my widowed mother being sent off to debtors' prison."

Alex clasps his hands together and leans forward. "You don't have to sign this contract. I can take you back to Mariah's if you wish."

"No," Dylan says, quickly, shaking her head. "I'll sign; I just . . ." She picks up a stylus and twiddles it between her fingers.

"No one here is going to hurt you or have sex with you, if that's what you're worried about," Alex says.

"That's most of it," she says.

"Well, let me know if you think of anything further. Also, while we're hammering out details, I'm required to offer you Dociline, if you'd like it. We're developing the new formula, so you'd inject an improved version that's not yet on the market."

Dylan turns her eyes on me. "Are you on Dociline?"

"No." I laugh, but nobody else does. My smile fades. "Isn't it obvious?"

Dylan faces Alex, ignoring me. "If I refuse, I won't end up like him, will I?"

End up like him. What does that mean?

"No," Alex says. "Elisha is special."

Wait. If we're both off-med, why should she end up any different? Is something wrong with me? I've done everything Alex has said. He wouldn't let anything bad happen to me. "Excuse me," I say.

"Not now, Elisha."

"O-okay."

Alex sighs and rubs his forehead. "Go see if Jess is downstairs. Maybe you two can get a coffee."

"Okay. See you later, Dylan." I wave, but when she doesn't look, I hug my arm against my chest. As I close the fogged door behind me, I wonder what I did wrong. She said she was happy to see me.

I take the elevator down a floor and scan for Jess. She's busy talking to another researcher, so I sit at a nearby station and wait. It lights up at my presence, bringing up my personal settings: the outline of piano keys and "Liebesträum no. 3." On a music staff, Franz Liszt's notes arc like waves above the melody. I can hear them if I close my eyes, feel Alex sitting beside me on the piano bench, at home. His hands guiding mine.

"Hey, you." Jess sits on the station beside mine. Her smile warms me. "What's up? Where's Alex?"

"He's upstairs with my friend, Dylan. He won her contract at—"

"—Preakness. I remember." She clicks her tongue. "So, you get kicked out?"

"I think I was in the way. Dylan didn't seem too happy with me, and Alex . . ." I don't know. He wasn't upset, but wasn't pleased with me, either. "He told me to find you, get a coffee."

"Well, he's the boss!" Jess hops down and leads me into the break room. Thanks to Alex, I can identify the soft glow of dials that adjust temperatures, open cabinets, and brew hot drinks. I reach for the latter, but Jess beats me to it.

"Cream and sugar?" she asks.

"Yes, please. I can do it if—" I glance up at the fogged conference room, where Alex and Dylan discuss her contract.

"Don't worry about it." Jess sets to work brewing coffee.

No one ever does things like that for me. Maybe a waiter or valet, another Docile, but Jess is a scientist. I wonder if she'll mind . . . "May I ask you a question?"

"Ask away."

"Why are you so . . . ."—"nice" isn't the word; plenty of trillion-aires are nice on the outside and monstrous on the inside—". . . casual? With me. Doing me favors and stuff. I don't mind the work; it's my job."

Jess leans against the counter. The rich scent of coffee—black, bitter, and nutty—fills the kitchenette. "You know that feeling when Alex doesn't want your help and you have to hold back?"

"Yes."

"That's how I feel watching you make me coffee. I can make it myself; I have two hands." She holds them up and wiggles her fingers as proof.

"I can make my own, too," I say.

"Yeah, but you do stuff for other people all day. It's nice to take a break every now and then."

"No one else thinks like that."

"Yeah, well, don't tell Alex I'm such a sucker." She chuckles. I check the coffeepot, then clasp my hands to remind myself not to help. "Can you keep a secret?" Jess asks.

"From Alex?" The notion gives me anxiety.

"No, he already knows."

Oh thank god. "Then, yes."

Still, Jess leans in and lowers her voice. "I started off as a Docile. Here, in Bishop Labs."

I gasp. "No."

"Yes. I inherited my parents' debt when they died and Alex's grandmother purchased it. I was such a curious little thing, she offered me an internship after my term. Put myself through school, with this place. When Alex offered me a research job, I knew I could help make Dociline safer and more in line with debtors' needs, if anyone could. He's extremely intelligent and his vision is better than his father's, but folks with direct experience should be involved, I thought. So, here I am."

"I've never heard of a Docile becoming a trillionaire, before."

"Because it's impossible without connections. You're looking at one out of two cases—at least to my knowledge." She grabs two mugs, cream, and sweetener, then pours a cupful for each of us. I don't ask who the other case is, even though I'm curious; the matter is obviously private. "So, that's why I don't mind doing Dociles favors. Alex does, too, but he can't let anyone know because of his fancy surname."

"He never does any favors for me."

"Never? He didn't win Dylan for you? I'd say that's a pretty big favor." Jess hands me a steaming mug. "Bigger than a cup of coffee."

Alex is quiet during the drive home, but my chest pulses with the warm thud of my heart. No matter where I look, I see Dylan staring at me—through me. I break the silence. "Can I ask you a question?"

"Yes."

"Is Dylan mad at me?"

"No," Alex says. "I explained the situation to her. She understands."

I unravel the diamond chain on my cuff and twirl it around my finger. "She acted like something was wrong with me, though. Is there?"

"No, you've been very good, lately."

"Then, why did Dylan ask if she'd end up like me, as if that's a bad thing?"

Alex stares out the window for a minute. "She hasn't seen you in six months." He slides a comforting hand over my leg. "Everyone changes; everyone grows. We're a new version of ourselves, every day."

I nod my head and replay his words. That sounds right. I have changed, but how could I not have? I'm surviving. If I'm honest with myself, life's easier, lately. Alex is warmer, time faster—which is good. Alex just said I've been very good. And his opinion is the only one that matters.

21

ALEX

Elisha's caseworker smiles for the first time—probably all day—when she sees him. Age lines crease her face. It's been six months since he first entered this building, since he met her—met me. Six months since we signed a contract. Since I paid off his family debts in exchange for the rest of his life. Dociles are required to visit home for a weekend every six months. This date felt like it would never come, and yet here we are: customers in this building where I'm usually in charge.

I make a point to make a good impression with Elisha's caseworker. With a quick glance at her name tag, I say, "Pleasure to meet you, Carol," and shake her hand before she can even stand up. "Alexander Bishop the Third."

She rises to meet me. "You must be Elisha's Patron." Carol is a middle-aged Latina woman, who manages to look down at me despite being a head shorter. She has the power to remove Elisha from my custody, if he were to say I violated any of his rights. But I haven't and he wouldn't, so she can't.

"I am," I say.

She doesn't smile at me like she does at Elisha. I know a fake when I see it. "I'll have to ask you to wait outside."

"I—" I know that, but by saying it, she makes me look foolish. "Yes, of course." I rub my hand over the back of Elisha's neck, keeping my eyes on Carol. "Find me when you're finished."

"Okay." He barely finishes the word before I peck a kiss on his lips. Used to public affections, he returns it.

"Thank you, Carol." I flash her a pretty grin and close the door behind me.

I consider asking my Patron Liaison, Charlene, whether I can have Elisha's caseworker changed. Haven't seen her since Preakness, but she's ambitious and I'm a Bishop.

The lone wooden bench is full of other Patrons. I join them, waiting like a husband whose partner is in labor. One at a time, their Dociles emerge, eyes still glossy as their last injection wears off. They're supposed to come at the end of their Dociline cycle so they're more honest. No on-med would speak badly of their Patron.

Finally, Carol and Elisha emerge from her office, animated with conversation. His demeanor snaps back like a rubber band when he sees me—*docile*. Carol has to tap his shoulder to regain his attention.

"I can take it from here," I say, smoothing a hand through his hair and down his back. Reclaiming him.

"Patrons shouldn't interact with their Dociles' families," Carol says.

"Anonymity of surname," I say. "Third Right. I know the rules."

"I know the rules, too, Dr. Bishop. I've worked here since you were a boy. You are not allowed to interact with your Docile's family."

"I'm not going to introduce myself to them, *Carol*. My family has been a part of this institution for a century. I don't need you to tell me what I'm allowed to do. I *am* this place."

"I should report this to my supervisor."

"Please do." I stare at Carol until her shoulders slump and the fire in her eyes goes out.

Finally, she turns to Elisha and says, "Are you sure you're okay?"

"Yes, just nervous to see my family."

That's not what she meant. She was giving him an out. I wonder how hard she pushed him to demonize me during his interview. I am definitely going to look into reforming some of their "rules," here, alongside the structural renovations.

"Thank you, Carol." I hold out my hand to her. "I assure you, Elisha is in good hands."

She forces herself to take it. I have no sympathy for her, having forced myself through far more precarious social situations. Who does this caseworker think she is, challenging me—in public, at that? She has no idea how hard I've worked with him over the past six months. The anxiety this whole ordeal has caused. I rearranged my whole life for Elisha.

"Don't forget to contact me if you need anything, Elisha," she says.

"I look forward to seeing you again in six months." I address her even though she ignores me. "Come on." I push Elisha forward by the small of his back.

You'd think I bent him over the wooden bench and fucked him, the way Carol glares at me. She can't do anything. Any inspector would praise the conditions in which I keep Elisha: well fed, educated, creatively enriched. Sexually satisfied.

I smirk to myself as Carol grows smaller behind us. She shouldn't work here if she can't handle it.

"Third floor," I tell Elisha as we near a recently fixed elevator, courtesy of Bishop Labs.

He presses the appropriate button and we rise, quickly, a soft tone signaling our arrival. Halfway down the long marble hall, there's a thick yellow line painted across the floor, up the walls, and along the ceiling, forming a bright square. Bold black text painted over the yellow states: **"NO PATRONS BEYOND THIS POINT."** On the other side, families huddle around plastic furniture and drink water from waxy cups. First thing Monday, I'm going to advise our contractors to make their area more comfortable. Show people we don't only care about the Patrons' experience, but the debtors', as well.

Elisha's eyes fix on a middle-aged man with a freshly shaven face who holds his daughter's shoulders while they watch another Docile cross the yellow line toward her family. The other Docile hugs her family with the awkwardly smooth gestures of someone still coming off their biweekly dose. When Formula 3.0 releases, that will not be an issue.

The man I assume is Elisha's dad rubs his daughter's shoulders, as if she's about to enter a boxing ring. When she glimpses us, her whole body tenses. Mine responds. I turn my back to them to avoid their gaze. If I haven't crossed the yellow line, why does it feel like I've broken a law?

"Take this." I stuff a thousand dollars into Elisha's pocket—cash withdrawn specially for this. I'll need to add him to one of my bank accounts as an approved spender, before his next visit home. "Two hundred for a taxi to take you and your family home. Another two hundred for your trip back, Monday morning; you can call this number." I hand him the card of a taxi service. "Another two hundred so they don't have to walk into the city, next time. Tip the drivers. I overestimated the cost, so no one would have to worry about having enough. Your family can keep whatever's left. I'll pick you up at the ODR at eight a.m."

Elisha pats his stuffed pocket, then stutters, "Th-thank you, I . . ." He shakes his head; he wants to refuse the money. "We don't have a phone. We can't—I can't call a taxi."

"Oh, um." Doesn't have a phone. It didn't even occur to me—everyone does. I try not to wonder what else his family doesn't have. "I'll schedule one for you, seven a.m. What's your address?" He does have an address. I hope. I fumble with the notepad on my phone more than necessary so I don't have to look at him.

"I can meet the car at Exit 31. On 83 South."

"Okay." I don't pry further.

Across the yellow line, his sister slips away. "Come on, Dad! Let me—"

"Go on." I want to kiss him, but shame stills my lips. The gesture would be inappropriate in front of his family. We are not lovers.

Elisha walks the first few steps before running. He crosses the yellow line like the end of the Preakness Stakes and throws his arms around his sister. I loiter for a moment, making sure he's okay. His dad looks him over, relieved that he isn't distant, like the other Docile. When Elisha pulls the money from his pocket, his father clamps his hands over the wad, as if someone might steal it. Elisha points casually in my direction, trying to explain. When his dad catches my eye, I know it's time for me to go. Carol was right.

22

ELISHA

"Are you . . ." Dad pulls me away from Abby and checks me almost as thoroughly as the doctor does.

"Am I what?" I ask, then realize. "Oh, no. I refused Dociline."

"Oh, thank god." He throws his arms around me. "I don't know if I could handle it—if you—"

I hold him tight, breathing in the sweat and firewood scent that lingers in the overgrown waves of his hair. "If I what?"

Dad lets me go and lowers his voice. "If you ended up like your mother."

I won't end up like him, will I? I flinch.

Alex's words kick in, and I recite them for myself as much as my dad. "You haven't seen me in six months."

"Tell me about it. We have a lot of catching up to do. Better start walking while it's still early."

"We don't have to." I take the cash Alex gave me out of my pocket and hand it to Dad. "I have money for a taxi."

He shoves the bills in his pocket, glancing at the other families like they might steal it. "Where'd you get that?"

I point past the yellow line. "Alex gave it to me."

"Your Patron?"

"Yes."

"And you took it?"

"Of course." But Dad doesn't seem to understand. "He wants us to have more time together."

When I glance over the yellow line, Alex is gone.

/ / /

Dad cringes when I pry two of the hundred-dollar bills from his hand and give it to the driver. I nudge Abby out ahead of us.

"Thank you, you can keep the change." I shut the door and wave the cab off. Dust and dirt form a cloud behind its spinning tires.

"We should have walked," Dad says. "Saved the money."

I hate how much his words hurt. His doubt and distrust. Why would he reject the gift of time that Alex has given us? But I hear worse from trillionaires, regularly, so if I can ignore them, I can ignore Dad.

I throw an arm around Abby's shoulders. It's only been six months, but already she looks taller, her shoulders broader, hands rougher. The first signs of acne dapple her perpetually sun-pink skin. Her bangs hang wavy and uneven over her eyes. She hugs me against her as hard as I do, her smaller fingers digging into my side.

"You turned into a teenager while I was gone. Next time I'm here you'll be a grown woman."

Abby laughs like I remember Mom used to. No wonder she took the same name. Dad's face remains blank.

"I've missed you," she says.

"I've missed you, too."

I push the front door open, relieved that I do not have to pass Tom to enter my own home. The single room that serves as our living room, kitchen, and dining room is exactly the way I left it, except—"Where's Mom?"

"She's with Nora," Dad says. "Abby, why don't you run and tell them Elisha's here."

Dylan and Nora Falstaff. David Burns. Abby, Elisha, and Abigail Wilder. My family. Our surnames sound foreign after six months of disuse; I make a point to remember them.

"Nora! Mom!" Abby breaks into a run, disappearing through the door.

Dad and I stand in silence. He breaks it by striking a match and lighting the wood in the stove. I hand him the kettle—still half-full—and we wait for it to boil.

"So, uh." Dad grabs two mugs and a metal coffee tin that no longer holds coffee, but leaves and buds for tea. "That was him, huh? Alexander Bishop 'the Third.'" He pronounces the suffix like it's make-believe.

My family got a copy of the contract in the mail, so Dad already knows the details. "Yes," I say, anyway.

Dad shoves mint and tea leaves into two little pouches and tosses them in the mugs. I take one and say, "Thank you."

"What's he do?"

"Alex?" I consider my answer carefully. I wouldn't lie, but the exact truth might hurt Dad more than help him. "Research," I say. "He's a scientist."

"How old is he?"

"Thirty."

Dad nods. "Could be worse."

I do not tell him how right he is. How lucky I am to be with Alex rather than Dutch or Mariah.

"He feed you?"

I laugh at that. "He has to. Second Right."

Dad holds his free hand up. "You hear things. I won't lie, I was relieved not to have to send your sister." Bubbling water interrupts us. Dad and I reach for the kettle at the same time. "I've got it." He pours steaming water into our cups.

I suppress the itch to help. To feel useful. "Thank you."

My tea doesn't have a chance to cool before Abby bursts through the door. Nora follows and points Mom in the right direction. "Come now, Abigail, you remember Elisha."

Mom wears the soft smile I see on every other Docile's face along with faded jeans and a World Foods branded tee shirt. "Hello, Elisha." She hugs me, gently, not at all like she hasn't seen me for six months.

But I squeeze her and kiss her cheek. "Miss you," I say quietly.

There's no catching up with Mom; we're not sure how much she remembers day to day, and she seems to enjoy everything she does equally.

"Come here, you." Nora pulls me into an even stronger hug that smells like sunflower oil and earth. Her brown skin is warmer than I remember, probably burnt judging by the state of my mother's; the two must've been in the garden under the sun, all day. "We're *all* happy to see you," she says, "even those of us who don't say it."

"Thank you. I'm glad to be—" *Home.* The word is "home," but it feels wrong. Even the letters don't come out right in my head. "—here. And to see you all." That part is true.

"Well," Dad says. "The farm was putting together a surprise party for you—"

"Dad!"

"David!"

Abby and Nora shout at the same time, jumping up from where they leaned against the wall.

"Oh, calm down," he says. "It'll still be fun."

They both huff and busy themselves with their own tea.

"Look, I thought we wouldn't be home until tonight. But since we took a taxi"—he strains to treat the word like any other—"everyone's still getting their work and party preparations done, your sister and me included. Do you mind spending a few hours with Nora and your mother?"

"Not at all," I say.

"And try to act surprised, later, will you?" He ruffles my hair—which I immediately fix—sets his mug down, and tugs Abby to follow him. She whines and drags her feet, letting the door slam behind them.

"Abigail, why don't you tidy up," Nora says. Not that there's much, but Mom will go over the same spots until you tell her to stop.

"Okay," she says.

Nora gulps her tea and stares at her boots, waits until the

only sound is the swish-swish of Mom's broom. "Dylan registered."

"I know."

She looks at me with hope in her eyes. "Did you—have you—"

"Seen her? Yes." I smile and relax, hoping my expression will comfort her. "She's safe."

"Thank god." Nora presses her hand to her chest. "I worried, you know? We didn't have too much debt left . . ." Not after her husband killed himself while under a Patron's care, she doesn't say. "But the creditors came by a few times, and we knew the cops would be next. You gave her that strength, Elisha."

My tea feels thick in my throat as I force it down. I wish I could've warned Dylan against trillionaires. Spared her the humiliation and Alex the trouble. They're not all like him.

"She's at Bishop Laboratories, now," I say. "I don't know if you received the new contract in the mail, yet. I know it's slow out here."

"I thought she was with some person named VanBuren, the one on all the TV billboards along 83."

"She was," I say. "But then Alex bought her contract for Bishop Laboratories."

Nora sits slowly and carefully in a chair, as if she's hurt. "Who's he?" She doesn't look hurt, but I worry she's stopped going to the doctor, now that I'm not here. I should tell Abby she has to make our family go. Untreated scrapes and sprains go a long way. "And what's Bishop Laboratories?"

"Alex is my Patron and Bishop Laboratories is his family's business. He's kind and fair." I hold Nora's hand in mine. "Dylan will be all right. I promise."

Dad and Abby come for us when the sun begins to set. Together, we walk down the dirt road toward the old barn. I can't remember it ever housing animals; we use it for storage, now.

The farm is quiet for a Saturday night. Normally, the adults lay out their haul while the children walk around with baskets, collecting groceries: greens, eggs, little rolls if there's a surplus. Paulo, who's worked with the sheep and goats for sixty years, always sneaks the littlest kids pieces of cheese until someone catches him. Cheese is actually worth something if we label it "artisanal." Not much, but something.

Dad looks at me, a muted smile on his face. "Remember to act surprised."

"I will," I say. But suddenly I find myself stopped. The others walk past me, not noticing they've left me for several yards. I stare at the rust-colored barn. "I haven't seen anyone in six months. What if they don't like me, now?"

"Why wouldn't they like you?" Nora asks, taking Dad's hand.

"I like you, Elisha," says Mom.

"Thank you." I look down at the seven-hundred-dollar tee shirt Alex bought me last weekend. The fabric was so soft and warm when I tried it on, he couldn't stop touching me. I remember thinking, as he bought me a dozen of the same shirt, his lips felt just as soft against mine.

"We're a new version of ourselves, every day," I say to myself.

"Uh, sure," Dad says. "As long as you're a surprised version of yourself in a few minutes."

"Of course."

"Good. Stay right there." Dad runs around to the side door.

I hook my index finger through the cuff on my left wrist and pull the diamond chain out. The sun shines brighter, here, unobscured by buildings and ships and billboards. My cuff sparkles under its evening light.

The big barn doors swing open.

"Surprise!" They bang spoons against pots and shake glass jars with pebbles inside. I jump back, nearly toppling over. A stampede of kids and dogs runs toward me, the adults waiting until they've cleared.

No one minds my expensive clothes or my styled hair, and once Abby discovers she can pull me along by my cuff, I'm her captive all evening. She wraps the diamond chain around her wrist and pretends it's a bracelet.

"Don't, Abby." Dad swats her hand away. "Leave that alone; it's not a toy."

"But—"

"They're bringing out the cake." Dad steers her in the opposite direction. "Go get us each a slice."

"Ugh, Dad!"

"Your brother will still be here when you get back, and all day tomorrow."

She drags her feet as she walks off. Such a teenager.

"Don't play with that in front of your sister," Dad says. "I don't want her to, you know . . ."

"Think that we can afford something this nice, I know."

He looks at me with a blank face, then hisses: "Idolize being a Docile." His voice softens. "Don't get me wrong, we're grateful for your sacrifice, but that's what it has to be: sacrifice, not inspiration."

"Of course, sorry."

Dad throws an arm over my shoulder. "You're a good brother. Don't let them change that."

Before I can respond, Abby pushes through a crowd of our neighbors with my promised slice of cake. "I did make this, in case you were wondering. So, you'd better like it. Even though it's not trillionaire cake."

"I'm sure it's better than trillionaire cake." I take the plate with my left hand so it will hide the cuff.

No one else mentions it, even though they take my hand to dance, deal me cards, and pull me onto an empty field for a game of soccer. By nightfall, most of the kids collapse in a pile with the dogs, exhausted from running around. Dad and his friends pass around a joint, while plucking out a nameless tune on a scratched-up guitar.

I walk over to an old piano that smells of mold, and slide my finger through a thick, sticky layer of dust. I pull a bale of hay out from under it, sit on my improvised bench, and rest my feet on the tarnished pedals.

"I didn't know your boy could play piano, Dave."

"He can't."

"Seems to think he can."

The first, low notes reverberate through the piano—through my fingers and the balls of my feet. Without the music tutor staring over my shoulder, "Liebesträum no. 3" flows through me at my own pace. Even when I close my eyes, I touch all the right keys—after months of practice, the music lives inside me.

Dad scratches a pick back and forth across a metallic chord on the guitar, cutting through Liszt. He howls falsetto. His audience claps.

I stop. When I remove my feet from the pedals, the notes cut off, sharply. Dad stares at me while he sings, crude lyrics rousing laughs from his friends. He strums his chords like he's trying to scrub a stain out of laundry.

I stand and tuck the bale of hay back under the piano. I know when I'm not wanted. "May I be excused for the evening?" I ask.

Dad studies a chipped fret. "Do whatever you want. It's your party."

"Thank you."

"Take your mother and Abby with you."

"Yes, sir." It's not until I'm halfway home that I regret my word choice. "Dad," I whisper.

I wake before the sun rises—wide awake even though I don't remember sleeping for more than an hour at a time. When I get up, it's more that I give up. Besides, it's time for my run.

My feet are used to hot, hard pavement, but I find myself dodging muddy potholes and tiptoeing over rocks, against a dark purple sky. My heart races even though my feet slow, as pinks and oranges brighten the morning. I thought the city had every color in the world, but it doesn't have these. It's not until the sun breaks through the clouds that I turn back.

I wave to my neighbors as I cut down the main path, alongside wheelbarrows and carts. Two playing dogs form a truce to chase me home until they're called back. I stretch and catch my breath against a tree. Dad and Abby will already have started work.

After washing up, I stand alone in the house, twiddling my thumbs. There's no schedule here, and without any homework to keep me busy, I'm not sure what to do. My fingers itch to clean off the piano and practice, but no one here wants to hear Franz Liszt.

Alex would.

My stomach growls. By now, most Sundays, I've eaten eggs, oatmeal, and a yogurt, not to mention coffee. There's no way I can cook in the mess of last night's party. I can't only wash one pot, though. That pot turns into every plate and utensil, then the counter, the stove, the floor. I rummage up a needle and thread to mend the growing holes in pillows and cushions until I can sit on our couch without worrying its guts will ooze out under my weight. Around noon, Abby stops in to make lunch. Together, the two of us finish cleaning. She shows me what food we have and I unwrap a small package of salted ham stashed away in the pantry. Perfect.

Dad finally comes in for dinner, holding Mom's hand. She smiles across the room at me.

"What happened, here?" he asks.

Abby spreads her arms like a spokesmodel. "We cleaned!"

Mom walks into my arms and hugs me, an easy smile on her face. "Hello."

"Hey, Mom. It's me, Elisha."

"Hi, Elisha. How are you?"

"I'm good. Are you hungry? I made dinner."

"Thank you, Elisha."

"Thank you."

Dad opens a pot on the stove and sniffs it. "You're welcome."

"Hmm?" I say.

"When someone thanks you, you say, 'You're welcome.' Or have you forgotten basic manners?"

"I haven't forgotten." But my face flushes. "Thank you, Mom."

Dad slams the lid on the pot. "You're welcome."

"I'm sorry," I whisper. "I only—I wanted to thank her for the compliment."

"Thank you for cleaning the whole house, Elisha." He overenunciates, staring at me.

My heart pulses through my entire body. The "Th" slips between my tongue and teeth. I bite down, cutting the word off before it fully forms.

"What do you say?" Dad's eyes are dark and narrow.

Abby leans closer and whispers, "Elisha, just say, 'You're welcome.'"

"You're welcome." I haven't spoken those words in months. They sound foreign. They feel wrong.

Dad nods. "So, what'd you do all day, clean? Something different, then."

"I also cooked dinner."

"Thank you, Elisha," Mom says.

"Thanks." I cover my mouth and squat down beside the counter, trying to hide my shame, but it consumes me. Hot tears burn the corners of my eyes.

Abby drops beside me; her voice softens. "It's okay." Her hand covers my cuff. "It's not your fault. He's being rude."

"Abby, go to your room."

"No. Elisha and I made dinner for you, Mom, and Nora."

"Fine." His focus shifts to me. "Elisha, go to your room."

I stand immediately, but Abby pulls the diamond chain out to stop me. "No, Elisha, don't. You don't have to do what he says."

"It's okay." I wipe at my itchy eyes, try to blink them back to normal. "You stay and enjoy dinner."

"I can't believe you're just going to leave," Dad says.

"You told me to leave." I look between them all. "Isn't that what you want?"

"No. I want you to act like a goddamned human being. Like my son."

"I am." I recite Alex's words. "I'm a new version of myself, every day."

"No, you're not. None of the guys can quit talking about that—" He flicks his hand through the air. "—that foofy trillionaire song you played last night."

"That's not a trillionaire song. It's Franz Liszt."

"'Frah-nzz'; excuse me."

"He's a Hungarian composer from the 1800s."

"Oh, you're smart, now, too."

"I—I've—" Was I not smart, before? Alex told me he chose me because I was smart.

"You are smart, Elisha." Mom smiles.

"Why don't you put your expensive shoes on and run back into the city where you clearly belong. Yeah, I heard all about your little run this morning. No one can stop talking about your cushy orange shoes and stretchy purple pants—whatever they are. Running around like a fucking bear's chasing you."

"I always run in the morning."

"Well, not here. Here, we work in the morning. What happened to my hardworking son? The one who raised a barn? Who helped birth three calves? When the stallion got tangled in the fence, did you stand around and wait for orders? No. You held its insides together with the shirt off your back. Now, you'd probably thank the damn horse for letting you watch it die." He grabs my hand and holds it up. "Probably don't even remember what it feels like to have dirt under your fingernails."

"Dad, stop!" Abby puts herself between us.

"I can't have you around her. Not like this." He gestures to my clothes. "I want Abby to go to school and get a job—a smart job—and not because of some trillionaire. On her own. What's-his-name can keep his money."

"His name's Alex."

"I wasn't asking."

"Sorry."

"What, you're not going to thank me?"

My mouth hangs open. Does he want me to?

"Hm?" He cups his ear and leans in.

Why doesn't he say what he means? Alex always tells me exactly what he wants. "Thank you?"

Dad's slow laugh fills the room. "You know what, Elisha? Go back home to the city where you belong. You're as much use to me as your mother."

"Thank you," she says.

"This is my home," I whisper.

"Is it?" Dad says. "You think you belong here, anymore? Look at yourself."

I hold up evenly tanned arms, and manicured hands that remember Liszt, Mozart, and Grieg. That give pleasure and pour champagne and grip the barre during ballet and barbells during weight training. I hold my cuffed wrist, pull the chain out, and wrap it around my finger.

Dad pushes Abby out of the way. "Go home, Elisha. Go back to your trillionaire. Abigail, get Elisha's things for him."

"Yes, David." She disappears into my and Abby's room.

I can't move.

"You're leaving," Dad growls.

"Dad, no!" Abby tries to sneak past him, but he stops her with an outstretched arm. "Elisha, stay. It's fine. You're fine."

"I'm sorry," I say. "Please, I can do better."

"No. You can't."

Mom returns, handing me the small designer bag Alex packed me. I take it, unable to stop myself from moving. The door grows bigger until I'm standing in the frame.

"And Elisha?"

I look over my shoulder.

"Don't bother coming back until you're the old version of yourself. I liked that one better."

His stare pushes me forward—out the door, down the

path, into the dark. He's right. Abby can't grow up wanting to be like a Docile—can't grow up to become me. That's why I left in the first place, to take the burden so she wouldn't have to. I walk until I can't hear her shouting my name, anymore. And then I run.

I slow when the pavement becomes darker and smoother when I hit Exit 20. It's too late and too far to make it back to Alex's, tonight. I wipe the dust and tears from my face, and take the exit. Lights are still on in Hunt Valley—not as many as in the city, but enough that I can see where I'm going.

A couple passes on bikes, dinging their bells so I don't step in front of them. I'm not sure what to do. Probably should've gone to Nora's or another neighbor's, but at the time I could only see the horizon, only see forward. And forward was far enough not to hear Dad and Abby fighting.

The balls of my feet pulse. I've never run for more than two hours, before, and especially not with a small bag. My shoulders ache. Thirst and exhaustion drive me forward even though my stomach is already in knots knowing I'll have to call Alex.

"I said, are you okay, sir?" Someone taps my shoulder.

I hurry into the light of the next streetlamp. When I look over my shoulder, I see a pale, older man hold up empty hands.

"I didn't mean to startle you," he says. "You looked like you might need a hand. I'm with Empower Maryland." He points to the logo on his shirt. "Just finished my shift at the center, but I can walk you there if you need some food or a place to stay."

I shake my head and teeter back. "I'm okay."

"Are you sure? It's free," he says.

I raise my voice. "I don't need Empower Maryland's help."

"Whoa, man, it's cool." He backs slowly away.

Roger's help earned me seventy minutes in confinement. Tom's help violated my family's privacy and trapped me inside an elevator. I already feel my heart beating faster. Hear Eugenia's *You're turning into one of them.* Dylan's *I won't end up like him, will I?* Dad's *You think you belong here, anymore?*

"I don't need Empower Maryland's help," I repeat while the man fades into the dark. "I need Alex."

23

ALEX

A low, soothing ring wakes me. The sound is soft and brings the lights up to a muted blue hue. "Who is it?" I mumble into my pillow.

"Unidentified caller."

That never happens. It could be someone from the ODR; their technology is adequate at best. But it's—I rub my eyes and force them open on the far wall—2:30 in the morning.

"Call location?"

"Hunt Valley, Maryland."

"Answer call." The signal switches over. "This had better be important," I say to whoever thinks it's a good idea to wake me up.

"Alex?"

I sit up.

"Alex, it's Elisha."

"I know who it is. Why are you calling me on your weekend off? And where did you get a phone?" He told me he didn't have one, so either he lied or he's not with his family.

"I was—" His voice shakes. "I was wondering if you could book me a hotel room for the night, or call the taxi to bring me home, tonight, instead. I didn't want to bother you. I'm sorry I woke you up."

"It's okay." I roll out from under the covers. My movement brings up dimmed lights. "What happened?"

"I—I'm not—"

He never hesitates to answer me. "Elisha, are you somewhere safe?"

"I don't know."

I bring up his microchip app on my phone. No location, no vitals—and he is obviously still alive. I refresh the app: nothing. Close it and restart. Read: *Application disabled for visitation weekends in accordance with Third Right. In case of emergency, please contact the Office of Debt Resolution.*

Fuck! I throw my phone onto the sheets and storm into the bathroom, Elisha's voice still in my ear. "Alex?"

"I'm still here. Tell me where you are; I'm coming to get you." I don't even brush my teeth, just tip back a capful of mouthwash.

"It's called the Valley Inn. It's up on that big hill, next to 83."

I know where he is: Hunt Valley, a little commerce center for people who can't afford the city. Lots of ex-Dociles getting their lives back together, recent university graduates trying not to default on loans, some farmers from neighboring towns peddling their wares. Those fucking Empower Maryland people have a center there. If they knew Elisha was there . . .

"Stay right where you are. I'll be there in half an hour."

"Okay."

"End call. Dial front desk."

Tom answers. "Dr. Bishop, how can I help you?"

"I need a car waiting out front in two minutes."

"Keep it running," I tell the driver, before hopping out.

"Yes, sir."

The hotel isn't a wreck. Generic cement blocks, well-tread carpet with a tacky red and yellow pattern, bland ivory furniture in the lobby.

"Welcome to the Valley Inn, sir. How can I help you?" The skinny bald white man at the front desk stares at my clothes, rather than meeting my eyes. Highly unprofessional. People like Tom are immune to higher-end styles. These people clearly are not. No one from

Baltimore City would spend the night in Hunt Valley. I'm probably the first person of class this concierge has ever interacted with.

"I'm looking for someone." I hold out my hand to illustrate Elisha's height. "About this tall, white, brown hair, freckled." I choose my next words carefully. "Wearing a bracelet on his left arm."

"You must be Dr. Bishop." He wants me to know that he knows who I am. How much I'm worth.

"In the flesh."

"He's waiting in the breakfast nook, down the hall to your right. We gave him a cup of coffee." The man smiles like he wants a pat on the back for showing basic hospitality.

"Thank you."

As soon as I walk off, another employee mutters something. Magazine pages flip—actual paper pages.

Elisha sits on the edge of a vinyl upholstered chair, clutching a paper coffee cup. At the sound of my feet, he looks up. "Alex."

"Come on, let's go." I motion him over.

The janitorial staff watch us while slowly restocking powdered creamer and sweetener packets. They wouldn't have hurt him—I don't think. His left shoe is probably worth a month of one of their salaries.

Elisha leaves the cup on the table and takes my offered hand. I kiss his forehead and squeeze him tight—only for a moment. We shouldn't linger.

I lead him back to the entrance and point to the black sedan. "Go wait in the car. I'll be out in a minute."

"Okay. Um, the front desk. They have my bag. I said they didn't need to, but they insisted, so . . ."

So, he didn't refuse, because he never refuses anyone unless I tell him to. For a split second, I worry that perhaps I've trained the fight out of Elisha. That he couldn't handle himself if something happened. I placate my nerves by vowing to hire him a self-defense instructor.

"I'll take care of it," I tell Elisha. "Go." As soon as he's safely inside the car, I walk up to the front desk.

The concierge closes his tabloid. His female coworker pushes it aside as he says, "How can I help you, Dr. Bishop?"

"I wanted to thank you for holding my Docile's bag and pay for the cup of coffee."

"Of course, sir." Both he and his coworker stare at the computer while he types. He nudges her. "The bag."

"Right." She runs off, failing to make his intended good impression.

"The coffee is on the house." He smiles at me. "Are you sure you wouldn't like a room? We'd gladly comp one for you and your Docile for the rest of the night."

"No, thank you. But I'd like to tip you for generously storing his luggage." Which couldn't have lasted more than an hour, nor could the coffee have cost more than five dollars, but the last thing I need is for Baltimore City to read about Alexander Bishop racing out to Middle of Nowhere, Maryland, to pick up his Docile at 3:00 a.m.

"Your staff do accept tips, right?"

The concierge looks at his coworker, who holds the hand-stitched leather suitcase as if it's a rucksack. Her nod is barely perceptible. He tilts his head. She narrows her eyes.

"Yes, sir, we do," the concierge finally says. "Did you want to put that on a card?"

They don't have the technology here for direct transfer, nor is this the type of establishment where I would keep my information on file. "Yes, thank you." I hand him the matte black plastic card.

He flips it over, searching for a magnetic strip, chip, account number, anything. He won't find any of that; it's embedded.

"You can swipe it anywhere." I smile to encourage him.

He laughs nervously and swipes my card. "There we go." He's trembling with nerves when he hands it back.

"Thank you."

He slides me a tablet that's attached to his computer by a cable. Even the ODR has this place beat. I pull a stylus from my pocket to save him the heart attack of scrambling for one.

I calculate his probable salary, his coworker's, and—who else has seen me, tonight? Perhaps a little extra for the two at the front desk. I settle on three numbers.

"Please divide the top amount between everyone on the hotel staff, for keeping such clean and comfortable accommodations. The two amounts on the bottom are for yourself and your bellhop, respectively, for your good deed and discretion."

The concierge grips the tablet hard to still his hand. Despite his precautions, it clatters to the counter when he reads the numbers. "Oh my, Dr. Bishop, we can't possibly—"

"Please, I insist. Is my bag ready?"

I know it is. The bellhop's been holding it, watching, for the past five minutes. She needs someone to shock her out of her stupor.

"Yes, Dr. Bishop—sir." But she doesn't move.

I reach out, taking the bag gently from her hold. "Thank you."

"You're welcome."

"Have a good night." I nod to the concierge and carry Elisha's bag out to the car.

Elisha huddles against the far side of the back seat. His shoes are scuffed and dirty. Sweat stains his shirt. He pulls on the diamond chain of his cuff.

I slide into the seat beside him and pull him against me. "We'll talk in the morning. Rest, now."

He relaxes in my arms as the car glides forward.

I call the lab Monday morning to tell them I'm going to be late, then cancel the tutor and shut off Elisha's alarm. He passed out as soon as we got home, but I've barely slept. Instead, I watch his chest rise and fall beside me. In my bed. Again.

I couldn't put him on the trundle, last night. He would have thought I was pushing him away, blaming him for waking me up. I want him to know I'll take care of him, especially in emergencies. It's not like anyone else lives here, and Elisha would never tell anyone.

My phone rings. Elisha's eyes fly open. I reject the call.

Elisha sits up; worry wrinkles his forehead. He shields his eyes from the light. "Alex?"

"Shhh, relax."

"I overslept my ballet lesson."

I knew I forgot something. Oh, well. The teacher still gets paid. "It's okay," I reassure him. "I turned off your alarm. I wanted you to sleep."

Elisha presses a hand to the bare skin of his chest. "Thank you." He doesn't ask what time it is. "My tutor?"

"Canceled."

"Oh. You're not at work."

"Don't worry about me."

"Sorry."

I don't want him to apologize. I want to know what happened, why he called me in the middle of the night. "First and foremost, understand that I am not upset with you. You should always let me know if you feel unsafe. You're my responsibility."

"Thank you." He bites his lip.

"I do want to know what happened."

Elisha looks down at the mattress and traces his finger in circles around the sheets. "My dad yelled at me. Told me to leave."

I assume that's the condensed version, but don't want to pry *too* deep and worsen his dejection. "Why?"

"He said I'm a bad influence on my younger sister."

I nudge his chin up. "I can't imagine you're a bad influence on anyone." He blends in seamlessly; I can't imagine him influencing anyone, at all. Except maybe other off-meds.

"Thank you." But he doesn't sound convinced.

"Hey, look at me."

I've never seen sadder eyes in my life. I kiss his wilted lips and he livens under my touch, arching his body against mine.

"Don't let it get to you. Your father doesn't understand."

Elisha's head falls back onto the pillow. "He told me I didn't belong there, anymore. But I didn't do anything bad. When I tried to play piano for them, they laughed at me. And they made fun of my morning run. It's not like it hurt anyone." He looks to me for the answers.

I sigh. These people are doing a number on his training. At this rate, his regular home visits will do more harm than good.

"Don't let him make you feel guilty about your hobbies."

"I told Dad I was a new version of myself."

Oh god, he didn't.

"And he said he liked the old version better. Not to visit until I changed back."

"I'm sure he didn't mean that. He was probably just surprised. He'll get used to you."

"I hope so."

"Hey." I put on a smile and sit up straight, hoping it will catch. "Let's ditch our schedules and get out of here. How does that sound?"

Elisha warms up to the idea. His eyes wander while he considers, lips tense for a smile, fingers gripping the sheets, ready to push off. "That sounds nice." By the time the words leave him, he's a new person, roused by my suggestion.

I pull him from the bed and toward the shower. Only a glance prompts him to undress beside me.

"How about I take you to a *real* hotel. One with a view and a nice restaurant—room service that will send up dessert at midnight, if we want it. Discreet staff, strong coffee, California king beds."

"I don't know what a California bed is, but it sounds wonderful," Elisha says.

"Oh," I say, pulling his body against mine as I turn on the hot water. "You'll love it. Believe me."

We clean and dress in casual clothes. The two of us have dressed up enough lately to last a lifetime. I'm packing my electronics when it occurs to me that Elisha still doesn't have a phone. We cannot repeat last night.

"Wait for me beside the elevator," I say.

"Okay." Elisha does as he's told, taking his overnight bag downstairs with him.

I duck quickly into my office, pull the bottom drawer open, and open the small black box from Javier. Tossing the card onto the desk, I delicately remove the strip of plastic to which the sticker-like phone adheres.

Elisha looks up at the sound of my feet on the stairs. I peel the device from its plastic backing and balance it on my middle finger.

"Open your mouth."

He does as he's told. I press my finger against the roof of his mouth, waiting while the device adheres. Elisha stretches his jaw when I back away. I pull out my phone and, as promised, the devices link.

"That is a phone. Sort of. All you have to say is, 'Call Alex.' Try it."

"Call Alex?"

He jumps a little and smiles when my phone rings. Even after six months, I'm still charmed by his awe of technology.

"Perfect," I say. "Exactly like you."

The bellhop takes our bags—to Elisha's surprise—when we arrive at The Douglass Hotel.

"Good afternoon, sirs," he says with such attention, I can barely tell he's on Dociline. This should be the norm. I wonder what instructions they give the hotel Dociles.

"Can I help you to your room?" he asks on autopilot, interrupting my thoughts.

"We haven't checked in yet," I say.

"Do you have a reservation, sirs?"

I smile and rest an arm around Elisha's shoulders. "Nope."

"Allow me to show you to the front desk, where an associate will assist you, sirs."

Together, we follow the bellhop Docile to the front desk, where he alerts a woman with a tight brown bun in a crisp gray suit.

"Dr. Bishop, a privilege. Would you like me to arrange a suite for you and your companion?"

"That would be lovely, thank you," I say, taking pleasure in her use of the word "companion." See, Dad? A Docile *can* be a companion. "This is Elisha, by the way."

"Nice to meet you, Elisha."

"Likewise," he replies, not straying from my side.

"Please, remind me of your name," I say, unsure whether I've met her before. Probably, since she appears to be the manager.

"Nguyen, sir. Prudence Nguyen." She shakes my hand.

"Thank you for taking care of us, Prudence. And, please, call me Alex."

"As you wish." She checks her computer again. "We can put you and Elisha in the Penthouse Suite, tonight."

"Perfect. You should have my account information on file."

"We do, sir—Alex." She smiles and bows her head, the slip well calculated. "However, your stay is on the house. We are honored by your patronage."

"Oh, you don't have to do that." I feel so at peace that my fake surprise is almost genuine. "Quite kind of you."

The manager completes our non-transaction and instructs the bellhop to take our bags. The latter disappears into a service elevator while Elisha and I ride up one that requires a fingerprint. Prudence directs us to place our fingers on the pad each in turn as we ride up.

The doors open to a short hallway, the private elevator opening opposite the service one. The bellhop Docile waiting with our bags in hand falls into line behind us. Again, at the door, we upload our fingerprints for access, and the door opens with the smooth twist of a brass knob.

The Penthouse Suite reminds me of my childhood home. Rich wooden floors; carpets, drapes, and couches in forest green, navy blue, and plum; pillows and linens embroidered with anchors and ships with raised sails.

Classic. Elegant. Simple.

Prudence dims the lights so that an apricot glow emanates from the translucent glass flowers that adorn the brass chandeliers hanging throughout the suite of rooms.

"Please let me know if there is any way we can further accommodate you," she says. "We have available a personal chef, classically trained pianist—"

I raise my eyebrows at Elisha, an inside joke. He's my own classically trained pianist, but it might be nice if we were both able to relax and enjoy the music.

"—personal shopper, tickets to the Baltimore Symphony Orchestra or any number of theater—"

I raise a hand and she stops. "Thank you, Prudence, we will let you know."

"Enjoy yourselves." She slips out, the bellhop close behind.

The door clicks shut. The light crackle from the fireplace colors our silence.

Elisha breaks the pause. "There are so many rooms."

"There's another floor." I bump my shoulder against Elisha's and speak softly into his ear. "Want to check it out?"

"Do—d-do *I* want to?" he stutters, flattered that I would ask his opinion.

"Yeah."

"Of course, I want whatever you—"

I don't give him a chance to finish, but take his hand and pull him along behind me until we're running up the circular staircase to the roof. Elisha's breathless laughter infects me and soon the two of us surface onto a canopied wooden deck with lounge chairs, tables, and a wet bar. The city surrounds us like a forest of painted marble and mirrored glass. Its inhabitants walk among the buildings like insects, boats sailing in and out before the sun can set on them.

"It's warm," Elisha says.

"It is." When I find the pool, it's even better than imagined. Clear water shows glittering tiles along its walls, large cobblestones on the bottom. The entrance slopes downward, mimicking a shoreline, and a stone platform in the center rises inches above the surface, for lounging. "Why don't we cool off?"

"I didn't bring a suit."

"You don't need one."

Elisha bites his lip, then unbuttons his shirt. He lays it neatly on a lounge chair. Watching him undress, I test my own patience; with one hand, I rub my neck and back, thread fingers in the ends of my hair while my other hand rubs over the crotch of my corduroys.

He continues stripping, setting aside boat shoes and belt and shorts, until all he's wearing is a pair of maroon boxer briefs. Unsure what to do next, he fidgets with them, eyeing the pool.

I realize I'm holding my breath when I say, "Go on." My lips barely move.

Elisha turns and carefully navigates the stone pathway between groomed gardens of grass and flowers. When he reaches the descending slope of the pool, he glances at me over his shoulder, then hitches his fingers into the sides of his briefs.

I watch them slide over the curve of his ass, down his thighs, and come to rest on the ground. Elisha picks them up, folds them in half, and tosses them onto a nearby chair. With one foot, he tests the water. Then, the other.

I cannot restrain myself any longer.

24

ALEX

I fumble with the buttons on my shirt, missing one that skitters across the patio when I tug my clothes off, not bothering to fold them like Elisha did. Luckily, he doesn't notice my haste. He wades deeper, stopping only at the sound of my feet splashing into the warm June water. I slow, trying my damnedest to appear cool and controlled. A man who knows himself and his place in the world. A Bishop.

A Bishop who's still catching his breath.

"How do you like it?" I try not to sound too eager and yet . . . I want to impress him.

Elisha looks out over the city. A breeze ruffles his hair. "It's beautiful."

"Better than the Valley Inn?"

"So much better." He looks at the water, unable to face me while he speaks. "Especially since you're here."

I take his hand and squeeze. I want him to know I'll *always* be here for him even when his own family isn't. It's my job to care for him—and I do. Care for him.

With a gentle tug, I lead Elisha deeper, until the water reaches his shoulders and my back hits the wall. I pull his naked body against mine. It's hot and smooth and I can feel his heart beating against my chest. I wonder if mine feels the same against his.

"Kiss me." I don't know where the words come from—not even sure I should be saying them—but there they are and I can't take them back.

"Kiss you?" Elisha hesitates. "I don't know how. I've never kissed you before."

It sounds silly, but it's true. Our mouths have met a million times, but it's always me who kisses him. "You never played piano before," I say, "never baked crème brûlée; du hast nie Deutsch gesprochen."

He laughs, nudging our noses together. With a look of determination, Elisha presses his lips against mine. The kiss is slow and unsure, like it's our first, like two teenagers experimenting behind the bleachers.

I feel his fingers tentatively glide over my cheek, brush the stubble of a day's neglect. When we part, we are both breathing hard. Then, Elisha smiles—loses his breath and catches it, again. He laughs a nervous laugh, a contagious one. Soon, we're both laughing. I splash him and tell him he can do the same and we're horsing around underwater, surfacing only so I can kiss him and he can kiss me back.

Across from me, Elisha lies splayed on the California king bed, still naked but dry after hours of fooling around like kids in the pool. He's better. Better off without his asshole father and neighbors who make him feel like shit simply for being who he is. I made him that way and I should reward him.

Without waking him, I slink out of bed and slip on boat shoes, shorts, and a button-down. I make my way downstairs to the concierge, who directs me to the closest bakery. It's a block away and smells like their ovens have been on for hours. I glance at my watch: 11:00 a.m. We never sleep this late, but clearly both needed it.

When I return to the hotel, the manager nods hello. "Late start, sir?" She smiles coyly, then corrects herself. "Alex?"

I cradle my cardboard coffee cup holder. A white handled bag rests in the crease of my fingers. "I figure we can afford to sleep in, every now and then."

"I'm glad to see you've found someone," she says. "I'm sorry, the tabloids, I shouldn't, but . . . the two of you seem genuinely happy."

I bite the inside of my cheek.

Found someone. The two of you. Genuinely happy.

I haven't found anyone. But that's none of her business, so I brush the comment off as quickly as possible. She can think whatever she wants. Her opinion doesn't matter.

The suite is still quiet when I enter. I set the coffee and pastries on the counter, sticking my nose in the bag for a preview. Dark chocolate coconut scones. Elisha loves baking with chocolate. I hope it will continue to distract him from his family.

I pause in the bedroom doorway. Elisha stretches his hands over his head. His back arches up off the sheets. He moans for no reason besides comfort, like a lazy cat, and settles back onto the bed. The bed we shared last night. Why wouldn't we? We share mine more and more often, at home.

The door hinges creak slightly when I push my way in. Elisha sits up, instantly, shielding his eyes from a beam of sunlight that managed to find its way past the curtains. Even the morning after, unwashed, hair tousled, smelling of chlorine and sex, he is perfect.

How dare his father say I ruined him. His talent and intelligence and beauty were always there, buried under the burden of debt. I dug him out. I brushed the dust away. I didn't ruin him.

I kick my shoes off and sit on the bed beside him. "How do you feel, this morning?"

"Good." He looks at my lips like he wants to kiss them.

Last night, though . . . last night was a special occasion. Last night, Elisha was hurting and it was my job to make him feel better. Now he knows he's safe and cared for, that my home is his real home and that I'm the only one who matters.

I touch my lips, remembering the pressure of Elisha's against mine. The hesitancy, the curve of his smile, the flutter of my heart in my chest.

He can't, anymore. Can he? Who will know? He wouldn't in public. Elisha knows his place.

"What are you thinking?" I ask.

"That I'd like to kiss you."

I'm correct, per usual. "Why don't you?"

"I'm not sure I'm allowed, this morning."

"Good inference," I say. "And how did you come to that?"

"You're always very clear with me. When you told me to kiss you, last night, it seemed limited to . . ." He shrugs. "Last night. I don't want to presume."

"Because?"

Elisha's eyes flick back and forth, for a moment. He's suspicious of my line of questioning.

"You're not in trouble," I say.

He leans back, relaxing. "I always do my best to be what you want. I don't presume because it's not my place to."

"No, it's not." I notice the edge in my own voice but can't stop it. I have no reason to be mad, so why am I clutching the sheets in my fists? "You'll do anything I say?"

"Yes?" Elisha's tone is uneasy, not unsure. "I always do."

"Because your obedience makes me happy."

"Yes." He bends his knees up to his chest, still naked. Even rumpled, he looks innocent. Even after this weekend, he behaves himself.

I shouldn't be angry—am I? Not half an hour ago I was over-whelmed with pride, and now I almost can't stand him. "What if I told you to fight me?"

"F-fight you?" He falters with his words. "I've never fought any-one before."

I stand. "Not a fistfight. I want you to resist me. Fight back."

"Why would I resist you?" Elisha asks, but he's doing it already, curling into a ball, tugging the covers up around him.

"Because I'm telling you to. It will make me happy."

"Alex—"

I grab his chin. "Do it. Now." I force my mouth against his, push my tongue past his lips. Kiss him through my sudden rage. It feels good.

It feels real.

Elisha pulls back, already panting.

"That's right." I lunge for him.

He scoots back on his elbows until he hits the headboard.

I reach for his head, again, but he ducks under my arm and rolls onto the other side of the bed. "Good boy," I say.

Elisha feels for the edge of the mattress, but not quick enough. I grab his calves and pull them out from under him. He flattens, unable to stop me from dragging him toward me.

When he kicks and pulls, it only heightens my arousal. Elisha pulls a sheet over his body and I release him. Slowly, I unfasten my belt and pants. He wraps himself up in a makeshift toga, unable to break eye contact.

With my free hand, I grab the sheet and pull. Elisha unwinds like a ball of yarn. Another swipe clears the mattress of pillows and blankets. It's just him and me.

Elisha twists from where he lies prone on the sheet. "Alex, please."

"Please, what? Isn't this what you want—what I want?"

"Yes, but—"

"But what?" I straddle his ass, using my weight to hold down his struggling form. "Don't argue. Do what I say."

A cry escapes Elisha when I wrench his arms behind his back. He fights in earnest. I loop my belt around his wrists, pull it tight, then fasten it. That doesn't stop him trying.

"That's it," I say beside his ear, licking the lobe before biting down.

I pull his hips up and slap his ass. Elisha cries out again, but it's part moan, and the sound of him stokes the fire brewing in my chest.

"I guess you really do get off on obeying me." I leave him with a few hard swats, then pick up the bottle of lube from the nightstand, where we left it, last night.

Elisha doesn't give up, taking advantage of my distraction. He sits up on his knees, but I push him down. The heel of my hand presses against his spine. My fingers dig into the soft flesh of his back.

I squirt the lube right onto my cock, not bothering with fingers. We just fucked. His ass hasn't locked up like some virginal nun.

I position myself between his legs and grip his thighs.

"Alex!" His arms twist into sharp, angular shapes against his back. The belt holds strong. "Alex." He's quieter, this time.

With a single thrust, I push all the way inside him.

This time, his response is more moan than cry. Still, he pulls at the belt. Every groan and strain sends splinters of pleasure under my skin. I plunge into him over and over, grinding into the feeling, sinking as deep as I can.

Elisha clenches around me while he fights. The tight heat ignites my orgasm. I anchor my nails in his hips and ride it out until the delight of afterglow sets in.

In my haze, I reach around and take Elisha's cock, still hard. He doesn't struggle while I finish him off. The mattress muffles the sounds of his orgasm. His come shoots up between his stomach and the bed. Hands bound, he rests in the mess when I release him.

I pull out and stand up. Elisha lies limp on the mattress.

I unfasten the belt and leave it loose. "Pack our things."

He fumbles out of the restraint and sits up, unable to look at me.

"Then, clean yourself up."

I close myself in the bathroom, fall beside the tub, and turn the hot on full blast. The glass basin fills in one minute. Soft neon lights illuminate the water. I drag my fingertips through the bath, stirring it.

I plunge one foot straight in, ignoring the burn that surges up my leg, then the next. I sink down, letting the water cover my hair and face. What am I doing? Pushing Elisha so he'll push me back? Testing him? I'm hurting him when all he's done is what I've asked.

I'm awful.

Bare feet pad over the tile as I wipe the water from my eyes. Elisha stops, looking between the tub and the shower. Thick lines circle his wrists, like bracelets.

He chooses the shower. Firing up a hard stream of water, he rinses away any evidence of sex. I watch through the glass partition as he finishes, shutting the shower down. But Elisha doesn't take a towel. He drips onto the mat, beside me.

"May I join you?" he asks.

I don't know why he'd want to. I can barely be this close to myself.

"Sure." I scoot back, making room between my legs.

Elisha kneels, facing me. He rests his hands on my thighs. "May I kiss you?"

"Why?"

"You look upset."

"For some reason, you don't." I slide my hands up his arms.

"Should I be?"

"You can't tell me you enjoyed that, whatever we just did."

"I did and I didn't. But you must have needed it, and I do lots of things I don't like, for you."

"Do you like kissing me?"

"Yes."

I press my lips against his before he can beat me to it. Elisha gives in. We part. My forehead rests against his, trapping beads of water between us. Then, before I can object, he kisses me with soft, gentle lips.

I pull back. "I didn't say you could do that."

"Not out loud," he says.

Elisha's right. But I shouldn't let him intuit my needs. I should stick to verbal and physical commands. I should establish clear boundaries with him. I *should*.

When we arrive home, I sit down at my desk. Elisha unpacks our bags. I watch him, through the thin crack of the door. This day may still be salvageable if I lock myself in my office and work from home.

A wave of my hand brings my desktop to life. I close old documents and swipe to bring up the ODR folder. My finger skips over a small white card, discarded on top of my work. I pick it up and turn the thick card stock between my fingers.

Didn't realize how much I missed you. If you ever want to reconnect, please don't hesitate to call. Yours, Javier.

My chest twinges with longing. I don't think for Javier, but perhaps. Perhaps for a relationship? I don't know. Mariah must've thought similar, since she invited Javier to join us at Preakness. She really does want me to find someone worthy of the Bishop name, whose company I'll enjoy, whom I'll be able to trust, and whom the Board will approve of.

Maybe I should call Javier. Just because it didn't break my heart to leave him doesn't mean he isn't worthy of partnership. And unlike some men on the Board's list, he works hard—in technology, at that. Isn't bad to look at, either. We're a good match. It certainly wouldn't hurt to be seen out with him every now and then, especially after the hotel manager mistook Elisha for a boyfriend.

Especially after the way he kissed me.

I need to revise my boundaries with him. Our relationship has matured. Now that Elisha is well trained, I no longer need to work so hard with him. We can both relax—well, he can, and I can get back to the lab more. Move Formula 3.0 closer to market.

"Call Javier," I say.

A soft ring fills the room. The connection clicks.

"Alex Bishop." I can hear his smile. "Wasn't sure you'd call."

I peek through the doorway as Elisha falls down on the bed, the literature tablet in his hands. He taps at the screen, scrolling to his bookmark.

"I wasn't either," I say.

"Well, I'm glad you did." Javier chuckles.

"Me too."

25

ELISHA

A tone interrupts the song I'm practicing for tomorrow's lesson, Mozart's "Alla Turca." I lift my hands from the keys.

"Answer call," Alex says from upstairs.

He's been bustling around the house all afternoon, despite my attempts to help tidy up. It's already clean, anyway. I decided it was best to stay out of his way.

I flinch when Tom's voice comes over the speakers. "Someone's here to see you, Dr. Bishop, a Mr. Madera. Would you like me to send him up?"

"Please do, Tom. Thank you." Alex stops atop the stairs and attaches a gold clip to a green tie that matches his eyes. He pulls on a dark gray blazer and smooths back his already-styled hair.

Both our attentions turn to the elevator when it dings. Alex hasn't told me he's expecting anyone. I can't decide who he'd want to clean and dress up for, but only in jeans. Nice jeans, of course. Alex doesn't own not-nice jeans. Even though he could make hand-me-downs look like they were designed just for him.

I smile at my own thoughts and stare at the piano keys.

"Hey there, stranger."

I look up at the familiar voice. It's Javier, the man from Preakness who was talking to Mariah and Alex after the race. His eyes wander up and down Alex's body.

"Hey," Alex says, a light smile on his lips. "I'm glad you came."

"Me too." Javier walks through the foyer, looking around at furniture and appliances like he's considering buying them. "Been a while since I've seen these walls." He touches one, lays his palm flat on the paint.

"Well, I hope it lives up to the memories. I'm sure you've encountered more luxurious homes, but I don't see the point," Alex says. "It's usually only me, here, anyway."

Only me?

I press down on the chord my fingers have been neglecting.

They both look at me.

"That's your Docile, right?" Javier asks. "The one who beat the on-meds, at Preakness."

I don't introduce myself.

"Yes, you'll have to forgive his manners. He's usually very well behaved." Alex glares at me.

I hang my head and rest my hands in my lap. He's right. I've embarrassed him in front of his guest. What came over me?

"Five hundred lines," Alex says. "'I will not be rude to guests.' After that, clean the upstairs. Finish before I return." He doesn't tell me how long he'll be out.

"Yes, Alex," I say, still unable to look at him.

"I've heard you have remarkable control over him, especially for an off-med." Javier straightens Alex's gold tie bar. The color matches his hair.

I wonder if Javier notices. I can still feel the strands between my fingers.

"I'd love to discuss my techniques, but—"

Javier smiles and offers his arm. "But this is pleasure, not business. I'm guilty, I know. Shall we?"

Alex summons the elevator, the doors part, and they disappear inside. I have no reason not to trust Javier. He seems like one of the kinder trillionaires. It's the way he touches Alex, like he has a right to.

I've seen others touch Alex—intimately, at that. I'm practiced at ignoring other Dociles while they ride his cock and suck him off.

I've always had the impression he doesn't like that. That he puts up with it about as much as I do.

But Javier is not a Docile, and they're each other's only company. And I have lines to write.

I retrieve the notebook from one of my drawers built into the side of Alex's bed, and sit at the writing desk. Five hundred lines. If I focus, I'll be finished in under two hours.

What could they be doing for two hours, this late on a weeknight?

I suppress the thought, quickly. It's not my business, and I don't have time to wonder if I also plan to clean the upstairs, before he returns.

The elevator dings. I look up from my folding. Alex is home. Finally. I fit the rest of his clothes in his drawers and gather the sponge and buckets from the confinement space. Although the freshly washed suits in Alex's closet disguise it, I don't dare let it go uncleaned.

Feet pound up the stairs. I stand, supplies in hand, as Javier crosses the threshold. What's he doing here at—I glance at the wall clock—midnight? But I don't ask. I just pledged five hundred times not to be rude to guests. I won't embarrass Alex twice in one night.

Javier eyes me. "Head down," he says. "Hands behind your back."

My breath catches in my throat. He's so casual with Alex, the confidence of his tone surprises me. My skin prickles; I can only obey. I drop my eyes to the floor in front of me and clasp my hands behind my back.

I can hear Javier rooting through Alex's now-immaculate closet. I only hope he isn't messing my work up so much that Alex thinks I didn't finish cleaning. Drawers slide open and shut. Javier walks around to the bedside and digs through another.

He moves behind me and pulls the chain out from my cuff. I hold still while he wraps it around my right wrist and secures it. The click makes my heart jump.

The only time Alex has restrained me in the past six months was the other night, at the hotel, and that was because he wanted to, not because he needed to.

Javier moves in front of me. "We won't have you interrupting us again. Open your mouth."

Is Alex angry with me? I wrote the lines he told me to. He doesn't usually get mad, afterwards. It's discipline; it's not personal.

As soon as I part my lips, Javier forces a hard rubber bit between them. He pulls it tight between my teeth, trapping my tongue. Another lock clicks behind my head.

What did I do wrong? I recount the past twenty-four hours, searching for any detail—any order I could have skimped on, any breach in my obedience. Wouldn't Alex have lumped my punishment in with the five hundred lines? What's so bad that he's sent Javier to administer discipline, instead?

Javier leads me over to the closet.

Alex can't even face me, himself. Probably because I interrupted him and Javier, earlier. How stupid of me. After all these months—after he's taken such good care of me, after he took me to that beautiful hotel—I can't even respect his personal life.

"In here. Go." Javier helps me into the confinement space.

Alex has never bound me in here, before. And he always gives me the emergency button. Does Javier know? Does it matter?

Heat rushes through my face, swelling at the corners of my eyes as I sink to my knees on the tile. Javier forces me down by the hair. My kneecaps dig into the floor. He pulls the top down, blotting out the remaining light. I barely fit in this position, and without my hands, my head bears the weight of my chest and shoulders.

Javier gives a final shove above me and I wince. A lock clicks, holding the lid and me in place. A string of drool slides down the corner of my gagged mouth.

"Alex!" Javier calls.

Feet run up the steps. They exchange muffled conversation and laugh at jokes I can't make out.

I close my eyes in the dark and try to shift positions. I can't. The dull pain in my face spreads throughout my head, slowly.

Why did I play that note? Why didn't I hold back? I only ever want Alex to be happy. He was happy with Javier. I interrupted his happiness, but I won't again. Not after this.

I deserve this.

ELISHA

Cries and moans interrupt the silence—the first sounds in at least an hour.

Wood creaks above me.

I'm only his Docile. I have no right to comfort or attention. This punishment will make me remember that; Alex knows I need it. He always knows what's best for me.

ELISHA

I can't resist the pressure on my bladder. Hot piss slides between my legs and runs a path to the little drain. After I *just* cleaned. I hope Alex doesn't notice the smell.

ELISHA

Heat sears my throat. My breath cracks my lips. I try to swallow, but my only saliva's dried to the side of my face. Shouldn't be much longer, now. Alex never leaves me in here for long. Then again, I'm usually better behaved.

ALEX

Lips kiss up my chest. I run my hands through sleek hair, then bring soft lips to mine. They're not Elisha's.

"Morning, sexy."

I open my eyes to Javier. Right, he spent the night. At least Tom will see him leaving. Unfortunately, he respects my privacy too much to tell the press. I sigh and stretch.

Javier changes directions. His tongue darts out, flicking over my cock.

"Mmm . . ." I relax back and let him suck me like one of Mariah's Dociles.

His head bobs up and down. He hums around my length, coaxing my morning arousal to its climax. I grip his hair and bend my knees, thrusting up to meet his pace.

It's not long before I come. Javier licks his lips and smiles up at me—not the light, happy smile I'm used to. It's mischievous and dirty, like he wants to ravish me. But I have no intention of letting that happen.

"How about some breakfast," he says. "I'm starving."

I sit up, but he lays a hand on my chest. "Don't get up. Doesn't your Docile cook?"

"Yeah, he does." I look down: no trundle bed. And he certainly didn't sleep in mine. "Elisha!" I call. He usually wakes up when I do, if not before. Come to think of it, I didn't see him last night when we got home, either. I grab my phone off the nightstand and open his microchip app.

I don't even realize how fast my heart's beating until his vitals show up normal. The GPS says he's here. I plant my feet on the floor, pull on my underwear, and head for the stairs. He must've slept on the couch. Maybe he's still asleep.

"Elisha!" I hold the railing, overlooking the first floor. No sign.

Javier rolls out of bed and joins me, wrapping his arms around my waist. He kisses the back of my shoulder and I jerk away. Something about the embrace makes my fingers flinch into fists. Just for a moment.

"I'll get him," Javier says, still holding me. "Why don't you get back in bed."

I stiffen. "How do you know where he is?"

Javier slides his hand up the back of my thigh. I grab his wrist before he can reach my ass.

"Easy, lover." He holds his hands up in surrender.

We are not lovers. This was our first date in almost a year, and just because we had sex doesn't mean I feel close to him. Sure, he's smart and attractive and wealthy, but he is quickly losing points for personality.

"Where's Elisha?" I release Javier's hand.

"If you get back in bed, I'll get him."

I am not bargaining with this man in my own home regarding my own Docile. "How about you get him now, and then"—once I know where he is—"I'll relax." I give Javier my best fake smile.

"Okay, okay." He walks back into my room, still naked, holding his hands up so I know I've won. "I just put him away for the night. It's no big deal."

I follow Javier. Put him away? Where's away? There is no *away*. This is not Mariah's house; I do not have Docile quarters.

Javier walks over to my closet and slides the door aside.

My bones are icicles.

He kneels down and fidgets with the lock. "How do you get this thing open? Is there a key, or . . ."

"Move." I push Javier out of the way.

This can't be right. Please let this be a joke.

ELISHA

A loud rapping sound wakes me. I shouldn't have let myself sleep. It hurts more when I'm awake.

Dim light floods the space. A lock clicks behind me.

"Elisha, it's me. It's Alex."

Alex. How can I face him, after what I did? He must be furious. I'm such a disappointment.

Pain shoots through my back as my arms fall to my sides. Pins prick my fingers back to life. The strap on my bit slackens, but the rubber sticks to my chapped lips. My skin rips, as it pulls from between my teeth. I shudder and groan.

"Into my arms, come on."

But my legs are cold and dead beneath me. Useless. Alex lifts me out of the cubby and carries me past Javier, to the bathroom.

My arms are too stiff to hold on to him, so I press my face into the warmth of his bare chest. I'll be anything Alex wants, even if that's invisible.

"I'm sorry," I whisper.

"No, stop that." Alex lowers me into the white ceramic tub, clothes and all. Warm water rushes down over my feet. "You don't have anything to be sorry for."

I have to be honest with Alex, tell him how childish it was for me to interrupt his date. "I—" But dry coughs scrape my throat.

"Shh, just relax."

The cold rim of a glass presses between my lips.

"Drink. You'll feel better."

I can't swallow fast enough. Water dribbles over my chin and cools the bathwater around me. I gasp and wipe my mouth. "I wrote my lines. I didn't get to show you, but I did."

"I told you to stop that." Alex leans over the tub and presses a warm hand to my cheek. "I'm the one who should apologize."

I don't know what to say. He never needs to apologize to me. It's I who can't live up to his expectations. It's not his fault; it's mine.

ALEX

Javier leans against the bathroom door. "Guess we're making our own breakfast."

I guide Elisha's hands to the glass. "Hold this. Finish the whole thing." As soon as I trust he won't drop it, I stand and face Javier. "*We* are not making anything. *You* are lucky I don't report you to the ODR for cruelty."

"For putting your Docile in his cage?"

"I don't keep him in a *cage*. He's not a wild animal."

"Then where does he sleep?"

I clench my jaw, glancing past Javier at my bed. The bed that has become our bed—mine and Elisha's—until last night. Changing the sheets won't erase that. I need a whole new fucking frame and mattress.

"Holy shit." Javier laughs. "You let him sleep in your bed, don't you?"

I don't have to justify myself to him. Just because the Board approved his GenEcs, a year ago, doesn't mean he's *someone,* and I'm still Alexander Bishop III. I can do whatever the fuck I want with my own Docile.

"What is that little cage even for?" he asks.

"It's not—" I lower my voice. "It's not a cage. It's a confinement space, and it's for discipline." It's no use. My whole body flushes with rage. "Did you even look at the dimensions before you crammed him in there?"

"I didn't cram him; he went on his own."

"Probably because he's trained to obey!" I lose control, shouting so loudly that Javier takes a few steps back. "How could he know you'd leave him in there overnight, when the most he's spent inside is an hour?"

"This is—I'd heard you were a little too into your Docile, but this . . ." Javier pulls his underwear and pants on.

"Do you have any experience with Dociles? You must not. Especially not an off-med. Elisha must think he's done something horrible to deserve eight hours in confinement. Fuck!"

"I don't have to work with Dociles to know they're not my equals."

"No, Elisha's better than you."

Javier rolls his eyes and slips his shoes on. "To think I was flattered when you called me again. *The* Dr. Alexander Bishop the Third giving me a second chance after he'd rejected so many others. I thought I might be the one to break through to you. But now . . ." He huffs a laugh. "Now, I know why you're still single. You treat your Docile like your goddamn boyfriend." Javier brushes past me, snatching up his tie and jacket.

"I treat him however I want. He's mine to do with as I please."

"That logic may work on the general public, but don't insult my intelligence; we're both men of science. It's obvious what's going on, here."

"That's enough." I do not need Javier to analyze my life. I'm perfectly capable.

Javier runs his hands down his jacket, perking his pocket square. "You tried to train an off-med. And you gave it a good go; you did."

"I said that's enough."

"But you failed. He's trained you."

"Enough!" I slam my fist against the wall monitor. Shards of glass grind into my skin, where I hold the web of cracks together.

Javier laughs.

I drop my hand to my side. Pieces clatter to the floor. A big triangle of glass swings free and crashes.

"If you're half as smart as I think you are, you'll send him off to your lab to live out the rest of his term. Forget about him before he—before *you* ruin your life."

I close my eyes.

Javier's feet pound down the steps. The elevator dings, opens, and closes.

And I still can't open my eyes. I want every cell that Javier's left behind gone from this place. I hear his words as clear as if he's here, still, feel them filling the room and pressing against my skin. Feel the weight of truth.

ELISHA

Alex erupts into the bathroom and turns the faucet to full blast, washing red from his hand. He's bleeding. Not so much that I need to rush for help. If he wants my help, he'll ask. I am right where Alex wants me.

"Elisha."

I turn my attention to where he kneels beside me. He has all of my attention for the rest of my life. "Yes?"

"Were you listening to that?"

The greatest thing I can give him is the truth. "It sounded like you were fighting, but I didn't pay attention to your words—they're not my business. I only heard something break."

"Okay." Alex warms his hands, then holds them out to help me. "Let's get you out of there."

When I stand, water rushes from where it soaked into my clothes. Alex peels them off with nimble fingers, one layer at a time, until I'm naked, then wraps a thick cotton towel around me. The pressure of his arms and the warmth of the towel comfort me. He dries my hair, examining it. His thumb grazes my brow.

When I catch his eyes, they're soft. Maybe a little sad. I don't like when Alex is sad.

Then, he whispers, "I can't."

ALEX

When I was growing up, my parents taught me what was acceptable to say and do, and where, and with whom. I learned from my teachers and classmates, my friends and coworkers. I was trained to go from a Board meeting to Preakness to Mariah's annual theme party in one day and not miss a beat. For thirty fucking years, I've banked acceptable behavior in my memory to pull from as required.

So, I know it's not my fault that I haven't realized it until now—the words I can never think, much less say aloud.

They're unacceptable. Elisha and the truth cannot coexist in my life as I know it. And what's more—*fuck*.

What's more, I've turned Elisha from a person who could return those words—those feelings—into a Docile who is incapable of doing so. The truth is moot. The words don't even matter.

"I can't do this." My fingers tremble as they smooth his hair. "I'm taking you back to your family."

Calmly, Elisha says, "I don't get another visit for six months."

"You're not visiting." I fear if I utter another sound, I'll be sick. I swallow, forcing down the rising lump in my throat. "You're going home to stay. To live."

I can't look at him. I press the towel into his hands and cross to my closet. Throwing the doors open, I scour for something to wear besides last night's underwear.

Behind me, Elisha doesn't move.

ELISHA

I take the knotted towel when he presses it into my grip. Somehow, I hold it. The air is too thick to pull into my lungs. Light-headedness settles and spreads until my skin tingles.

Alex rummages through his closet. Picks out clothes. He's getting dressed so he can take me back to my family. What about my contract? My debt?

Doesn't he want me, anymore?

"I don't understand," I say.

But Alex doesn't answer. He continues putting on his boots like I'm not even here. I won't be, soon.

I won't be here.

No.

"Alex, please."

All he says is, "Get dressed."

"What should I wear?"

"I don't care."

Every day, Alex picks my clothes for me. If he doesn't have time, he gives guidelines. Something tight, long sleeved, yellow, warm.

I unravel the towel and fold it into a square. My stomach feels like I've drunk sour milk. If I move, I'll throw up. If I speak—I open my mouth, but immediately close it. Alex doesn't want me. Am I that much of a disappointment?

"Please tell me what I've done wrong," I say. "Please, and I'll fix it. I will."

Alex removes a small leather suitcase from his closet and starts packing my clothes inside. He tosses a pair of underwear at me.

"Put those on."

I slide the fabric slowly over my legs, drawing out every chance I have to please him.

"And these." Alex fires jeans and a tee shirt at me.

I barely catch them.

"Hurry up." He robs me of my time. "Get your things; we're going. Dial front desk." He addresses me and the phone in the same breath. "I need a car. Five minutes." He pauses. "End call."

I can't. I can't do this. My limbs stiffen and cramp. Pain slices through my chest. I can't breathe. I'm going to pass out.

I speak the one word that is supposed to stop the pain. "Midnight!"

ALEX

It takes me a moment to realize he's not referring to the time. He's using his safeword. He's never used it before. Doubt he would even if he should—not that I would ever hurt him. Probably just doesn't understand. "I'm not touching you; why are you using your safeword?"

Elisha clutches his jeans between his fists. His lashes flutter, weighed down with tears. "For some reason, you can't see how much pain I'm in. I can't bear it."

This can't be happening. A throbbing settles between my eyes. I try to pinch off the pressure before it builds, before I burst.

Elisha doesn't feel anything for me. He can't. I ruined him. And now I've hurt him. "Fuck!" I can't wipe the tears away as fast as they're coming. "This is why you have to leave! Because I—" What's the point in denying it? I'm fucking done for. "I love you. I love you, Elisha. And you can't love me back."

"Why not?" he asks, softly.

"Because." Is he even capable of understanding the explanation? "Because you're not you, anymore. You're not Elisha Whatever-Your-Surname-Was. You're just Elisha, my Docile. A drone." He understands that word; it hits him like a fist. "And that's my fault."

ELISHA

I gasp for air. It escapes faster than I can breathe it in. He's wrong. Why is he lying to me? He told me I wasn't a drone.

"This is my fault," Alex says, again.

I shake my head. "You said people change. I'm just a new version of myself." My voice wobbles as sobs take me.

"If I'd told you the truth, it would've wrecked you. None of this has been an accident. I planned all this." He gestures at me. "From the length of your hair, to your morning alarm, the words you're allowed to speak." Alex raises his voice. "Do you really believe you have any free will left? Prove me wrong. Show me there's a sliver of a human being left in there. That I haven't fallen for my own creation."

I don't move, worried that the wrong word or gesture will prove his point. How do I know what's right? Alex knows everything about me. Everything except—

ALEX

"Wilder," Elisha says, toying with his cuff. "My name is Elisha Wilder."

I ready my breath to tell him off, again, but can't. That was—that was not what I was expecting. Maybe there's a person under there, after all.

I clear my throat and hold out my hand.

Elisha eyes it, then grips it firmly.

"Alex Bishop," I say, shaking his hand. "Nice to meet you."

"Please don't make me leave," he whispers.

And the illusion is gone.

I drop his hand. I want him to shake off this persona he's created for me. I want him to lunge at me, scream at me for taking him from his family. For humiliating him, for hurting him, for scraping away his identity and leaving this obedient slate of a person in his place.

"I have to," I say. "Every minute you're with me, you lose yourself a little more. I won't have it. Hopefully, if I take you home, you'll figure out who you really are, again."

"This is my home."

Elisha parrots one phrase after another, like an on-med. Like a windup doll. Only his are loaded with sympathy and emotion. Maybe a dose of reality will set him straight. I'll force him home, if that's what it takes.

"No," I say. "This is *my* home. You live here because I let you."

His eyes become red and glossy.

"Please don't do this, Alex. Please." Elisha grabs for me, dislodging the suitcase. "Please. I can't live without you."

I shake him off. "You'll learn." He'll have to.

"My dad doesn't want me. Everyone out there hates me." He cries, unabashed.

"I'm sure Dylan's mother will take you in—What's her name?"

"Nora Falstaff."

"I'm not supposed to—" know her surname. But what does it matter, now?

I hate this. He can't know how much I want to hold him and kiss his face until the tears stop coming. Normally, I would. In a better world, I'd strip him bare and caress every inch of Elisha until he forgot all his troubles. Until all he could think of was me and how good I make him feel.

But we can't love each other. I can't be his only source of happiness. Can't be with someone like that. Never mind what my peers and the press would think—what my family would think, the Board. Everyone.

Never mind that I haven't just crossed the yellow line, I've fucked it good and rough.

Even if I managed to escape all that, it still wouldn't be right. I am Dr. Frankenstein and I've fallen in love with my own monster—my perfectly behaved, beautiful monster.

This is for his own good as much as it is for mine.

38

ELISHA

"Alex, don't do this. Don't. Please don't," I beg, curling my hands against my chest, dying to touch him but not allowed.

"Stop it!" Alex shouts, inches from my face.

I flinch, squeeze my eyes shut. His voice rings in my ears.

"Stop that this instant," he says. "I have never seen such outrageous behavior from a Docile."

I pull back, clutching my shirt to keep from reaching for him.

"Pick up the suitcase and follow me. And I don't want to hear another sound."

Does he want me to disobey, to show him I'm me? I'm not something he made. I'm Elisha Wilder and I'm staying here because I want to. Not because I have to.

Or maybe Alex will change his mind if I listen. He's never liked my disobedience before. Maybe he'll remember why he loves me if I'm good. He always says I'm perfect, regardless of others' opinions.

"Got it?" Alex says.

I nod, silent as instructed.

During the drive, I remain silent, as promised. Alex sits on the other side of the car, staring out the window. I tap my feet against the floor and pull at the diamond chain on my cuff.

"Which exit?" is all he says to me.

"Thirty-One."

Every exit we pass, I wait for him to tell the driver to stop and pull off, turn us around. Wait for Alex to pull me into his arms, and take me home. He has to. He knows I have no place where we're going. Alex said, himself, they don't understand who I've become.

"Here," Alex says, and the driver takes the exit. My exit.

I clasp my hands to keep them still. Every part of me that can jitter does: fingers, legs, teeth, heart. If I stare at the floor, maybe, when I next look outside, we'll be home. I'll have imagined this whole nightmare. Maybe Alex will realize he's made a huge mistake. That he needs me as much as I need him.

"This is it," he says. "Pull over."

The car slows to a stop. Nausea rolls through me, unsettling my stomach. My throat feels thick and clogged. I have to get out of here.

I pull the car door open, stumble a few feet, and retch bile from my empty gut. My stomach muscles burn as they clench over and over.

I want to go home. I want to lie in bed with Alex. Feel his arms around my waist, lips on my neck. This is all my fault. I should never have interrupted his date with Javier. I'd write ten thousand lines, spend hours on the rice, all day in confinement, if it meant I got to stay with Alex.

I don't want freedom if it means being alone.

39

ALEX

It hurts not to comfort Elisha. After a minute, he stands and spits, face paler than usual. Against my better judgment, I rub his back and offer him a bottle of water from the car. He rinses out his mouth, then takes a few, slow sips before giving it back.

"I'll be back in a few minutes." I return the bottle to the driver through the window. "Keep it running."

"Yes, sir."

"Let's go." I hold out my hand to Elisha.

You'd think we were magnetic the way he latches on to me. Normally, I'd lie to myself and justify the touch. God, I am so good at that—lying to myself, rationalizing the last six months with Elisha.

I feel the excuses arming themselves, in my brain. That I'm only holding his hand so he won't escape—I know he won't. He got in the car, remained silent, followed me this far. Or that I need to comfort him, as if that's even possible at this point. My touch won't ease his pain once I let go.

My motive is simple and selfish. I want to feel our bodies flush against each other, because I love him. All I can offer, now, is palm to palm. It's not enough.

"Which house is yours?" The words taste bad in my mouth. My house is his house. His home. But I told him that's not true. I took that away from him.

"Over there." He looks to a small house built on the foundation of another—long since torn down—with salvaged bricks and stone. Cement fills the gaps and lines a small window.

No one loiters by the house. In fact, the dusty road is practically empty. It's not even lunchtime; everyone's probably working. As we approach, he clutches me tighter. I can't risk running into his family.

I run my fingers over the rose-gold cuff around Elisha's wrist with its unbreakable diamond chain. Eye a water pump between his house and his neighbor's. Finger the lock and key in my pocket. Yes, that'll do.

40

ELISHA

I hold down my words along with the water in my stomach. Alex notices everything; he has to see how good I'm being, how all I want to do is hold and kiss him, beg him to keep me forever.

But I'm not. I'll keep silent as long as he wants me to.

When he grasps my hand, I squeeze his, reassured by his touch. Alex wants to touch me. He wants me. *Keep me. Please keep me.*

We walk toward my house. No one's home. I don't have a key, any longer. Good. More time with Alex, while we wait. He can still change his mind.

I stop beside Alex. He pulls his phone from his pocket and fiddles with the screen before writing something with his stylus.

"Sign on this line. Date beside it." He hands it to me. His name's already scrawled across the document.

I can't read straight. The words curl together and blur on the screen. I make out *term completed . . . debts settled . . . stipend to continue.* I can't sign this.

"Not a word," Alex says. "You're still mine until this document is executed. Don't disappoint me now."

I won't. I'll be good for Alex. I always am. He'll see. He'll keep me.

I slide the stylus over the slippery surface. I haven't signed my full name in six months. The letters jumble together. What's the date? I copy Alex's.

I can still cross it out. I can take it back. I can—

Alex pulls the phone and stylus from my hands. He taps one

of his rings to the screen, says, "Turn around." I grab the water spigot, so I won't fall over. Feel the warm metal around his fingers as they press between my shoulder blades. Hear him say, "Confirm microchip deactivation."

Now. He's going to take me back, now. I obeyed him right up to my signature—to the dead microchip beneath my skin. I was good.

ALEX

"Come here." I open my arms to Elisha and he holds on to me as if he'll fall off the face of the Earth, otherwise. "I want you to stay here, with your family. Find yourself, again. Figure out who you were before me. Okay?"

Elisha's full weight suddenly hangs on me. I lower us slowly to the ground, glancing around. We shouldn't attract too much attention. In the distance, a dog barks at squealing children. A woman bikes past, her eyes on the path.

"Hey, everything's going to be all right." I smooth Elisha's hair back from his face and wipe the tears from his cheeks. My kisses comfort him like they always do. It's a horrible trick, but I have to play it.

Elisha holds me and kisses me. I want this. I wish it were real, that this was Elisha Wilder kissing me, touching me, loving me. It's not.

Quickly, I pull the chain from his cuff and wrap it around the water pipe. With a click, he's locked in place.

Elisha's eyes widen in horror.

"Be good for me." I extricate myself from his arms, trying not to look at him as I place the key in his mailbox. Someone will happen by soon and free him. But I can't chance him following me to the car. I need a head start.

"Alex." His voice rides an incoming sob.

"Be good." I can only whisper. Any louder, and I'll cry, too. I cannot cry in front of him, now.

42

ELISHA

I grab my left arm and pull as hard as I can, until the cuff digs into my flesh. "Alex, please!" I fold my fingers in and try to slide the cuff off, but it's too tight.

The pipe. I can break the pipe. I kick it, but it doesn't budge.

"Alex, come back! I need you!" I sink to my knees for better leverage, but it's no use. My throat burns as I scream his name over and over. "Please." I sob and pull at my hair.

"Please, I was quiet. I didn't talk. I didn't talk for you. Please, I can be good. I can . . . Tell me what I've done, I'll never do it again. I won't. Please, I need you."

ALEX

I pull the car door open and glance back at Elisha. Dirt sticks to the sweat on his arms. He blinks away tears and dust. He sniffs and clears his throat.

"Please, give me a chance. I just want to make you happy!" he shouts. "I can love you back. I can."

No. He can't.

ELISHA

He left me.

"Elisha! Are you hurt? What happened?"

He's gone. He left me. Alex is gone.

"Elisha, where's the key?"

I finally close my eyes. "It hurts." Dust and gunk clog the corners of my eyes. My forehead throbs.

"What hurts? Elisha, please answer me. Are you okay?"

Be good. How can I be good for him if he's not here? I need to lie down. Maybe if I wake up, he'll be beside me.

"I found it, in the mailbox. One second, I'll have you out of there."

Soon, I'll wake up and this will all have been a bad dream. He'd never leave me. He knows I need him.

Cold water floods my nostrils. I choke and cough until the burning at the back of my throat fades. My hands and knees shake as I struggle to hold myself up.

"Thank goodness. I thought you were a goner."

"Am I home?" I ask.

Blurry brown arms wrap around me. "You're on the farm, Elisha."

"No . . ." He's still gone. I'm still here. I don't want to be here, anymore. "Please don't make me. I can't. Not without him."

"Who?"

"Alex. I need Alex."

"He's not here. It's me, Nora. Do you remember me, Elisha?"

I am beyond pain. The aftershocks linger in my chest. How did this happen?

"Come on, let's get you inside and washed up."

She hauls me to my feet. "Hold on to me. There you go."

The road behind us winds into a dark fold of trees. A small shape speeds out of it, toward us—a car? Alex? A bicycle. I grab on to the water pump as my last hope withers.

"Midnight," I say. "Please, midnight."

"It's the middle of the day, Elisha."

I shake my head. "No, please, it hurts. Make it stop."

"Oh, hon." She pries me upright, again. "I'm afraid I can't fix that."

"Elisha, I brought lunch. Potato soup. Paulo even snuck me a bit of cheese. Everyone's asking about you."

A cracked ceramic bowl clanks onto the little table beside me. Nora leans down until her eyes are level with mine.

"You have to eat, sweetheart." Her pudgy palm flattens against my forehead. "It's been three days." She sits on the couch beside me and smooths her hand through my hair.

"Am I still here?"

"Yes."

"I don't want to be."

"The fresh air will do you good."

I stare at my running shoes, bright aqua against the unfinished wood floor. Nora and my mother sit opposite me, legs folded, hands clasped.

"Those are pretty, Elisha." Mom smiles.

I say, "Thank you," but don't move.

"Why don't you put them on," Nora says. "See how they feel."

Put them on. An easy command. I slip the right one over my sock and tighten the laces. The light material hugs my foot. "Thank you, that does feel nice." The other feels even better. Almost like I can jog downstairs, grab a protein drink, and run around the harbor.

I pinch my lips together. This can never be home. Not because we don't have a second floor, or a fancy refrigerator, or because the harbor is any nicer than the reservoir. But because Alex won't be here when I return.

"Go!" Nora slaps my back. "And don't come back till you've run around the entire reservoir."

"Yes, ma'am." I stand and adjust my workout clothes. The tight spandex comforts me, like someone holding me.

The sun will be setting soon—hopefully not too soon. I used to be able to predict the sunset, but city lights changed that. Out here, I wouldn't be able to see my path if it weren't for the neon light my shoes give off. My feet are the loudest things on the road.

I run.

I run even though I don't know where I am or how far I've gone. I run until I lose my rhythm and can no longer count my breaths against my footfalls. I run until I can feel each swollen toe throb against my shoes. I have to stop, but I can't. Need to build my stamina. How far is the city?

When I walked to the ODR, the first time, it took me ten hours. Twenty minutes per mile, about thirty-five miles. I can run a five-minute mile, but not for that long. If I pace myself, maybe nine minutes times thirty-five miles. That's five and a quarter hours. Only five and a quarter hours separates me from Alex.

I slow to a stop beside the faded red barn. It's too dark to run anymore, tonight. Maybe tomorrow. If I reach the apartment, Tom might let me in. But would Alex even take me?

"Excuse me."

I jerk upright and search for the voice in the dark.

"Sorry." A woman in a cheap pants suit emerges from the barn with a tablet under her arm and a stylus stuck through her ponytail. "Didn't mean to scare you. I was just finishing up work—it's too dark even with a lantern." She holds up one of the LED lanterns Empower Maryland gives out to communities who can't afford utilities.

When I still don't respond, she walks closer, shines the light on her rosy cheeks and frazzled hair. "You're Elisha, right?"

"Yeah."

She nods, knowingly. Does everyone know? I don't want to deal with their questions and prying.

"Are you okay?" she asks.

"I'm fine," I say so she'll leave me alone.

"Okay." She pulls a small card out of her back pocket and hands it to me. "If you want any help, we're here Tuesdays and Thursdays for legal and financial planning. On the weekends, tutors stop by the school."

"School?" I glance at the card: *Verónica Vasquez, Empower Maryland.* "Oh."

"Yeah, Eugenia—sorry, you probably don't know her, one of our Directors in the city—allocated some funding for us to repair an old Parks building out here and turn it into a schoolhouse. It's not accredited or anything, yet. But it's been good for the community."

Eugenia kept her promise. Even though I was useless to her. She seemed angry, at the time.

"Thanks. I mean . . ." Verónica will expect me to sound grateful, but I have nothing to offer except exhaustion. "I'm glad," I say so that Verónica will leave. She does with a wave.

The last time I pocketed one of these cards, it earned me seventy minutes in confinement. Now there is no consequence. Even that feels wrong—the wait for something to happen, some human response, *any* response.

I go into the barn and shut its wide door behind me. There are no animals in here; this one's reserved for storage and occasional work or gatherings. Along the wall rest bags of seeds and beans and other dried goods stamped with the Empower Maryland logo.

I rip open a bag of rice, push it over, and spill its contents across the cement floor. I fall to my knees and let the grains push deep into my skin. No clock times me, here. I close my eyes while the pain infects every bone and nerve in my body. Until I remember what it's like to feel.

Nora hands me a plate when I walk through the door. "You can't skip meals if you want to keep running like that."

I stare at the fluffy, yellow pile of eggs. My stomach gurgles.

"I thought you always did what you were told." Nora winks and guides me to a place at the table, then goes back to scrubbing pots. "You're letting me down, kid."

Letting her down. First Dad, then Alex, now Nora. Dylan's still at the Silo. I'm running out of people I care about—who care about me.

I eat as quickly as possible. The eggs stick to my mouth when I swallow them. "May I be excused?" I show her the empty plate.

She sighs and waves me away. "Go on!"

"Thank you." I wash my plate, then head back outside. I haven't been okayed to work, yet, and almost everyone else does, so there's little to do. Not that I feel like doing much, anyway, without Alex.

I pull a clean towel off the line and head for the reservoir. A hundred years ago, the EPA told us we weren't allowed to swim in it. We're probably still not, but it's faster and easier rinsing off than trying to bathe regularly.

I pry off my sweat-soaked clothes, fold them, and set them on a rock. Warm water swallows my legs as I wade in. The cops can arrest me, if they really care. No one ever notices we exist until we owe them money.

I hold my breath and duck, sealing myself underwater. Down here, I can't see or hear or smell. But I still ache. When will it go away? When will I learn to live without Alex, like he said I would? I could sink to the bottom and stay there forever. My lungs burn as I surface, gasping for air. Voices drift over the water from the shore.

"Are these clothes?"

"They feel weird."

"Fucking tight-and-brights."

A man snickers. "Probably so some trillionaire can cop an easy feel."

They see me before I can swim away, a group of four guys with sweat-stained sleeves rolled up over dirt-stained arms. I know them like I know everyone in our community; we've worked together our whole lives. But standing on the shore, they might as well be standing on the surface of another planet. I rub a hand over my smooth, soft skin, under the water. They're hairy or stubbled, their skin rough, bodies thick and muscled.

"These yours?" asks one.

It takes me a minute to remember back past Alex—has it only been six months? Micah, that's his name. He helps build and fix houses. Helped me and Dad add the second room on to Nora's house once Mom started spending more time there.

"Yes," I say, still treading water.

Another of the guys holds up the spandex pants and stretches the leg as far as it'll go. He laughs. "What are you, some kind of trillionaire?"

Another, "No, man, I heard he's some trillionaire's pet."

Another, "Think you're better than the rest of us, huh?" He slingshots my clothes into the water, and stomps them to the bottom. He spits where they sunk, then leaves.

Micah stops and turns back, letting the other three wander off without him. They don't seem to notice. I stop moving and let gravity pull me deep. Maybe when I come back up he'll be gone.

The water churns and bubbles around me. Arms hook beneath mine and haul me upward. I open my eyes and sputter at the surface. Beside me, Micah wipes the hair from his face and the water from his eyes.

"It's okay." He offers his hand. "I'm not going to hurt you. Come on. Let's go inside. You shouldn't be swimming; you . . ."

Could drown. *Might drown yourself.* That's what he's thinking. "I can swim."

"I know you can."

I take Micah's hand and hold tight while we kick back to shore. Already I feel dread creeping back into my body. He's right. I can swim, but I can't be trusted to come back up.

I fish for my wet clothes, but Micah takes them and wrings them out. His own hang soaked on his body, only his shoes kicked aside on the shore.

"Here." He hands mine back before putting his boots back on.

"Thanks." The damp material fights my efforts, hanging heavy on my skin.

"I'll walk you home."

I shake my head so fast, I confuse Micah.

"I can't. I'm staying with Nora and she's helping care for my mom and I can't tell her what happened."

"Okay. You can come back to my place." He puts his arm around me, taking us the long way so that no one will see.

Micah lives alone in a one-room house that's part of a row, built like that to keep the heat in, during winter. When we enter, he sits me on a stool and turns on a small fan to clear the humidity.

Micah hands me a pair of drawstring shorts and a tee shirt. I stand and strip the wet clothes from my body, dry off with the rough towel. I'm slipping my legs into the holes when Micah turns. Hundreds of people have seen me naked or worse. Nakedness doesn't mean what it used to and Micah's eyes don't linger on me. He walks over dressed in sweat shorts and a tee shirt, from which the hair on his chest pokes out.

"Here." He hands me a tall glass filled with dark liquid and a shrinking chunk of ice.

"Careful," he says. "It has a bite."

Alcohol burns my tongue; fresh mint soothes it. The face I make before taking another sip makes Micah laugh. This time, I'm prepared and welcome the hit of rum. "Thank you."

When the glass is half-empty, I rest it on the small table beside me. Micah sits on his bed: a mattress stacked on two plastic pallets.

"Do you want to talk about it?" he asks.

I shake my head. "Not really."

"Makes sense." He sets his mug aside, empty. "I was a Docile, too. Didn't refuse Dociline, so I don't know exactly what you're going through, but . . ." Micah punctuates his sentence with a shrug.

I gulp down the rest of my tea before the ice can melt and take the glass to the sink.

"You don't have to wash that," Micah says. "Unless you want to."

In the basin, where he can't see, I set the glass down and curl my hands into fists, fighting the urge to wash up after myself.

Unless you want to.

What do I want?

. . . want to.

I don't want anything.

. . . you want to.

Nothing except Alex. To be with him. Make him happy.

"Elisha?" Micah's voice is closer.

My hands won't stop shaking. They won't stop. *Stop.*

I pick up the glass. It bangs against the metal basin until I press it against the bottom, hold it still, hold myself still.

"Elisha, it's okay. You don't have to wash it," says Micah. He's behind me.

"I don't have to," I whisper.

Micah reaches around and takes the glass from my hand. He sets it dirty on the counter. Alex would never leave a dirty dish out.

But Alex isn't here.

Alex left me.

The crushing sensation begins in my chest and spreads through my stomach, grips my shoulders, weakens my knees. The room loses its color; the fan whirs louder; the air hums around me.

He left me.

I can't do this.

I can't.

45

ALEX

Elisha's dirty bathwater still sits in the tub. The closet cubby reeks of his piss. The bed—I can't even look at. I want to burn it to ash, then scatter it across the city.

I can't be here. Not where everything reminds me of Elisha or how Javier hurt him. How I broke him.

"Call Jess." I close my eyes as a soft ring fills the house.

"Hey, Alex, what's up?"

"I, uh, I need . . ." I need Elisha. He's not here, anymore. That's over. He's better off, now. I need to move on. "Can I crash at your place for a few nights?"

"Yeah, sure. You bringing Elisha?"

"No."

"You sure he'll remember to feed himself, if you're not there?" She laughs.

Numbness envelops me.

"Alex?" Jess clears her throat. "Are you okay?"

"No."

"I'm coming over."

"Don't. I'll be there soon. End call."

And I'm alone, again. The house is silent without Elisha. No shuffling of bare feet on hardwood, tinkling of the piano, scribble of a pen over paper. Not even the idle tapping of his foot or the scrape of his teeth while he bites a stylus, studying.

I walk through my bedroom, slowly. Touch the soft cotton

bedspread, sleek polished table. Elisha's notebook still rests open to five hundred iterations of *I will not be rude to guests.* I flip back through the pages. Through dozens of punishments and addendums to the rules he copied down to memorize. Notes about how I like my coffee and favorite wines. Habits I dislike. I stop on a page where he wrote: *Alex's opinion is the ONLY one that matters.* Two underlines emphasize the point.

As I continue toward the front, a wallet-sized photograph slips out. In it, a young boy stands between his mother and father. A baby stares with curiosity toward the camera. Fourth Right: Dociles are allowed one personal item. Doesn't matter for most—they don't remember the items once they inject.

I tuck the photograph back inside and close the notebook. Walk downstairs, through the living room, and past the piano. Stop beside the kitchen. I reach into the cabinet above the refrigerator and retrieve the bag of uncooked rice and metal tray Elisha uses for punishments. It clangs against the marble floor. The grains scatter across its surface like raindrops as I pour them out—not too many. Enough so that when I take off my pants and drop to my knees, I feel each one where it burrows into my skin.

I close my eyes while the pain latches on to my nerves and climbs up my thighs. Pain I inflicted on Elisha for asking a question or touching his own hair without permission. No cuff or timer holds me accountable. No amount of time will ever atone for what I've done to him, but I remain until tears break free of my lashes and stream down my cheeks. Until the ache in my body mirrors the ache in my heart.

I ride the elevator down with only my phone and wallet. With dried eyes and dimpled knees. The notebook tucked under my arm.

Tom looks up from his desk. "Can I help you with anything, Dr. Bishop?"

"Yes, actually. You may want to write this down."

"Yes, sir." His stylus hovers over the front desk, ready.

"I need Maintenance to deep clean the upstairs bathroom—everything, with bleach where it's safe. I'd like the bed linens—pillows, pillowcases, sheets, and comforter—thrown into the incinerator."

"Yes, sir." He writes almost as fast as I speak.

"The mattress, I realize, is used, so I won't be offended if you decline, but you're welcome to it. There's easily a decade left on it. Better be; I paid a hundred thousand dollars for it."

Tom looks up, mouth slightly agape.

"The frame is like new. You're welcome to that as well. Hire movers to take them—to the dump, if you don't want them. Either way, send me the invoice."

"Dr. Bishop, that's awfully generous, but I can't—"

"The nightstand, as well. Once the furniture is out, I'd like that space deep cleaned, including the closet. There is a small cubby space in the floor that requires particular attention."

"Yes, sir. Anything else?"

I picture the still, tepid water in the tub. Shards of the wall monitor I broke scattered on my bedroom floor. Metal tray with its scattered rice, grains littering the floor where I picked them out, unable to make it to the tub. I do not want anything here.

"You know what, get rid of any furniture that isn't attached. Everything: lamps, rugs, tables, curtains. Keep whatever you'd like. Sell it. I don't care. I don't want it."

"Dr. Bishop." Tom sets down his stylus.

"And this." I slap Elisha's notebook down on the desk. "Destroy this first. Incinerate it."

Tom rests his hand on the leather cover, then looks at me with concern in his eyes. "It's none of my business, so I hope you don't mind me asking, but are you okay?"

"We'll see," I say. "Give me a few days."

"Whoa, look at you." Jess holds the door open.

I don't linger on the threshold, instead making my way into her modest kitchen. The door clicks shut behind me. Jess jogs to keep up while I sit on a lime-green chair.

"So." She stands beside me. "Did you want to talk over a cup of tea, or . . ." She squints. "Whiskey?"

I set my sunglasses on the sturdy, wooden table and massage my irritated eyes.

"Or we could just sit here and pretend you haven't been crying."

"Tea sounds good. I can make my own." I rise, but Jess pushes me back down.

"You know you're wearing a hoodie, right?"

I glance down at the clothes I bought on the way over: light denim jeans, salmon tee shirt, baby-blue sweatshirt. The hood swallows my head like a cave. I could pull the drawstring tight and disappear inside.

"I needed something new."

"Well, you got it." She wanders over to the stove, puts the kettle on, and readies two bags of green and purple tea.

"So, what's the occasion?" She takes the flamingo-pink chair, beside me. None of the furniture matches, here, and yet the house is a whole.

"I took Elisha home."

"Didn't he just visit?"

"For good. Contract fulfilled. Debts paid."

She doesn't respond. My phone vibrates against the table. Mariah. I shut it off and flip the display over.

Jess clutches the tiny silver sugar spoon in two hands. "Why?"

"Why do you think?"

The kettle whistles. Jess hurries out of her seat to tend to the tea. She returns a minute later, setting a yellow teacup in front of me. My fingers are too big for the dainty handle, so I take the whole cup in my hand. The hot water tests my nerves through the thin porcelain.

I stare at the bottom of my cup through the swirl of steeping tea. "Please say something."

"No," she says, drawing my attention. "I want you to say it."

I inhale the lavender and spearmint steam rising from my mug, hoping it will clear my head, or at least calm me. I should take something, but then I'd feel better, and that's almost like forgetting. I have to say it. Sooner or later, I will have to say it.

"I love Elisha." I let the words hang in the air. "Or I'm in love with him—well . . ."

"Well?" When I can't answer, Jess reaches across the table and rubs her hand over the arm of my new sweatshirt. Anyone else would chastise me.

"I would be if he was capable of loving me in return. It's kind of a two-way thing, being in love with someone, isn't it? But he's not really him, anymore. He's whatever I made him."

She squeezes my arm.

"When did you figure it out?" she asks like she realized long ago. Javier did in one night. Guess I was the last to admit it.

"Too late." I close my eyes. Dylan's words ring through my brain: *If I refuse, I won't end up like him, will I?* Then Elisha's. "He asked me if something was wrong with him, and I told him everyone changes. Not like that, though. He's so far gone he doesn't even know it."

Her spoon chimes against the teacup as she stirs it. "What are you going to do?"

I know what I have to do, even if it hurts. Even though my feelings are hurtling forward, I need to stop them here. "I'm going to move on. That's what I told him to do." I still hear him—can't stop seeing him kneeling in the dirt, straining and crying—screaming for me, that he loves me.

"You told Elisha to move on?" Jess raises her eyebrows. "How's he supposed to do that?"

My shrug morphs into a vague gesture as I think. "I'm still giving his family a thousand dollars every month. He can get a therapist, or—"

"Get a therapist? Alex, he can't dress himself!"

"I can't be the one to pick out his clothes every morning, Jess!" I bang my hand down on the table. "Believe me, I wish he could do it himself, but that's my fault. Don't you understand? Every second he's with me, he becomes *more* dependent on me. Someone else has to fix him because I can't."

We both sip our tea, diluting the energy in the room.

"You can stay here as long as you want; you know that," Jess finally says. "But the longer you do, the more people will talk."

"I know." I can't look at her when I say, "I'm having my house gutted. That excuse will hold up for a while."

"Holy . . ."

"Jess." I flick my eyes up to meet hers, desperate that she understand. "Everything reminds me of him. The piano almost had me in tears."

She drums her fingers on the table. "You need to keep busy. Because—I hate sounding like Mariah—" Jess sighs and rolls her eyes. "You can't be seen crying over this."

"I know." I do. And yet it doesn't make sense. Why can't I feel sad? Why can't I love Elisha, miss Elisha, be with Elisha? He's not a debtor or Docile anymore, but that doesn't mean anything to my parents.

"Come on," Jess says. "Before you get any other bright ideas. Let's go to the lab. You can lose yourself in a pile of paperwork."

She's right. I need to focus on something—anything besides Elisha. Because right now her support is all that's stopping me from driving back out there.

A text lights up my phone. *Alexander Bishop, return my calls this instant.* I can only ignore Mariah for so long.

Jess looks up from her tablet, on the other side of my desk, where she is standing guard over me. "You might as well take her call. She's not going to stop."

The phone only rings once before Mariah answers. "Are you fucking crazy?"

"Hi, Mariah. How are you?"

"I have only ever tried to help you, Alex."

"I'm fine, thanks for asking."

"I've literally handed you men. Multiple times."

"I'm a little busy, right now. Can we reschedule this lecture?" I drag my finger over an open document on my SmartDesk, scrolling through it without reading. Jess glances at the surface, monitoring my work upside down.

"Absolutely not. Are you aware that you were photographed checking into a hotel room with your Docile—"

"What?" I patronize that hotel because they're discreet. I didn't see any photographers. Not that I was looking, I was—I wanted to help Elisha—I . . .

"And not any old hotel room, the fucking Penthouse Suite, like it was your goddamn honeymoon."

"I-I don't—"

"I know you're avoiding me, Alex, but you can't avoid this. Open your goddamn feed and look. They're everywhere."

Jess can only hear one side of the conversation, but she watches me close spreadsheets and databases in favor of my browser. My news feed assaults me with photos of myself and Elisha—photos taken through blurred ferns, across rooftops, and through windows.

Alexander Bishop III and His Docile Check into Penthouse Suite.

Image: two well-dressed men in a posh hotel lobby, the older man's arm draped casually around the younger's shoulders, pulling him close.

Bishop and Docile Caught Horsing Around in Penthouse Pool.

Image: two men embracing in a swimming pool, wet chests pressed together. The younger man holds the older man's face. The two stare at each other's lips, only inches apart.

Alex Bishop and Docile Share a Romantic Night at The Douglass.

Image: through a crack in the curtains, two men lie together on a California king bed, their limbs indistinguishable.

The Morning After—

"Alex, are you listening to me?"

I remember Mariah and, with a touch, close all the windows on

my computer, leaving its generic Bishop Laboratories wallpaper.
"Yeah, I'm here." But when I close my eyes, I am back at The
Douglass with Elisha. I'm holding him in the lobby, kissing him in
the pool, embracing him like a lover in bed.

"You've really fucked this one up," Mariah says. "You might've
saved it, if you had only dated the smart, attractive man I all but
dropped into your bed. But no. Thank god I made him sign an NDA
before he went out with you, because he tells me you called Elisha
better than him and then kicked him out."

"He hurt Elisha," I say, quietly.

"Listen to all the fucks I give. Literally, listen."

Silence.

"Mariah—"

"No. Do not speak. Every word further damages the company
your family and its Board members have worked so hard to build."

"Mariah," I shout, "I sent Elisha home!"

"What?"

"I amended Elisha's contract. His debts are paid, his term
served. I took him home. It's . . ." I have to say the words for her
and for me. "It's over."

"Well, that's the first good news I've heard in six months. But the
following still stands, so listen carefully. I am offering you one last
chance to clean up this horrific mess you've made."

I sigh. "What do you want me to do?"

"Propose to Javier."

"Excuse me?"

"The Board and our legal team have approved his GenEcs."

"Did you not hear what I said? He hurt Elisha!"

"And you're hurting this company! Your family's company, Alex."
More silence.

"Now's the time to decide. Which do you care about more: Elisha
or Bishop Laboratories?"

I don't answer. I'm not sure, and I don't think I should have to
choose. Business and pleasure exist on different planes; that's why
the phrase "business or pleasure" exists. The stress between my

eyes is like a spike being pounded into my skull. I press the spot to ease the pressure.

"The Board is having a Proposal prepared for your personal attorneys' review. I expect it executed, notarized, and returned within one week."

"Whatever."

"You did this to yourself, Alex." The phone beeps, and Mariah is gone.

She's probably right, but I can't decide if I care. I care that Bishop Labs doesn't crumble, wasting generations of my family's work. And I won't lie to myself; I like owning nice things, eating gourmet foods, and doing whatever the fuck I want. I'm not going to give up everything and move out to Prettyboy Reservoir with Elisha. That's it. That's my decision, like I said. I'm moving on.

"I don't want to talk about it," I tell Jess, who is doing a terrible job of pretending to write a report.

"I didn't say anything." She looks around, innocently.

"Fuck!" I slam my fists against the SmartDesk; documents fizzle out before returning.

In a week, I could be engaged to Javier, the man who locked Elisha in confinement overnight. I refuse—and yet might not be able to. There has to be someone better, someone I don't have to rush to propose to. The Board will give me time; Mariah's being rash. I need time to decompress. Unfeel all this. Forget Elisha. Fall out of love.

The Proposal arrives in a few days, as promised. Tom calls to let me know, since I didn't answer when he buzzed my place. I've spent three nights on Jess' couch, under a pile of pink and green designer quilts decorated with owls and elephants.

I take the package from Tom. "Thank you." I'm glad when he doesn't mention that I'm wearing sunglasses inside or the same clothes as when he last saw me.

"You're welcome, Dr. Bishop. There's something else waiting for you, upstairs. Well, someone."

I take my sunglasses off and hook them on the neck of my sweat-shirt. Look at the elevator. "Someone?" He wouldn't let a stranger into my house.

"He asked me not to tell you." Tom leans closer. "Your father. Act surprised."

I *am* surprised. I only talked to Jess and Mariah—not that it's anyone's business what I do with my Docile. Ex-Docile. "I won't give you away," I say. "Thanks, again." I tuck the package under my arm and head for the elevator.

For thirty seconds, I enjoy the silence, wishing it would carry beyond these doors. When they open, I'm not prepared for how cavernous my apartment looks. How unlike a home. The hardwood floors stretch wide like an endless beach, the two-story-tall windows opening over the vastness of the city like an ocean. I feel insignificant.

"Oh, hello, Alex." Dad looks up from a newspaper, a steaming mug in his hand. "Hope you don't mind, I helped myself." He presses down on the newspaper and it collapses into the countertop, where he sits. Dad saw the paparazzi photos from the hotel, if Mariah did. Probably showed the whole Board. Oh god, what if he's come to fire me? "Your Docile wasn't around."

"No," I say. "He isn't."

"How's that going, by the way?" Dad sips his coffee.

He must know, if Mariah is sending me GenEcs. "It's going nowhere. It's over."

"So, it's true, then."

"Yeah." I set my envelope down on the counter. "It's true. I sent Elisha home."

"I'm proud of you, Son."

"Why?" I slump onto the stool across from him. "I failed."

"For your ambition. For recognizing failure. For moving on."

When he says "moving on," I reflexively look at the envelope of GenEcs.

"You do not need to marry Javier Madera."

"Thank god."

"I did mean what I said about moving on, though. I have a

designer coming over with some craftspeople, shortly, to assess this . . ." His eyes wander over the barren surfaces. "Situation. Recommend a new look."

I know I need a bed, at the very least, but the idea of someone rebuilding on this burnt ground—I thought getting rid of everything would help. I don't know that I want to make this a new home, as if Elisha never happened.

"In the meantime, you are I are going to the ODR."

"For work?" I ask.

"No," Dad says, "a meeting with Charlene. To find you a new Docile. An obedient one, who respects you and recognizes the advantages of Dociline. Come on, Son." Dad sets his mug down, stands, and rubs my shoulder. "Let's get you back on your feet. Reimagine your life."

Reimagine my life without Elisha, he means. Pretend I didn't break a person. *Fuck.* I take Dad's mug over to the sink, so I don't have to stand beside him. So I can close my eyes. Wait for the tears to reabsorb. I did the right thing, sending Elisha home. I'm doing the right thing, moving on.

The Office of Debt Resolution is closed to the public, by the time we arrive. I was here with Elisha only, what, a week ago? Two? Despite the completed renovations, it feels even more depressing, now, with holograms displaying new Docile profiles and testimonials neatly stenciled onto the wall:

"I paid off my PhD in only three years as a Docile. Nothing but opportunity lies before me, now."

"With the streamlined matchmaking and interview process, I was able to find the perfect Docile in a familiar environment."

A line of Dociles walk past on the new royal-blue carpet, wearing "ODR"-monogrammed scrubs. Their artificial smiles give me goose bumps.

Charlene approaches, tablet in one hand, white cane in the other, its laser scanning the path. "Two Dr. Bishops! Always an honor,

Lex." She tucks her tablet under her arm, then shakes my father's hand. "And Alex."

"Likewise," I say because I can't manage *my pleasure* or *delighted*. I'm not. Not that I ever was before, but faking it requires energy I'm trying to conserve.

"I'm sorry to hear things didn't work out with Elisha, but I've curated a wonderful selection of Dociles for you to interview, this evening."

"That sounds lovely, Charlene, thank you," Dad says.

Normally, I'd demand to see the profiles in advance. Whittle them down until only the best remained—but what do I know? I broke my last Docile. Maybe, this time, I should trust Dad and Charlene.

During my first three interviews, I try to perform—try to smile and look alert. The debtors are attractive and smart, well groomed and personable. Most of that doesn't matter, since, according to their files, they've all pre-agreed to inject Dociline.

The fourth debtor's chair scrapes the floor—and my nerves—when he pulls it out and sits down. When I do not give him my immediate attention, he says, "Are you okay?"

"Yes." I straighten up and clear my throat. "I'm fine." I don't tell him it's not his business. He doesn't deserve my anger; none of this is his fault.

The debtor apologizes, anyway. He's a few inches shorter than me, high cheekboned, dark skinned, and muscled. I wouldn't mind his mouth on my cock and I suppose that's all that matters, since he'll be on Dociline.

I'm lying to myself. Of course that's not all that matters, but as much as I want to, I can't fake caring about him. I wish I did. How much easier it would be . . .

"Why are you here?" I finally ask.

"To pay off my debt."

Not what I meant and he knows it.

"College debt," he adds. "Turns out a philosophy major isn't what it used to be."

He can say that again.

"I assume, since you've been selected for me, that you're gay or otherwise interested in men?"

"Pansexual."

"Even better." Easier to share him, not that it really matters. I keep forgetting I won't have to train the new one. It's almost too easy, Dociline.

"W-why's that?" he asks.

My phone rings before I can not-answer his question. My caller ID speaks calmly into my ear. "Incoming call from Alexander Bishop."

"Hold on; I have to take this."

Incoming call from myself? "Call location?"

"Unmapped location, Baltimore County, Maryland."

"Answer call." The line connects. "Who is this? I know you're not Alexander Bishop."

46

ELISHA

I'm no longer holding myself up. I am held tight, whispered to, laid down on something soft. Someone is holding me, squeezing. It stills me. I want the pressure, like suspenders and bits and bow ties and leather. Like Alex holding me tight against him, telling me everything's going to be all right.

"It's okay." A whisper. "Elisha, it's okay. Breathe."

Breathe. I remember to breathe, shaky breaths that are wet with snot and saliva.

"Here, take this."

I take the soft cloth and blow my nose, clear my throat. A glass of water is pressed into my hands, then moved to my lips.

"Can you hold it?"

"Yes," I whisper.

Water dribbles between my lips as I drink. Soon, the glass is empty and color returns to the room. I recognize Micah's face opposite me.

"I'm sorry," I say.

He takes the empty glass and sets it on the small table. "Oh god, no, Elisha. I'm sorry. I didn't know—I'm not sure what I said. . . . Are you okay, now? Okay isn't what I mean. Of course you're not okay."

I know what he means. "I know where I am and who you are."

"Good." He rests a hand on my shoulder. "Do you want me to take you back to Nora's?"

Want. Why does he keep asking me questions when I have no answers for him? If Alex were here, he'd know what was best.

"Maybe you should just stay here."

Breathe: in and out.

"That sounds nice," I say.

"I can sleep on the floor or keep you company. Whichever you need."

Company. I know what that means. I can keep Micah company like I did for Alex. It won't be the same, but that's okay. It will still feel good.

I pull the borrowed shirt over my head while Micah watches. He continues to stare while I untie the shorts.

"What are you doing?" he asks.

"You want to sleep with me."

"Not—not like that. Elisha, I meant keep you company. Make sure you're okay."

I stand with my thumbs hooked in my waistband and flush with embarrassment. "Oh."

Micah helps put my clothes back in place until I'm snug on the bed, once again. He holds me flat against him, breath rustling my hair. Micah doesn't want me to please him; I can't tell if I've done something wrong. So few people want nothing from me.

But his grip eases the pain, so I focus on breathing: in and out.

"Hey, Elisha!" Micah walks past, while I tend Nora's garden.

I muster up a smile and wave.

"I'll see you later, right?"

"Yeah." I watch him walk off.

"Looks like you're finally settling in," Nora says. "Making friends."

"I guess." I rip out a handful of weeds by the roots and set them aside. The past few nights, Micah has come for me and I've followed happily to his bed, where he's held me until I've fallen asleep. It's hard without the city noise.

"Well, you always bring a smile to my face, kiddo." Nora gathers up the weeds in a burlap sack. "Get inside and wash up for dinner. Your father's coming over."

My arms go limp. He hasn't spoken to me the entire week I've been back—at least, that's how long Nora says it's been. I've barely glimpsed Dad. Haven't seen Abby at all.

Maybe he's changed his mind. Maybe he'll help me.

I race inside to grab a towel, then out to the bath. I'll never be as clean as Alex had me, but if I scrub hard enough I just might show Dad I'm underneath all this. I'm here.

My hair's still damp when he knocks. The table isn't set. *Shit.* A fork clangs to the floor. I can't even hold everything. I've set more complicated places than this.

"Good to see you, Nora. Sorry I haven't been more helpful, lately." Dad hugs Nora and kisses her hair.

"Don't you worry about it." Their lips meet; then she shoos him into the kitchen.

I stand tall with my hands by my sides. Lifting my eyes to meet his is like lifting a two-hundred-pound weight. I'm going to buckle; it's only a matter of when.

Dad nods in my direction, but doesn't speak to me, as if he's counting me. Mom wanders in from the garden with a small bundle of flowers.

"Those are lovely, dear." Dad takes the bunch and holds it out to me without acknowledging my presence.

I take them, fill a little glass with water, and sit them on the table in their new vase. When I smile at Dad, he neither smiles back nor shows his approval. I give up and sit down, joining the others at the table. Their words all mush together. I'm still not used to paying attention to others' conversations, so my name startles me.

"Elisha?" Nora glances sideways at me.

"Sorry, I was distracted. What did you say?"

"She said, you've been making friends." Dad sticks a forkful of cabbage in his mouth and chews it like a horse.

I scramble for an answer. "I met up with Micah after a swim, the other day. He used to be a Docile, too, so he's helping me."

Dad shoves another clump of cabbage into his mouth. "Yeah, I heard he's turning you into his own personal Docile."

"That's nice," Mom says.

"David." Nora glares at him.

"What? You know it's true. He was that trillionaire's pet and now he's Micah's."

"We decided to let Elisha heal in his own way."

"Heal." Dad wipes his mouth on a rag. "Heal from what? Drinking out of gold cups, sleeping on special foam beds—"

"I'm sorry," I say, before he can finish. "I'll do whatever you say, but please take me home." The word feels weird. This doesn't feel like home. "At least let me see Abby."

"Absolutely not."

"David!" Nora stands.

"I won't have her turning into one of them!" He gestures between me and Mom.

"Please." I stand with them. "I'm not an on-med. I'm not a drone."

Dad wipes the sweat from his forehead. "No, if you were, I might pity you. Look at her."

Mom smiles up at us, folding her hands in her lap. Her brown curls are soft and bounce on her shoulders. She still styles it every morning, like she was programmed. I look down at the city clothes I still wear even though no one's told me to. I still run every morning.

Do you really believe you have any free will left?

"I don't know," I tell Alex. Why isn't he here? I already feel dead.

"Great, now he's talking to himself." Dad throws his hands up and walks away.

"What if I am like Mom?" I look at her. She's always so calm and happy, no matter what people say about her. Hopefully, I can adjust as well as she has. I wonder if she misses her Patron. "At least she's always happy."

"I can't take any more of this." Dad pushes the door open and heads into the dark. He paces back and forth.

What did I do wrong? I barely spoke, barely moved—and only to help. I look to Nora for the answer, but she huffs and glares at my dad. I didn't mean to anger anyone.

"I'm sorry," I say. "I can do better."

"Don't worry about it, hon; you're doing fine," Nora says. She doesn't take her eyes off him. "It's your father I'm worried about."

He circles back and stops with one foot inside. His face shines with tears. "I'm only going to say this once, so listen good." He wipes them away. "I loved your mother and I loved you."

Loved. Past tense. Over, done.

"We didn't expect what happened to her and I have to face that, every day, the *thing* that used to be my wife. But at least I had you and Abby, right? Well, I don't anymore. All I have is a confused teenager, who thinks this"—he waves at me and Mom—"is normal. Acceptable. And that she can get a job in the fancy fucking city and grow up to be a happy drone, like her brother.

"I am sorry," he says. "I'm sorry I let you go. It should've been me. Then, at least I could've been with my wife, again. A happy Docile couple."

Happy. The word stabs me through the heart. Tension grips my neck, the ache spreading through my hands and head, bending me to its will. I thread my fingers through my hair, trying to squeeze the pain away. "I knew how to make Alex happy, but not you, Dad. It's not enough for you that I gave up my family and my freedom and my future." I push myself to look at him. "Why am I not allowed to be *happy,* now? Why are you only happy when I'm suffering?" The ache—the want—builds in my chest until it releases with a sob and a shout. "I was happy with Alex! He cared for me. He wanted me around. He said he loved me. Do you?"

"I love you, Elisha," Mom says.

Dad looks at his feet. "I love my son."

"But that's me." I slam my fist into my chest. "I'm still me, just a new version."

"I prefer the old version."

"I know; you've told me. Don't worry; I prefer the old you, too." I press the wet corners of my eyes before they overflow. "And I miss Alex. Why am I not allowed to say that, here? Why can't I love him?"

"Because it's not real," Dad says.

"But it feels real to me. Isn't that what matters?"

"The voices sound real to crazy people."

"I'm not crazy," I whisper. "I'm hurt. I hurt everywhere."

Mom begins clearing the table, taking dishes out from under us. No one else moves or speaks.

"I know I'm different," I say. "But I'm not gone. I'm still in here." I curl my finger against my sternum. "I need help. I need someone to love me and be patient with me."

Nora clears her throat. "Maybe we're not the best people for that."

"You've been patient." I reach for her hand and she squeezes mine harder than I expect.

"But your father's right. I've let you slip into old habits. You're not taking care of yourself." She points at me. "And I know you're not sleeping."

"It's too quiet, out here."

Nora's hand slides up and pats my shoulder. "Go to your room, Elisha. Take your mother with you."

For one second I consider staying. But I've spent all my energy arguing with Dad and doing what Nora tells me is comforting. I lead Mom into my room—hers, really, since I've been sleeping at Micah's. But I don't mind sharing with Mom. She's the only one here who's always happy to see me.

"You look tired, Elisha," she says. "Would you like me to turn down the bed?"

"Yes, please," I say, not denying her the chance to feel useful. I wish someone would do the same for me.

Mom pulls a thin sheet down and I settle onto the bare mattress. When she pulls the sheet up and tucks it around me, it's almost like we're both real.

"Thank you," I say.

"Thank you," she says, before helping herself to the old pullout couch.

On the other side of our thin wall, Nora and Dad argue. Might be enough sound to lure me to sleep. Mom smiles when she closes her eyes. Always content.

"Mom?" My voice rouses her.

She doesn't care. "Yes, Elisha?"

"Are you happy?"

"Yes, thank you. And yourself?"

"No. I miss Alex."

"I'm sorry."

"It's not your fault. I'm too scared to run into the city. What if I get there and he doesn't want me?"

"I love you, Elisha."

"I love you, too, Mom. I wish I could at least call Alex, talk to him. Tell him I can love him."

"Who is this?" Alex's voice fills my head. "I know you're not Alexander Bishop."

"Maybe I am crazy," I say. "Your voice sounds so real."

"Elisha?"

Hearing my name in his voice tenses my body with want. "I wish you were here."

"Elisha, you shouldn't have called me."

"I know you're only in my head, but . . . I do love you. And I need you. No one here *needs* me. If you don't, either, what's the point?"

His voice doesn't answer.

"I don't care if I'm hearing things," I whisper, so Mom will fall back to sleep. "Please stay with me."

No answer, again.

I sigh. He's—

"I'm here," he finally says.

"Thank you." Alex is all I want. Now I have him. He has me— just tonight. Tomorrow he'll be gone again, and that will hurt too much; I can't stand it, anymore.

I reach into the bag Alex packed me and pull out my razor. He bought it for me, like everything else. With the press of a button, the used blade drops into my palm. I hold the sharp side against my wrist. One slice. That's how Nora's husband, Riley, died, right on some trillionaire's bathroom floor. His body was pale as ash when they brought him back.

"Please stay with me," I whisper.

"I am." Alex's voice surrounds me.

For once, I'll be what everyone wants: out of the way.

I wince at the first cut, at the white insides of my skin before blood floods the line. The sting shoots up through my arm. My heart quickens, as if my body wants to pump all the blood out of me.

"Elisha, what are you doing?"

"I cut myself." I flex my arm and the blood runs onto the mattress. The buzz in my skin deepens to a tingle.

"Where?"

"My wrist."

"When?"

It's not bleeding as hard as I thought it would. Maybe I did it wrong. I can't even manage to disappear. "Just now."

"Elisha, listen to me."

That's all I want to hear him say. I hug my pillow as if it's any substitute for Alex. "Always."

"First, put down whatever you cut yourself with."

His voice makes it okay. I set the blade on the bed, next to me. "Okay."

"Do not hang up the phone. I want you to put pressure on the cut. Can you do that?"

"Yes." I clamp my hand over my wrist. It's all I have. The blood is slippery and sticky between my fingers.

"Good. I want you to talk to me."

"About what?"

"Anything. What have you been doing?"

"Running, mostly."

"That's fun." He sounds distracted. Even the Alex in my head is too busy for me. "What else?"

"I made a friend. His name's Micah."

"Does he run with you?"

"No, I'm too fast."

Alex chuckles. "Of course you are."

I smile to myself. He's happy, now. I'm happy. "He helped me, though, slept with me. It was okay. Not like being with you."

"Remind me to kill this Micah kid when I get there."

"If you're coming here, you'd better hurry." When I close my eyes, relief surges through my head. I am so tired—of trying, of caring, of existing. Of neighbors gawking and Dad fighting. "I'm about to fall asleep."

"Do not go to sleep, Elisha. Understand? How does your wrist look?"

My eyelids weigh heavy, as I peek. "Fine. I don't think it's bleeding, anymore."

"Is anyone else there with you?"

"My mom is, but she's asleep. Dad and Nora are fighting about me. I'm at her house."

"Do not hang up the phone. I'll be right there."

"Okay." It was easier with Alex. Here, I'm exhausted.

"And stay awake."

Then, for the first time, I break my word to Alex. I fall asleep.

47

ALEX

"Elisha?"

Silence.

"Elisha, answer me." I unfog the privacy glass for a second, then reset it. Charlene is gone. Dad sits at a table in the waiting area, talking on the phone and reviewing documents on his tablet. He was *proud* of me for taking Elisha home and moving on; he won't understand. None of them will.

"You should go," says the debtor I was pretending to interview.

"You fucking think?" The feelings I've spent the past week suppressing rush to the surface like a buoy forced underwater. Relief and pain hit me at the same time. How stupid to think I could move on like the last six months didn't happen. Like Elisha means nothing to me.

He stands. "I'll vouch for you. Tell him you went to the restroom or something—whatever. That you said you'll be right back. Should give you a head start."

"How much debt do you have?" I ask.

"Two hundred thousand."

"Your name?"

"Liam Greene."

"Liam Greene, go home."

"I can't just—"

"I'll pay it. If you cover for me, I'll pay it."

"Really? I—are you sure—"

Already I'm drafting a virtual check on my phone. "Yes."

"Thank you."

"Don't." I crack the door. Dad paces down the hallway, still talk-ing. He is going to be so disappointed in me. "I have a lot to make up for." I slip between the door and its frame, closing it quietly, not taking my eyes off Dad.

He stops at a window and speaks to the glass as if it's whomever he's on the phone with. I cringe at the pattering my shoes make in this echo chamber of a hallway, then speed up as if I can escape the sound.

As soon as I round the corner, I run down the marble staircase, not waiting for the elevator. How can I stand still when Elisha is bleeding out forty fucking minutes away? I grind my teeth to keep from screaming.

My car waits at the end of the block, but I can't risk taking it. Behind it, a row of taxis. I open the back door of the last one in line and rap my knuckles on the dividing plastic.

"Eighty-Three North. Fast as you can."

"Yes, sir." He looks in his mirror and backs out. Not fast enough.

"I'll triple your rate if you can get me there in less than thirty minutes." I slide my card through the reader in an act of good faith.

"What's your exit?" he asks.

"Thirty-One."

"You got it."

"Call nine-one-one," I say.

"Me?" the driver asks.

"No, I'm talking to my phone. You drive."

The operator answers after one ring. "Nine-one-one, what's your emergency?"

"I need you to meet me at Prettyboy Reservoir off 83 North. Exit 31. Fast as you fucking can."

Dust billows around the car when it slides to a stop. I push the door open and run.

Nora is his neighbor. His house is beside the water spigot, where I left him. People wander out of their homes at the wailing sound of the approaching ambulance. I collide with a cheap wooden door that can't possibly still lock. It swings open easily. Elisha's father and a middle-aged Black woman, who I assume is Nora, stand in the small kitchen. Her finger still points at his chest; accusation lingers in her eye.

"Where is he?" I ask.

"Who?" she says. "And who are you?"

"Where's Elisha!" I shout.

"You're the Patron, Alexander Bishop." Mr. Wilder glares at me, fingers twitching at his sides.

"I don't have time for this." There are only two doors in the whole damn house. He's got to be behind one of them.

Dad and Nora are fighting about me.

I shove past them and fling open the nearest door. Shouts erupt behind me. On a faded twin mattress, Elisha lies with his eyes closed. Blood stains an almost floral pattern around his wrist. The razor blade sits neatly beside him, where I told him to put it.

"Wake up." I drop to my knees beside him.

But Elisha doesn't respond to my command.

"I said wake up!" I reach for him, but EMTs push between us.

Nora wraps her arms around me, pulling me back. "Let them work," she says.

They rush back and forth. Their figures blur into one giant mass.

"It's my fault," I whisper. "I did this."

She doesn't deny it.

An EMT cracks the door and sticks her head out. "Any of you family?"

We all stand.

"I'm his father," David says, and the EMT leads him into Elisha's room.

Nora stares me back down onto the couch. "Wait your turn."

That man disowned Elisha. He shouldn't get a say. "He—"

"Don't." She narrows her eyes at me.

I ball my hands in my lap. "If I could go back and undo it, I would."

"Maybe. But you're still the one who took Elisha from his family."

I stare at her for a minute. Twice as many wrinkles line her face as my mother's. Her stained tee shirt says: "Be Crabby," but I bet she's never eaten a good crab cake.

"You're Dylan's mother, right? Nora Falstaff? I'm not supposed to know your surname unless Dylan volunteers it, but Elisha told me—I didn't mean to."

"It's fine," she says. "Surnames are the least of our worries, now."

"No. I've violated Third Right. I don't know how much sway I have over Dylan's contract, but I'll tell our contracts manager I fucked up. She should get to go home."

Nora lets out a *hmpf.* "Your toys are less fun to play with once you realize they're people, aren't they?"

I want to like this woman. I do. "It's more complicated than that."

"I may not have birthed Elisha, but I am as much his parent as David is. I am his family. And what you've done to him is . . ." She looks at the ceiling, shaking her head and wiping the corners of her eyes with callused fingers.

I swallow and look at my feet. "Unforgivable."

"At least you know it." Then, she pats my leg. Reassurance I don't deserve. "Elisha will get through this. He's a good boy."

"I used to tell him that, all the time. Happiest I've ever seen him."

"How sad." She says it like she means it. "You'd like Elisha. I hope you get to meet him."

I bite my lip to keep myself quiet. It doesn't matter that she's right. I don't really know Elisha. I only know the person I made him into. But I can't believe it was *all* a lie. Who knows what Elisha might've become if he could've afforded private tutoring, a university degree, formal arts, and athletic training. He might've liked the piano, regardless. Maybe I only helped the keys under his fingers.

The EMTs emerge with their gear. "He's going to be fine," one says. "Just be careful with him."

"Thank you." I shake their hands. "You can send me the bill." After I sign the paperwork, I show them out.

Nora ladles broth into a mug and sets it on the table. "You're going to be here awhile."

"You don't have to feed me." My stomach growls, while I try to remember the last time I ate.

"I don't care if you have a hundred billion dollars, Dr. Bishop. I'm still a mother and you're still a son."

I sit, smiling for the first time since I arrived. I have more than a hundred billion dollars. "Please, call me Alex."

"All right, then, Alex, eat. No one's child goes hungry in my house."

"Yes, ma'am." I glance over my shoulder at Elisha's door before sipping the warm broth.

Still closed.

When the door finally creaks open, Nora and I both look up. It's David. Alone. He beckons Nora over, speaks quietly into her ear, and rubs her back before he walks off, not giving me a single look.

Nora stands between the open door and its frame. "Alex, why don't you take a walk. Get some fresh air. I won't forget about you."

She wants privacy—I get it. And I don't blame her. She watches me stand and leave the small house, closing the door behind me. I stand in front of it, for a minute, eyes closed, listening for Elisha's voice. Any hint that he still exists. I hear only a murmur in Nora's comforting tone and the creak of hinges.

Then, I leave. Shove my hands into my pockets and kick a stone across the dirt path before following. I don't want to stray too far. Can't be too many people in Elisha's community who want to talk to a Bishop. The ones whose company holds their loved ones' contracts, whose laboratory manufactures Dociline.

They wouldn't take it if they didn't think it was useful. I wouldn't keep working on it if I didn't feel the same. If he'd taken it, Elisha would never have . . .

I round the side of the house and look over the potted herbs. Not sure how long they need me gone, I stop and smell each one. Pluck a mint leaf. Chew on it, while I walk. A woman sits on a stool behind the next house, a bucket of laundry between her knees. She stares straight ahead with a calm smile on her face, not once looking at me as I draw closer.

I nod politely, acknowledging her. "Hi."

"Hello," she says in a soft voice that reminds me of my elevator.

I stop. This is Elisha's house. I face the woman. "Pardon me, but are you Elisha's mother?"

"Yes, Elisha," she says, still raking a shirt over the washing board.

He'd said she was disabled. Like she was still on Dociline, despite having come off it a while ago. But she seems normal to me, pleasant enough. "I'm Alex." I hold out my hand and hers rises to take it, straight from the wash, still dripping and soapy.

"Hi, Alex."

When she doesn't introduce herself, I say, "What's your name? If you don't mind me asking."

"My name is Abigail."

"Nice to meet you, Abigail." I let go of her hand and she returns to her washing. There's something about the way she looks at me, or how she doesn't. Her eyeline passes an inch to the right of my face, off into the countryside. "Would you mind if I asked you a few questions?"

"Okay."

"Elisha seems to think the Dociline never fully left your system, though—" I gesture to the laundry. "You're clearly fine."

"That's nice." Her gaze lingers off to the side. Response unsettling, but not indicative of anything. Yet.

I'm nervous when I ask, "What's your favorite color?"

"Yes."

My stomach drops. "What did you eat for breakfast?"

"I like breakfast."

"But, what did you eat?"

"Okay."

Oh no. A chill works its way up my spine, in the humid evening air. That is not an answer. It's a canned phrase. "Abigail—"

"My name is Abigail."

I squeeze my eyes shut and press my fingertips against my forehead. Elisha told me she was like this, and I called him a liar. I punished him for lying to me, because it couldn't be true. Dociline shouldn't do this to a person. If she has another condition—something I can treat. Actually help her. I would, for Elisha. To help him, one of the only ways I know how. I should ask. If I can help—

I stumble when someone grabs the back of my shirt.

"You get the fuck away from my wife!"

Pain explodes through my face—transforms into a dull throb that burns through my cheek and pounds in my eye socket. I can feel my heartbeat in my teeth. When I crack open my eyes, Elisha's father is massaging his hand.

He kneels beside Abigail, sliding a hand over her cheek. Looks into her eyes as if there's anything in there.

I struggle upward, holding my jaw. "I can—"

When he jumps to his feet, I hold my hands in the air and back up. Something warm trickles from my nostril. Blood or snot. I wipe the back of my hand against my nose, wincing at the sharp pain that shoots up the middle of my face. Yep, blood.

"I don't think she's well. I can help her. Or I'd like to try. If you'd let me—"

"The fuck you will."

I brace for his attack, but he stands like a wall in front of Abigail.

"You think you can help her? You did this to her! You broke her, and my son." Tears well up in his eyes. He wipes them away, wipes the sweat from his forehead through his hair. "I don't ever want to see you again, Bishop. You stay the—"

"David!" Nora slows to a stop, in the middle of the dirt path. Her glare catches David as if a spotlight. She pushes her sleeves up, wipes her arm across her forehead, as if that will wipe away the stress and exhaustion of the situation.

David softens. His shoulders slump as he appeals to her. "I don't want him near Abigail, Nora. Or Elisha."

"I could help her," I say before David can continue. While I have Nora's attention. She seems the more reasonable of the two. "If you let me bring her to my laboratory, I can run some tests and—"

"No." She crosses her arms. "If I had it my way, you wouldn't be allowed within a mile of my family. But Elisha's asking for you."

"Absolutely not," David says.

I resolve to see Elisha whether or not his father gives me permission, before Nora says, "You didn't exactly help Elisha when he asked you to, David. Despite everything, Alex rushed up here to help Elisha when he called. If Elisha wants to see him, he can." She gestures for me to go, like air traffic control.

I stop listening when I round the corner. David's right. I did break Elisha. Abigail . . . I swallow any thought of that being my fault, my family's fault. That there could be others like her, out there. We don't observe Dociles after their contracted terms. ODR regulations don't allow us. Maybe they should. I don't know, anymore.

All I know is Elisha's waiting for me when I go to him. Standing in the middle of the room with his arms folded, trying to hide his bandaged wrist. On the other, he still wears the rose-gold cuff I locked on, six months ago.

He opens his mouth to speak, but fails. Bites his lip. Glances at the bloodstain on the bed. Now that I'm standing in front of him on as equal a footing as possible, I don't know what to say, either.

"I didn't do it right," he says, quietly.

"Good," I say. "I never wanted this. I wanted you to heal, but . . ." Shame warms my face. I run a hand through my hair and

force myself to look up from my feet. "It was stupid and selfish of
me to think you could do that on your own, especially here. For
me to abandon you after months of training and expect you to find
your feet without help. I'm sorry."

"I'm sorry," he says, in a voice just like his mother's.

"No. You have nothing to apologize for." I work up the guts to go
to him. Take his trembling hands in mine and kiss his fingers until
they relax and warm. He smells different, like earth and salt and
grass. Like blood. I hold his right arm, fingers and elbow, examining the bandage around his wrist. "It's okay if you don't know what
to say. But don't be sorry. This isn't your fault."

"Okay."

"Fuck." I sigh, tightening my hold. I feel him wince, and jerk my
hands away, remembering his wound.

"Did I do something wrong?"

This is harder than I thought. "No. You don't have to please me,
anymore, Elisha. You can say what you feel. You don't have to say
'okay' or 'sorry' if you don't mean them. My opinion doesn't matter,
anymore."

"Oh." He chokes the syllable out and steps back. "But you came.
Why . . ." He looks to me for permission to ask the rest of his question.

"Ask. Ask me anything you want." I deserve an inquisition.

"Why did you come?"

"You called me. Did no one tell you?" They may not have known.

"No." He shakes his head. "I heard your voice in my head. I
thought—I thought I was imagining you."

"No." I reach out for him, gently this time. "I'm real."

Elisha wraps his arms around me and buries his head in my chest.
His body shudders. My chest warms with his breath and tears. I kiss
his forehead and wait until he unwinds. When I feel his breathing
steady, I loosen my hold. Allow him to step back.

"I should go." I hate myself for saying it, but it's what's right. I
have to let him recover. I don't hold his contract anymore and his
parents clearly don't want me around. Not that I could stay here, if

I wanted. Dad knows I'm gone—I snuck out in the middle of an interview. My mother's probably heard. Mariah, Dutch, Jess? I didn't tell anyone where I was going.

"Okay." Elisha wipes his nose on his sleeve. "I'll get my things."

My heart plummets. "Elisha, you can't. I can't." I clear my throat. "Believe me when I tell you I want nothing more than to bring you home with me."

"Then, I don't understand."

"I hurt you, Elisha. Every second you're with me, I hurt you more—change you more. You become less of yourself. That's why you can't be with me."

"But I can't *not* be with you. I don't know how." He looks away, blinking rapidly. "I need you. I love you," he adds, quietly.

"I know you think you do."

"Why would you say that?"

"Because it's true. I changed you. Made you feel loyalty or admiration. Made you dependent. I want you to be able to make your own decisions."

"Then, why won't you let me make this decision? I want to go home with you."

"Do you, though? Would a rational person want to go home with someone who hurt them?"

His eyes wander while he works out the correct answer. "No? I don't know? I can't stay here. Please, I don't know how to—what to—" Elisha crosses his arms and digs his nails into his skin. Closes his eyes. Creases his forehead.

He's right. He can't stay here. Fuck, he tried to kill himself because he couldn't function without me. He needs to be guided back to himself. Can I do this, though? Untrain him? Teach him how to be himself when I don't even know who he was?

"When will I be rational?" Elisha twirls the diamond chain around his finger—a lingering reminder of my patronage.

The real answer is that he won't be rational for a while. But he needs to know he has agency. "Now," I say. "You're capable of making decisions right now."

"Then I want to go home with you, please." He can't resist that "please."

And I can't resist him. "Okay. As long as your father says—"

Elisha's already shaking his head before I can finish. "I'm not a dependent. I don't need his permission."

My face relaxes into a smile. It's almost like having a real conversation with him. "Okay. But it would be respectful to tell Nora where you're going, since she cared for you. Go find her. I'll gather your things."

"Yes, Alex." And like that, Elisha's back in old habits.

Once Elisha leaves to find Nora, I call a taxi. Don't want to call my building for a car and risk my father showing up. He won't—can't—understand our relationship.

"You're taking him back, aren't you?" A girl in her early teens leans against the door, arms crossed. Wavy brown hair hangs in her face.

"Yes," I say. "But it was his decision."

"He's not very good at making decisions, though, is he?" She kicks at the floor with leather boots that are too big. Like they belonged to an older sibling. An older brother.

"You're Abby."

"None of your business."

I sling Elisha's small bag over my shoulder. "Fair enough."

She follows me outside. "When are you bringing him back?"

"None of your business," I say, without stopping. The taxi texts to let me know it's close.

"Of course it's my business. He's my brother!" That stops me. She sighs. "Yes, I'm Abby, and yes, I know who you are. It's not fair that he's going back into the city with you when I'm not even allowed to see him. Our dad hasn't let me talk to him since he's been home. He doesn't want me becoming like him and Mom."

"Their situations are different."

"Yeah, but they're both your fault."

I resist the impulse to defend Dociline. To tell Abby her mother is an outlier. That she probably had a pre-existing condition she should've alerted her doctor to when she was considering Dociline. Now is not the time.

Elisha closes the gate to a small garden and jogs toward us. From the other side, the taxi pulls up.

"So, when are you bringing him back?"

"I don't know. Honestly. When he's better and only if he wants to return. It's up to him."

"Better?" Abby crosses her arms. "Do you even know what that means?"

No, but I don't say that.

"I think he'll be better when he hates you," she says. "Because he should."

I said the same to Jess—and myself—but when his sister says it, a shiver ripples over my skin.

"There you are," Elisha says, coming up behind Abby. "Nora didn't know—"

She hugs him so hard it muffles his words. I turn around, give them a moment. The taxi doesn't. It honks and I wave at the driver, hoping they'll wait.

I feel Elisha beside me. When I glance over my shoulder, Abby's heading toward their house.

He'll be better when he hates you.

He sits beside me in the cab—in the middle seat, so he can lean against me—and I hold him tight. He rides the rest of the way into the city with his eyes closed. Fixed on the back of the scratched leather driver's seat, mine remain open.

I rouse Elisha when we pull up to my building—our building. Rain patters against the window. I need to start thinking of "mine" as "ours" if we're going to be truly equal. Elisha's not the only one who needs to change.

"Wait for me inside," I say, then add, "if you want." We've been alone for less than an hour and already I'm fucking it up. Elisha thinks I'm equipped for this, but I could very well not be.

"Of course I will." He squeezes my hand, then runs through the rain, closing the door behind him.

I press my index finger to the payment pad and wait for a beep that doesn't come.

The driver swivels in her seat and taps the machine. "Finger-print reader is wonky, sometimes. You have to run your card."

I swipe my matte black card.

We wait.

"Maybe the other side," she says, leaning even farther into the back seat to look. Her plastic flamingo earrings dangle in the way of my view.

Any side should work, but I go through the motions so she has no reason to doubt me. Finally, the machine beeps an affirmative jin-gle. The driver's dashboard lights up. She slides back into her seat and taps it, processing the payment or whatever cab companies do.

"I've got a message from your bank. Says your payment requires secondary authorization?"

Before I can tell her the problem's on her end, the dash beeps again.

"Wait, there it goes," she says. "If you want to leave a tip, now's the time, hon."

Tacky.

I breathe in and blow out my revulsion before leaving a one hundred percent tip. "For your trouble," I say, then get out and slam the door behind me.

Elisha stands under the marble awning. His eyes dart nervously at the front doors.

"What's wrong?" I ask.

"Nothing." He puts a damp arm around me.

For the first time in months, I can't tell if he's lying. He wouldn't—not so soon.

But he *could*.

I have to choose to believe him, now. Believe that he tells me the truth because he loves me. I kiss the top of his head. Thread my fingers through his.

When we push the front doors open and walk into the lobby, Dutch is talking to Tom. He's drenched and disheveled, shirt sleeves pushed haphazardly over his elbows, hair sticking up, bow tie hanging loosely from either end of his collar.

"Thank god you're both here," he says, voice breathy and tired.

Elisha tightens his grip on my hand. Maybe this is why he was nervous. I pull him closer for comfort.

"What's going on?" I ask.

"Your father's on his way. I need to get Elisha out of here, before he arrives."

48

ELISHA

No! I think the word but can't say it. Can't push enough air from my lungs or press the flat of my tongue against the roof of my mouth. The word is going off in my head like fireworks. *No, no, no!*

"No."

Did I say it? Dutch and Alex and Tom are all looking at me like I said it. My mouth is open. Throat still hums with the echo of speech.

"No." I say it again. "I don't want to go."

Alex squeezes my hand. "You don't have to."

"But you should." Dutch approaches slowly, his eyes on mine. "You have no reason to trust me, I know. But you do have reason to fear Lex Bishop. You're a debtor, Elisha. And his son is in love with you, regardless of the circumstances. You're bad for his business and his family."

Alex's grip tightens, his shoulder bumps mine, as he inches closer.

"He asked me to set an alert on your accounts so he'd know when you got back in town. If I know you're here, so does he. Didn't you notice the secondary approval on your credit card? I had to give that."

Alex clenches his jaw. Looks hard at his dirt-spattered leather boots. "He's right, Elisha. My father isn't your friend. It would probably be best if you weren't around when I talked to him, but I'll let you decide what you want to do."

Dutch glances between his watch, the front door, and me. Tom taps at his computer desk as if he's been busy this whole time. Alex stares resolutely ahead. And I don't know what to do. How do I feel so alone in this room full of people and how do any of them expect me to choose?

"I want to go home," I whisper, loud enough that only Alex can hear me. "What if we go home and lock the door and get under the covers?"

"I got rid of the covers." Alex's voice sounds flat. "And the bed. Everything, really. Dad and I were going to refurnish it, before I went to you."

Everything. He got rid of everything. Nothing's the same— never will be. People change. This is a new version of us. I miss the old version. "Can't you come with us?" I ask Alex.

He shakes his head. "I need to deal with my family, but I'll see you soon."

I can do this. I can make decisions, now. Right now. I can say something—*say something.* I am capable of loving Alex and of making decisions. Do I want to meet Lex Bishop like this? Be alone with him? Be alone with Dutch?

"You won't touch me," I say to Dutch, not quite a question.

"No. Not without your permission."

Does he mean it? I've never known him to lie and he wouldn't lie in front of Alex. Alex trusts him. I can do this. Alex wants me to go with Dutch, anyway. I can handle myself. I can make decisions.

"Okay," I say, finally. "I'll go with Dutch."

"You're making the right choice," Dutch says. Then, to Alex, "I'll take care of him, don't worry."

"I know you will," Alex says, before wrapping his arms around me.

I bury my face in his neck, breathe in the scent of sweat and earth on his skin, from the farm, while he waited for me. He loves me. When our eyes meet, I kiss him like I did that night at the hotel. *Kiss me,* I hear him say, and press my lips hard against his with the hopes we'll meld together and disappear from this place, but we don't.

Behind us, car doors slam.

"Now," Dutch says. "We need to go, now."

Reluctantly, I trade Alex's hand for his. Let him whisk me through a service hallway and out into the back alley. Into a car. As the engine revs to life, as Dutch glances out the window and slams on the gas, my hands shake so hard, the metal ends of my seat belt won't fit together, no matter how many times I jab them at each other.

Where are we going? I wait for the answer, not realizing I haven't asked. Dutch's eyes dart back and forth over the road, the car jolting similarly between lanes and around pastel buildings. *Rule number six: don't ask frivolous questions.* I don't need to know. It doesn't matter. Alex trusts Dutch to make decisions for me.

He pulls onto 83 North, slides into the left lane, and flies past a row of slower cars. By the time we pull off 83 onto the Falls Road exit, I still haven't asked and don't intend to, despite my worry. The buildings are smaller, here. Colorful in different ways. All brick, instead of marble and flagstone. Fewer pastels and nauticals, more brights and flamingos. We pass a street strung up with lights, crowded with casually dressed couples and groups of friends lingering outside shops and restaurants.

We turn off the main road and the scenery quickly changes to rows of houses built alongside one another, with tiny fenced-in yards and alleyways between them. Compared to the farm, they're beautiful. Uniform appearance, no patchwork of materials. Second floors, evergreen grass, painted mailboxes, and porch furniture with floral cushions.

We drive under 83, bumping over poorly filled potholes, passing more houses lined up in rows. Dutch pulls into a parking lot full of cars that are dented or scuffed with squared edges and bumper stickers.

He gets out and I do the same, trailing several feet behind him, in the rain. Despite the trust Alex has placed in him, suspicion and discomfort ball up in my gut.

Cold, fat drops of rain follow us between towering warehouses. Overhead, people stand on a fire escape talking and smoking, like it's a porch.

I don't like it here. This isn't safe.

I reach for the hand beside mine, then bump into Dutch and remember he's not Alex. "Sorry," I mumble, and back away.

"It's okay. I don't blame you for not wanting to be near me."

My forehead wrinkles. All of this understanding, today. Why now? And why should I believe him, after everything he's done to me, to his own Dociles, and others'?

Dutch nods at several people loitering beside a rusty metal door. Their conversation drifts off when I pass; their heads turn to follow me. I grab Dutch's arm with both hands and, this time, don't let go.

"I want Alex," I whisper.

"I know you do."

The metal door thrusts open into our space. A white person with a ring pierced through the middle of their nose looks at us. "Lock it behind you," they say.

I go in with Dutch, still holding on to him. We stop while he closes and locks the door and I survey the entranceway. People lounge on scratched-up, mismatched furniture, talking and laughing like I haven't seen since the party Dad threw me on the farm.

Street clothes are different, here. They're dresses over leggings and sneakers or joggers and sweaters that hang off their shoulders. Nothing tucked or buttoned or tied. None of the free, branded clothing that corporations donate in the counties.

I am thankful to be wearing jeans and a tee shirt but am secretly afraid someone here will know how much they cost. Then, I remember the feel of Dutch's starched sleeve and the embroidered bow tie that hangs from the collar. If they don't mind him, they won't mind me. Right?

Dutch waves at a woman sitting behind a desk. She slides a large pair of headphones back over her coarse, wavy hair and looks up at him.

"Is Eugenia here?" he asks.

"Yeah, but Roger's chatting with her about some ODR information Carol sent over," the woman says. "I'll let her know you're looking for her." A sensor on her right ear cup flashes when she taps it.

"Both of them, please."

K. M. SZPARA

"Sure thing." The woman goes back to work on her tablet.

I follow Dutch deeper into the warehouse space, over area rugs with fraying edges, past shelves loaded with paper books.

"Up the stairs." He wiggles his arm, signaling me to let go so we can fit up the narrow staircase. "After you."

The metal stairs squeak underfoot. I hold tight to the railing, but Dutch doesn't bother. He waits a step behind me while I walk slowly to the top.

Lofts line either side of this floor, like the second floor back home at Alex's. These are much bigger. At one end, people walk to and from an enclosed bridge that reaches another warehouse. Everywhere I see people at work on portable computers, beneath the awnings of the lofts, behind glass walls, most wearing gloves and coats. Like the Silo, but less sterile.

I stop at the top of the steps, unsure where to go. Dutch nudges me toward another, smaller set of steps that lead to the loft on the right. At the top of these, unfinished walls form rows of tiny stalls on either side of an aisle. Curtains shield most interiors from passersby, but some are drawn back. I don't want to be rude, but can't help glancing inside at people studying or reading. When I pass two women talking, half under a blanket on their pullout, I avert my eyes, give them their privacy. I trusted Alex to keep me safe, to know what was best for me, so I learned to suppress my curiosity for him. But nothing here is safe and every corner pings my urge to know more.

"In here." Dutch pulls back a curtain to reveal a pullout couch fitted with sheets and pillows, along with two small stools. Three books and a photo rest on a plank of wood painted red and fastened to the wall on metal brackets. The books aren't mine, but I recognize the picture of my family. Dad, when he loved me. Mom, still herself. Abby, a smiling baby. Me, a proud teenager. *One personal item.* I wonder how he got this from Alex, but don't dare ask.

"Have a seat." He gestures to the makeshift bed.

I hover beside it, cross my arms. Why does Dutch want me on a bed?

"I told you, you're safe here. I'm not going to touch you—no one's going to touch you—without your permission."

I don't move.

"Fine, stand there." Dutch ducks out of the stall.

Did I do the wrong thing? Alex said I can make my own decisions, but maybe that only applies with him. I don't know.

I press my hands against my forehead, hoping to stop the low throbbing that threatens to overtake me. In the dark of my palms, the room spins and I sink onto the thin mattress for support.

What if I made the wrong decision coming here?

The curtain rod screeches. I open my eyes to see Dutch return with one of his Dociles. The man from Preakness. From Mariah's party.

The two of them pull stools toward the edge of the bed and sit, their legs too long for how close they are to the floor. "Elisha, do you remember Onyx?" Dutch asks.

"Yes."

He grips the edge of the stool between his legs and eyes me over. He wears torn black jeans and a flannel shirt with the sleeves pushed up over his elbows. I've never seen him fully dressed before, especially not in such casual clothing.

Onyx nods and says, "Hey."

My heart nearly spills from my mouth when I open it to speak. "He's not—you're not . . ."

Dutch and Onyx look at each other and then back to me, expectantly. Why won't they say it for me? I'm trying but—I'm going to have to say it myself. I hope they don't get mad.

"You're not on Dociline."

"No," Onyx says. "Never was."

The room spins again. I draw my knees up to my chest, squeeze them tight until my blood slows and my toes begin to tingle. We had sex. At Mariah's, she and Dutch and Alex made us. Onyx did everything they told him with a smile, with sleek submissive motions only someone on the drug is capable of. I thought Onyx was on Dociline.

And I thought I was taking advantage of him. I was sick with myself. I hated myself for all the things we—

He's seen me naked, kissed me, touched me.

He remembers.

"Elisha." Dutch waves his hand in front of my face.

"You lied to me."

Onyx wavers back on his stool as if he's debating the point. "Kind of."

"Kind of?" I tighten my grip on my legs, trying to steady my trembling hands. "I—"

I feel Onyx's lips on my neck, the warmth of his tongue. Deliberate hands, hard cock smooth against mine. He knew what he was doing. He knew, and I can't decide if that makes it better or worse.

"I can explain," Dutch says.

I glare at him over the tops of my knees. "I had nightmares for weeks."

"I'm sorry; let me start there. Let us both start there." Dutch clasps his hands together and leans forward like he's going to tell me a secret. "I'm sorry for the way I've treated you and for not being able to bring you into the know, earlier. We wanted to—Eugenia tried—but Alex was just too damn good at his job, like he is with everything." Dutch's scoff turns into a laugh. "Micromanaging perfectionist with brains, a good name, and money. Dangerous fucking combination. In order to maintain my cover, I did some shit I'm not proud of. You don't have to forgive me."

"Me neither," Onyx says. His voice lacks the perfect, almost musical control I remember. "But I don't regret what I did. I'm just sorry I did it at your expense."

"Okay," I say, because I've no other words. Even theirs blend together like liquors in a trillionaire cocktail.

Dutch continues. "Onyx and Opal pretend to be my Dociles—to be on-meds—so we can keep tabs on trillionaires, hear the shit they'd only say around on-meds. In order to convince people like Mariah and Alex that Onyx and Opal are on-meds, they have to act the part. Unfortunately, that includes sex."

"Alex doesn't know, then."

Dutch drops his eyes to the floor.

"Do you only pretend to be a trillionaire?"

"Yes and no," he answers. "I have the money. Not as much as Alex, mind, but Bishop Labs does pay me and I do earn it. Don't keep most of it, though."

"He almost solely funds Empower Maryland," Onyx says. "And not just this office. The food banks and tutors, legal aid, career assistance . . ."

My tongue sticks to the roof of my mouth when I swallow, throat dry, lips chapped. I feel Dutch's cock invading my mouth, taking up space inside my body that doesn't belong to it. The impression of his fingers on the back of my head. The bitter taste of his come mixed with floor polish.

Onyx has long since finished explaining, but Dutch makes no further effort for my attention.

"You didn't have to treat me like that," I say, finally. "You could've been nicer. Jess was nice. Please tell me she wasn't lying, too."

"No," Dutch says. "She's not involved in this."

At least that wasn't a lie. I wonder if she'll talk to me still. If she can get me in touch with Alex.

"Jess can afford to be nice, but I have an image to keep up. Dutch Townsend doesn't give a shit about Dociles." The condescending smirk I remember tugs at his lips. He leans back on the tiny stool, straightens his legs, crosses his arms. "Nor does the general public, for that matter," he continues. "Most of them stopped fighting a long time ago. Just like you did."

"I don't know what you mean."

"We've both agreed you're not stupid, Elisha, so I want you to think. You were a person when you refused Dociline. Interacting with you now, there's little left."

I cannot relax.

That's not true. "I'm still me." The words come out weaker now than they did with my father. "Just a new version."

Relax and I might as well inject Dociline.

"This is a waste of time." Onyx stands up and pulls back the curtain. "Bishop fucked him up real good."

"I can hear you!" I snap.

Onyx regards me momentarily before disappearing through the curtain.

"Ignore him," Dutch says, once we're alone. "You have enough to worry about."

"When will I get to see Alex?"

"I don't know."

That answer isn't good enough, anymore. It can't be. Alex told me I have to think for myself, now. Ask questions. Ask, "Why?"

Dutch raises his eyebrows in surprise, but doesn't mention it. "Because it's not up to him. Alex is a dreamer—as idealistic as a trillionaire can be within his limited world view. And I've got to hand it to you, he's definitely in love with you—at least, his version of you. That combination is deadly to Bishop Laboratories; you have to understand that the rich will do anything to preserve their privileged lifestyles."

Fear creeps under my skin. I have to ask for Alex. It's easier when it's for him. "Anything like what?"

"Sometimes you cut off a branch to save the tree."

"What does that mean?" I say, louder. "Where's Alex?"

Before Dutch can answer, the curtain slides back. Onyx holds its edge, catching his breath. "There's a cop here, a sheriff."

Dutch looks over his shoulder. "Why?"

Onyx looks me directly in the eye and says, "She's here for Elisha."

49

ALEX

The side door swings in Dutch and Elisha's wake, as my father enters the building. He smooths nonexistent water droplets off the shoulders of his blazer, hair still dry and perfectly coiffed.

"There's my son," he says, putting out his arms for a hug. "I was worried. You didn't tell us where you were going."

I embrace him, stiffly, wishing I'd asked Dutch for more information before he took off. How much does Dad know? Is he angry? Will he sympathize if I explain? Dutch sounded nervous, if not scared. I'm not *scared* of my family, but I am nervous. At the Board meeting, Dad told me to find a partner or a Docile. I'm sure those values don't overlap, in his mind.

"Sorry," I say. "It was an emergency."

"I saw." He brushes at the wet spots my clothing leaves behind. "Dutch helped me review your accounts. A taxi to the county? Emergency services? I hope everyone's okay."

He doesn't say Elisha's name, but that's what he means.

"Sort of." Should I tell him? Declare my intentions? I've never done anything my family wouldn't approve of, before.

"Why don't we talk about that in the car." He holds the front door open for me.

I take a moment to glance back at Tom, who's doing his best not to pay attention. I can't catch his eye, but I see him shake his head ever so slightly, before turning back to his computer.

Suddenly, I want to do what Tom's suggesting, to get away, to do anything but get in that car. But I can't *not go* with my own father. We need to talk about Elisha. About my future. I'm his son; he'll come around.

I follow Dad back out into the rain. His driver, a young person dressed in black, holds a black umbrella over our heads as they escort us through the rain into the black limousine. Feels like we're going to a funeral.

After the driver closes the door behind us, Dad slides his fingers up the length of a control panel and the partition follows suit, giving us privacy. Then, he taps a side panel and it opens to reveal a crystal decanter of Macallan.

The tension in my body diffuses. Dad is ready for a serious talk, or he wouldn't be breaking out the good stuff. I reach over and take the decanter while he removes two glasses and sets them on the tray. "Sixty-two year?" I don't usually drink Scotch, don't usually have the time, frame of mind, or anyone to enjoy it with the way he taught me to. I hand the bottle back to Dad and he pours for the both of us.

"Your mother gave me this for my birthday, along with the glasses—Lalique."

He hands me one and I admire the crystal engraved with *ABII*. Middle names dilute the family name, Grandma said. Like ice in a sixty-two-year Scotch. The tinted windows of the limousine block most of the morning light, but still I hold the glass up, admire the rich cherry color and thick legs that run down the sides as I rotate it. "Beautiful."

"Tastes even better," Dad says, tilting his glass toward his nose.

I raise the glass, anticipating aromas of toffee and apple, vanilla and oak. The car jostles over a pothole and the glass bumps and splashes. Scotch burns my nostrils; I cough and thumb my tingling nose. Dad glances at me and smiles, holding his own glass out to calm its contents.

"Cheers," he says with a nod.

The Macallan tastes of raisins and dried figs, oak and cigar leaves. Reminds me of the hotel where Elisha and I stayed. Of an

autumn evening together, curled up on a plush couch with throw
blankets and a good book. I want that for us so badly.

"Alex." Dad cradles his glass. Sighs. Purses his lips when he
looks at me. "Your mother and I are worried about you."

I drop my eyes to the glass resting on my knee. Here comes the
disappointment. I failed them—failed my namesake. The company. The Board. Not to mention Elisha. "I'm sorry," I say.

"Don't be. You're not liable; none of this is your fault."

My skin tingles. This conversation is going down a road I don't
want to travel. Beyond the rain-dotted window, the concrete walls
that surround the beltway have been replaced by an awning of trees
and overgrown grass.

Dad takes a long, slow sip of his drink, sets it in a cup holder, and
clasps his hands. "We have good reason to believe Elisha specifically
targeted you, and refused Dociline, so that he could seduce you—"

"*Seduce* me?" What the fuck?

"—so that he could convince you to deem his contract fulfilled
and send him home debt-free, with a healthy stipend."

"That's—" the opposite of what happened. I feel like we've crossed
into an alternate universe. "Why would you even think that?"

"I know it's difficult for you to see, from the inside. We care about
you, Alex, your mother and I and many more people, and we're concerned about what's happened to you. We want to help you get better. And we want Elisha to pay for what he's done."

"He hasn't 'done' anything. I'm the one who—"

"Don't you find it suspicious that he would sign with a Bishop
after what he alleges our product did to his mother? A brazen lie,
but motive nonetheless."

"Motive?" I can only repeat fragments of his assertions, the
ideas too bizarre.

My father leans forward, holding eye contact, filling the space
between us. "He manipulated and defrauded you."

"I can't believe what I'm hearing," I say less to my father and
more to myself.

"I know. He hurt you, Alex, but don't worry." He settles back in his seat, reaching for his tumbler. "Our attorneys are going to take care of this. We've filed a lawsuit against Elisha and his family for financial, emotional, and medical damages."

Words escape me. How are the Wilders supposed to have hurt us financially? They have no money. And I am not the one who needs emotional and medical care. I should be paying for *Elisha's* care.

"You need help, Alex. You need somewhere free from Elisha's influence."

"He didn't influence—I'm the one who—" I dig my fingernails into the heel of my hand until I can feel the sting of the marks they'll leave behind. Why did I get in the car? "You can't do this."

"It's for your own good." Dad looks down at his Scotch, tilts the glass back, and finishes it. "I'd hoped you'd understand. We love you, Alex, but it's clear you're no longer yourself."

"Stop the car. I'm going home. Elisha's *actually* hurting and he asked me to help him."

We stare at each other. The car maintains its speed. "Elisha is no longer your concern."

"He's the only one I'm concerned about!"

"Clearly!" Dad gestures at my rumpled clothes. At pushed-up sleeves and dust-stained slacks. Sweat stains and wrinkles. "We were ready to trust you with the future, Alex, but you can't take care of yourself, much less an entire company. We—" He takes a deliberate breath and smooths a hand down the front of his shirt. "We've assigned a conservator to manage your estate."

"What? How—you'd need a judge to—"

But Dad knows plenty of judges. I've seen him entertaining them at Preakness, donating to their reelection campaigns, making sure they listened when Bishop Laboratories wanted to weigh in. Dad sighs, disappointment radiating from his posture.

"I was gone for a day and you had me declared incompetent?"

"Going forward, Dutch will approve your spending and allowance, in addition to his CFO duties. It's only temporary."

"Until what? Until I make the romantic decisions you want for me?"

"Until you're better!" Dad raises his voice. "You can't see how you've changed, Alex. You used to care about going to work. About your future. I know how hard you prepared for that first Board meeting, even though you weren't quite ready, yet. Remember how eager you were to talk about your plans for Dociline with me, at Preakness. Lately, all you care about is Elisha—not about your work or your family." He shakes his head. "I've informed the Board that you'll be taking a leave of absence, for the foreseeable future."

I fix my eyes on the floor and bite my tongue. If I speak, I'll scream. My fingers wander to the door handle. I could pull it. Jump out of the car. Run back to the city—Elisha did it.

"That you're considering jumping out of a speeding car proves my point."

I clench my jaw, enforce my own silence.

Hours pass. My fingers grow stiff and cramped, holding the Scotch glass that I refuse to either bring to my lips or hand back to my father. I do not look at him, even when we turn onto a lush campus. In the distance, a brick mansion towers behind a wrought-iron fence with the words "Ellicott Hart" emblazoned in bronze.

I hear the driver put his window down and speak to someone in a guard booth, before the gate squeaks open and we pull through. This is the kind of fence that keeps people in. As soon as it closes behind us, I know I'm not leaving. I told Elisha I'd see him soon.

The car stops with such grace, I don't notice until Dad opens his door. I can't follow him. If I do, it's as good as consenting to the story he's concocted, a story in which I'm the victim.

The driver opens my door. I don't move.

"Alex, please." Dad peers into the car. Behind him stand a row of people in suits and doctor's coats. One holds a tablet.

The last few hours of pent-up anger uncoil when I finally acquiesce. Right foot, left foot. I look my father in the eye, then slam the monogrammed Lalique glass to the ground. It shatters; Macallan sixty-two year bleeds across the concrete.

50

ELISHA

The last time the cops came for me, they took my mother and burned their mark into my flesh. I wrap my right hand over the rose-gold cuff that's hidden it for the past six months—not that I could ever forget.

"Just one?" Eugenia asks. She and Roger are walking toward us, from the end of the hall.

I step back when they arrive, making room for the people who got me in trouble every time I saw them. An hour in confinement for that card Eugenia slipped into my pocket without telling me. Alex's hand urging me down into the dark. Javier's force, my body bending to fit in the space. My legs and shoulders twinge with memories of pains and cramps. Of the cold, hard tiles against my cheek. The slotted grate pressing against my knees. The scent of my own urine.

"I deserve this," I whisper, pressing my fingertips into my forehead. Squeezing my eyes shut.

"Elisha, are you okay?" I hear Dutch say. "Back up. Give him some room."

"We don't have time for this," Onyx says.

Roger huffs, then says, "Why not? Make the sheriff wait."

"What cop is going to wait outside until they're ready?"

"Guys." Eugenia's voice ends the bickering. "Go keep an eye on her, while we wait for Elisha."

I hear the two of them grumble at each other, as they walk away. I open my eyes on the palms of my hands. Doubt presses on my shoulders.

"Take your time, Elisha." Dutch's calming voice confuses me. Is this the man who promised Alex to take care of me or the man who watched while I licked his come off the floor? How can he be both? He seems caring, now, and feels more like Alex than anyone else here. His clothes, his demeanor, the way he carries himself.

"What if she takes me away?" I ask. "I don't want to go."

"We won't let that happen, Elisha," Eugenia says, though I know she can't promise; she's never protected me. Cops do whatever they want. I've seen it and I'll never believe otherwise.

I say, "Okay," anyway, because agreeing is easier, and hold my hand out to Dutch. "Will—" He wants me to ask. I can do this. "Will you walk with me?"

He glances at Eugenia before answering. "Yes, most of the way. The sheriff can't see me here, or I could be exposed. The Bishops own the police, and I'm no good to Empower Maryland if the Second fires me for conspiring with the enemy."

With an "Okay," I take his hand. Allow myself to feel comforted by the one familiar person in this place. A person carrying Alex's trust. While we walk, I imagine Alex's trust holding my hand.

Downstairs, people crowd around the door. A tactic, Eugenia explains, to prevent the sheriff from slipping in or seeing inside. At some point, Dutch squeezes my hand, then lets go, disappears into the crowd, and Eugenia replaces him by my side.

"I'll talk to her, for you," she says.

"Okay." I follow her, closely, through the crowd as it parts for us.

There, on the other side of the door, stands the sheriff. A uniformed, middle-aged woman, with enough bulk that she could haul me off with one hand. She leans against her brown car, reviewing the papers in her hand. When Eugenia and I step out into the daylight, she looks up as if we're bothering her.

"Elisha Wilder?" Slowly, she walks over.

"Yes." I scold myself as soon as I answer. If I were smarter, I'd have asked why, first. Alex would've asked why.

"This is for you." The sheriff thrusts the papers into my hands.

Reflexively, I close my fingers around them, but I can't focus long enough to read them. "What is this?"

"A summons, complaint, and request for trial," she says. "You have thirty days to respond."

I feel Eugenia reach over and lift the summons. She reads while I watch the sheriff leave. When her car roars to life, I release my held breath with such force that I stumble into Eugenia. I'm still here. The sheriff didn't take me.

"Don't worry," Eugenia says. "We'll represent you pro bono."

I don't know what that means—don't know what any of this means. I wish Dutch had been able to stay. He would know. Eugenia asks too much, goes too fast. I don't even know what she's talking about. I should. Alex would want me to, even Dutch.

"Represent me?" I look over my shoulder as if one of them will be waiting there to answer. Instead, I meet Onyx's eyes. He folds his arms, kicks at the gravel, looks between his shoes and me. He looks worried. Makes me feel even more nervous.

"Pro bono, for free." Eugenia folds several pages over, exposing a document with the word "**COMPLAINT**" in bold black letters. Above, my name, my mother's and father's names. "Defendants."

What do we need to defend ourselves from? Realization sears itself into my skin. "Are we being sued?"

"Yes."

I trace my finger up the page farther. Stop. Suck in a sharp breath and read the names out loud. "'Alexander Bishop the Second as Personal Representative for Alexander Bishop the Third. Alexander Bishop the Second o/b/o Bishop Laboratories. Plaintiffs.'" Words I don't know and am afraid to ask the meaning off. "Plaintiffs," I say to myself.

"That means the people who filed the complaint," Eugenia says. "The ones who're suing you."

My fingers tremble. The words blur. Alex's name is there, with the plaintiffs. "O/b/o?" I ask instead of what I want to, which is why Alex is suing me.

"On behalf of," Eugenia says. "The Second is suing you on behalf of the Third and Bishop Labs."

Alex is suing me. Why is Alex suing me? Why would he do this? He loves me. He told me so a few hours ago. Kissed me and said he would see me soon. Maybe it was all a lie—no, Alex doesn't lie to me. But there are no rules anymore. We can lie to each other. Did I hurt him? What did I do?

"Elisha?" Gently, Eugenia presses her hand against my back, and presses me toward the front door of Empower Maryland. "Why don't you go inside and I'll ask someone from our legal team to go over this with you, so it's less scary, okay? Onyx can take you to the meeting room. I know you're not ready for this, but your trial could be an opportunity. With our help, you could make an impact."

"Okay," I say because it's easy. Being my own person hurts too much. I need Alex. Want to make him happy—that makes me happy.

I close my eyes and breathe in, imagining the feel of his hand on my back, instead of Eugenia's. Of his soft *good boy,* and even softer lips, pressed against my forehead. Why should an opportunity hurt so much?

I'm grateful when Onyx leads me inside, taking the burden of decision away. I follow him past the couches, up to the second floor, and through the computer stations. Everywhere we go, people stare. I don't like when they stare. Never have.

I focus on the stack of papers in my hands, while we cross the metal bridge, into the second warehouse. It creaks and shifts under our feet and I can't help but look at the two-story drop down and wonder what it would feel like to crash into the cement.

"This way," Onyx says, nodding toward a row of offices. They're only a step above the tiny bedroom stalls. Their walls are better finished, and rise on all four sides. The one he takes me to has a real door. Instead of a pullout couch, inside, a table and chairs.

A woman wearing a green pants suit stands when we enter. She extends a hand and says, "Nice to see you again, Elisha. I'm not sure if you remember me. I'm Verónica. Vasquez," she adds, as if I know enough people that a surname will make the difference. "We met while you were on a run. In the old barn, in Prettyboy. I'm an attorney."

"Right." I remember, now. I remember scattering grains of rice that dug deep into my knees. Feel the pain shooting up through my legs and back. "Nice to see you again."

She offers me a chair. Onyx sits with us, his elbows on the table as he leans nearer the stack of papers.

"I'm going to read this over," Verónica explains, "and then we'll go through it paragraph by paragraph, together. How does that sound?"

"Good, thank you." The relief of being in an expert's hands dissolves through me like ice dropped into hot tea.

I twirl the chain of my cuff around my finger, while she reads. Her face remains calm, head nodding every now and then, finger tracing a line, turning back a page to double- or cross-check—whatever it is attorneys do.

A hand clamps firmly down over my left wrist, stopping my fidgeting. Onyx catches my eye. Loosens his grip.

"Sorry," I say, slowly letting the diamond chain disappear back into the band.

"Don't be," he says. "You haven't done anything wrong."

Then why is he stopping me? What are the rules here? I don't understand. But I don't ask frivolous questions. I say, "Okay," and clasp my fingers together to curb their temptation. Onyx's hand slides back into his own space, but his eyes remain on my cuff.

"Okay, this is pretty simple," Verónica says, finally looking up at me. "First, to ease your anxiety, let me assure you that Alex—your Alex—is not suing you. It's his name on the document, but this isn't his doing. It's Lex Bishop's, his father's."

"Okay."

From the corner of my eye, I catch Onyx shaking his head. He and Verónica exchange a look.

"Elisha," she says, "I know you're not used to asking questions, but you're going to have to, if you want to get through this trial. It's going to hurt more if you don't understand what's happening. Plus, you'll be able to help us provide you and your family a better defense if you can give us all the facts. You want that, right?"

"Yes."

"Good. Then why don't you ask me a question after each point I explain to you—even if you don't have one. How does that sound?"

"Okay." I can do that.

"Good. Now, Alex isn't the one who's really suing you; his father is." Verónica looks to me for a question, her face unlined, tensionless. No pressure, and yet . . .

"Um." I pull the ring of my cuff, again, dragging the diamond chain link by link until Onyx's hand closes over it. I look at the ceiling and bend my fingers enough that the ring slides free and the chain contracts and Onyx's hand disappears. "Why?"

"Why, what?" Verónica asks.

"Why is Lex suing me in Alex's name? Why not do it in his own?"

She sounds pleased: "That's a good question. Lex is suing you in Alex's name, it states, because Alex was declared temporarily unfit to stand trial."

A short burst of laughter escapes me. When I look between Onyx and Verónica, neither of them gets the joke. "Unfit? Alex. *My* Alex. No. He always knows exactly what he's doing."

"Elisha." Verónica uses my name, once again, with the tone that signals she's going to explain something basic to me. "Lex is extremely powerful and influential. He knows everyone who runs the city, on a political and judicial level. Donates to their election campaigns and to their foundations. If he wanted a favor, they wouldn't hesitate. Not to stall a law he didn't like or endorse a candidate or—"

"Help Lex hurt his son." My voice fades to a whisper. If he can have a judge call my Alex unfit, there's nothing he can't do.

"Exactly. I would guess Alex is fine and has nothing to do with this complaint. He may not even know about it."

"If you defend me, though, won't that hurt Alex even more? You said he might not know what's going on. I love him. I don't want to hurt him—What if he thinks I'm hurting him? I could never." I shake my head, clasp my hands in my lap. I only want to make him happy. For us to be happy.

The door swings open and Eugenia enters. She leans against the wall, watching like a hawk perched on one of the old power lines.

"Alex is a plaintiff. You can't hurt him by defending yourself. There are not usually legal consequences for a plaintiff, if they lose," Verónica says, as if Eugenia isn't here.

"Okay," I say, feeling stupid for having asked. Alex always told me what I needed to know; I'm not good at guessing.

"Good." Verónica smiles, pleased with me. "Now, in brief, they're alleging fraud."

A silent minute passes before I remember to form a question. I know what the word means, but can't think how I've defrauded Alex. I've never lied to him, not even when he thought I had. Not even when he wanted me to.

So, I ask, "What kind of fraud?"

Verónica moves her finger from paragraph to paragraph as she explains. "Lex alleges that you targeted Alex to get close to Bishop Laboratories, in an attempt to punish them for hurting your mother."

"Okay."

"Okay, what?"

I forgot "okay" is no longer enough. "I meant that I understand, but that's not true. I don't understand that; I didn't target Alex."

"And you don't believe Bishop Laboratories hurt your mother?"

"No, I do believe that. That part is true."

Eugenia catches Verónica's eye, as if they have a secret. Neither shares it with me.

"Good," Verónica says. "You need to be clear on that point. It's very important. They're going to depose you—like an interview that can be used in court—and you will need to answer questions with as much specificity as possible. Their attorneys will use your words against you, in court."

I feel my heart beating faster and take a deep breath before the rest of my body can catch up. "Okay." I close my eyes and breathe slowly. "Okay, it's okay."

"It *is* going to be okay," Verónica echoes. "You're not alone. Eugenia, Onyx, and I are here with you, and many more people will support you and your family, going forward."

"Thank you." I push my middle finger through the loop on my cuff, but don't pull. I can feel Onyx's eyes on me. "What else does it say?"

Verónica moves her finger to the next paragraph. "It alleges that you refused Dociline so that you could seduce Alex."

Seduce Alex? I hear the words—know both of them, but . . . They don't belong here. I'm supposed to ask if I don't understand, but all the answers I imagine are wrong. I don't want to ask. Don't want this lawsuit. Want Alex back.

"Are you still with me, Elisha?" Verónica asks.

I whisper, "Yes."

"It says you convinced him to amend your contract, freeing you from your obligations while also paying off your debt—cheating Alex out of his three million dollars."

"That's not what happened," I say. "I begged him not to take me home, even though I've never asked Alex for anything like that, before. I never would have dared, but . . ." I feel the swell of tears in my eyes. "It hurt." Remember the sharp jab of my own finger against my sternum. "He did it, anyway. I was quiet the whole time, like he asked, I thought if . . . if I was good, but he made me sign it. I didn't even know I was signing my contract until it was too late. I never wanted it. I wanted to stay with him, be his Docile. Alex left me."

"I'm glad to hear you say that. I intend to argue the exact opposite of their assertions; that it was Alex who manipulated you. I'd like a behavioral expert to examine you—I assume they'll do the same for Alex—to show that you're the one struggling; that you did not render Alex unfit for trial by way of seduction."

Beside me, Onyx snorts. "Imagine a Docile seducing their

Patron. How? The power differential is incredible. Even for an off-med, the influence Alex held over Elisha's life and family."

"Yes, but that's how they've declared him unfit. Knowing the Second, he only would've had to ask a judge. I guarantee they're going to parade his family and friends out to say Alex isn't the person he was before meeting Elisha." Verónica looks at me. "The implication is that something must have changed him, and he spent a lot of time alone with you over the past six months."

"I didn't seduce him," I say, to make sure I'm heard. They have to understand. "I love Alex—and he loves me. He told me."

"I know you think that, Elisha." Verónica uses my name like I'm a child.

I'm not. She's my attorney. She should believe me. "It's true."

"Okay," she says, but I can tell she doesn't. Why can she say "okay" when I can't? Why do I have to do more than her?

"I'll be the bad guy," Onyx says, turning his chair to face me. "Elisha, you're not well. Whether he meant to or not, over the past six months, Alex has conditioned you to behave the way he wants you to. To follow his rules. To speak and act in the manner that suits his lifestyle. You're not the person you used to be."

"People change, every day." I hold up Alex's words like a shield. He used to protect me.

"They do," he says, "but not like this. He brainwashed you. You need to unlearn what he taught you, if you're going to make it through this trial. There's a real danger that you'll end up back in debt. You could be forced back into the Docile system. Your parents could go to debtors' prison, Elisha. This is serious."

Back in debt. Prison. Words I understand—and can Alex's dad really do that? I signed a contract. I registered for the ODR, left my family. I did everything right and, still, Lex can take it all away from me. From my family. I look between the cuff on my left arm and the bandage on my right. The familiar urge to disappear reasserts itself.

"Can I interrupt?" Eugenia pushes off the wall and paces alongside the table. I'd forgotten she was there.

"Certainly," Verónica says, looking askance at Onyx.

"No one is going to prison. I just talked with Dutch, as well as the rest of our budget committee, and we've agreed to set aside the three million dollars to satisfy your family's debt, should you lose, on the condition that we make certain strides with this case."

Eugenia stops between me and Verónica. "That money could build several schools, resolve a dozen folks' debts, upgrade infra-structure in struggling county towns—all of that is important and meaningful. But public perception is priceless. We've been trying, for years, to convince this city that Dociline and the Bishops are hurting them, not helping. If we can do that here, other states will follow."

She squats down, meeting me at eye level. "Help us prove that the Bishops are the frauds and Empower Maryland will cover you, regardless of the verdict. No ODR, no debtors' prison. Are you in?"

Am I? I can't afford an attorney on my own. Can't defend myself without Empower Maryland or Verónica. Despite how lost I feel, this situation is familiar. That someone is asking my consent as if I have a choice. Pay to see a doctor or suffer. Register with the ODR or go to debtors' prison. Go down on Dutch or be humiliated—punished. Impossible choices I've made, if you can call it that.

I know when I say, "Yes," it's the same, here.

"Good." Eugenia smiles as she stands and makes her way to the door. "I think this is going to be good—for all of us."

51

ELISHA

Fighting is more than Verónica filing our answer, I learn. If I'm going to help them fight the Bishops, I shouldn't be wearing the clothes Alex bought me. Onyx takes me to the donations closet: a room as big as Alex's house, packed with clothing, and, already, I feel overwhelmed. Why can't Verónica tell me what's best to wear for a trial? I don't know and can't pick. A rack of colorful clothes blurs into a rainbow as they slide past, startling me. I jump when Onyx appears on the other side.

"Ask me for help," Onyx says, a challenge.

"With clothes?"

"No. Ask me to help you deprogram. If you're going forward with this, you can't act like a Docile. I'm not sure you want it. Do you know how frustrating it is to engage with you?"

"I'm sorry?"

"You know you can't function without Alex and yet you insist you're not brainwashed, so which is it? Are you so far gone that you can't exist without Alexander Bishop or are you an independent person, capable of making your own decisions? Dressing and feeding yourself? Having dreams and desires? Able to ask basic questions and stand up for yourself?"

"I don't know, okay?" I say. "I don't know. I need Alex. I . . ." I look at the endless racks of clothing, or an impossible number of decisions. "You're right. I don't know what to do without him. I miss him. I miss doing what he tells me. Making him happy—that made *me* happy. But I also know he's not here, for whatever reason, so I need to be able to function without him. He told me, when he was taking me back to the farm, that I needed to find myself. Learn how to be myself again. I'm not sure what that means or how to do it alone. But if that's what Alex wants, while he's gone, I'll do it. I'll try."

Onyx stares impatiently at me. "So are you—"

"Please help me," I say before he can finish. It feels important that I ask before he can tell me to, again.

"Help you, what?"

"Help me"—I still can't say "deprogram"—"learn who I am, again. How to exist without Alex. How to pick out my own clothes." When he doesn't immediately respond, I say, "Please."

Onyx, with a smirk, says, "Okay, I'll help you. Pick something."

"For what?"

"For yourself. But good job asking a question."

"Thank you." I wonder how much goodwill that will earn me. Not enough. Maybe if I ask another. "Where will I be wearing it?" Context matters. I would never wear the same outfit to Preakness as to the Silo or eating dinner in.

Onyx shrugs. "Around. Doesn't matter. Pick whatever you like the best."

I don't know what I like the best—and don't believe him that context doesn't matter—but I don't tell him that. What I like are the clothes that Alex bought me. The outfits he picked for me. I liked the tee shirts that were so soft he couldn't keep his hands off me, and the pink-checkered button-down he always called cute.

"Go on." Onyx nudges me gently forward.

I decide to browse, first. There's no rush. This is an exercise. Nothing's riding on it. Besides, I've never shopped for myself, before. On the farm, I wore whatever clothing was donated—usually branded, unless Empower Maryland was in the area—and Alex bought all my clothes for me, after we signed our contract. I've literally never seen so many clothes. I have no idea where to start.

"Underwear," I say to myself, cracking a small smile. That's an easy one. I find a row of underwear—not used, thankfully. Donated new, in plastic packaging. Alex hates plastic. He probably wouldn't like any of these.

There are styles to accommodate all types of bodies and genders. High waists, full coverage, briefs, boxers, something that looks like two pieces of string tied together.

"Going for the thong, eh?" Onyx calls from a row over.

I wasn't, but I feel the heat of blush on my face, as I set it back on the shelf. Would I wear that if Alex gave it to me? I would, I think. I don't think I would like it, but if he did, that would make up for it.

Instead, I find myself eyeing a pack of boxer briefs, not unlike those I'm wearing, now. The package says they're ultra-flexible and the man in the picture is holding a gym bag, so I assume they're for exercising. Can I wear them if I'm not exercising? I think I can. There are no more rules. I can wear whatever I want. With my heart pounding in my ears, I tuck them under my arm and move on to the next section.

"I'll hold that for you," Onyx offers. When I hand them over, he says, "Solid choice. What's next?"

"I don't know." I bite my lip and try not to tug on my cuff. "A shirt?"

"What kind of shirt?"

"Um."

"A tee shirt, button-down, long or short sleeve . . ." He gestures to a different section. "Blouse?"

"No."

"You could forgo a shirt, altogether, if you wanted to wear a dress."

"I've never worn a dress before."

"Nothing's stopping you."

"I don't know." I run my fingers down the silky black fabric of a cocktail dress. "Not for me—or not for me, now, at least."

"Fair, but worth considering," Onyx says. "So, what kind of shirt are you looking for?"

"I think it depends on the pants."

Onyx jogs backwards over to a different section, and I follow. "Pants it is, then."

"Comfortable pants."

"Sweatpants?"

I shake my head. "No."

"Why not?"

"Too casual."

"But you're not doing anything formal."

"No, but I'm around a lot of other people, and I want to look nice."

"What if you try them and love them? Go on. Try them on." Onyx thrusts a pair of heather-gray sweatpants into my arms before I can object.

They *are* soft. Comfortable, too, I'd bet. He's right. I should try them on, if only to know I don't want to wear them.

"Do you need me to turn around?" Onyx asks.

"You've seen me naked," I say, the edge returning to my voice. I don't have the energy to be angry with him, anymore. I should be. He deceived me—made me feel bad for him. But, off-med, he knew what he was getting into. He made the choice to be with me, then.

"Just because you've experienced something once doesn't mean you have to every time. You have agency, now, Elisha. You can give consent. Try it." He asks, again, "Do you need me to turn around?"

Before the choice can overwhelm me, I answer, "No. No, it's fine. You can stay. I don't mind. Really."

"Okay."

Onyx holds out an arm for me to steady myself on while I take my pants off. He holds them, as I slide into the legs of the sweatpants. The cotton feels soft and warm on my legs. The elastic not too tight around my hips or ankles.

"Do you like them?"

"Yes." I'm not lying, either. "I do." I shift from one leg to the next. Shove my hands into their deep pockets. "But not for now."

"You can keep them for later."

"Really?" I feel like a thief, taking more than I need for right now.

"Really. You're allowed to have more than one set of clothes. At the least, you're going to need a few sets of casual clothes, pajamas for sleeping—those stalls aren't the pinnacle of privacy—and suits for court."

"Court, right." The reality of why we're here spoils the moment like old milk poured over fresh oats. I'm picking out clothes so I can go to court because Alex's family is suing mine. A jury is going to judge me. I can't look like a fraud. I should pick out something I'd be proud for Alex to see me wear. That he'll look at and think, *That's my Elisha. My good boy.* I don't tell Onyx that, in case it's wrong.

With one swift motion, I pull the sweatpants off and drape them over Onyx's waiting arms. I actually feel most comfortable like this, in underwear and a tee shirt. The gentle compression. The freedom. Is there anything like that I can wear in public?

I look through jeans—ripped jeans, black jeans, baggy jeans. I don't love them. I feel more at home in the slacks section, flipping through pinks and greens and blues. With these, I can wear button-downs and bow ties and belts and—

"What are these?" I hold up a pair of, well, they look like my exercise bottoms, but nicer. I'm not sure they count as pants. They're stretchy and soft, sort of like the sweatpants, but much more form-fitting.

"Leggings," Onyx says.

"How do you wear them?"

"On your legs and over your ass."

"Okay."

"Oh, come on, I'm messing with you." Onyx flashes a smile, a dimple forming on his left cheek. "You mean, what do people normally wear them with."

"And on what occasion."

"They're considered casual, but you can dress them up with the right top and accessories. Want to try them on?"

"I think I do."

"Might want to put your new underwear on, first. Once we get these leggings on, you might not be able to get them off. You might not want to."

"Okay," I say, because that sounds nice.

"Do you want me to turn around, while you change your underwear?"

"No, it's okay." I push them down to my knees, then step out. Onyx's mouth hangs open as if he's going to say something, but he doesn't. Instead, he clears his throat and glances between me and a nearby rack of ties. I'm used to people seeing me naked. I'm surprised he's not more so, himself, acting the part of an on-med.

"I'm not holding your dirty underwear," he says, remembering himself. "Put them in the package."

I take the new pair out and put my old pair in. They're almost indistinguishable, except for the color. I pull the new ones on, stretch and flex, and know I made the right decision. "I like these," I say, smoothing my palms down the front of my thighs.

"Good," Onyx says. "Leggings?"

It takes a bit of maneuvering to get them on correctly, but once the fabric is untwisted and unbunched, they bend and move as easily as my underwear. I bend my knees, lifting each as high as they'll go. "They're nice. No pockets, though." I mime pushing my hands into side pockets.

"Yeah, but what are you carrying around, really?" Onyx says. A fair point.

"What kind of shirt do I wear with these?" I look down at my legs. They look long and athletic. I feel the urge to run my regular route, around the harbor. The route that begins and ends in Alex's home.

Onyx shrugs.

"You're not going to tell me, are you?"

"No."

The shirts section is the largest in the whole closet. Since I don't know where to start, I choose the closest rack. I know what I *don't* like. I can work from that. From the rainbow of tee shirts, I pull several that are long and colorful. I'd prefer something a little nicer, but they are comfortable. Most of the button-downs stop awkwardly at my waist, where they want to be tucked into slacks and belted down or strapped on with suspenders. I trace my fingers down the front of my chest, where those lines would lie.

"Why do you keep doing that?" Onyx asks. He's been mostly quiet, not wanting to influence my decisions, so the question startles me.

I don't have to answer him. Should I not, to prove it? Before I can decide, I feel the answer coming up in my throat like vomit. "I miss the feeling."

"Of what?"

"Straps. Suspenders, harnesses." I rub my hands over my arms and squeeze my own shoulders. "I like the pressure. I miss it."

"Clothes aren't the only way to meet that need," he says. "But that's for a different day."

I assume he's talking about sex, from the way he shrugged off the topic, and I decide to move on as well. From the rack, I pull a button-down that's longer than the others, with a floral print that Alex would've picked out. "This one," I say, holding it up.

This time, I don't wait for Onyx to offer to turn around. I take off my shirt, toss it on the floor, and pull the new shirt on. The sleeves come down around my hands, but no matter. I roll them up one, two, three times—up to my elbows. Button the black buttons up the front, stopping short of my neck. I'm not going to wear a tie or bow tie. I can leave it open.

"How do I look?" I ask Onyx, holding my arms out to my sides. The shirt stops in the middle of my thighs, almost like a dress.

"Pretty damn cute." His eyes trail up and down my body, like I've been looked over, so many times before. "I'd fuck you."

"You already have."

He shrugs. "I'd do it again."

I look down at my bare feet so I don't have to look Onyx in the eyes. "Can—can I ask you a question?" It's personal. I'm not sure I should.

"Of course. Whatever you want."

"Why do you keep saying stuff like that, to me? I know you were talking about sex, earlier, too." I fiddle with the cuff of my shirt so I won't play with the cuff around my wrist. Onyx doesn't like that.

"It's called flirting." He winks.

"Aren't you, um." I look in the direction of the first warehouse, where Onyx and Dutch had talked to me about their relationship. "With Dutch? Does he mind?"

"Nah, we've negotiated that we can flirt with and fuck other people; we're poly. He has another relationship with Opal, but she and I aren't a thing. We all live together because of the fake Docile shtick."

"Cool," I say, and then, "my parents are poly, too," because I don't know what else to add. "My mom and dad are each other's primary partners, as are Nora and— Well, her husband died while he was a Docile. They all loved one another. Now that Nora's husband's gone, and my mom's no longer herself . . ."

"What about you?" Onyx asks, breaking the silence. "Ever consider multiple partners?"

"Before I sold our debt, I'd never considered any partners, to be honest. Didn't have the energy, after taking care of the farm and my family and community. But now . . . I don't know. I don't think there's enough space inside me for more than one relationship at a time."

"You don't have to be in love with someone to fuck them. You know that."

"I do, I—" I know because Alex and I fucked multiple times before I fell in love with him. I'm afraid to say it out loud. Afraid the words will undo all the work I've done so Onyx and Eugenia and Verónica will believe me, that I love Alex, now. I didn't always, though, and now I wonder whether or how much it colors my memories of him. The notion is uncomfortable.

Onyx dumps the rest of the clothes I've picked out, along with my dirty underwear, into my arms and says, "You don't have to figure it all out, now. I was curious, is all. Seems like we're done here, though."

"Yeah, this is good." I readjust my hold. I'm leaving here with more than clothes. With doubts, but also with help. Maybe, a friend.

The rest of Onyx's "help" is harder. He never tells me what to do, and the constant guessing stresses me to the point of inaction, more than once. Other people at Empower Maryland follow his lead and bombard me with questions, all day.

"What do you want?"

"Are you sure you like that?"

"Maybe you only do because Alex told you."

"Try something different."

"Why?"

"Why?"

"Why?"

"Stop!" I shout, during dinner. Everyone stops. Eugenia, Onyx, Roger—half a dozen other people I've just met. They're all staring at me, these people I don't really know—who don't know me or what I've been through.

"Please, stop," I say, softening my words so they won't think I'm losing it. Regressing—I'm trying, but I'm shaking so hard, my utensils clang onto my dish when they fall from my hands. "Sorry, I'm sorry."

"Elisha, it's okay," Eugenia says. "We all know how hard you're working."

I grip my cuff to try to make my hands stay still. "I need a break; I need—"

Onyx pushes his chair out from the table with a loud screech and takes my hand. "I know what you need."

I go with him, without question. I don't need to know where we're going or why, because he does. I am happy for him to take the lead, because I can't right now. I follow with trust—without knowing or caring where we're going—and soon I find myself in a room with no windows, a desk, and a standard-issue pullout couch. A thin, expensive-looking tablet rests on the desk. A flannel shirt hangs over the arm of the unfolded sofa.

"Take off your leggings, then put your hands on the desk and look at the wall." Onyx releases me, then locks the door.

Several days ago, I'd have been afraid, but I'm not, now. I remove my leggings, leaving my shirt and underwear on, then place my palms flat on the desk and train my eyes on the gray wall. Beside me, I hear a drawer open and shut. Hear the creak of Onyx's feet as he paces back and forth. A soft shuffling of cloth.

"If I'm going too fast or too far for you, I want you to say the word 'yellow.'"

"Okay."

"And if you want me to stop, 'red.' Do you understand?"

"Yes," I whisper.

"I can't hear you."

"Yes, I understand," I say louder. *Always answer aloud when people address you.*

"Good. I'm going to touch you, but I'm not going to fuck you, do you understand?"

"Yes," I repeat, the monotony comforting. "I understand."

"Good. Spread your legs wider." Onyx toes my feet until they're where he wants them.

I feel the reassuring tension of rope wrapping around my left ankle and the cinch of movement and tightening. A quiet moan slips from between my parted lips, as my eyes flutter closed. When Onyx does the same to the right, slivers of pleasure embed themselves in my legs like splinters.

"Are you going to be loud?" Onyx's hand slides to rest on the right side of my ass. The thick, flexible fabric of my new boxer briefs the only thing separating his palm from my skin. He pushes it down.

"I . . ."

His hand disappears, leaving a cold echo in its place. Then, a hard slap and shock of pain that resonates through my body. I shudder and curl my fingers against the wooden surface of the desk. Arch my back. Whimper.

"Yes."

"Good," Onyx says. "You're so pent up." His palm collides with my ass again; fingers dig into the flesh. "Let it out."

I suck air through my teeth, hissing. Holding my breath until his next slap knocks it free from my lungs. I welcome his switch to the other side and pull at the ropes around my ankles when he returns to the right, hitting the throbbing spot over and over until my limbs tingle and I can't hold myself up anymore.

My elbows thud against the desk, as I fall onto my forearms. I rest my sweaty forehead on the backs of my hands and catch my breath.

Onyx slides his hand over the swell of my ass, up my back, and rests it on my left shoulder as he bends over, beside me. "How are you feeling?"

"Good," I whisper.

"Do you want more, or do you want to stop?"

"I want to stop."

"Too much pain?"

I shake my head. "Can't stand up."

"Okay, let me untie you. Don't move yet." Onyx's weight disappears, but I feel his fingers at my ankles, the warm friction of rope sliding against my skin, and cold heat of blood rushing back into my feet. I don't move until he returns and says, "Easy, now."

Slowly, I bring my feet closer together. My knees wobble, but Onyx puts an arm around my waist, carrying some of my weight. "Would you like some water?"

"In a minute."

"Do you want to lie down?"

I nod. Onyx helps me to the pullout couch, where I sprawl on my stomach. "Thank you," I say.

"Any time you need something like this, let me know," he says. "Will you be okay while I get you some water?"

I nod, my energy gone, my body tenderized. If Onyx returns, I don't know. I'm asleep before he can.

52

ALEX

When Dutch comes to visit me at Ellicott Hart, I'm allowed a pair of red shorts without a belt, a blue-and-white-striped long-sleeved shirt, and casual loafers without laces. A mockery of sailing wear. After trying to leave, twice, I've been labeled a danger to myself and others. My suite has been downgraded to a dormitory-sized room with furniture that's fixed to the walls and floor. My restricted internet, disabled. I'm surprised they let me have visitors at all.

"You've looked better," Dutch says, as we stroll through a gated courtyard.

We've been given the space to ourselves, but I can still see the orderlies watching us from a distance. I glance at the locked wrought-iron gate, wondering how quickly I could scale it.

"I hate it here," I say, smiling as we pass a security camera poking out of a hanging flowerpot.

"I heard you trashed your first room," Dutch says calmly, but tight-lipped. Unimpressed.

I hate that I feel the need to prove myself. He should be on my side. "They filled it with comforting clothes and photographs and books. It smelled and felt like home—home before Elisha. They wanted me to forget."

"So, you destroyed it."

"Yes."

"Well, if you want to get out of here, you need to chill out," he scolds me.

"But—"

"No. Stop." Dutch glares at me. "I'm sure it feels good to rebel, but you aren't helping yourself, which means you're not helping Elisha. You do still care about him, right?"

I lower my voice. I don't think anyone can hear me, but the confession feels illicit, here. I'm supposed to be conforming to my father's standards. "Of course I do."

"Then calm down. Play along with"—he waves his hand in the air—"whatever they want from you. I'm serious. If you want to get through this trial without sending Elisha and his family to debtors' prison—" I open my mouth to object, but Dutch cuts me off. "Yes, that could happen, so you need to play along."

"With their lies?" Frustration creases my forehead. I am barely keeping myself from trashing this garden, too. Its marble busts of old rich Marylanders. There's even one of my grandmother.

"Yes," Dutch snips.

I want to hit something—have wanted to hit something since Dad kidnapped me and dropped me in this fucking place. "I'm tired of playing along. That's all I've done my whole life."

"Then you should be good at it. Stop acting like someone who needs to be controlled, or they'll do what they need to do to control you. A locked room, restraints. Dociline. I heard you went full Mr. Hyde when your expert interviewed you. You're making their case for them. They're arguing that Elisha changed you."

"He did."

Dutch draws a breath, then huffs it out, as if he was about to say something. Presses his closed fist against his lips, then points at me. "Not like you changed him, though. You *brainwashed* him. Your attorneys are claiming Elisha *seduced* you, as if they're the same thing."

"He didn't seduce me. He shouldn't even love me."

Dutch rolls his eyes. "No shit."

Even though I just said so, it hurts when Dutch agrees. Just because I know I don't deserve Elisha's love doesn't mean I don't want it. I want him so badly—more than anything. I'd give it all up,

I think, to have him back. Bishop Laboratories. The penthouse. The money.

I rethink that last one. Giving up my money means up giving up freedom. It means helplessness. Means this. I don't know, when it comes down to it, if I'm brave enough to do that, even as much as I love Elisha.

"How's he doing?" I'm afraid of the answer. That he's either *better* without me—flourishing away from my influence, like I wanted—or *worse*. Depressed, suicidal. I should want the former, but I miss him.

"He's—Onyx is—" Dutch clears his throat. "We're helping him."

Nothing in that sentence sounds right. "Who's 'we'? You and Onyx? Your Docile is helping with Elisha?"

Dutch clasps his hands and sits on a nearby bench. Taps his heel on the ground. Bites his lip. *Fidgets*. CFOs don't fidget.

"What's going on?" I sit close to him. "Tell me. I can handle it."

"Can you?" he says, as if to himself.

"Things literally can't get any worse. So, yeah, I want the details on Elisha."

"Okay." Dutch smiles—another fake for the cameras. "I'll tell you, but you can't react badly."

"Fine." I maintain my facade for anyone who might be watching. "I promise."

"Elisha's at Empower Maryland."

I feel the heat rise in my chest, and it's an effort to keep my promise, not let it show on my face. "I'm sorry, what?"

Dutch sighs. "I knew you'd be upset."

"How'd they get him?"

"I drove him there. Alex . . ." Dutch looks me dead in the eyes, the echo of a smile still on his face. "I work with Empower Maryland."

I know I heard him say he works with Empower Maryland, but those words clash with my image of Dutch Townsend: Bishop Labs' CFO, Patron of two Dociles and partaker of everyone else's. One of my closest and oldest friends—how—even if it was true—

I don't know how to respond, especially not in public. So, I keep smiling until the muscles in my cheeks grow sore. "Is this a joke? Did Dad tell you to say this for some reason?"

"Why would he do that? He doesn't know. No one does." Dutch glances nervously around the garden. Fiddles with cuff links no Empower Marylander would deign to wear, straightens a tie they'd roll their eyes at. "For once, I'm being honest with you."

I still can't believe it, much less form a coherent thought. Say anything that isn't *What the fuck?* "You work with the people who protested at our senior prom. Who regularly print trash in the *City Paper* about me?"

Dutch nods.

"For how long?"

He shrugs. "Does it matter?"

"Yes!"

"Shh!"

"Yes," I whisper. "You're one of my best friends. I've confided everything in you and you've been lying to me. For, what, months?"

I wait.

"Years?"

Dutch stares at me, jaw clenched. "Sometimes I forget how privileged and sheltered you are."

"What's that supposed to mean?" We work in the same place, live the same lifestyle, hang out with the same damn people. How can he say that to me as if I'm a different monster than he is?

"It means we're not the same person, Alex. At no point during our friendship did you ever stop and think that I might have a different view of the world after growing up in the fucking Silo? I mean, I guess we were friends as kids, but I don't remember. I went on Dociline when I was *seven* and didn't get off until I was twelve. Do you realize how much therapy it took for me to feel semi-normal again? I'm still dealing with it, for fuck's sake. Your parents owned me, Alex. It feels weird calling what we had 'friendship.'"

Dutch's words hover between us like an invisible barrier. Ages seven through twelve. When I was a kid and Dutch was one of three people who played with me, regularly. I knew on some level that he was on Dociline at the time, but also didn't. We were kids and, surprise, my parents didn't teach me to pay attention. Even now, I remember them fondly. Those years are a gaping black hole in his life.

"You were a child, so I can't blame you for not comprehending that Jess and I were incapable of refusing to play with you. But, for fuck's sake, Alex, you're an adult, now."

He looks directly at me and I don't dare avoid him.

"Jess and I worked our asses off at the lab to pay for college and graduate school and we still ended up with debt. Luckily, once you had your degree, you were handed the highest-paying job in the company and brought us along with you."

"Because you deserved it," I say.

"Of course we did, but that's beside the fucking point. Lots of people deserve the job your parents handed to you. People as qualified, who work as hard as or harder than you, Alex, and have no chance of achieving your success. I'm grateful for the opportunities our friendship's provided, don't get me wrong. But we do not have the same worldview."

"You've always seemed content. You love your life, the parties, the work—at times it seemed even more than I did. If I'd known you were unhappy . . ." I don't have a right to feel hurt, but I do. "You could've told me."

Dutch laughs to himself. "Could I have? You can only barely understand now because, for the first time in your life, you can't fix something by throwing money at it."

I look down at my laceless shoes, ashamed. "I've only ever tried to help."

"I know and you're still my friend, but you have a lot of work to do. Both out there"—Dutch gestures toward the city, then touches his chest—"and in here. This trial is a big deal. If you want to help, if you actually consider yourself my friend and Elisha's partner, then listen to my advice. Play along with your attorneys and get out of here. Be quiet. Trust that we have everyone's best interests at heart."

"I trust you," is all I say, afraid that more will get me in trouble. I don't want Dutch to hurt, don't want him or Jess upset with me, don't know if I even deserve them, anymore. Don't deserve Elisha. He's right. I should focus on getting out of here rather than throwing tantrums. Being selfish.

"Okay. Good." Dutch pauses, glances at his watch, and rests his hand on my shoulder. "I have to go. Please don't do anything stupid." With that, he leaves.

I breathe the humid summer air deep into my lungs and relax against the bench. Trust Dutch. Trust Elisha. Trust a group of people who hate me and my family and everything we stand for. I have to try.

53

ELISHA

I wait in one of the empty offices, for our defense expert to arrive. A psychologist, Verónica told me. Someone we hired to examine me and provide a report. I can't help but wonder whether the psychologist has also seen Alex, and how he's doing. I wish someone would tell me where he is and when I can see him, again.

A knock on the open door startles me. I shift on the wooden chair, reminding myself of the bruises Onyx gave me, yesterday. They still hurt. I like them more than I thought I would, even more because no one has to know, unless I tell them.

"Elisha Wilder?" A tall Black man with graying hair pokes his head into the room.

"Yes." He's a doctor and I'm no one. A debtor. A Docile. Not either, anymore, even though I don't feel like myself free of those words. I'm not sure if I'm supposed to stand. I rise enough to shake his hand when he approaches the table.

"I'm Dr. Gerald O'Connor. You can call me Gerald."

"Nice to meet you," I say, returning to my seat.

"You as well. Do you mind?" He gestures to the chair opposite mine.

"No."

"Do you know why you're here?" he asks, while removing a tablet from his briefcase.

"Yes," I say, relieved to be able to answer at least one of his questions correctly.

He retrieves a stylus, taps and slides it a few times over his tablet, before resting. His attention is on me, now. "Why don't you tell me—in your own words."

"You're going to ask me questions to see how I'm doing." I can do this. I can answer questions. I don't even have to ask any of my own. This is easy.

"I am. Your attorneys hired me to perform a psychological evaluation."

I want to ask if he's talked to Alex, too. "Have . . ." There are no rules. Ask.

"I'm sorry?" He pushes the side of his ear forward.

Nothing came out. I wasn't confident. I can do better. "Have you spoken with Alex?"

His forehead scrunches up. "I'm sorry?"

"Are you examining Alex, too?"

"Oh, Elisha, I'm only examining you. The plaintiffs will hire their own expert to examine Alex, if they want. You do know you're opposing parties in this lawsuit, yes?"

"I do, sorry." My face burns with embarrassment. I shove my hands between my knees. I'm wearing colorful slacks today, a button-down shirt, and a jacket. A tie with a gold clip. Suspenders. The compression feels like armor.

"Are you concerned about Alex?"

"Yes. Only because I haven't seen or heard from him for a while and I miss him."

"You miss the person who's suing you."

"Alex isn't really suing me. His dad is. Alex loves me."

"And do you love him?" Gerald looks at me over the golden metal frames of his glasses.

"Yes?" I say, more like a question than I mean to. My breath catches, like there's a "but." Gerald tilts his head as if he is also expecting more. "But no one believes me. I'm not even sure Alex does, to be honest." I dig my fingernails into the heels of my hands, under the table. "Is this the kind of stuff I'm supposed to tell you? I'm sorry. I don't usually talk this much. I'm usually better behaved."

"You're perfectly fine, Elisha. Would you mind telling me why people—Alex, even—say you can't love him?"

I bring my hands onto the table and clasp them, so I won't hurt myself in front of him. I know the answer to this question. "Because I was his Docile."

"But you refused Dociline."

"Yes."

"So, you were fully aware of everything happening to you. Unlike other Dociles, you were capable of getting to know Alex. Perhaps, even, of falling in love?"

I know this one, too. Alex's words burned themselves into my brain. Into my heart.

Because you're not you, anymore. You're not Elisha Whatever-Your-Surname-Was. You're just Elisha, my Docile. A drone.

Do you really believe you have any free will left? Prove me wrong. Show me there's a sliver of a human being left in there.

Every second you're with me, I hurt you more—change you more. You become less of yourself. That's why you can't be with me.

"But I can't *not* be with you."

"I'm sorry?"

"I don't know how."

"Elisha?" Gerald leans his elbows on the table. "What were you saying?"

I struggle to lift my eyes. "I can't love him because I'm not me. At least, that's what people tell me. I don't know who else I'm supposed to be. I'm still me, just different. People change, all the time."

"That they do. Can you describe to me, in your own words, how you've changed since meeting Alex Bishop?" Gerald writes something on his tablet, then relaxes back in his chair and folds his hands in the same position as mine.

This sounds like a question I can get wrong, so I look for the right answer. "I've learned a lot," I start. "Alex paid for me to see tutors in subjects I'd never even heard of. For athletics and arts."

"Anything else?"

"Um." Everyone else seems to think I've changed. What's different about me, and what's wrong with being different? "I dress nicer."

"Quite fashionable. Did you pick that out, yourself?"

I bite my lip. "Yes, but it took me a long time. Hours. I think Onyx got frustrated with me. I'm not good at picking out my own clothes, yet."

"What does that mean? Did you not pick out your own clothes when you lived with Alex?"

"No." I huff a laugh. "Alex did. He knows what he likes."

"And was that okay with you? Did you like having your outfit decided for you, every day?"

"Oh yes. It's a huge relief." I'm able to relax my hands, stretching my fingers as I think about the clothes laid out on the bed.

"What else did Alex decide for you?"

I shrug. "Everything. How I styled my hair, where I stood or sat, whether I spoke and what I said, who touched me, where I slept, who I slept with."

"So, it would be safe to say that Alex told you what to do."

"Yes."

"And you listened?"

"Of course."

"How did that make you feel?"

"Good. I liked making Alex happy."

"Was there ever a time, for example, when you first met Alex, that you didn't like making him happy?"

The question stumps me. Not because I don't understand, but because I don't remember. My early days with Alex are a blur. In my head, I run through the times Alex punished me. I know I disobeyed, and I try to remember whether it was on purpose.

"He didn't believe me when I told him Dociline hurt my mother. I didn't like that, because I was answering his question honestly and he told me I was lying. I was trying to follow his rules and he didn't believe me." The anger of writing a hundred lines overwhelms me. My cuff chained to a desk in the Silo, surrounded by thousands of Dociles while I wrote how *I will control my attitude*.

How *I will not lie to Alex.* How, afterwards, he took me to bed and made me call myself his good boy. The shame burns across my cheeks, all over again. I look away, so Gerald won't see.

"I'm sorry to hear about your mother. You can tell me about her, if you'd like, Elisha. I'll believe you."

"Thank you, but I'd rather not." I'm surprised how easy it is to say no. How right it feels.

We're silent, for a moment. Gerald out of respect, I think.

"I don't think I liked him, at first," I say, looking past Gerald. It's easier if I don't look at him. "But he was so good to me. He cared, like no one else did. I know it sounds stupid—everyone tells me it is—but he cared more about me the longer we were together. When I was sad, he spent time with me. Asked me about my feelings. Laid with me or gave me pleasure. Made me forget."

"He sounds like a good Patron."

"He was."

"What changed when he amended your contract? When he took you back to the farm."

I feel the hollowed pit in my chest. The place where Alex scooped my heart out and left me empty. "It hurt."

"The records I received show you attempted suicide."

He knows. Why is he even asking, when he's read about me at my worst? "I didn't listen."

"Didn't listen to what?"

"Alex. I heard his voice. He told me to stay awake. But I fell asleep. I couldn't keep my eyes open any longer." A sob hits me like a wave. I gasp, shudder. Close my eyes. "Back on the farm, no one wanted me anymore. Not Alex or Dad, and I wasn't allowed to see Abby. Even Nora told me to go. I was exhausted. I wanted to disappear. Thought it might be easier for my family. That it would stop the hurt."

"Have you ever felt like you wanted to disappear, since then, or only that once?"

"I think about it sometimes, but I don't want to leave if there's a chance I'll be with Alex. He didn't want me, then, but he wants me, now. I know he does."

"I'm sure you'll get to see him, again," Gerald says, before reaching into his briefcase. "Can you do one thing, for me, and then we're all finished?"

"Yes."

He sets two thick cardboard boxes with clear lids on the table. Inside each, I can see a different pocket square. The one on the left, red with tiny blue bicycles embroidered on it. The right, purple with pastel orange flowers. "Choose one."

I look between them. "For what?"

"For you. You can have one. My treat."

"Oh." This is a test. Gerald is a doctor, and this is a test, and it's going to be used in court and *what if I get it wrong?* If Alex were here, he'd know what to do.

54

ALEX

After Dutch leaves, I start to play along. I pass all their tests, pretend to have realized the error of my ways, and act like I'm glad to be suing Elisha. It works. I hate myself, but it works.

I'm given my suite and shoelaces back. My belt and the right to leave my room for meals. Attorneys arrive, not long after, to prepare me for my deposition. The older, a partner named Reginald Moore, who doesn't tell me to call him Reg or Reggie. He wears a black suit, matching oxfords, and a jade-green tie. His associate, Gabriela Hemsworth, wears a charcoal-gray skirt suit. Serious, professional clothes, both of them. I'm underdressed and embarrassed, but act polite and accommodating. This is another test. Hopefully, if I'm a good witness, I'll be allowed to leave.

I almost feel like my old self when we sit down, together. Ellicott Hart lets me into the conference room like someone who can be trusted not to throw a chair out the window and jump. Like someone who doesn't need to be controlled.

When they leave, I stand with the energy of someone who's also going home, only forgetting I'm not once we're in the foyer and several security persons take a step closer as if I'm going to make a run for it. I watch them go with want building behind my sternum. To go home. To my apartment the way it was: soft lights framing a floor-to-ceiling view of the harbor, scent of roast lamb wafting from the kitchen, taste of an accompanying spicy Syrah, the cool crumple of a down feather comforter as I climb into bed, and Elisha.

That place doesn't exist anymore. I destroyed it.

Tonight, while I try to fall asleep, my mind replays childhood memories of Dutch and Jess. Guilt colors the image of three kids chasing one another around the Silo. Of playing scientist, with beakers and goggles, baking soda and vinegar. Food coloring—only until we stained my dad's desk.

Dutch doesn't remember this.

I'm unsure whether I ever fall asleep. Whether they're memories or nightmares that keep my brain on edge, through the night.

My attorneys—though it feels wrong describing them as representing my interests—schedule my deposition at their downtown office. I should look pitiful, not deranged, they explained. Wounded, Reginald suggested. Not a difficult look for me to pull off.

Each of my attorneys pulls a tablet from their briefcase, while I sit awkwardly between them. Nothing in my hands while they scroll through documents. Gabriela prints one wirelessly, a small stack of papers materializing on the conference room table. The firm must have a vault like mine and Bishop Labs'. I feel ashamed for missing the luxury of being able to conjure papers or jewelry, like the halo I made for Elisha's angel costume. Feel ashamed for remembering how beautiful he looked and for missing him like that.

When the conference room door opens, and the defense attorney enters, my nerves begin to tremble beneath my skin. A court reporter slips in, while all the attorneys shake hands and discuss logistics, situating herself at the head of the long oak table.

Then, I see Elisha. He's scanning the room, nervously. Smoothing down a black floral tie—did he pick that out himself? It looks stunning against his white shirt and tweed jacket. When our eyes meet, I realize I've been staring. Am I allowed to shake his hand, like the attorneys did? I don't think so. My lips parts with words unspoken, kisses withheld. Before I can make a decision, an arm reaches out and steers Elisha into a chair.

"Would you like something to drink, Alex?" Gabriela snags my attention.

"Water, thanks," I say, my eyes flickering back toward Elisha.

She sets a cold glass down on a coaster, in front of me, and finally I have something to do with my hands. I take a sip, nearly sloshing it onto the table.

Get it together, I think in Dutch's voice. I wish he were here. He always knows exactly how to behave in public. His advice earned my privileges back, at Ellicott Hart. Hopefully, it'll earn me a ticket out of there, altogether. I'm sure a review will get back to my father if I nail this deposition—or if I fuck up it up. I can't go back.

"Ready to get started, Verónica?" Reginald asks, clicking the top of his stylus.

"Yes." She sets an actual three-ring binder on the table, along with a legal pad and two pens. Somehow, her supplies look more impressive.

"I'm ready, too," says the court reporter. "Go ahead, whenever you'd like."

I'm still watching Elisha when his attorney introduces herself to me and asks me if I've ever been deposed before. I have to force my eyes on to hers while she explains how this works.

"It's okay to say you don't know the answer, if you don't. You can ask me to repeat myself, if you don't understand, and ask for a break, at any time."

"Okay."

"Can you state your full legal name for the record, and spell it?" she asks.

I give her my name, and my address. As I answer, I imagine the empty penthouse and feel like a fraud. Technically, I still own it. But if Verónica Vasquez visited, she'd find cold marble counters, expanses of hardwood, and air absent of piano. I answer her questions about where I grew up, my education and work history, all by rote. I almost forget she's cross-examining me, until she asks when and where I met Elisha. At the sound of his name, he looks up at me.

"We met in January of this year, at the Office of Debt Resolution. I'd set up an interview with him."

"How did you come across him?"

"I reviewed the debtor database."

"Did you specially select all the debtors you saw that day or were some selected for you?"

"Objection," Reginald says, without looking up. "You can answer."

He told me they might object, for the record, but it still throws me. Why am I giving information that could be used against me? "Most of the debtors were selected for me. When I arrived, I met with Charlene—"

"Can you tell us who she is? In fact, please assume we don't know who anyone is."

I look between Reginald and Gabriela, the latter of whom nods. "Charlene Williams works at the ODR—the Office of Debt Resolution," I add. For the record. "She was assigned as my Patron Liaison, to curate a selection based on my data. Dozens of debtors register, every day. There's no way someone like me has time to look through everyone. What if I missed the perfect match?"

"So, Elisha was on this curated list that Charlene gave you, when you arrived?"

"No," I say, with a hint of surprise in my voice, as if I'm realizing the answer, for the first time. "She'd used information from my father and the Bishop Labs Board. Her selections didn't suit me."

"Then, how did you end up arranging an interview with him?"

I remember, now, charming Charlene. Not that I conned her; she knew that by helping me she'd gain my favor and possible advancement. She was ambitious. We both were. I tell Verónica how she showed me the larger database, how I picked Elisha's profile.

"Given the events you just described, would you say Elisha 'targeted' you?"

I hear Reginald's deep, gruff voice, from beside me, again. "Objection. Phrasing."

"Okay." Vasquez clasps her hands in front of her and leans on the table.

I know what she was trying to ask, and she's right. Elisha didn't target me. I targeted him. I knew what I wanted. I'm used to getting it.

"Did Elisha have a similar chance to review profiles and select those he wanted to meet?"

"I assume so."

"What do you mean by that?"

"I've never participated in the ODR as a debtor, but I know they're supposed to be able to pick who they meet. I assume because I can't speak for him. I don't know what he did that morning, before I interviewed him."

"But you would say that you went out of your way to find Elisha's profile, correct?"

"Yes." I do my best to remain expressionless. Inside, I'm rooting for Verónica Vasquez.

"Thank you. Now, Elisha refused Dociline. That's an undisputed fact." I nod. "How did that make you feel?"

"I was shocked. I don't know if that answers your question."

"There's no wrong answer," Vasquez says. "Is that everything, or . . ."

"No. I was nervous." Gabriela told me to emphasize how surprised I was, how I struggled to adjust to living with an off-med. I'm so used to portraying confidence, despite the truth, that being vulnerable actually feels good. "There was a lot of pressure on me to perform. To show the Board and my father—the whole world, really—that I could handle a Docile, with or without Dociline."

"How did you respond to those nerves?"

I shrug. "I formed a plan."

Verónica leans forward, smiling hungrily, like a predator ready to pounce. "What kind of plan?"

I feel the defensiveness creeping up inside me. I know where she's going with this, and I don't want to let her paint me as a creep. I made a plan because I needed one.

"'Plan' may be an exaggeration. I came up with a set of rules, to help us function together. You have to understand that Elisha was a stranger to me, at the time."

I glance at him when I say his name. He quickly looks down at the table. Why won't he look at me? Did I hurt him that much? Has Empower Maryland already turned him against me?

I think he'll be better when he hates you. Because he should.

"Alex?" Vasquez says, angling for my eyes.

"Sorry." I don't look at my attorneys. Don't want to see their disappointment at my hesitation. They're probably noting it, to share with my dad, later.

"You were explaining your rules, and how Elisha was a stranger—"

"Right. I came up with a set of rules. You wouldn't let a stranger live in your house without establishing basic ground rules. People do that with roommates—and you're supposed to trust them. I didn't know or trust Elisha, yet, so the rules were strict, but not out of line with the behavior of my friends' Dociles."

"So, how many rules would you say you came up with?"

"Probably half a dozen. I'm not sure how many." Elisha would know the exact number. I resist asking him—and looking at him. "I created rules over time, as I needed them. Things like, don't bite your nails. Stuff you don't think of until you're at the Governor's charity event and your Docile is standing beside you, chewing on his fingers. It's unsightly," I say, and hate myself for meaning it. For feeling the urge to correct him, still.

"Did you feel in control of the situation?"

"Sometimes," I admit. I've never shared my anxieties about training Elisha with anyone other than Jess. I couldn't, even though I doubted myself. I know my lack of confidence will play well into Dad's narrative of what happened, and it's the truth, so I say, "Less so, in the beginning. Honestly, I had no idea what I was doing, and was under severe pressure to act as if I did. The Board"—I don't say "Dad"—"threatened to remove me as CEO of Bishop Labs if I proved incapable of handling a personal Docile."

"Did you continue to feel like that? Like you had no idea what you were doing?"

"It would surface, every now and then. I am human." I smile for effect. "It got easier the more I got to know Elisha. His habits, interests, tendencies. Once I came to trust him. The better I got to know him, the easier it was for me to—" Control him. That's the answer, but I can't say it. I'm supposed to be the one who was seduced by Elisha. Dutch said I should go along with it. Elisha must know. He'll forgive me, if I . . . Will he? "—live with him."

My answer falls flat. Falls short of the truth and yet passes for it. For the first time since this deposition began, I'm afraid to look at him.

55

ELISHA

Verónica had told me, if I wanted to attend Alex's deposition, I would have to follow the rules. And I did want to attend, because I wanted to see him. Wasn't sure if I was supposed to admit that to my attorney. I definitely wasn't supposed to admit how much the promise of rules tempted me. Onyx never gave me rules; he barely gave me mealtimes.

When I entered the lush conference room at Betts, Griffin & Moore, I felt confident. Recited Verónica's rules silently to myself.

Don't speak unless spoken to—especially not to Alex, his family, or attorneys. Don't look happy to see him. If you feel like you're going to cry, cry. Don't be afraid to take a tissue. Refuse any food or beverages offered to you.

Since I followed the rules, my mouth is gummy and dry. I spend more time staring at Alex's glass of water than at Alex, which is probably good. If I look at him—if our eyes meet for more than a second—I'm afraid he'll see how much I miss him. How much I fucking *hurt*.

So, I listen. I don't look. I listen while Verónica points out that, if anything, Alex targeted me at the ODR, and that Alex was the one who made the rules. Hear Alex admit he was nervous. That he didn't know what he was doing.

Alex told me his opinion was the only one that mattered. I always thought that meant he knew everything—he seemed to. I never knew he was under so much pressure.

"What's your opinion on Dociline?" Verónica asks.

Alex shifts. "Can you clarify what you mean?"

I hold my breath. He shouldn't have to clarify; he should know. I need him to get this right.

"Do you think it's good or bad? Effective, or needs improvement? That it helps or hurts people?"

"Objection," says Alex's attorney. The man. I think he's Moore, but don't know because I was told not to speak to him. "This is a fact-gathering deposition with regard to Dr. Bishop's relationship with Elisha Wilder. We're not here for his opinions on Dociline."

I shrink, but Verónica doesn't back down. "Dr. Bishop is an expert on Dociline and Elisha not only refused it, but alleges it harmed his mother. Dr. Bishop admits that Elisha's refusal to take Dociline put him under pressure from his parents to keep Elisha under control. Dociline, and Dr. Bishop's opinion regarding same, is relevant, and I'd direct your client to answer my question."

"Go ahead," Moore says. "If I think this veers off path, I'm going to file a Motion to Quash."

"You do that," Verónica says. "Dr. Bishop, your opinion?"

I close my eyes. Beneath the table, I clasp my fingers so tightly the bones ache.

"I, uh . . ." He pauses so long I think he might not speak again. "I think it's a wonderful invention that I'm honored to have participated in developing. It's changed a lot of lives. Helped a lot of people."

His answer rings in my ears, overpowering the sound of Verónica's voice. The edges of my vision fizzle to gray as I fixate on the wall behind him. That's what he thinks? After all this time? No, he's supposed to play along with his attorneys. Please let him be playing along and not mean that. I close my eyes and breathe, like Onyx and I practiced.

The shuffle of papers brings me back. Verónica's taking something out of her binder. "I'd like to mark this as Exhibit B."

"What is it?" Moore asks, leaning on the table, as if he's about to leap across it and tackle the papers from her hands.

"Alex Bishop the Third's laboratory notes on Formula 3.0. Alex, would you please read that last paragraph onto the record?"

"Sure." He takes the photocopy, glossing his eyes over the text before finding his place. "It says: 'I'm still not happy with version 3.0.7 and would prefer to abandon the attempt, altogether. Every Docile who injected 3.0.7 fell so deep into its thrall that caretakers had to instruct them to perform basic bodily functions. It's unsafe and, frankly, makes more work for Patrons. 3.0.8 is only mildly better in that the Dociles can survive on their own. They still need to be told to eat and drink, though."

"Formula 3.0.8 is the current formula—the one headed for the market—is it not?"

"I—" I can't watch Alex grasp for words. I don't know what I want him to say, whether I want him to have the answer or for him to stumble. To give up. "I honestly can't answer that question since I've been off the project for some time, now."

"Would you consider Dociline dangerous?"

"Objection," Moore says. "Leading the witness."

Verónica continues as if he didn't interrupt her. "Would you describe the formula you just read about, Formula 3.0.8, as dangerous?"

Alex looks directly into Verónica's eyes as if he's expecting her to give him the answer. "Yes," he says, slowly. "Any drug that prevents a subject from eating and drinking unaided poses a danger to the person's health."

"And, did you recently visit Elisha's family?"

"I did."

"Did you meet his mother?"

"I did."

He did? He didn't tell me that. Then again, I wasn't well and he was focused on my health and I didn't think to ask. Haven't thought to ask since, either. I listen for his assessment over the pounding of my heart.

"How would you describe her?"

Moore interrupts again. "For the record, any response my client gives should reflect that the cause of Abigail Wilder's condition is unknown and has not been attributed to Dociline." He taps Alex's shoulder. "You can answer."

I risk looking directly into his eyes—letting him see I'm listening. I know I'm not supposed to, and the guilt surges hot through my body as I hold his gaze, but I need to hear this. Need him to tell me more than I need him to tell Verónica.

"I met her in the garden. She was washing clothes, but not well. Her actions were repetitive, her task never finished. When I spoke to her, she answered almost without context. Like a doll programmed to repeat a handful of phrases. She seemed peaceful," he says.

I remember thinking the same. The surge of jealousy that no one minded that my mother still acted like a Docile, but I was expected to come out of it, instantly. Why couldn't they have let me be?

My eyes burn with tears. Verónica said to cry, if I needed, but I don't want to in front of Alex's attorneys, or her, if I'm honest with myself. I don't want to cry in front of people I don't know and can't trust. Why won't they let me talk with Alex, alone?

"What did you say to Abigail when you met her?" Verónica asks.

If I watch Alex, it's like the rest of them aren't here. Like it's only us.

"I, uh . . ." He fiddles with his cuff links. "She wasn't capable of engaging in a coherent conversation, so I spoke to her family instead, to David and Nora. I offered to help her."

"Why would you do that?"

"I like helping people," Alex says. "That's always what's motivated my work on Dociline. Abigail certainly isn't going to get the treatment she needs, in the county."

"Do you have any theories as to what happened to her?"

In that instant, I watch Alex's face change. The muscles at the corners of his eyes and mouth relax. "No. I only met her for a few minutes. It would be wildly inappropriate for me to speculate about the cause of her condition."

"Would you say she acted similar to an on-med?"

"There were similarities." He stiffens. "But that is by no means a diagnosis."

"Understood," Verónica says. "Since meeting Elisha, has your opinion on Dociline changed, at all?"

I hold my breath.

"I think there's still hope for Dociline."

Hope. When I blink, Alex blurs—my thoughts blur. He still thinks there's a good version of Dociline. Dutch told me Alex would have to say things he didn't believe. How am I supposed to tell if this is one of them? He was always honest with me. I don't like this version of Alex. Didn't like it when I was his Docile and he tried to prove how much *good* it was doing. How innovative he was. I watch his lips move, but can't process the sound. Close my eyes. Breathe.

"Thank you," Verónica says, beside me. "Just one more question and then I'm finished here." I am glad those are the words I hear next. I don't know how much more of this I can take. "Do you love Elisha?"

"No."

"Alex?" I say out loud before I can stop myself. Verónica might scold me, but this is important. How can he say— They told him to say that. It's not real. This is what he's supposed to say. It'll be fine. It'll—

"You told your own expert that you did love Elisha," Verónica says, ignoring my outburst.

"I was mistaken." Alex looks straight at Verónica, as if I'm not in the room. As if every one of his words isn't crushing me. "I've had time away from Elisha—time to reflect. To realize that, even though I did feel strongly for him, it wasn't love."

I can't listen to this, anymore. I'm not going to cry in front of these attorneys—in front of Alex. He'll know I can't take it. I'm not strong enough, yet. My leather chair glides silently over the carpet as I push away from the table, stand, and leave without looking back. Why would Empower Maryland do this to me? Why would they make me watch?

56

ALEX

When the deposition finally ends, Dad shows up and debriefs with his attorneys. I watch them through the glass wall, hands folded in my lap, attempting to look as cool and patient as possible. Well behaved. The chair where Elisha sat is still turned toward the door from when he leapt out of it. I want to sit in it. See if the leather is still warm. If it still feels like him.

When he finally dismisses Gabriela and Reginald, Dad enters the conference room, alone, walks over to the bar cart, and pours me a whiskey. He didn't give me good news the last time we drank together, so I'm not expecting any now.

"You did well, Son." Dad clinks his glass against mine, sitting untouched on the table, then drinks.

Did well means I betrayed Elisha. I wonder if I can ask Dutch to tell him I didn't mean it, the next time he visits. Whenever that is. All I can bring myself to say now is "Thanks."

"Your doctors and I think you're well enough to check out of Ellicott Hart."

I lift my eyes to meet Dad's, feel a smile tugging at my lips. Maybe I'll be able to tell Elisha myself. "I can go home?"

Dad looks at his drink while he responds. "Well, I don't know about home, yet. Your mother and I would like to have you close by. For your safety."

"You want me to move back in with you and Mom?" There goes any hope of talking to Elisha. Living with my parents might be worse than Ellicott Hart. I don't have the energy required to constantly please them.

"Oh, no." He throws back the rest of his whiskey, a signal that this conversation is over. "Nothing like that. We discussed some ideas with your doctors and think the lab would be a good place to start—you still have personal quarters there. Correct?"

"I do." Behind several layers of security to trace my comings and goings. Eyes on me at all times. The Silo, no matter how luxurious its accommodations, is little better than Ellicott Hart. The only advantage is its location in the city.

"Good." He pats my back and stands. "Dutch has agreed to remain your conservator, so he will continue to manage your spending and approve necessary travel. I think it'll be good for you to have something to focus on, even if we can't have you working on Dociline. Lots of paperwork to do at the lab!" Dad clicks his tongue and winks at me, then disappears.

I give him a few minutes to leave. There's nothing I want less than small talk with Dad or, heaven forbid, further discussion of my deposition. At least I'll be reporting to Dutch rather than the doctors. Will he let me see Elisha or does that go against his plans with Empower Maryland? He's still my friend.

I reach for the speakerphone in the middle of the conference table. The room mutes my voice from passersby, engineered to keep conversations private with its carpet and fabric paneling.

"Hello?"

"Hey, it's Alex," I say, peeking out into the reception area. Only the receptionist remains, my attorneys having returned to their offices. "I need a favor."

57

ELISHA

I sit beside Verónica, in the legal clinic, while she tells Eugenia about the deposition. How Alex disclosed information that showed he manipulated me, rather than the alleged opposite, but that he still believes in Dociline. I don't digest most of their conversation, Alex's words still weighing on me. I have to see him.

"Excuse me," I say quietly, so they won't get mad, but they keep talking. I take a deep breath and say, "Excuse me!"

They stop and look at me. Eugenia raises her eyebrows with an air of pleasant surprise. "Yes, Elisha?" she asks.

"I want to see Alex."

"We would advise against it," she says, any trace of pleasantness disappearing from her face. "After how much he's hurt you—you're making such good process."

"Besides," Verónica adds, "you're opposing parties in a lawsuit. You shouldn't communicate with each other except through your attorneys. That's my job, to represent you. He can use your words against you, Elisha."

"He won't," I say, with as much confidence as I can muster. I believe what I'm saying, but will even more once I can talk to Alex. Confirm that he didn't mean what he said during his deposition. That he still loves me.

"Why don't you go see what Onyx is up to, instead," Eugenia says. "Work on deprogramming some more; your deposition is coming up, you know."

"Okay." I don't mean it, but I know they won't question it. Despite their efforts to undo what Alex did to me, they like it when I obey them. It feels wrong.

Verónica stands and opens the door for me. "We'll check in later, Elisha."

I say, "Okay," again, and leave. Look over my shoulder to make sure she closes the door. Find Onyx, but not for their reasons.

He's talking on the phone when I peek inside Dutch's office. "Uh-huh," he says to whomever he's talking to, looking up at the sound of my feet. "Got it. Love you, too." He sets the phone down and says, "Hey, how'd the deposition go?"

I would tell Onyx "okay," too, but he'd fight me on it. "Mostly well, but Alex said some hurtful things."

"You expected that, though." He licks a red sauce from his finger, then bites into his sandwich.

"Yes, but that didn't make it hurt any less." I should go ahead and ask, now. Get it over with; Onyx would want me to. "I need to see Alex. I was wondering if you could help me. Eugenia and Verónica said I shouldn't."

"Why do you think I'm going to help you go against your attorney's advice?"

"Because I'm making this decision on my own and I'm going to try with or without your help." I fold my arms so Onyx can't see them shaking with nerves. I can do this. "I need to know that Alex still loves me. Otherwise, what's the point in . . ." going on? Continuing to wake up every day in this place that isn't my home and put myself through the pain of trying? "I still think about hurting myself, sometimes. I don't want to."

"That's good to hear. And it sounds like you know what you want." Onyx smiles. He looks impressed and the warmth of his validation spreads through my chest.

"I do."

Turns out, Dutch had called Onyx, while I was talking to Eugenia and Verónica. Alex wanted to see me, too, but it was my conversation with Onyx that finally convinced them to help us. Dutch, Onyx explains, has been appointed Alex's conservator, so he's the only one who can arrange for us to meet.

Together, we walk down the road from Empower Maryland, past the row houses, and into the parking lot of a coffee shop. People walk in with laptops tucked under their arms and out with sweaty plastic cups of iced coffee. Onyx looks from his phone to me and says, "Well, this isn't weird at all. Meeting up in a parking lot, behind your attorneys' backs."

"Thank you for helping me," I say, hoping he isn't doubting his decision.

"Of course," he says, but that wouldn't always have been his answer. Onyx watches the black car that pulls into the parking space beside us.

Dutch steps out, looks around, holds the door open for Alex. As soon as he has two feet on the ground, I throw myself into his arms. He stumbles back as I bury myself in the dark of his hold.

"I didn't mean it," he whispers. "I'm so sorry."

"I know," I say. "I hoped."

"I can't stay long." When I pull back, Alex is looking around as if there might be snipers posted on the coffee shop. "Could we talk in the car, maybe?"

I follow Alex into the car and close the door. Reach out and press the lock. The action is simple, but still feels strange. Not my place to lock us in. But I've done it and it's done and I'm not undoing it.

"I lock doors now." I regret my words immediately. How pathetic. Who's proud of locking a door? Couldn't I have started with something more impressive?

Alex shifts, inside the dark car, so that we're facing each other. Our legs overlap. Fingers touch. He takes my hand in his. "I'm proud of you."

"You don't have to be. It's stupid."

"It's not stupid," he says, quickly. "People deserve privacy, space, control over who can access them and when."

I shake my head. "You're right. You're always right."

"Please don't—that's—I'm not always right," Alex says. "Rarely so, evidently. And look at you."

He glides his hands over my button-down; it's my favorite. The bright floral pattern reminded me of him; that's why I picked it out of the donations closet. If I'd known Alex was coming, I'd have put on jeans at least, but I was too anxious when I got back to put on anything but leggings, tight and comforting.

"I picked these out myself," I say.

"They're perfect." He runs his hand through my hair and leans closer until we're both staring at each other's lips.

I bite mine.

"Can I kiss you?" he asks.

"Yes."

Our foreheads touch, warm against each other, when we kiss. Alex's lips are as smooth as I remember, but he stiffens against me. Our eyes open, mouths part. Kissing him feels as good as I remember, and yet he feels tense. Off.

"Are you okay?" I ask.

Alex looks at his lap.

"You don't have to tell me, if you don't want," I say, "but you seem different. I know I'm different, too, so I understand, but I—I want to make sure you're okay." Maybe I shouldn't have asked. He'd tell me if he wanted me to know, right?

"I, uh." Alex flattens his palm against his forehead and presses. Lines crease his face. "It's embarrassing."

I don't know how to reassure Alex that he doesn't need to feel embarrassed in front of me, that I'll love him no matter what happened, and that my feelings are probably just as stupid. Onyx isn't the best instiller of self-confidence.

"I'm afraid you won't like who I am," I blurt out. One of us has to take the first step. Maybe mine will help Alex. "I'm afraid you only loved the person I was and that without the clothes and the comfortable bed and fancy parties or hobbies, you'll think I'm boring or . . . I don't know. I miss a lot of who I was before. I'm worried you'll miss it, too—so much that you realize you don't love me, now."

"Well, I'm afraid you won't like who I am, now that you have a choice." Alex squeezes my hand. "I'm afraid you only loved the person who could pay for your tutors, dress you in nice clothes, and teach you piano. I can't do anything for you, anymore." He holds his open palms out as if his money is slipping through his fingers, right before him. "I don't know who I am without it." Alex is looking past me.

I open my mouth to tell him he's wrong. That stuff makes life easier and softer and more comfortable. That money allows you to work out for fun, make art, and try food you can't grow in your backyard. But he's more than his bank account; he's smart and caring and creative. I love Alex because of who he is, not his ability to throw money at things.

"I'm not allowed to go home—not sure I have a home, anymore." He snaps out of his daze, then, looking directly into my eyes. His are so green. "My family placed me under a conservatorship. I don't have access to my own money, can't leave my quarters at the Silo without Dutch's permission, or see anyone he doesn't want me to. He's my friend, but he still answers to the Board; there's only so much he can cover up."

I force myself to swallow. To imagine life without Alex. Only Empower Maryland. Only working and fighting. Always tired, always alone. I remember what it felt like to give in. Close my eyes, and fall asleep, unsure if I'd wake back up. To stop swimming and sink. For the water to swallow me up.

No, I am here with Alex. He still loves me. I have to keep working so I can be better, for him, and fighting so that we win this lawsuit. So I can keep my family out of debt and out of prison.

"You *can* fix things without money," I say. "You have a really good education and have spent your whole life around and working with Dociline. Didn't you just say you're staying in the Silo?"

"Yeah."

"So, you said during your deposition that you offered to help my mother." I bite my lip. He's hurt me multiple times, on this front. He can't, again. "Did you mean that?"

"Of course I did." Sincerity lines his forehead as he sits forward.

I am so nervous to revive his idea, but I'm on the path now. I'm going to say it. "What if I could get her into the city?"

"You would do that?" Alex's face lights up with an eagerness I haven't seen in a long time. "I'm sure Dutch would figure out a way for me to see her—help her."

"Alex, wait!" I take a deep breath. "I need a minute." And I take it, closing my eyes and going through the breathing exercises Onyx taught me.

In, two, three, four, five.

Out, two, three, four, five.

"I know I brought up the idea, but I need you to tell me that you believe me and I need you to mean it. Tell me you believe that Dociline hurt my mother." Of course I want my mother back to the way she was before Dociline took her, but Alex needs to prove himself to me, first. He's never believed me. Why should I believe, now, that he's genuine? That he's not going to treat her like a science project?

Alex purses his lips. "I believe it is likely that Dociline contributed to your mother's disability."

"That's not enough. Is that enough? I don't know. I'm supposed to be decisive. Alex isn't always right. This—"

Alex's lips press gently against mine, stilling them. Calming my thoughts.

He's barely an inch away when I whisper, "I said all that out loud, didn't I?"

"You did."

"Sorry."

"Don't be. You're working through a lot, but I'm not going to lie to you. Partners don't lie to each other."

Did he just call us partners? I don't dare repeat it, in case he decides to take it back.

"I want to help, but I won't draw any conclusions without examining your mother. I think that's fair."

I'm nodding my head before I can get the words out. Onyx would tell me to stand my ground, but maybe Alex is right. If he and I are going to be equals, I can't demand things from him any more than he can of me. Onyx doesn't know everything any more than Alex does.

"Okay," I say.

Alex sighs relief, then glances at his watch. "I have to go. Already stayed longer than I should have, but I needed to see you. To apologize."

"It's okay," I say because I mean it, not because I think I'm supposed to. "And I think this is a good idea. I'll see if I can convince Dad and Nora to let Mom come visit me in the city."

Alex nods along, enthusiastically. I've only ever seen him this driven at the lab. "Ask"—he holds his breath while he thinks— "someone you trust if there's somewhere private, in the city, where we could set up a miniature lab. Nothing fancy. Somewhere to draw blood, administer trial drugs to counter the effects of Dociline."

"Okay." I can do this. I like this—this *having something to do.* Alex used to be my purpose. Maybe helping Mom can be, instead. "I will."

"Good." Alex bites his lip. Hard. As if he's stopping himself saying something. Then repeats, "Good."

With that, I pull the door handle. It doesn't open.

Alex presses a button and a soft click sounds in the car. "You lock doors, now."

"Yeah." A smile tugs at the corners of my mouth as I pull the handle successfully. "I lock doors."

58

ALEX

When the door to the Silo closes behind me, I know I won't be leaving any time soon. My palm sweats where I grip the handle of a suitcase we stopped to buy on the way here. Dutch needed a cover story for our outing and I needed clothes and a new phone, after Ellicott Hart confiscated mine. I regret the impulse to throw everything away. Would've been nice to bring a little bit of home with me to the Silo. Here, everyone looks at me. They know I was sent to a mental health facility. That I'm incompetent.

Without looking anyone in the eye, I take the catwalk over to the elevator and ride it down to the third floor. At least I have some privacy here. Some space to breathe and be alone.

Panels on the walls light up as I roll my suitcase through my office and past the workstation where Elisha wrote a hundred times that he would control his attitude, that he wouldn't lie to me. He didn't. I was the one who lashed out because I didn't want to hear his truth. No one had ever challenged Dociline to my face, before, except Empower Marylanders, and I'd always been taught they were rabble-rousers. Elisha wasn't one of them. Hearing it from him? How could I not feel defensive?

I still remember what he wrote in his notebook when I asked what relaxed him: being alone, the outdoors, and stars. I hope he's getting them, now. I'm the one who took them away from him, to begin with.

As soon as I start hanging my new clothes up in the armoire, someone knocks on the open door. "Hey, you." Jess pokes her head in. "Need any help moving in?"

"You heard, then?" I say with a halfhearted smile.

"Yeah, along with the entire state." She returns my smile. "But I'm glad you're back. Is Lex letting you do real work while you're here?"

I scoff. "No. I'll be chained to a desk, all day. They might as well stick me with Dociline." I pause, my suitcase half-zipped.

Jess stares at me with familiar anticipation; after years of working together, she knows when I've had an idea. "What?"

I want to ask Jess to help me with Abigail. Jess was on Dociline, as a child, and is one of the few people I trust, anymore. I look out over the Silo, at Dociles and researchers sitting opposite one another at workstations—at the hundreds of doors—and it hits me all at once that there's a person behind each one with a whole life before this, with a story like Elisha's, and people who miss them, and it makes my skin crawl.

I touch the glass wall and it frosts over, hiding my discomfort. "Do you have a minute? Will you sit with me?"

"I'm kind of busy, but . . ."

"Please."

She looks at her watch. "I haven't eaten lunch, yet."

"Call front desk." I wait until they pick up, eyes glued to Jess. "Hi, yes, would you please order two—no, make that three—steak-frites, from City Grille? They have my card on file." I assume lunch is an approved work expense. "Thank you. And send Docile number OFM58297 to my office, when the food arrives? Cheers."

Jess sits at the small dining table in the corner. "Lunch with Dociles? You really have turned over a new leaf."

I roll my eyes while I join her. "I—You'll see. Before she arrives, I need to apologize to you."

"Okay." She looks skeptical.

"I've always thought of you as my friend—one of my three best friends—but that's not entirely earned. Dutch visited me while I was at Ellicott Hart—"

Jess' face flushes with guilt. "I would've but—"

I hold up a hand to stop her. "I'm not chastising you. I wasn't keen to have visitors in that state, anyway. Dutch came to help me with this fucking lawsuit—teach me how to help Elisha, while also avoiding a permanent stay at Ellicott Hart.

"He reminded me that you and he were on Dociline for several years, when you were kids and I"—my eyes fall to my lap—"wasn't even really aware. Not until now. I knew, when I was a kid, but I never stopped to think about it and no one encouraged me to. I didn't realize you never chose my friendship. Didn't realize the difference between me working in the lab for fun and you two working so Dad would pay your university tuition. Through high school and college and graduate school, while we were getting our doctorates, I never stopped to think that we were different.

"I'm sorry for assuming we were friends, when you didn't have a choice in the matter. For never checking in with you or recognizing that our childhoods were completely different. I wouldn't blame you for not wanting to be my friend, any longer. If you've felt"—I dread saying it—"obligated."

Jess is silent for longer than feels comfortable. Until I'm squirming in my seat, wondering if I should leave. I want her help, but she would deserve some space—to cut me out of her life, if she wanted.

"Thank you for saying that," she says, finally, looking directly at me. I feel naked under her gaze. "Dutch and I fought over it, a lot, during university. Why we stayed, why I continued to work on Dociline and he continued to manage your family's money. Whether we were doing the right thing. I know he's been seeing a therapist for decades—I did, too, for a long time. But I made my peace with this place. I decided to accept you as you were and do my best to help Dociles through my research. But I honestly never expected to hear an apology like that from you."

"I would never have thought to say it." I huff a little laugh. "Apparently, I have a lot to learn."

"Well, I accept your apology on the condition that you keep learning and don't grow complacent, again."

"I won't!" I almost shout. "No, I'm trying. In fact, I have a favor to ask you, so soon after apologizing."

"Well, you're buying me a steak lunch, so I guess I can hear you out." Jess leans back with a smile on her face and I know we're going to be okay.

"I met Abigail Wilder, when I was in the county."

"That's Elisha's mom?"

"Yes, so this is all off the record."

Jess makes a show of zipping her lips. "I promise not to tell your superpersonable lawyers."

"Abigail acts similar to an on-med, still, but she shouldn't. She's been off Dociline for years. I want to create some kind of supplement or—"

"An antidote."

I cringe—hopefully only on the inside—at the term. Dociline isn't poison. "More like a counteractive agent. Something that can neutralize the effects, so she regains her agency and doesn't require constant care. I only interacted with her for a few minutes, so I don't know her full range of symptoms, if she remembers anything, what's going on in her blood and brain."

"I'm assuming you have a plan."

"Kind of." I tilt my head side to side, weighing my options. "Elisha's going to see if he can get her into the city and find somewhere—a neutral location—where we can set up a small work space. Nothing fancy."

She raises an eyebrow. "You want me to help you undermine decades of your family's work on Dociline?"

"Uh, I don't know if I'd say 'undermine'—"

"Because hell yes, I will."

Suddenly, I'm confused. I wanted her to say yes, of course; I am asking for her help. It's the enthusiasm that I don't know how to handle. "You've helped put Dociline into the hands of debtors for years, now. You literally design our formulas—my dad loves you. I thought I'd have more trouble convincing you."

"I'm a bit surprised, myself." She leans back in her chair, gazing past me. "I don't think it's practical or even healthy to immediately unravel the fabric of society. What would all these debtors do tomorrow, if we told them Dociline was no longer an option? We'd have to rethink the Docile program, which, yes, but where do they go until then? Debtors' prison?" Jess crosses her arms and looks square at me. "It was rough on me, Alex. I lost five years of my childhood, five years of personal development that I struggled to make up. I stayed at Bishop Labs because I thought I could shape a drug that would make it easier on other kids. That someone who had personal experience with Dociline should be involved with its future. I think what you're proposing is a natural evolution and I'm in for the same reason."

"I'm honored to hear that." I hazard a smile as my face warms. Am I allowed to feel good, right now? I do. For the first time in a while, I feel energized.

"Don't get weird about it, Alex." Jess rolls her eyes, but she's smiling, too.

A knock on the door interrupts us. "I've got your overpriced dead cows." That can only be one person.

"Come in, Dylan." I slide a third chair out and gesture for her to sit down. "Sit." When she doesn't move, I say, "Or don't. The steak will taste just as good if you eat it standing up."

She drops the paper bag in the middle of the table and sits down. "I'm joining you because I want to, not because you said to."

"Okay." I hold up my hands. I'm not trying to coerce her. Never have. I'd have sent Dylan home when I went to visit Elisha, if I thought the Board would let me. Unfortunately, I blew my one chance at amending contracts on Elisha, and look what happened to him.

I catch Dylan up on what's happened since she last saw Elisha—and find her hungry for news. I never realized how much of the outside world the Bishop Lab off-meds miss; there's no news, no television or tabloids or tablets, for them. They live in controlled environments.

She saws through the medium-rare steak while I tell her I took

Elisha home. Stuffs it into her mouth while I say the word "love" out loud, over and over. Chews and swallows while I tell her about Ellicott Hart and the lawsuit. When I tell her my plan, she stabs another piece of bloody meat with her fork and eats it. I look to Jess for help, but she shrugs.

"I was wondering if you wanted to help us," I ask forthright. "Help us help Elisha's mom."

"I'd do anything for Abigail," Dylan finally says, wiping her mouth on one of the cloth napkins that were delivered with our meals. "She raised me, too, you know."

"Is that a yes?" I ask.

"I'll stay to keep an eye on you. Abigail needs help." She looks at Jess, next. "And I trust you less, Dr. Docile. How can you work here?"

"How could Elisha sign a contract with a Bishop? How could you?" Jess replies. "They make our world. It's a privilege not to interact with it. A privilege not all of us have."

A slow thirty seconds pass before Dylan says, "Fine," smiling out of the corner of her mouth. "Then I'm not going to feel guilty about interacting with this steak."

"As you shouldn't." Jess holds out her hand to Dylan, who shakes it. "Welcome to the team."

Several weeks pass before I leave the Silo. A car picks me up and drives me to my attorneys' office, where I sit like a decorative plant while they depose Mariah. I try not to invest myself too much into the questions—I can't answer them or talk to her about them. I know she thinks I've been fucking up my future, but I still value her opinion. Always have. And when Gabriela asks about my and Elisha's relationship? This feels like judgment day.

"How did Elisha affect Alex—if at all?" Gabriela asks.

"Not much, at first," Mariah says. "Of course, it was a shock to all of us—Alex included—when Elisha refused Dociline. No one does that, especially not when their Patron is a Bishop. He either was completely ignorant or knew exactly what he was doing."

"Objection," Vasquez pipes up. "Conjecture."

Mariah looks to Gabriela for direction. The attorney nods. "Let's move on to what you do know. Did your friendship with Alex change at all, after he signed Elisha?"

She licks her lips, waits, then says, "Yes. It was slow at first, as they got used to each other. He was nervous bringing Elisha around, like someone with a new dog they're afraid will pee on the carpet. But after a while Alex began to bring Elisha with him everywhere. Might sound normal, but consider that Dutch and I almost always leave our Dociles home, unless we're attending a social function where their presence is relevant. For example, Dociles are commonplace at Preakness, but they come along to race in advance of the horses and then are put in the barn. Alex's sat at the table with the rest of us. It was like they were on a date."

"We—" I say, catching myself before I can finish my sentence. "Sorry." I fold my hands in my lap, feeling my attorneys' disapproval. I want to defend myself, but could it be true? Were we on a date? I'd never thought about it that way, before. That in some way, I was courting Elisha. He certainly wasn't courting me. That would imply he had a choice.

"Over the six months they spent together, I lost my friend to Elisha." Mariah's eyes flicker over but only meet mine for a moment. Does she mean what she's saying or did the lawyers tell her what to say? "I've known Alex almost thirty years, but lately? I don't know . . . he becomes more like a stranger, every day." Mariah wipes her finger at the corner of her eye. Is she crying? I can't tell if it's an act. "I rarely saw him, during that time. Either he was staying in with Elisha or he was bringing him along, and, when he was there, Alex only had eyes for Elisha." With a little sniff, Mariah looks at me. "I miss you."

"Will the record please note that Miss VanBuren is looking at Dr. Bishop."

"Got it," the reporter says.

"Are we finished?" Mariah pushes her hair behind her ears and begins to stand. "Or can I take a break?"

"Absolutely," Gabriela says, but Mariah is already pushing the conference room door open.

Before anyone can stop me, I go after her, jogging down the hall. "Mariah!"

She doesn't stop.

"Mariah, please, wait." I slow as I fall into place beside her. "Can we talk?"

"Now you want to talk?" When Mariah looks at me, her eyes are pink and watery. She wipes the pad of her finger across her cheek to catch a falling tear.

I pull my pocket square out and hand it to her.

She sighs, reluctantly taking it and dabbing at her face. "Are you sure you wouldn't rather talk to Elisha?"

"I wouldn't *rather* talk to him than you. He's not the only one in my life I care about."

"Doesn't feel that way." She leans against the wall.

I glance over my shoulder to make sure a herd of attorneys isn't flocking our way, then lean against the wall and lower my voice. "I'm sorry. I am. I know I've changed—quickly. But this isn't—" That's not true. It is Elisha's fault, but in the best way.

"You're lying to yourself if you don't think this is Elisha's doing."

"No, I know it is, but it wasn't intentional. I'm not a victim; I just *changed*. On my own, naturally."

"If you say so."

I sigh.

"You tried to run out of Ellicott Hart naked, Alex. You almost attacked a psychologist. You've been freaking out," she says, the tears welling up, again. "And why? For your Docile? The Alex I know would never lose control like that." She blots her face dry, then pushes the silk wad into my hand. "I think we should take some space from each other."

Even though she's right, the words sting. "I think that's a good idea."

Mariah disappears into the restroom, leaving me in the hallway, holding a pocket square stained with makeup and tears. Whether or not I meant to, I hurt her. Not like I hurt Elisha or Dutch or Jess, but Mariah hurts and it's my fault. I hope, someday, she'll realize why I did it.

59

ELISHA

I'm relieved when Verónica says I don't have to attend Mariah's deposition and elated when Onyx suggests we take the day off. "Will you—" drive me to Prettyboy? Too presumptuous. "Are you—" free? He's probably too busy for me. "Can I ask you a question?"

Onyx snorts and crosses his arms. "Three takes, huh?"

I scowl, feeling defensive and hurt. "I did it, didn't I? You know I'm trying."

"I know." He smiles and leans back in his chair. "And, yes, you can ask me a question."

"Are you free today?"

"You're really going to work your way backwards, aren't you?"

"Yes," I say with confidence.

"All right, then. There's shit I need to do, but I could be tempted to play hooky. What've you got in mind, Wilder?"

I like when people use my surname. It reminds me that I have one. "Will you drive me out to Prettyboy?"

Onyx lifts his eyebrows. "I thought you didn't get along with your dad."

"We used to get along." I bite my lip. "It's complicated."

Onyx hoists himself up out of the old armchair and holds his hand out to me. "You can explain on the way." That's his way of asking. He never just *takes* my hand, as if he has a right to touch me, even though we've been friends for a while, now. Friends? I think we're friends. I should ask. *Ask.*

I take Onyx's hand and let him lead me out of the lounge and into the parking lot. Ask. It's a hard question. What if he says no?

When we stop beside one of Empower Maryland's cars, I ask, "Are we friends?"

"Yeah," Onyx says, letting go. "I think so. What about you?" We make our way to opposite sides of the car, then slide into the front seats. I'm still impressed that he knows how to drive.

"I think so, too." I take extra care buckling my seat belt to let the blush on my cheeks cool. I made a friend on my own.

"Well." He looks over his shoulder as he backs out of the lot. The cars here don't have cameras, like Dutch's did. They're old and boxy, but they work and that's what matters. "Then I guess we're friends."

"Thanks."

When Onyx puts the car into drive, he looks right past me, at the road. "For what?"

"For being my friend."

Onyx doesn't respond, only smiles—wide and tight-lipped, as he speeds away from Empower Maryland.

"So," he asks, "what's with the field trip?"

"Couple things," I say, starting with the easiest. "Verónica mentioned it would be easier if my family was in the city, for the trial, and I'd rather be the one to ask than her or Eugenia. I've hoped for weeks that Dad would realize I'm getting better and can be a part of our family, again."

"Makes sense." Onyx looks in the mirror, then back at the road. "What else?"

"I want to help my mom." I work up the courage, then say, "Alex thinks we can help her."

I jerk forward, the seat belt cutting into my chest as Onyx hits the brake harder than he should.

"Stop sign," he says, as if I don't know the real reason he stopped so suddenly. Slowly, the car rumbles to life. Onyx looks both ways and we continue normally.

"You just said we're friends. I know you don't like Alex, but I

could really use your support. After his deposition, he offered to
help my mom. Said he wouldn't rule out Dociline's influence—of
course, I know it's Dociline, but Alex was raised on this stuff.

"I had to listen to his deposition. He still believes in Dociline,
even though he doesn't like the current formula or direction the
Board wants to take. But look how different he is—at the disruption
he's caused among the most powerful people in Baltimore—after
spending time with me. Imagine what working directly with my
mother could do to him, especially with his new view on things."

I roll down the window and let the roaring wind take over when
I run out of words.

After a minute, Onyx rolls his window down all the way, then the
back windows. "Did you practice that speech?" he shouts.

"No!" I shout back. "I just said what I was feeling!"

"Well, it was badass! And right!"

With that, Onyx pushes a button on the dashboard and music
floods the air. A loud, catchy song with more soul than trillionaire
beats and none of the twang I'm used to from guitars. He sings
along as we drive, his rich voice wailing over the wind. My hair
whips out the window and tangles. It's getting so long.

After a while, he shouts, "I want to make a stop real quick!"

"O-okay!" the word erupts from my chest. "Where are we
going?" The question surprises me so much, my face slackens. I
hadn't even hesitated, just asked. I was curious—am curious.

"Don't die from shock, over there." Onyx rolls up the window as
we pull off the highway. "You ask questions, now."

My smile resurrects. "I ask questions, now."

We pull off the highway at Exit 27, Mt. Carmel Road, and turn
past a small gas station and convenience store into a shopping center that looks like it was busy a hundred years ago. Unlit signs top
storefronts with large Xs taped over the windows, except for one.
From the entranceway, I'd guess it used to be a grocery store, but
now?

Onyx parks, then opens the hatch while I get out. "Someday,
I'll teach you to drive. No one knows how, anymore." He tosses

me a trash bag that's soft, but heavy, when I catch it. "Talk about freedom."

I smile at the idea, as I follow him to the storefront. I'm not sure even Alex knows how to drive. The rich don't have to, because they pay professionals, and debtors don't have the opportunity. Bikes cost less, are easier to repair, and don't require licenses or ID or interacting with the government at all. Lately, I've preferred my own two feet, but it wouldn't hurt to learn how to drive. I bet Alex would be impressed.

"Is Betty in?" Onyx asks a tattooed person, when we walk inside. I quickly realize this isn't a store at all. It's a donation center—bigger than the one at Empower Maryland.

"That you, Onyx?" a voice shouts from the back.

"Yeah!" he hollers back. "Just dropping off two bags of winter gear." He lowers his volume as a Black woman with dreadlocks and a warm smile nears. "I know it's tropical outside, still, but I don't want anyone to be surprised when the temp drops."

"Shucks, hon." She kisses his cheek, then takes the bag off him. "Who's your . . ." Her sentence dries up when she looks at me. "Wilder, right?"

My surname still feels like a secret I'm supposed to keep locked deep down inside me. The sound of it is both freeing and terrifying. Like I've broken a rule that shouldn't exist in the first place.

"Yes," I manage to say, my mouth dry with nerves. "Elisha Wilder. Nice to meet you."

Betty sets Onyx's bag down on top of a pile of coats, then takes mine. "I heard you were a bit worse for the wear, but you look good, kiddo."

"Thank you," I say, glad when the words come easily. How did she hear? And how did she know my name? From Onyx. He must've told her we were coming. But *worse for the wear*? "I'm getting better."

"Glad to hear it," Betty says. "We're all rooting for you." She sets my bag down.

"What do you mean?"

"Your trial." She grabs a folded-up newspaper from one of the shelves and holds up the front page. "I read—we all read—that interview Mariah VanBuren gave to *The Baltimore Sun*."

I stare at the full-color photo of myself in one of the suits Alex bought me, probably at Preakness or a party or who knows where. Beside it, another photo of Alex dressed casually and looking sad. Beside his photo, I look sharp, confident.

Betty reads the headline. "'Alexander Bishop's Ex-Docile on the Warpath.'" She raises an eyebrow. "It's all about how you targeted the Third and manipulated him in revenge for what Dociline did to your mother. Of course, they throw 'allegedly' in there every three words and VanBuren makes the Bishops sound like our saviors. This article is supposed to spook anyone with a hint of debt into thinking their only option will be debtors' prison, after you destroy the ODR." She shakes her head and turns back to our donations. "Don't worry; I only believe the *City Paper*. And, like I said, I hope you kick Bishop's ass."

Onyx catches my eye, sees that I'm barely there. "You ready to go?"

I shouldn't be surprised by Mariah's article—but the words still hurt. They're out there, in bold black print, alongside photos used out of context. This is the opposite of what Eugenia asked me to do, during this trial. People can't believe this, can they? "Yeah," I say, ready to put the article out of my mind. I have too much else to focus on: myself, Alex, my mother, my upcoming deposition. "I'm ready."

"Thank you!" I shout, hoping Betty can hear over the crinkle of trash bags.

"'Thank you'?" Onyx says as he leads us back to the car.

I say, "Yes," and don't explain myself. "I know you're trying to help, but, please, don't make me justify everything I say and do."

"All right, then." He gets in the car, with a satisfied smile, as if that's exactly what he wanted me to say.

I think I got what I want, but it's hard to tell with Onyx. Instead, I say, "I can't believe she knew about my trial."

He shrugs. "Pretty much everyone knows."

"I've lived out here my whole life. We don't get a lot of news—on purpose. Only thing that matters is keeping away debt collectors and cops."

"Fair." Onyx pulls back on the highway, leaving the windows up and the music down, this time. "I've spent most of my life in the city—you're the expert. This is big news, though. Empower Maryland's been pushing Bishop Labs for years without much response. Somehow, you pushed them hard enough to get one."

"I didn't mean to."

"I know."

"Are you going to knock?" I can hear Onyx masking his annoyance. We've been standing in front of my house for five long minutes. My clenched fist raised to knock, arm beginning to tingle from loss of circulation. I held my breath, until I couldn't.

"No." I grasp the doorknob and twist. This is still my house. I'm not breaking in. I push the door open and stop. Onyx bumps into me.

"Dad." I didn't expect to see him. It's the middle of a Wednesday. He should be out working. "What're you . . ."

He holds up a sandwich. "Ever heard of lunch?"

"Right."

"Can I come in, or . . . ," Onyx says, right in my ear.

"Sorry." I step inside and he follows. "Dad, this is my friend Onyx. He's helping me."

"Is he?"

"Yes. I lock doors now." Why did I say that? Dad isn't Alex. He won't care, doesn't want to hear about my progress. I can't apologize, though. That'll make it worse.

"Nice to meet you, Mr. Wilder," Onyx says before my dad can respond. "I work with Empower Maryland."

"Burns, not Wilder." Dad actually shakes his hand. "But you can call me David. Are you hungry?"

"We already ate, but I wouldn't mind some coffee, if you've got it."

"How about tea?"

"That's fine."

I force myself to stand still while Dad gets a mug and canister, from the cabinet. Why do I have to stand here, like I'm invisible? I want to help. It's okay to help. Dad won't mind.

Slowly, I walk over to the stove, pick up the kettle, and fill it with water. Not looking at my father. Not looking at Onyx. Only at my hands and the sink and the column of water that streams from the faucet into the spout.

Beside me, the gas clicks five time before the flame whooshes on. Eyes on the grate, I set the kettle on it like a target. Dad walks away. I take a deep breath.

He didn't push me away. Wasn't angry. Okay. This is okay.

Dad leans against the wall. "So, what brings you out this way, Onyx?"

Onyx nods at me. "Ask Elisha. I'm just the chauffeur."

Dad scoffs and shakes his head. "Knew it had to be something like that." He looks at me. "Too good for your own two feet?"

"N-no. I just wanted to get up here quickly and—"

"I'm not his driver." Onyx folds his arms, forehead scrunching at the suggestion. "It was just an expression. Elisha's my friend and he can't drive, so he asked for my help. Something wrong with that?"

Dad opens and closes his mouth. The kettle whistles. While he tends to it, Onyx flips him the bird. I cut my hand across my neck. Onyx shakes his head and drops the gesture.

"Actually, Dad." It feels so weird talking to him, again. "I want to talk to you about the trial."

He hands the steaming mug to Onyx without a word. Lately, I prefer his silence.

"I'd like to bring our family into the city," I say, not breaking that contact. It's the first time we've really looked at each other since I left. Maybe he sees me, now.

We all turn at the sound of the door thrown open. "Elisha!" Abby runs into my arms. "Are you better?" she whispers in my ear.

"Not all the way," I say to her, "but I'm working on it."

She releases me. "So, what's going on? And who'd you bring with you?"

"Onyx," he says. "Nice to meet you . . ."

"Abby." She holds out her hand to him. "Elisha's sister."

He shakes it. "I'm with Empower Maryland. Helping your brother out."

She looks between him and me. "What happened to Alex? I thought he was helping."

"Something came up," I say, before Onyx can snark or explain. Dad's barely listening as it is.

"The lawsuit?" she asks. "Verónica told us we didn't have to worry. She would handle it."

"No—I mean, yes. But that's not why I'm here."

"He wants us to move into the city," Dad says. I'd almost forgotten he was there.

Abby's eyes light up. "Can we? Dad, can we go into the city?"

"I'll have to confirm with Eugenia, but we have some housing connections. I'm sure she'll agree this is an excellent use of resources," Onyx says.

"Nora, too," Abby says. "She's family and Dylan is still in the city."

I'm nervous knowing Dad will come, too, after all the fights we've had. But it would be great feeling like part of my own family, again.

"Let us move into the city, Dad," Abby says. "Please."

The three of us stare at him, while he stares at the floor. "Fine," he says, finally. I can almost feel the room breathe. "But only if Nora agrees to come, too, and only for as long as the trial. Once it's over, we can discuss staying longer. And by 'we,' I mean Nora and me."

"Ahhh!" Abby throws her hands over her head and runs back outside. "Nora, Nora! Guess what?" Her boots thud over the doorway before the door slams behind her.

"I think she's excited," Dad says with a smile.

A *smile*. I almost fall over at the sight. "Yeah, I think so, too."

Dad walks slowly toward the door, grasps the knob, and looks back at me. "It seems like you're on the right path, Elisha. Please don't make me regret moving our family into the city."

Our family.

"I won't."

"I need to ask you another favor." I feel bad asking for so much from Onyx, but there are so few people I trust. "If you don't mind."

He chuckles. "You can *ask*."

I roll up the car window so he can hear me better. Tall, brightly painted buildings begin to crop up around us, as we drive back into the city. Even though it's been my home—felt more like my home than the county—for over six months, it's weird to think I'll officially live here, soon. That my family will live here. In a real apartment, not a curtained-off room at Empower Maryland or someone else's house.

Though I still miss Alex's, sometimes.

"Elisha?"

"Sorry. I, uh . . ." Ask. "Was wondering if you could help me find a place where Alex can work with my mom? I don't want Eugenia or my family to know. It doesn't have to be fancy. Alex said we only need space for a few chairs and a makeshift workstation. Clean would be nice, but I can clean it up myself."

"I noticed you didn't mention that to your family—that Alex plans to help your mom."

"No. Dad was barely willing to move for my sake; imagine if I brought up Alex."

"I'm not saying it was the wrong move." Onyx doesn't say what it was, though.

I fold my hands together and stuff them between the soft second-hand denim that stretches over my knees. I'm better at picking clothes I like, now, but didn't want to wear something that would remind Dad of trillionaire fashion.

"I'm not sure I can help you find a work space—not because I don't want to. I don't have the resources or knowledge. Official Empower Maryland stuff? Sure. Off-grid? As much as I dig, I'm going to have refer you to someone else."

"Can I ask who?"

"Isn't that what you're doing now?"

"You know what I mean."

Onyx doesn't take Empower Maryland's exit. He's going to follow 83 to its end—into the heart of Baltimore City. "If you want to disappear from Bishop Labs and Empower Maryland, you're going to need someone who's wealthy enough to independently own property. Who already knows you and wants you to succeed. Who likes Alex Bishop but won't tell on him. You need Dutch Townsend."

60

ALEX

"What do you think?" Dutch walks into the empty apartment with his arms outstretched. He stops under a ceiling fan and twirls for effect. "It's small, but that's what you asked for. I figure you can set up in this kitchen-dining-living area. Use the cabinets to store all your science *stuff.* Even has a little backyard."

He walks toward the small French doors and turns their handles. Walks outside, leaving me alone in the space. The first floor of a powder-blue row home split into apartments, it's not like anywhere I've ever lived, and yet?

I look at the front door as the lock whirs, then clicks. When Elisha crosses the threshold, I imagine him coming home to me. The space is big enough for two and I like that it doesn't have monitors and SmartSurfaces everywhere. I've had enough of work and news intruding in my personal space.

Dutch peeks his head back into the living area. "That you, Elisha?"

"Yeah." The last time we saw each other, he threw himself into my arms. This time, he takes my hand and kisses me quickly. A peck on the lips as if he doesn't have time.

"What do you think, good?" Dutch asks him. "I hate buying foreclosed homes—usually, I give them back to the family—but this one was clearly abandoned. Didn't even take their stuff. Empower Maryland came for anything useful, this morning. The rest went to the dump."

"It's nice," he says. "But I don't know what Alex needs." I hear an undercurrent of irritation in his voice. Didn't Dutch say he was coming from his family's new apartment?

"I'm going to step outside." Dutch looks between us, aware that he's in the middle of something, then heads for the front door. "Give you two a chance to look around. Talk it over. Let me know when you're ready to head back to the lab, Alex."

"Sure thing," I say.

The door closes, dead bolt whirs back into place.

"You did it," I say, hoping my enthusiasm is catching. "You got her here."

"Yeah. Whole family, actually. Empower Maryland hooked us up with an apartment, nearby." Elisha doesn't look as excited as I assumed he would be. I remember what a dick his father was to him. What if things haven't gotten better? "Actually." He sighs and wipes sweat from his forehead. "I'm having a hard time."

I squeeze his hand to remind him I'm here for him. I love him and want him to succeed. "Do you want to talk about it?"

"Everything's wrong," he says, his irritation finally bubbling over. "All I've wanted for months is for my family to be happy and secure. For my dad to accept who I am, now. To be allowed to hang out with my sister. For Nora to be closer, for Dylan. I was there. In our new apartment—it's really nice. Clean, spacious, close. It has new furniture and linens that remind me of yours. Not as soft, but still comfortable."

"I'm sure they're perfectly fine." I chuckle, but Elisha's face is still hard and creased.

"I felt like an alien. Like I'd landed on someone else's planet."

Damn. "I'm sorry to hear that."

"I've always shared a room with Abby, but for some reason I felt claustrophobic in there, with her. Trapped. She led me around like I was a Docile. I am not a Docile, anymore."

"She was probably trying to help," I offer, hoping to calm him.

"I guess." Elisha's fingers twitch against mine, as if itching to pull away.

"She hasn't spent a lot of time with you, lately," I say. "Give her a chance to catch up."

"Am I supposed to pretend it doesn't bother me?"

"No." I take his other hand in mine and watch his muscles tense beneath his freckled skin. Does he not want to touch me? Am I blowing this? I'm trying. I am trying so hard to speak thoughtfully with him and respect his space. "Talk to her. Like you're talking to me. Be honest."

"I was being honest with her. This is how I feel." Elisha yanks his hands away. "I don't want to share a room with my sister. I don't want her to hold my hand. Either she's guiding me like a child through my choices or she's treating me like I can't make my own. I just want to be treated normally."

He turns and walks through the empty kitchen, to the French doors. They still hang open to the warm, humid air. I shouldn't follow—or should I? I want to go after him. I love him and he's clearly angry, but I don't think my presence is soothing him, right now.

"I know. You deserve to be." I rest a hand on his back, feel its heat radiating through his tee shirt. Then he turns to face me and my hand slides away without fanfare. Like he didn't notice and didn't care.

"Nora doesn't think so," Elisha says. "Not while Dylan's stuck at Bishop Labs."

"Elisha, there's nothing you can do about—"

"I know!" he shouts so loudly, I stumble back. "But it's all I can think about when I see her, now. That it's my fault." He groans. Runs his hand through his hair and leans against the doorframe. "Then Dutch called and Dad asked where I was going—don't worry; I didn't tell him."

"Can I ask what you told your father, instead of the truth?"

Elisha shrugs. "Nothing."

"Nothing?" I try not to sound surprised.

"Yeah, nothing. I don't have to tell people where I'm going and what I'm doing, anymore. They all want to know and I can't handle it."

"They're only asking because they care." Like I'm doing. He wanted normal conversation; this is normal. It is normal that I want to know where he is. Just because he doesn't have to tell me—doesn't have to tell his family or friends—doesn't mean we don't want to know.

"If they cared, they would understand that I can't tell them."

"Elisha, they're treating you normally. It's normal for people to want to know where their loved ones are."

"Would you stop saying my name like that? That's how Abby says it. Like you have to explain to me how the world works!" He's shouting again.

"I-I'm sorry." I don't know what to say. How to fix this or if I even can "I didn't mean—"

"I thought you would understand. I didn't bare my feelings so you could explain why they were wrong. I wanted your support."

"I *do* support you." Desperation pulls at my voice. "I don't even know how this conversation turned into a fight."

"I don't know. Maybe it is me." His eyes drop to his hands. "Maybe I'm the broken one who can't interact with normal people, anymore."

"You're not broken, E—" I stop. Purse my lips. Don't say his name because he just told me it bothered him. I am trying to do the right thing. "Tell me what you need and I'll do it, I promise."

Elisha squeezes his eyes shut and digs his fingers into his forehead. I watch him breathe. Slowly, purposefully. "I need you to side with me, without humoring me. I need to be allowed to come and go when I please without telling anyone where I'm going. I need space and to be able to fill it, on my own."

Then, before I can respond, his face falls. He looks away.

The realization sours my stomach like old milk. Slowly. Nauseating me. I can't help him. Doesn't matter that I was there for all the shit Elisha went through; it wasn't the same for me. I was the bad guy. I can't believe I ever thought I could untrain him. How naive.

"I have to go," he says.

"Do what you have to." I don't want him to leave, not like this, but what choice do I have except to let him go?

"I, um." He looks around the room as if expecting to find an escape hatch. Something to latch on to. A lie. "I have to prepare. For my deposition. I'll talk to you later."

I make space for him to leave, not trying to stop him with my body or words. I don't believe him, but I don't question him. He clearly doesn't want me to. Elisha says he wants normal, but I'm worried, now, he has a long way to go. And I can't help.

61

ELISHA

Empower Maryland is only a few miles away. When I arrive, sweat sticks my clothes to my body and my hair to my forehead. Onyx isn't the person I'm supposed to see, but he's the first.

"Did you run here?" He looks me over. "We can get you a bike from donations."

"I need your help."

"With what?"

I step close enough that I can whisper into his ear. "I need you to hurt me, again."

"Let's go to Dutch's office." He holds out his hand and I take it, walking with him. Walking together. Not like Abby, who *took* my hand. Who guided me with patience and pity.

I grip Onyx tighter.

He closes the door behind us.

"We're going to have a real conversation." He lets go, pulls out a chair at the small table, and sits down.

I sit across from him. "Okay."

"I shouldn't have hit you, earlier. I thought I was helping you."

"You were."

"In the moment, yes. But aren't you and Alex still working out your relationship? I don't like Alex, so I ignored him to help you, before, but that was shitty of me." He claps a hand over his heart. "I expect people to respect my relationships. I'm a hypocrite when I don't return that respect, even if I don't like them. If anything, that's worse."

"But I asked you to."

"Yes, but you didn't ask Alex."

"I don't need his permission, anymore. I thought you, of all people, understood that."

"It's not about permission, Elisha; it's about communication."

"I know how monogamy and polyamory work."

"Then, you're cheating."

"No." Am I? I'm not.

"If you're unable to negotiate the terms of your relationship with Alex, maybe you should reconsider whether you should be together. I'm not judging you for being with him." Onyx holds up his hands. "I definitely did when you got here, but I understand, now. I'm not going to narc on you, but I'm not going to cheat with you, either. We can be friends but I'm not going to play with you while Alex still thinks you're in a relationship." Onyx slaps the table as he stands. "Think about what you want. Talk to him. I'll still be around."

When I finally sit down with Verónica, I'm hollow. All my emotions poured out for Abby and Nora and Dad and Alex and Onyx.

She goes over the questions Alex's attorneys are likely to ask me. About my permission slip and debt history and my mother's disability. About my feelings for Alex. About every time we had sex. Details. Am I okay with going into details?

The details will matter, Verónica says, when she cross-examines me. Alex's lawyers are out to prove that I seduced him—with intent. Intent implies agency.

I didn't have agency, Verónica says. Not the first time, not the last. I didn't and I'm still struggling to find it. If I can say the word, I should. If I can say he raped me—only if that's what I think happened.

My legs are numb when Verónica excuses herself. My fingers cold, on the table. I still don't know what to say—what's real, what counts, who's to blame. But tomorrow, it goes on the record.

62

ALEX

The click of heels nears me. Gabriela says, "We're ready."

I hate seeing Elisha while we're surrounded by attorneys, especially after the way we fought, the other day. We haven't had a chance to talk and now our words and actions will be monitored and regulated, anger and irritation marinating while we're forced to act professionally. Expected to align with our respective "sides." I know the questions Reginald's going to ask him. No one should have to answer those, much less in a room full of strangers, while a court reporter records every word.

"Alex?"

"Yeah, I'm coming."

She holds the door for me as we leave behind the humidity for air conditioning, polished marble, and elevators. We don't speak as the car rises to the top floor. Bishops don't hire mid-level law firms.

Gabriela walks a step ahead of me, opening the door to the office for me—I don't even stop, simply glide between the doors, into the conference room, across the table from Elisha.

He's wearing a crisp white shirt, light gray slacks. Navy belt, matching loafers. No tie. Top button undone. Linen pocket square in his blazer pocket. I try not to stare at his exposed throat. At his growing hair, long enough to tuck behind his ears. At the tension in his jaw. He doesn't look at me. Looks at the table. At his hands— clasped so they won't tremble, I assume.

Elisha looks good. Humble. A strategy, surely, but not a lie. I grit my teeth as I sit to remind myself not to speak to him. I wish we'd had a chance to speak after Dutch showed us that house. Our makeshift lab. The place where I'm going to undo what my family probably did to his mother. I want to ask if he's okay, after he ran out. I didn't know what to say then and I don't know what to say now, except *I love you and support you.*

"Are you ready, Elisha?" Vasquez asks. The court reporter's fingers hover over the outline of her keyboard, where it's projected onto the table.

"Yes."

I can't tell if he means it. Does he know what he wants to say? What he thinks about me? What our relationship meant and means? Answers not yet spoken curdle in my stomach.

"Why did you decide to register with the ODR?" Reginald asks.

"I had to. We couldn't fend off the debt collectors much longer. Dad was seriously thinking about sending Abby."

"How much debt did you have?"

"Three million—and that's after my mom spent ten years paying some off."

"She was a Docile?"

"Yes," Elisha says. Clipped. Aware of where this is going.

"Was this family debt?"

"Yes. Two million on my father's side, one million remaining on my mother's."

"When she sold off that first million, did she also refuse Dociline?"

"No." He doesn't give them more. He knows they're going to use it against him. Across the table, Vasquez stares at Elisha, willing him not to give. Not to feel. Willing away his anger. My attorneys aren't allowed to lead him on.

"How is she now?"

Elisha purses his lips. He looks frustrated with Reginald's reaction before he's even answered. Reasonable, I suppose, when you're used to people not believing you. "She acts like a Docile, still. An on-med."

"Why do you think she acts that way?"

"Because of Dociline." Elisha sounds exhausted when he answers, as if it's the hundredth time, today. "I don't have scientific proof, but she was normal when she left and when she came back . . ."

"She was like an on-med? How did you feel about that?"

"Sad. Angry."

"Did you ever tell Alex about your mother?"

"Yes."

"How did he respond?"

Elisha catches my eye for half a second, then returns to Reginald. "He called me a liar and punished me for it."

"You've already stated you don't have scientific proof, but in your personal opinion, was anyone to blame for your mother's state of being?"

"Lots of people."

Reginald tilts his head. He wasn't expecting a nuanced answer. He was expecting anger. "Lots of people?"

"Yeah. The federal government for enacting the Next of Kin laws. Debt collectors and cops for forcing us to choose between the ODR and debtors' prison. Bishop Labs for inventing and producing Dociline. The State of Maryland for creating our debt resolution system, and the people for accepting it as normal. For perpetuating it."

"Bishop Laboratories?" There. Elisha gave my attorney enough to latch on to—but how could he not? We're at fault.

"Yes."

"Did you know Alex was affiliated with Bishop Laboratories before you signed with him?"

"Carol, my caseworker, explained who he was after he made an offer, but I didn't know during our interview, no."

"Do you remember how many offers you received, after your interviews?"

"I'm not sure of the exact number."

"That's okay," Reginald says. "Can you give us a ballpark? More than one? Five? A dozen?"

"More than one." Elisha shrugs. "Maybe three or four."

"Then, knowing who Alex was, why did you accept his offer?"

"He offered to pay my family a stipend of a thousand dollars per month, for every month I was with him."

"How long was that?"

"My whole life. Long enough that, if my family saved, they might not fall into debt again. Enough for my sister to go to a better school, get a better job. Enough that we could afford better medical care for my mother."

"Is that the only reason?"

"The stipend? No, but it was one of the biggest factors."

"Humor me," Reginald says, scooting his chair closer to the table. He leans onto it casually, as if he and Elisha are talking over drinks. "What else factored into your decision?"

"I remember receiving an offer for a shorter term, but it was hard labor. I knew I wasn't going to take Dociline, so personal comfort was a factor. During our interview, it was—" Elisha looks at me as if for permission.

"It was?" Reginald redirects his attention.

Elisha slides his finger through the ring on his cuff and pulls the chain. "It was heavily implied that Alex was going to have sex with me. I'd heard about trillionaires signing Dociles as . . ." He hesitates. "Personal companions."

A companion. That's what I'd called him. What I told my parents and the Board I thought Dociles could be. That's what Elisha became, but that's not what my friends would've called it.

"So, you'd already planned to refuse Dociline?"

"Yes, but I'd planned that for any scenario, no matter who I signed with. Whether I'd be cleaning houses or building them. My decision wasn't specific to Alex."

"Okay. So." Reginald counts on his fingers. "The stipend, quality of life as an off-med. Anything else?"

"Not that I can put a name to. Chemistry? I liked him. He seemed fair. Kind. Like he was interested in me as a person and was less likely to abuse his role as a Patron. I'd heard stories of Dociles injured during their work for bigger corporations—injuries they couldn't even remember sustaining because of Dociline. Their contracts would end, the drug would wear off, and they'd have lost a toe. I had offers like that, for shorter periods of time. Good offers, my case manager told me. But all I had to go on, during those interviews, was my gut. Alex didn't seem like the kind of person who'd abuse our contract."

"Despite Alex being CEO of the corporation that made Dociline."

"Objection," Vasquez says. She looks at Elisha and nods. "You can answer."

"Yes, despite the Dociline connection. I knew, legally, he couldn't make me take it. I'd researched my rights."

"That's smart. Most debtors don't think they need to know their rights."

"That's because most debtors take Dociline. They wouldn't know a violation of their rights if it slapped them in the face."

Reginald laughs. "I like you, Elisha. You're smart."

He looks at Vasquez, unsure what to do with a compliment from his opposition. My attorney called him smart. My attorney wants Elisha to look smart enough to manipulate his Patron, in an environment where he is mostly powerless. Elisha just wanted to survive. To provide for his family. I'm already angry on his behalf.

When Elisha says, "Thank you," I watch him retreat into himself. Into the safety of learned behaviors.

"Let's move on," Reginald says. "Do you think Alex would have developed feelings for you if you'd taken Dociline?"

"No."

"Why?"

"Because Dociline turns people into drones. It's like asking me why Alex didn't develop feelings for his refrigerator, if his refrigerator could suck his dick."

"So, you're saying it's inevitable that Alex would have developed feelings for any Docile he'd signed, who refused Dociline?"

"I'm saying it's possible."

"Did you reciprocate those feelings?"

I hold my breath. He's got to hurt me here—say that he was incapable of returning my feelings. If he doesn't, it'll hurt his case.

Elisha pulls the chain on his cuff again, then stops and puts his hands in his lap, as if he's been caught. "I don't know."

That's not the answer I was expecting, and Reginald is just as surprised. "Why not?"

"I've been told I was incapable of loving Alex. But it felt so real. Which was it? I don't know. I'm sorry, I can't answer your question."

"That's okay," Reginald says. "I want to ask you about Dr. Javier Madera. Do you know him?"

Elisha's whole body tenses. "Yes."

"Where did you meet?"

"Preakness."

"Do you remember your initial impression of him?"

"I had just won the race for Alex. Javier came over to say hi to Alex. Then, I went to clean up and change. I didn't really have time to form an impression."

"Sure, sure," Reginald says. "A win like that is sure to release some endorphins."

"I suppose."

"Maybe some pride."

"I—"

"Objection," Vasquez says, exasperated. "You're clearly leading the witness."

"I have a point." Reginald calmly sips his coffee.

"Then get to it, already."

He rests his cup back on its coaster. "Were you jealous of Dr. Madera?"

Elisha looks at me, his lips parted, lungs full of air. *Yes.* The answer is yes, but he can't say it. *I know,* I try to tell him. *I know the real answer. You can lie. I won't mind. Please lie.*

"No." His voice cracks. "No, I only wanted to make Alex happy and that meant winning the race. If he wanted space, I always gave it to him. It wasn't my place to take it up."

My chest clenches as Elisha belittles himself like I haven't heard since he was my Docile. He's been making such progress—I don't care if it's at my expense. I want him to heal. Please don't retreat.

"Did you ever see Dr. Madera, again?"

"Yes."

"Can you describe what happened?"

"He came to Alex's house and then they left together."

"Anything notable happen while he was there?"

"I interrupted them, on the piano."

If I close my eyes I can hear the chord Elisha slammed on the piano. The disgust in Javier's voice.

"Why?"

"It was an accident. I apologized and accepted my punishment."

Why didn't I speak up for him, then? I knew he was jealous. I'd taken Elisha to a fucking hotel suite. We'd played in the pool. And I'd sided with Javier because it was easier than admitting I was falling for Elisha.

"Did Dr. Madera ever return?"

"Later that night."

"Did you interact, then?"

"He came into Alex's room while I was cleaning and said he wouldn't have me interrupting them, again. I didn't question him. I assumed Alex knew what he was doing."

I can't watch.

"What did Dr. Madera do?"

"He bound and gagged me, then put me into the confinement space."

"Were you in the midst of fulfilling a punishment when this happened?"

"I was."

I bite my tongue so hard I taste blood. What Javier did wasn't normal or okay. I guarantee he didn't tell me because he knew I wouldn't approve. But Reginald thinks it's fine to get all this on the record, and I know plenty of judges who'd agree with him.

"What happened when you completed your punishment?"

Elisha looks at the glossy tabletop while he answers. His face slack. Body hunched. "Alex pulled me out—I couldn't stand up on my own."

"Was Javier still there?"

"Yes."

"What happened, then?"

"Alex kicked him out."

"Did Alex tell you why or say anything to you?"

"He said he loved me. That he was sorry he'd let Javier hurt me."

"Thank you," Reginald says. I'd grown to love and favor Elisha over my trillionaire friends. Point proven. "I'm finished with questions, for the time being. Would you like a break, Elisha? I could use another coffee."

"Yes, please."

Like a flock of startled birds, the reporter and attorneys rise, sliding their coats onto their arms and into the air. Across from me, Elisha remains: small and alone.

ELISHA

By the time Verónica begins cross-examining me, I'm freshly flayed. My flesh already peeled back. Nerves exposed. I take off my blazer and roll up my sleeves to relieve the heat of anxiety. Rest my arms veins up on the table. A cuff on my left wrist, long, thin scar on my right.

"I want to ask some follow-up questions about your time with Alex, Elisha; is that okay?"

"Yes," I say because what way is there but through? I agreed to this as much as I agreed to be Alex's Docile. Choices I've been fooled into thinking were my own.

"Would you categorize your sexual encounters with Alex Bishop as consensual?"

"Which one?"

"The first one."

She wants me to say no. "I knew what was expected of me when I signed with Alex."

"But did you want to have sex with him?"

Get on the bed.

"I was nervous."

Don't hide your body from me.

"I'd never had sex with anyone, before."

"And how did you feel afterwards?"

I see Alex's bedroom as it was in January: imposing bed, soft sheets, dim lights. Inescapable. Hot.

"Confused. Angry with myself."

"Why?"

"I wasn't sure if I was supposed to have enjoyed myself, or if I even did."

"Okay, what about the second time?"

"I don't remember it. I'm sorry."

"Which do you remember?"

"I remember—" My breath catches in my throat.

I'm at Bishop Labs, my cuff chained to a desk in Alex's office suite, writing lines.

I will control my attitude. I will not lie to Alex.

The linens on his bed are white with a navy-blue monogram: "ABIII." My fear replaced with his tongue and a bargain. My obedience for an orgasm. And I fucking said it.

I'll be your good boy.

"No."

"No?"

"No, it wasn't consensual. I didn't want to tell Alex I would be his good boy, but I didn't have a choice. We were at Bishop Labs, on his bed, and who was I among thousands of Dociles? How could I say no, when he controlled my family's stipend?"

"Do you remember any other times?"

"At Mariah's party—not with Alex. With Dutch Townsend and his Docile, but Alex expected me to."

"Didn't you sign a consent form, though?"

"What choice did I have but to sign it?" I snap at Verónica, as if she's the one who made me sign it. "Should I have let the cops haul my family off to debtors' prison?"

"Objection," Moore says.

"Acknowledged." Verónica doesn't look at him. "Elisha, can you recall any of your later sexual encounters?"

"At the hotel. The Douglass. I can't remember if we actually had sex that evening, but we made out in the pool. The next morning, we definitely fu—" I suddenly remember I'm in a room full of attorneys. "Had sex."

"Would you describe either of those encounters as consensual?"

"I don't know."

"Why don't you know?"

"Please stop." I dig the heels of my hands into the shiny wood table and squeeze my eyes shut. "Stop asking questions."

"Do you need a break?" Verónica asks.

"No, I want to explain."

"Mr. Moore, do you object?"

"Not yet," he says.

"Then the floor's yours, Elisha."

Breathe in through my nose, out through my mouth. Long, mindful breaths. Count:

One, two three four five.

Five, four, three, two, one.

"I don't know because I'm not okay. I haven't been okay for a long time, but I didn't want it to be true. Alex said I couldn't love him back and—" I feel my voice waver. The prickly heat of tears. "He was right. You can't love someone if they're in control of you. Alex was in control of me."

"Objection," Moore says, but no one stops me.

I look at Alex as my vision blurs. "Love is equal. I don't know what I felt, then. Loyalty, fear, adoration, safety. And now? He's the only one who knows exactly what I went through. He changed me."

"I object to—"

"We get it, Reginald," Verónica snaps.

"I've been struggling to adjust to life without Alex because I don't know who I am without him. That's not love. Partners are equal. You called us partners." I talk to Alex as if he's the only one in the room. He's the only one who matters. "But we're not."

"I know," he whispers, his own eyes pink.

"It's too hard."

"I'm so sorry."

I stand up. The court reporter looks between me and Verónica and Mr. Moore. "Alex Bishop raped me. You want that word on the record, so there you have it. How could I consent when I had no choice but to say yes?"

The court reporter's hands still.

"Are you getting this? This is what you all want—for me to realize how truly Alex fucked me up. Well, I have. Alex Bishop took advantage of my body and mind. But Lex Bishop put us in this position, and Alexandra Bishop before him, and the ODR before her. And I'm done being a part of it. This is over."

Halfway to Empower Maryland, I stop and turn around. I don't live there, anymore, and I don't live on the farm. I live in Mount Vernon, in a painted building, with my family. They'll only gloat, if I go home, now.

God, I fucked that deposition up. Moore will probably get the whole thing thrown out—I can't do that, again. I'm dry. These are onetime emotions. I need—I need—

I open Dutch's texts and repeat the address to myself. Think of the empty space with its double-door patio. No furniture. No people. Only sunlight and peace.

I enter the code, the lock whirs, and the door opens. Alex leans against the kitchen counter, no longer wearing his suit jacket. His face red and blotchy. Hair erratic.

He straightens when he sees me. "I thought you might come here."

I let go of the door. It slams shut behind me. "I didn't think you would."

"I'll leave." He picks up his jacket.

"No, wait." I have to do this. I have to do it now, while we're alone. While it means something. "I need to tell you something."

"I'm listening." Alex sets down his jacket and clasps his hands.

"I let Onyx hit me. He was helping me deprogram, but one day at dinner, I was so overwhelmed I almost lost it. But he knew what I needed. Showed me what healthy pain could feel like. Catharsis." I've only heard that word, before, but it fits itself into my brain like the last piece of a puzzle.

It takes all my concentration not to play with my cuff. I don't want him to see me like that. Don't want him to know that I still have the habits he gave me. "The other day, I asked Onyx to do it, again, and he said no. He said he shouldn't have done it the first time, either, and he was sorry. He wouldn't help me cheat. I hadn't stopped to think it through."

"It's okay," Alex whispers.

"Fuck." I turn around. Face the long living room window. Feel the warm glow of afternoon sun on my face. The tickle of tears down my cheeks. I press my fingers into the corners of my eyes as if that will hold back the sobs.

"I can't be with you, anymore, Alex. You hurt me, even if I can't always tell how. Which parts of me are me and which parts are you." I squat down. My knees hit the floor.

Over my own gross, wet wailing, I hear the pad of Alex's feet as he comes closer. The soft thud of his knees on the floor beside me. Feel the warmth of his arms as he pulls me onto his lap and kisses my forehead and I allow it. Falling into him like water into a container; I fit.

"I'm sorry." I can't stop myself saying it.

"It's okay," Alex whispers against my skin. "This is okay."

"I'm so scared."

"That's okay, too." He wipes the hair from my face and kisses my temple. His lips are wet. "You're going to do just fine without me, Elisha Wilder. You're going to be amazing."

64

ALEX

Elisha falls asleep in my arms, on the floor. We lie together, unmoving as the sun sets, coloring the pale wooden floor orange, then red, then purple. I stay awake, trying to memorize his weight—as if I've never held him before—and the soft herbal scent of his hair where his head fits against my neck.

The press of his fingertips against my shirt, where they held tight only a few hours ago. I should leave before he wakes up. He shouldn't have to face me again—to feel like he needs to say anything. He's already said it all. The truth.

Gently, I untangle myself from Elisha. Slide my suit jacket under his head. Press one final kiss on his forehead.

Leave.

As I ride the glass elevator down to the bottom floor of the Silo, Jess runs to meet me. "Thank goodness you're okay," she says before the door's even fully open. "When you didn't come back, yesterday, I worried they'd sent you away, again."

"Elisha broke up with me."

"Oh." Her brow furrows. "I'm sorry."

"I'm . . . not." I walk with Jess to a small meeting room where Dylan lies on the table, hair like a dark corona around her face, feet propped on a chair. She tests the chair's flexibility while she reads from a tablet, bending its back with her sneakers.

"I'm heartbroken for a thousand reasons—most of which are my fault. But, more than that, I'm happy for Elisha. I really am."

Dylan drops the tablet on her chest. "Did he dump you?"

"Yeah," I say. "He did."

She tilts her head back and shouts at the ceiling, "Thank god!"

"I'm glad you're both doing well." Jess squeezes my shoulder. "Or well enough."

"Thanks." I smile with closed lips. I know this is the right path—in my head and my heart. If I focus on helping Abigail and securing the win for Elisha, without getting myself sent back to Ellicott Hart, I may be able to forget the lingering hurt. "So, we have a place to work. Officially."

"Yeah?" Jess' face lights up.

Dylan sits up so fast, she kicks the chair over. "Will I get to go?"

I fix my hands on my hips and take a deep breath, hoping the words will come to me before my lungs explode. They're burning by the time I give in and answer, "I don't know. I'm barely allowed to come and go, without a good excuse. Dociles don't usually leave the Silo."

"Most of your Dociles wouldn't know if they left the planet."

I chuckle. "I don't make the rules, anymore. Ask Jess if you can come. She has more clout than I do."

Dylan swivels to face Jess. "Can I come?"

"We'll see," she says, but she's smiling. "Where is it? *What* is it?"

"It's an empty, first-floor apartment about ten minutes' walk from here. I don't think we're going to have many chances with Abigail. She and her family moved into the city, so they're close, but—"

"My mom, too?" Dylan jumps to her feet.

"I haven't been to see them, but I assume. She's part of the family."

"I'm going. I'm going to see Abigail and my mom."

"We can't tell Nora about this; I'm sorry. That's a hard line. No one can know."

"But she's so close."

"I know." Jess puts her arm around Dylan's shoulder. Jess never touches people unless she's really close with them. "Alex is right, though. If she thinks we're hurting or taking advantage of Abigail—all it would take is an ounce of distrust for this to end. We've got to think of Abigail, of former Dociles in her situation, and everyone on Dociline. After that, I'll see what we can arrange with your family."

"Fine." Dylan leans sideways into Jess' hug. "How can I help?"

"You can be my lab assistant." Jess smiles with a mischievousness I don't normally see from her.

"What does it pay?" Dylan asks.

Jess raises her eyebrows at me.

"This is off the books and I don't have access to my own bank accounts, so—"

"Fifty dollars an hour," Jess says, "full medical coverage."

"I'm a Docile. You're required to cover my medical expenses."

"Okay, you two." I step between them. "We have a ton of work to do. Jess, can you text Elisha? Arrange to meet him and his mother at our safe house. We need some of her blood."

65

ELISHA

I wake up sore and alone. Face tight with the salt of dried tears. The scent of Alex lingers as I sit up from the floor.

His jacket. I shouldn't take it—and, yet, I can't stand to throw it away. I stand and fold it. Place it in one of the kitchen cupboards. I'm grateful he left me this peace.

My phone vibrates in my pocket. Empower Maryland gave it to me after Verónica insisted I remove the one Alex put in the roof of my mouth. Dozens of missed calls and texts fill the screen, from Verónica and Nora and Onyx and Eugenia. Only one from Dutch that says: *You don't owe anyone anything. Take your time.*

I clutch the phone to my chest as if it's my own beating heart. There is someone I owe something: me. I owe myself a goal. One that isn't tied to Alex or my family. I could help people—people like me. Debtors.

I scroll through my few contacts, ignoring the constant feed of messages. My thumb rests on Eugenia's name. She'll be able to point me in the right direction. Bet she'll even be impressed I'm taking the initiative.

"Hey, Elisha," she says, answering the phone. "I'm glad to hear from you. I heard you left your deposition—"

"I did." I cut her off. "Sorry, I don't want to talk about it, right now." I lock doors. I ask questions. I set boundaries. "I'm okay."

"Well." She sounds surprised. Hopefully, *good* surprised. "I'm glad to hear that. Is there something you wanted to talk to me about?"

"Yes, I've been thinking of ways I can work on myself. Figure out what I want to do."

"Okay."

Just say it. She might think it's stupid, but if I don't say it, it'll never happen. "I want to apply for a job helping debtors, at the ODR." The words barrel out of me, and are met with silence. It's a fight not to rush to fill the space before Eugenia finally speaks.

"I think it's great that you want a job, but I'm not so sure about the ODR."

My fears settle at the base of my throat. They force out my "Why?"

"The ODR is aligned with Bishop Labs, Elisha. You know that."

"My former caseworker reports to you all." Carol's the one who told Empower Maryland I was going to refuse Dociline, in the first place. She's the reason Eugenia slipped me that card—the card Alex found. Spent seventy minutes in confinement—*Stop*. I need to stop thinking about that. I need to not punish myself for thinking about it, either.

"Carol has been helping Empower Maryland for many years. She provides us valuable insider information. It's a risky job. I'd rather not put you back in the enemy's grasp."

"Okay," I say because I don't know what else. Sometimes Eugenia makes me feel powerless, again.

"Hey, I have an idea." Energy courses through her voice. "Why don't you come work for us? We pay everyone a living wage. You'd get to directly help debtors without being overseen by the Bishops. I think we have an opening in our donations closet. The job's yours, if you want it."

"Sure," I say, before I have time to think. "That sounds great." Is it? It's true I'll be helping debtors and I hadn't thought about the ODR working with Bishop Labs, but Eugenia gave me the donations job without asking what I was interested in. I didn't even have to apply. Instead, I'm still doing as I'm told.

/ / /

Jess drives to our neighborhood—I like that we're neighbors—parks, and walks up to my family's new apartment with me. When our doorperson calls me "Mr. Wilder," Jess snickers.

"What?"

"Nothing. You're very fancy, now."

"I am not." I try not to blush as we step into the elevator. "But I like when people use my last name. I didn't have one for six months."

"I get it," she says. Sometimes I forget Jess was a Docile, too.

The elevator dings our arrival.

"Nice building," she says, following me.

"Thanks. I have to warn you, though." I unlock my front door, clenching my stomach and shoulders as I prepare for anything. "I'm not sure who's home."

The door creaks open.

"Maybe no one," Jess whispers. If she thought there was no one, she wouldn't whisper.

Bare feet swish down the hallway and Abby slides into the living room. "Oh." She stops. "Hey, Elisha."

"Hey."

"Who's this?"

"This is my friend Jess. Jess, this is my sister, Abby."

"Nice to meet you." Jess smiles and nods a half bow, like she often does with strangers.

"You too," Abby says, cautiously. "How do you know each other?"

Jess and I look at each other. Should we lie? We don't need to lie. I don't want to—I want things to be good between us, again. Abby is my sister.

"I was a Docile, too," Jess says. "When I was a girl. Now, I work with them."

I hold my breath.

"Cool," Abby says. Then, to me, "You didn't come home, last night."

"No. I had something to take care of." Please don't make me explain. I can't think about Alex, right now.

"Okay," she says, to my relief. "Dad and Nora aren't going to be home for a while. He's taking care of some paperwork so I can go to a city school, and Nora's with a career counselor. Can I help you with anything?" She asks as if she was scared to. I know that, now. Just like I'm trying, so is everyone else.

"No, thank you." I shouldn't stay angry with my sister. She wants to help me. She wants—she wants to *help*. "Actually, can you keep a secret?"

Jess shoots me a look.

"It'll be fine. We can trust her."

"Trust me with what?"

"Let's sit down." I perch on the edge of a firm emerald-green ottoman. Slowly, Abby sits on the matching couch. Jess leans against the wall, arms crossed, eyes narrowed at me. "I really appreciate that you're trying to help me, but I'm not sure you're the right person, if that makes sense?" I tuck my hair behind my ears, nervous she won't understand. If I didn't love her, I wouldn't have put myself through all this, in the first place. I hope she knows that.

Abby purses her lips and eyes Jess, as if she's come to take her place. "If that's what you want. Is this about the room? I can share with Mom if you need your own space."

"It is and it isn't. I'm embarrassed, Abbs. I know I don't have to be because it's not my fault, but I did a lot of things while I was a Docile that I don't want you or Dad or Nora to know about. And because I can't talk about them with you, I can't explain a lot of my needs. Communication is something I'm working really hard on; I hope I'm making sense."

"You are. I just feel left out. I don't know how to help."

"That's what I want to talk to you about, actually. It's a secret—a *really* important secret, Abby. You can't tell anyone, promise?"

She nods. "I promise."

"Okay." Butterflies fill my stomach. If Abby tells on us, this could all fall through. Say it. I need to say it. "Jess and I are trying to help Mom get back to her old self. To do that, Mom needs to go with Jess for a while. She's smart—she's a doctor and scientist. But, more importantly, I trust her. I need you to trust her, too. Or, at least, me."

"Where're you taking Mom?"

"Not far. A safe space where Jess can work alone and then she'll bring Mom right back. Dad and Nora won't even notice—and they can't."

Abby eyes Jess one more time, then looks at me. "I trust you, Elisha."

"Thanks. That means a lot."

For a moment, neither of us speaks.

"Sooo, do you really think you can help Mom be her old self?"

"Honestly, I'm not sure," Jess says. "But I'm hopeful and willing to do the work."

"Okay, then." Abby looks between us. "I'll go get her."

66

ALEX

Jess hands me a long tube of blood. "Abigail's, I assume."

"Yep," she says, gently patting her sweater pocket. "And there's more where that came from."

"You're really getting into this secrecy thing." I sit at a workstation, long abandoned. Dylan volunteered to talk the overnight caretaker's ear off. She's good at that and we need as much privacy as possible. Besides, I like the lab at night. The quiet. Nowhere in the city is this big and open and empty.

"I'm basically a spy."

"Hate to break it to you, Jess." I rip open a testing kit and begin setting up. "But we're the lab nerds who help the spies."

"Good enough, I guess. Not sure I'm cut out for fieldwork, anyway."

"Why's that?" I grab a pipette and begin the dilution. Hard conversations are easier when you can't look at the other person for fear of spilling your solution.

Jess leans against the wall, beside me. "My deposition sucked."

"It did?" I hold the tiny vial between my thumb and forefinger, inverting it several times, while I listen.

"Yeah. Your attorneys kept asking me about my Docile history as if that made me some kind of traitor. Though . . ." She gestures to my work. "I suppose I am, now."

At that, I do stop. "You're not a traitor because you were a Docile. I was never a Docile and look at me. Spurned my intended husband, fell in love with my Docile, and am now literally trying to help my opposition. You were a Docile and you work at Bishop Labs. You're allowed to have your own reasons."

"They asked if I ever helped Elisha. If I ever gave him information you'd told me in confidence—as if I would ever betray you like that." Jess sinks onto the seat beside me and leans against the countertop. Hands me a small tube of Abigail's blood without my having to ask. "No matter what I said, Gabriela gave me this look like I was a hanger-on. The kid your mom tells you to play with even though you don't like them."

"You know that's not true, right? This place would shut down without you. Gabriela and Reginald only care about crafting my father's narrative."

"Is that part of your father's narrative, though? That I don't care about this company? That I helped your Docile manipulate you?" Jess sighs. "I used to like your dad."

"I did, too. I'm sorry you got caught up in all this."

An unexpected voice fills the room: "Caught up in all what?"

A chill slices through my body as my dad walks into the room, hands clasped behind his back while he peers over our work space. Heat follows the cold. The heat of being caught. Of horror. What if he *does* fire Jess? What if she's right, and all my reassurances were only motivational bullshit?

I stand quickly. Too quickly. Lie. I need a lie. Or a partial truth.

"The lawsuit," I say, drawing Jess' gaze. "I felt bad taking Jess away from her work. She's got a lot going on with the development of Formula 3.0."

"I came to thank her, actually, for her time. Her testimony was valuable."

Jess puts on a smile. She's not like me; she's not a good faker—that's what I like about her. "I'm glad to hear that," she says. "Anything to help the company."

"And I'm glad to hear that." Dad's smile is genuine. "What's all this?"

Jess and I survey the countertop, covered with tubes and

half-empty vials, damp paper towels, and a discarded pipette. She can't take the fall for this. I have to.

"I thought I'd help out. Like I said, she's missed work for the lawsuit, which is my fault, really. And, to be honest, I miss being hands-on in the lab. I know I'm only supposed to be doing paper-work."

Dad picks up the tube of Abigail's blood. Holds it up to the light. Tilts it back and forth, slowly. Does he know? He can't know. We didn't label it. Jess and I used to work late into the night, together, all the time. He'd pop down from his office, like he is now, and send us home to bed, never mind that he was here just as late.

"You're correct." Dad sets Abigail's blood gently down on the counter. Neither of us dares reach for it. "You're only supposed to be doing paperwork. If Jess can't handle her workload alongside the trial, she can discuss that with me."

"I'm fine," Jess says. "I don't need any help."

"Good. Do you mind cleaning this up while I see my son to his quarters?"

Quarters. Like we live on a boat or in a sprawling multiwing mansion. Like he doesn't mean "put my son to bed," like a child. Might as well have security escort me out.

"No problem."

"I really am sorry," I say, once we're out of earshot. Dad presses the call button on the elevator. He doesn't look at me and I'm not sure how much groveling I have left in me.

"I want to believe you, Alex." The doors chime as they open. Dad steps inside. When I join him, I feel like I'm stepping into the chamber of a gun. "You seem to be improving—that's why your doctors and I thought you could handle living here. Please don't prove me wrong."

When we reach the third floor—my floor—the doors open and Dad gestures for me to get out. I do, without hesitation. I don't say good night or that I'll behave myself or anything else. I walk through the fogged doors of my office and into my bedroom. Closed velvet curtains black out light from the Silo, mimicking a real home.

I feel guilty making the comparison, but I can't help wonder if this is what it was like for Elisha. Debt and stipend held over his head, Ellicott Hart over mine—implied threats. As I flop down on my bed, I remember how I manipulated him, on these monogrammed sheets, into calling himself my good boy.

With one grand movement, I tear off the linens and stuff them under the bed. Tonight I'll sleep on the bare mattress.

67

ELISHA

I sit in the stairwell behind the donations closet, pulling the chain on my cuff while I wait for Onyx to answer his phone. Today, I organized a dozen bins' worth of incoming clothes. Helped a sprawling family that reminded me of my own pick out clothes for the coming winter. I know I'm doing good, here, but a part of me still wishes I'd had the idea on my own. I feel stuck. Need to get out, for a bit.

"Hey, what's up?"

I jump to my feet when Onyx answers. "Hey, it's Elisha."

"I know. Your name shows up on my phone."

"Right."

"So, what's up?"

"Um." I can't say it in this cavernous closet, where sound bounces off the metal walls like a rubber ball. And there are people all over Empower Maryland who might be listening. "Is there somewhere we can talk in private?"

"Yeah," he says. "Why don't you come over? Dutch and Opal are here, but they're working. They won't bother us."

"Come over . . . to your house?"

"Yeah."

I've never been to Onyx's house, before. I only ever see him at Empower Maryland. I don't know why I assumed he lived there, because I did. He has a family. He's with Dutch and Opal. Dutch has a house; I know that. Obviously, Onyx lives there, too. Why didn't I think of that?

"I'll text you the address. You can get here, yourself?"

"As long as you live in the city. I'm coming from work."

"Yeah. We live in the city." Onyx chuckles. "I'll see you soon." He hangs up.

I check the address he texts me, then start walking. When I'm close—when I've ripped my sweater over my head and rolled up my sleeves—I see why he laughed. Of course Onyx lives in the city. How quickly I've forgotten Dutch is still a trillionaire, whether he acts the part or not. I give my name to the doorperson, then ride the elevator up to the top floor. Another penthouse. I feel like every floor takes me further back in time.

The doors open into a room with couches that circle a brick hearth, floor to ceiling. Chimney and all. Opal looks up from one of the couches, where she's sprawled with her phone and a tablet. Then, Onyx walks over, wiping his hands on a dish towel.

"Hey," he says, tossing the towel onto a nearby counter. Like in Alex's house, every surface is clean, except where there's work. "You've met Opal, right?"

"Yes, but not since Alex amended my contract." She's as beautiful as Onyx. Body thick and muscular. Pale skin spattered with freckles. Hair spilling down her shoulders and back.

She waves, pushes a pair of thick-rimmed glasses up over her nose, and says, "Nice to see you on the other side!" Then, looks back at her phone.

To our left, the stairs creak. Dutch appears, moments later, at their base. Unbuttoned shirt hanging from his shoulders. Unfastened belt in his hands. Barefoot. "Hi?" he says, more to Onyx than to me.

"I can speak for myself," I say.

"I know." He buckles his belt. "But I'm still wondering why Onyx invited you into our home. That's between him and me."

"Oh." I feel sheepish, now. "Sorry."

"It's fine," Dutch says. "I know you're still learning. In the meantime, anyone going to tell me what's going on?"

"Elisha asked if we could talk in private. I don't think he has anywhere that fits the bill, so I figured why not here? I'd have mentioned it, but I didn't want to interrupt you while you were working."

"You know I don't like inviting people over." Dutch begins

working the buttons on his shirt through their holes. I find myself watching his fingers with interest. "But I guess we trust Elisha not to rat us out."

I startle at my sudden inclusion in the conversation. "I would never tell anyone about your private lives."

"You can't be seen coming here," Dutch says. "Especially not while this charade of a trial is still going on." He tucks his shirt in and slides his bare feet into loafers beside the elevator doors. "I have to go prepare for my deposition; it's tomorrow. Jess said they put her through the wringer. Opal, would you mind coming as my Docile to this networking thing at seven? It's going to be boring, but I really shouldn't show up alone and Onyx is clearly busy."

"No prob!" She rests her chin on her hands and blows him a kiss. Not good enough, apparently, as he walks over and presses his lips to hers.

I turn away, unsure I should watch such an intimate moment. I can do that, now. I don't have to watch.

I hear his footsteps near Onyx and me, then the sound of another kiss. "Have fun, you two," he says, heading toward the elevators. The doors open and he steps inside. "Make good choices!" They close. He descends.

We're alone—except for Opal, but she's so deep in her phone, she wouldn't notice if the ceiling caved in.

"Do you want to go to my room?" Onyx asks.

"Yeah, that would be great." I follow him upstairs and down a long hallway. All of the doors are closed except for one, a bathroom.

Onyx opens the last door and holds it for me. "After you."

I don't walk far—can't without stepping on something. Clothes, hardcover books, poster board.

"Sorry. I don't have many people over." He kicks a path from the door to the bed. "Do you want to sit down?"

My eyes immediately find a maroon love seat and coffee table, instead.

Onyx notices. "There's fine. Didn't mean to imply anything." He clears another path with his foot and sits on one of the crushed velvet cushions, patting the other. He leans back against the arm, curling his left leg against his body. The other dangles over the edge.

I sit.

"So, what did you want to talk about?"

"I broke up with Alex."

"Oh." Onyx's eyes widen. "Wow. Big step. How do you feel?"

I breathe deep through my nose. "Good? As long as I don't think about it. It's hard. So much reminds me of him. It would be easier if his father hadn't sued me."

"It wouldn't be Baltimore if the Bishops didn't have their hands in everything." Onyx shakes his head. "Well, I'm glad to hear it. Did you want ice cream and sad movies, or . . ."

"Is that something people do after breakups?"

"Pretty standard."

"Well, I'm not hungry and I've already cried enough over Alex. I came here to ask you for something different."

"What's that?"

My eyes drop to our knees. They almost touch where the cushions meet. I remember what he felt like naked. Hand wrapped around both our cocks.

"Would you have sex with me?" I ride the wave of heat as it spreads down my neck and shoulders. Into my chest. I know he can see me burning, but I don't look away.

Onyx doesn't scoff or laugh or leave—he doesn't react at all, for a minute. "What kind of sex?"

"Um."

"I will, for the record, because I'm your friend and I think you're cute, but I also think this is an opportunity for you to learn how to negotiate a relationship. So, Elisha Wilder, tell me what you want me to do with you."

I can answer this. I've had sex lots of times. As I run through them in my head, I try to separate sex from Alex, the bodies from the feelings.

"I like penetration."

"What kind?"

I can't blush any more than I already am, so I answer honestly. "Anal."

"Giving or receiving?"

"Receiving."

"Have you ever given, before?"

"No."

Onyx clicks his tongue and sinks his fingers into the thick of his curls. "Maybe you should."

My muscles reflexively tense. "Please don't treat this like I'm picking out an outfit. I might not know everything I like, yet, but fucking someone isn't like trying on a shirt."

"You're right." Onyx grins and drapes his arms across the corner of the love seat. "So, you like it up the ass. What else?"

"I liked it when you hit me."

"Impact play. Check."

"I like feeling secure. Kind of tight? I don't know how to describe it—like the tack I wore at Preakness, or a snug suit."

"Okay, okay." Onyx looks past me, thinking. "I'm not an expert with rope, but I definitely have some, as you already know."

"And . . ." He's going to think I'm pathetic. "I've never really made out with anyone."

Onyx cocks his head. "You didn't, with you-know?"

"When I was his Docile, it was as if my mouth was a fruit he was tasting. After that, we barely had time or energy. It's been frantic."

"Got it. Any hard limits besides penetrating someone?"

"No, but going down on someone else is a— Soft limit? Is that a thing?"

Onyx purses his lips as if he's trying not to laugh. Sits forward.

I scrunch my forehead up and match his stance. "What?"

"I swear I respect you so much for this; but you're really too innocent for as much fucking as I'm sure you've done."

"I don't know all the words because I didn't have a say."

"Well, you're figuring it out, now. I accept your limits. Any medical conditions I should be aware of?"

"No."

"Me neither." Onyx's gaze slips from my face, down my body.

I can't stop staring at his mouth. At the swell of his lips. "Is that it?"

"No," he says. "Before we do this, I need you to understand that you and I are friends who are about to fuck. That's our relationship. I'm not looking for anything else, right now, but I think both of those things are awesome. Agree?"

"Agree."

He counts on his fingers. "Safewords, like before. 'Red' means stop; 'yellow' means slow down. Got it?"

"Yes." I lick my lips. Bite them.

"Good."

"Green."

Onyx doesn't move, but we are so close.

"That means—"

He presses his lips against mine with such force that we topple, me onto crushed velvet. Him on top of me. Onyx bites my bottom lip hard, when he draws back—draws a cry from between my pulsing lips.

"Oh god," I say, eyes drifting upward as my back arches and Onyx's teeth scrape against the soft skin of my neck. He sucks as hard as he bites and I can feel the heat of blood swelling under my skin. It hurts and I love it. My body squirms beneath his, clothes out of mind as our limbs wrap around one another.

Then, his hands slide under the hem of my button-down and I become desperate to undress, fumbling with the buttons while struggling to keep my mouth on his. Onyx holds his body away from mine, giving me space to finish. Every button a lifetime until I'm free.

"Bed?" he asks, as we catch our breath.

"Yeah."

I take my pants off, fold them, and set them on the couch as Onyx walks down the cleared path on the floor. With one swipe, he knocks a pile of clothes off the red plaid sheets. A flannel that's soft and warm when I lie on them, my pants halfway off. Onyx stands while he undresses, tossing his clothes wherever as I watch. No hamper in sight. No rules.

"Wait." He places a hand over mine before I can remove my boxer briefs. "Lie back. On the pillows," he says as I scoot into place. "That's it. Now, hold your hands together."

Onyx runs over to a closet and pulls a length of sky-blue rope from inside. He uncoils it as he walks back over, swiftly doubling the length. I lose track of his motions as he wraps my wrists. Every cinch makes my cock twinge. When he pulls the loose end around a bedpost and ties it off, I lose the ability to lie still. I writhe for touch—for *his* touch. Even the sheets send pleasure through the downy hair on my thighs.

"How does that feel?" Onyx lowers himself for a kiss.

My eyes are still closed when I answer, "Good." It's tight enough, somewhere that matters. Not everywhere. I can take more, but this is enough, for now.

Onyx's mouth makes its way down my chest. Pausing to roll my nipple between tongue and teeth. To lap at the curve of my navel—I gasp, that spot never explored. His fingers curl inside the hem of my underwear, then pull it slowly down—over my hip bones, over my thighs—exposing the trail of thick brown hair that's grown from my abdomen to my hardening cock, and inside my thighs.

Onyx's body is smooth, not a hint of stubble. Should I have continued grooming? Maybe that's what everyone in the city does. I tug at my hands, unable to cover myself, now. He can see what I've done. I look away.

"What's wrong?" Onyx asks, his mouth an inch from my ear. He slides his hand up my thigh, fingers spread so that they glide through the short hairs. He grips and tugs, so close to my cock. I thrust up.

"Nothing," I say.

"Then, why won't you look at me?"

"I'm embarrassed. Ever since I stopped living with Alex, I've let my hair grow—everywhere. What if that's wrong? What if you don't like my body this way?" I pull at my hands again, but the rope doesn't budge.

"Do *you* like it this way?" Onyx says.

"Yes."

"Then, so do I." He kisses my hip bone. My pubic hair.

I gasp.

Onyx slides his tongue slowly up my shaft, leaving a cool trail of saliva. "Anyone ever go down on you?"

My "no" evolves into an "ohhh," as he engulfs the head of my cock. I want to tell him I've never experienced anything so *much* so wet and warm and all over, but I can't speak. Can barely breathe. I dig my heels into the mattress and raise my hips.

Onyx pushes them down and holds me there. "Wow, you are bad."

The word hits me like a bucket of cold water. "Red," I say, before I can stress over it. "Please don't call me bad or good."

"Got it," Onyx says, lips free only long enough for those words before I watch my length slide between them. I close my eyes and let myself feel his fingers at the base of my cock, sliding to meet his mouth where it stops. The soft suction, swirl of his tongue around the head.

He kisses the side of my shaft, still holding it, hand unmoving. The hyper-glow of pleasure emanates from my groin, down my legs.

"I'm going to help you up and then I want you to hold on to the bedpost. How does that sound?" he asks, question hot against my skin.

"Good."

"Good." Onyx slides away and I feel the tension of the rope change as he unfastens it from the post. "Up." He pushes gently at my back until I'm sitting, then kneeling. Cock bobbing between my thighs as I shuffle toward the corner of his bed. It's not like Alex's, in the middle of his room. Not like an altar on which rituals are performed during the dark of night.

As I grasp the wooden bedpost, as Onyx winds the rope around my wrists and the post, as he fixes me in place, I feel like a normal person in his friend's room. A lived-in room, pieces of his life scattered on the floor and furniture.

I gasp. A sting spreads across my ass. I grip the bedpost tighter.

"On a scale of one to ten, I want you to tell me how much you're hurting."

He slaps me again, open palm resting hot against my skin.

"Um." I can't think.

Onyx hits me, again, the heat compounding. I shudder and moan. "A number, Elisha, or I'll stop." Another hit.

I don't want him to stop.

"A five?"

Soon, I'm a seven, then a nine. Trying to flex away from the sting of his palm. It hurts. I know it hurts, but I want it to hurt. I want more, want him to take me to ten. Instead, I feel the cool absence of Onyx's hand and the shift of the mattress as he moves. I rest against the cold surface of the wall. Breathing. Waiting.

"How're you feeling?"

Before I can answer, Onyx nudges my legs apart and presses a finger against my hole. It's cool with lube and smooth. Covered in something unfamiliar.

"Good," I say. "What are you wearing?"

"A glove."

"Oh." Alex and I never used protection.

"Honestly," he says, wiggling his finger around the tight ring of muscle. I gasp and lean against the post. Onyx moves closer, cornering me while he strokes what feels like every pleasure nerve in my body. "It's easier cleanup. If you looked around my room, you noticed, I need all the help I can get."

I laugh, low throaty notes that dissolve into moans as Onyx's finger slides deeper inside me. He doesn't waste time finding that spot—I thought it was a trick only Alex knew. That I would never—

"Oh fuck, I can't . . ." My knees buckle when Onyx takes my cock into his other hand.

"No, no, no," he says, quietly, lips on the back of my neck. "Stay up. You can do it."

My thighs burn with effort, but he's right. "Please," I say, searching my brain for the right words—any words. "What is that?"

"You mean this?"

I shudder again as Onyx brushes the spot. "Yes."

"Didn't have an anatomy tutor, I take it."

I shake my head, unable to verbalize my *no.* Thankful I no longer have to.

"This"—he continues stroking the spot—"is your prostate. It's situated between your dick and your bladder and can be stimulated several ways. Let me know if you ever want to try sounding."

"I don't know what that is."

He chuckles. "Then I won't explain until we're both dressed. Don't want to risk you losing this." Onyx begins stroking my cock again.

I lean back against his bare chest. Allow my head to loll back on his shoulder, while he plays my body like a piano.

"You can come if you want to," he says. "You don't have to wait for me."

I hum, satisfaction buzzing through me. If I weren't tied down, I might float away—but I don't want that. Don't want only to come. "I want you to fuck me."

"Oh yeah?" Onyx removes his hand from my body and the glove from his hand, then grabs my waist. His erection presses hard against my bare ass.

"Yes." I arch my back, rubbing against him.

He disappears, again. I look over my shoulder to see Onyx roll onto his back and slide his trunks down his legs and toss them onto the floor with everything else.

He reaches over the end of the bed and returns with a foil packet, which he rips open, then discards the foil. "Ever use a condom?"

"No."

"Then, watch." He pinches the tip, demonstratively, then rests it on the head of his circumcised cock. Slowly, he unrolls the length of rubber down his shaft, until it nestles against his body. It's so thin, I can still see his dark skin through the translucent material. "Got it?"

I nod.

"Ready for it?" He smiles.

I do, too. "Yes."

I'm bracing myself against the bedpost and widening my stance when Onyx positions himself behind me. With little effort, he pushes his cock inside me, loosing a string of curses as he slides in to the hilt. I have missed this feeling. The stretch, the fullness. Being joined to another person. I squirm against him, losing myself in a burst of pleasure.

"How's that feel?" I ask.

Onyx's voice cracks. "Good. Really fucking good, Elisha."

With both hands on my hips, he draws back and thrusts in, again. Again and again and again. I clench when he pulls out, drawing moans from the both of us.

Onyx kisses my neck, leaning his weight on me. Bending me forward, my full weight on the post. He kisses me with teeth, marking my skin. I expose my neck to him, needing more. The pain feels magnificent. Onyx bites me, again, then grabs a fistful of my hair and pulls, wrenching my head back even farther. I scream—desperate and satisfied at the same time.

"Was that a good scream?" He digs his tongue into the hollow of my shoulder bone.

"Yes," I choke out. "Please," I beg. "Please touch me."

"I am touching you."

"Please." I thrust my cock into the open air.

"Tell me what you want, Elisha." He holds my hips flush against his body and I squirm around his length.

"I want you to touch my cock. Please. Please, I want to come." I thrust again, but this time his hands finds me. Warm and nimble.

I give myself over to Onyx. Wholeheartedly, I *feel*. His cock inside me, his hand around me—I am so close. My body has never been stimulated in so many ways in so short a time. His pelvis bumps into my bruised ass, forehead rests against my sore neck, lips occasionally forming kisses against my slippery skin.

I hold on to the bedpost inelegantly. I don't want to free myself, but every time I struggle, pleasure jolts through my arms and down between my legs until the feeling sends me over the edge.

"I'm going to—oh god." My body buckles. Hips buck of their own accord. I glow from the inside out. Throw my head back and cry out as if my body is no longer my own. I forget. No longer on this bed, in this room, on the top floor of a building in the center of Baltimore City. I'm raw energy, exposed.

Then, I'm in Onyx's hands. His body cradles mine, thighs and chest my relief. As I come down from my orgasm, I grind down on his cock, one last time, drawing a hiss from between his teeth.

"Easy," he says, pulling slowly from my body.

I look over my shoulder. "You're still hard."

"Such powers of deduction." He rolls the condom off and tosses it.

"I want to help."

"You don't have to."

"I know," I say, feeling empowered by the option. "I don't have to do anything I don't want to, but I want to."

"Then tell me what you want to do."

"I want to suck you off."

Onyx raises his eyebrows. "That's a soft limit; are you sure?"

"Yeah." I nod. "I know what I'm doing."

Onyx and I hold each other's gaze for a solid thirty seconds. I don't falter. He's judging me. Wondering whether I'm capable of this kind of decision so soon. I am. I pick out my own clothes. Lock doors, when I want privacy. Go to work, in the morning. Broke up with Alex. It's not always easy, but I can make my own decisions.

"I believe you," Onyx says. He reaches around to untie my hands.

"Wait!"

He stops as suddenly as if his life depended on it.

"Don't untie me all the way, only from the bedpost."

He smiles and begins unwinding the rope from the post.

"I like this," I say, as Onyx winds the extra rope around my wrists and ties it off. "It makes me feel secure."

"I mean, I'm into it." He helps me onto my knees, beside the bed, and sits, legs spread, on the edge. Rolls a new condom down his shaft.

I lick my lips. I've never gone down on anyone wearing protection, before. I hope I can get him off; I *want* to get him off. I still like making people feel good.

Onyx holds the base of his cock with one hand and brushes my cheek with his other. Hesitates. "Elisha, I really don't want to fuck this up."

"You won't," I say with as much authority as I can muster. How do I make people take me seriously? "I know you're having trouble believing me because of the relationship I had with"—I can say his name; it doesn't mean anything—"with Alex. Just because I learned about myself with him doesn't mean everything I learned is wrong. I'm allowed to want this until I don't."

"Fair enough," Onyx says, then tilts his head sideways. "I have an open-mouth gag, if you—"

"Oh, put your dick in my mouth, already, for fuck's—"

Onyx grabs my face and thrusts into my open mouth. I bend closer, taking his full length down my throat. I am grateful Alex trained away my gag reflex. Onyx gasps with surprise, holding the sides of my head tight as my lips meet the base of his cock. I swallow, flexing my throat and tongue around his length.

"Fucking hell." He throws his head back.

This new condom tastes like plastic cherries, but I suck on his cock like it's the sweetest treat I've ever tasted. I dart my tongue over every ridge, every vein. Every time he moans I go harder, faster, my head bobbing rhythmically between his thighs.

His breathing speeds up and his grip tightens. I let Onyx take control, pursing my lips around his shaft as he fucks my throat like he fucked my ass.

He doesn't announce when he's coming, but I feel it. Part of me wishes he wasn't wearing a condom, so I could taste him—swallow his come. My reward for a job well done. Maybe someday.

We don't move for several minutes. Onyx leaves his cock in my mouth while it softens and I suck lightly, teasing out the dregs of his orgasm. I'm happy to be a warm, comfortable home for his afterglow.

Finally, he reaches down and pulls the condom off as he pulls his cock from my mouth. "You're too good at that."

"Thanks," I say with a smile.

This time, I let Onyx free my hands. Warmth reclaims my palms and fingers as he works. It felt good when he tied them and it feels good when he unties them, as if it's not an undoing, but a natural progression. A completion.

We flop onto the bed beside each other and he hands me a tissue to wipe the come off my chest and cock. I flex my jaw.

"Where should I . . ." I glance over the edge of the bed at a trash can piled high with wrappers and tissues and condoms.

"Overflowing." Onyx closes his eyes and smiles. "Good luck."

"Okay." I balance the tissue on top of the bulging trash can, then close my eyes, too. Feel Onyx pull the comforter over our naked bodies. He rolls over, curling up against my back. Drapes his arm around my chest. Kisses one of the bite marks on my neck.

"Ouch." I don't mean it.

I feel the heat of his laugh against my hair. "Your ass is so warm."

"Gosh, I wonder why."

"You like it."

"Yeah," I say, feeling the pull of sleep. "Thank you. For all of this."

"Anytime," he says.

I fall asleep thinking how safe I feel. How I've felt that before. I wonder whether that was real, if the safety was an illusion. Alex would've protected me. I never felt safer than in his arms. I think that's real. I decide it doesn't matter, now.

68

ALEX

I'm making myself a mediocre shot of law office espresso when my phone rings. And though I'd rather be most anywhere besides attending another one of my friends' depositions, I like talking on the phone even less.

"Who is it?" I ask, and the caller ID answers.

"Dr. Jessica Pearl."

"Okay, answer call." Before she can speak, I say, "I only have a minute."

"Right," she says. "Dutch told me he was being deposed at ten a.m. Wonder if they'll treat him like a traitor, too."

He *is* a traitor, but I don't tell Jess that. It was cruel of my attorneys to treat her like one, without reason.

"So, what's up?" I ask.

"I want to start testing these counteractives on people. I had some luck, this morning, applying them to samples A, C, D, E, and H, but they're in tubes, Alex. We can't ask if their memories are coming back. It's all theory until we have test subjects."

"We can't use the lab Dociles."

"I agree; that's why I'm calling you."

"Okay, I'll do it," I say.

"Do what?"

"Dylan'll help. I'm sure she'd love to stick a Bishop with a needle."

"You're going to test them on yourself?" Jess says, disbelief in her voice.

"Plenty of notable inventors have tested their own progress on themselves."

"Yeah, but—"

"I'm not going to risk injecting Abigail with something else that could hurt her." I look around the office kitchen, suddenly aware of how loud my voice is. "Her family doesn't deserve that, after everything."

"Okay," she says.

"I've got to go. I'll be over, afterwards. Could you take a look at your results from this morning and write up detailed memos for each of the samples?"

"Will do. Talk to you later."

"Later." I tap my ear and the signal cuts off.

I swallow the entire espresso in one go; its heat slides down my throat and burns my stomach. I cringe, set the tiny cup in the sink, and grab a mug from the cabinet.

Ever since I started living in my office, I've stopped sleeping. During the day, I hide. Even though everyone knows I'm mostly stuck there, I don't want to remind them of it. Don't want to feel the shame of being deemed too irresponsible to govern my own life. I work after everyone goes home. Jess stays, occasionally, but not as often as she used to. I think she's emotionally exhausted, and I don't blame her. She shouldn't have to give any more than she already has. Dylan, despite her snarky facade, is happy to pass along anything she and Jess worked on, during the day. And she stays with me well into the night, listening while I talk myself through our options.

"Hey." Dutch walks over to the counter beside me and grabs a mug. We place them beside each other in the espresso machine.

"Hey." I should warn him. "I don't know if Jess told you how her deposition went—"

"I heard."

"Then I don't have to warn you that they might try the same on you."

"They can try." His hand trembles while he makes his coffee

selections. Americano, double shot of espresso. He shoves his hands in his pockets while the machine whirs to life.

"Are you okay?"

"Yup." He doesn't look at me.

"Dutch."

"Alex?"

The machine sputters, pumping black liquid into his cup. My latte finishes, foam topping it off.

"What are you planning?"

"The less you know . . ." He sips his drink.

My stomach churns. "I don't like this. Whatever it is."

"Latte that bad?" He smiles, but I can tell he's nervous.

"Please don't do anything stupid."

"Everything I do, I do with purpose." He leans against the counter beside me, looking into the hall. A file clerk passes, carrying a precariously balanced stack of folders. "Do you trust me?"

Without thinking, I say, "Yes. Always." Doesn't matter who else he's working for, Dutch will always be one of my closest friends.

Gabriela peers into the kitchen. "There you two are. We're ready to get started." She motions, then walks away toward the conference room.

Dutch transfers his Americano into his left hand and holds out his right to me. I look between it and his face, unsure what he's pulling. Finally, I take it and shake his hand.

"It's been a pleasure working with you for so many years, Alex." With that, he follows Gabriela.

Oh no.

I hurry after him, waiting in the line of attorneys filing into the conference room. "Dutch, do we need to talk?"

He doesn't answer. Doesn't even look at me.

"Please don't do this," I whisper before we're separated to opposite ends of the long conference table. I don't even know what he's planning, but I'm terrified for him. Terrified to be without him, if I'm being honest with myself.

First Elisha, now Dutch? Jess is struggling and Mariah hasn't spoken to me since she published that interview with *The Sun*. I don't have friends left to lose. Already I feel the black hole of loneliness inside me expanding.

Beneath the table, I bounce my feet. Unseemly. I'd have scolded Elisha for it, but I can't stop. I'm too nervous. I worry if I pick up my coffee, I'll spill it.

"Please state your full name for the record."

"Dutch Townsend."

My coffee goes cold while Gabriela gives her opening spiel. While Dutch answers her preliminary questions. Each question a bomb, each of his answers the delicate cutting of a wire.

He doesn't become defensive when she asks about his history as a Docile and she doesn't press him. Dutch is our CFO. He's on the Board. He's my conservator. I assume Gabriela will want the same story from Dutch as from Mariah.

"How did you react when Elisha refused Dociline?"

I remember. He was furious. Now I'm not sure how much of an act that was. Will he tell them? Is that his plan?

"I'm not proud of my reaction; it was disruptive."

"Please elaborate."

"I told him off for refusing Dociline in front of Alex's party guests. Like I said, it was inappropriate."

"Did you have a chance to meet Elisha, after that?"

"Yes."

"How would you describe his demeanor?"

"He seemed nervous and unsure, most of the time. Looked to Alex for direction. Didn't know how to interact with people of class, in social situations—not at first, anyway."

"Oh?" Gabriela sits up. "Can you explain what you mean?"

"Sure." Dutch clasps his hands and leans forward on the table. "The first time I really spent with him was at Mariah VanBuren's costume party. He asserted himself when he shouldn't have—there was a noticeable difference between him and the other Dociles. They obeyed happily and performed well. Elisha looked like he'd rather have been elsewhere and had to be scolded for misbehaving. Not a great look."

"And later?"

"I admit, I didn't see him much, but he attended Preakness with Alex and boy, was there a difference."

"Explain, please."

"He was much better behaved. Almost indistinguishable from the other Dociles present, except . . ."

"Except?"

"Well, there are stables at Preakness specifically for Dociles, before and after they race. Alex had Elisha sitting at our table and wearing a suit instead of tack."

"Would you consider that typical of Alex?"

"Eh." Dutch tilts his head side to side while he thinks. "It wasn't atypical of him to bring Elisha along to events the others didn't. He liked having Elisha around and it was his right to, so he did. I can't say whether he'd have done the same with an on-med because the only other Dociles he controlled were those at Bishop Labs."

"During her deposition, Ms. VanBuren credited Elisha with changing Alex. Would you agree or disagree with her assessment?"

"I would agree."

"I'll ask you to elaborate, again."

Dutch looks down the table at me. "Of course. I think Elisha changed Alex for the better."

Gabriela's eyes widen. "You do?"

"Yes. For the first time, Alex was forced to see what debtors go through. It's a shame that it was at Elisha's expense, but he changed, all right." Dutch's lips curl into a smile. "He spent so much time training Elisha that he accidentally got to know him. Accidentally fell in love with him. Well, whatever was left of him."

Gabriela looks nervously at Reginald.

"Please, elaborate, Dutch," he says to himself. "Don't mind if I do. You see, Alex had no fucking clue what to do with a real human being. Someone with feelings and instincts and a family. Someone with agency. He only knew he had to gain control, to protect himself and to please his family and the Board. That's what Dociline's all about—that's what the ODR is about." He smiles and holds up his hands like it's not his fault; he's only the messenger.

"The Docile system exists to give the wealthy control over debtors. To satisfy that need for control, Alex forced Elisha into submission by threatening to stop the stipend, stipulated in their contract, to his family. He used that leverage in a calculated fashion to establish rules and enforce corporal and emotional punishments. He called it training, but Alex brainwashed Elisha, slowly, over a period of six months.

"You asked me if Alex changed; they both did. Alex changed because he began to view Elisha as a person he cared about while those around him viewed him as a cocksucking robot. Elisha changed because his behavior was forcibly modified."

The court reporter stops typing.

"Did you get all that?" Dutch asks her.

Vasquez shoots her hand into the air like an overeager schoolgirl. "I'd like to cross-examine the witness."

The lab is quiet when I return. Most of the lights are dimmed, except Jess' office, where someone sits across from her. Laughter bubbles out from the open door as I near them. I knock, ceremoniously, on the wall, then step inside. Dylan turns around, holding half a sandwich in her hands.

"Oh," she says, then turns back to her meal.

"Hey," I say to Jess, not trying to win Dylan's affection. She *has* been nicer since Elisha broke up with me.

"How'd it go?" Jess wipes her mouth and sets her own dinner down.

I take a deep breath. Can't believe I'm about to say the words out loud. "Dutch got fired."

"What?" Jess stands. "He—why?"

"He told the truth."

"I told the truth and they didn't fire me. Yet."

I lean against the doorway, too tired to stand on my own. "You didn't tell them that I forcibly brainwashed Elisha and that Dociline and the ODR are means for the rich to control debtors."

"Damn," Dylan says. "Is this dude single?"

"No," Jess and I say at the same time.

"Okay, okay." Dylan returns to her sandwich. "I was kidding, anyway."

Jess holds the sides of her head as if it needs keeping on. "Does he believe all that? He must. But he's worked here for so long! As long as I have. He has Dociles. And he . . ." She looks at me. "He fucked Elisha at Mariah's party."

"I know."

"Like, Dutch *humiliated* him."

"I take it back," Dylan says. "I don't like him, anymore."

"I don't get it," Jess says. "He's always seemed to really believe in the Docile system. He loves his job. Never gave a shit about anyone beneath him."

"About that." I'm not sure how much of this is mine to tell, but it's not like Jess isn't going to find out, soon. Not like the whole city isn't going to find out. I watched Dutch walk straight from Betts, Griffin & Moore into the waiting arms of Chadwick Bell at the *City Paper,* and Bishop Labs isn't going to let him spew his story without fighting back. "Dutch has been working with Empower Maryland—for years, as far as I can tell. He told me, recently. I was as shocked as you are."

Jess sinks down onto her desk chair. "Mariah is going to tear him apart."

"I hate to change the subject so abruptly, but the fewer allies we have in this company, the more urgent it is that we move forward with Abigail."

"Right." Jess is facing me, but her eyes are focused somewhere in the distance. Like she's staring into another plane of existence.

"Jess, you okay?"

"Yup." She focuses. "Let's get moving."

Dylan stuffs the end of her sandwich in her mouth and follows the two of us to one of the storage rooms. Instinctively, I stand in front of the retinal scanner. The display reads:

DR. ALEXANDER BISHOP III
CHIEF EXECUTIVE OFFICER (PROBATION)
ACCESS DENIED

"Right. Of course." I step aside so Jess can handle it. "After you." She passes the scan. I'm more embarrassed that I stepped up first than that I failed.

Once inside, she unlocks another cabinet and rummages around. Her arm disappears farther inside, until she's standing on her toes, shoulder deep.

"Do you want me to—"

"Nope," she cuts me off. "I've got them."

I shove my hands in my pockets so I won't be tempted. The hardest part of helping, I'm finding, is knowing when not to.

Jess pulls out several bottles, handing some to Dylan, holding the remainder, herself, as she re-locks the cupboard. "We should not do this in a conference room; your dad really can't walk in on this."

"Makes sense. We can go up to my office. There aren't any cameras in there. That I'm aware of."

Jess nods and the three of us take the elevator up to my third-floor suite. I'm glad my working office is the first room, so we don't have to pass through my bedroom and remind everyone I live here, now.

I take a minute to make sure all the glass is frosted, while Jess and Dylan spread out the bottles on my desk. With several swipes, the papers on my desk return to their digital forms and collapse into the SmartTable.

"Dyl, will you grab at least six each of alcohol swabs, needles, and syringes from the supply closet? Twenty-two gauge, if you can find it. Twenty, if you can't."

"Got it." She runs off.

Jess spreads five bottles evenly across the desk. Behind them, she places a vial of Dociline. "This probably isn't the same formula version that Abigail injected, since that was some time ago, but since we only keep limited quantities of the previous generations for historical purposes, any that went missing would be more obvious."

"Good call."

"I really don't want to get fired, Alex."

"I really don't want you to get fired, either, Jess."

"Glad we're on the same page. These are the prototypes Dylan and I tested this morning that returned favorable results. No idea if they'll actually work on a person."

"We're about to find out."

Dylan returns with a handful of supplies, dumping them on my desk.

"We didn't have any twenty-two-gauge needles?" Jess asks as she opens a syringe.

"We did, but twenty is a bigger needle, so it'll work faster."

"You mean it'll hurt more," I say, rolling up my sleeves.

"They do?" Dylan asks with a sly smile. "I had no way of knowing."

"All right, you two." Jess draws Dociline into the first one.

I swab my arm with alcohol and hold it out to her. I've injected Dociline recreationally, before—most of us have. When we were younger, Mariah and I broke into her parents' study while they were at a fundraiser, and got into their stash. We did not stop to think that one of us should be sober. Consequently, we flopped down on her couch while it sunk in, then did nothing for the entire evening.

That's the thing about Dociline; you're not motivated unless someone else gives you direction, and if you take an actual dose, you forget. We didn't take enough to forget the talking-to her parents gave us or the month we were grounded. We did take enough to march upstairs silently and go to bed without dinner when they told us to.

Lab employees are occasionally fired for indulging, but the

actual addiction rate is relatively low, since those who abuse Dociline check themselves into a rehabilitation facility as soon as
they're told.

As Jess injects me, I relax into my chair and watch her, intently,
waiting for my memories to fade and bliss to settle in. It's nice. I
feel tingly. Airy. Everything is so wonderful. So warm.

"How're you doing, Alex?" asks a woman holding a syringe.

I must be Alex, so I say, "Nice, thank you." Every word feels better than the last.

"All right, he's—"

"Hey, Alex, do a dozen jumping jacks."

I stand and jump, counting to myself. It feels rewarding, doing
what they tell me.

"Now push-ups—a hundred." She smiles.

I drop into position and begin pressing myself up from the floor,
enjoying the burn in my muscles. When I reach sixteen, the first
woman says, "That's enough. You can stand, Alex."

"Aw, come on," the other says. "Next I was going to have him tell
me what a massive tool he is and dance across the room."

"You're on the clock."

A sigh. "Fine."

"Now." The first woman, again. I wait, listening for my name.
"This is a terrible testing method, since each previous dose will
still be in him when we inject the next. But that's how we're going
to have to work on Abigail, since there's only one of her and we're
running on limited time. I know you're not going to remember
this, Alex, but I feel weird not telling you, this is prototype A."

"Okay."

"Hold out your arm."

I do, watching as she injects me with something. I don't know
what it is, but it's what she wants and that's wonderful. After she
withdraws the needle, they both watch me. I sit still, waiting for
whatever they're waiting for.

"How do you feel, Alex?"

"Nice, thank you."

"Dammit, we're going to have to come up with better questions," she says to the other person.

"How about personal questions?"

"Sounds good. You're going to have to introduce yourself. He won't know who you are."

"Got it." They lean forward. "Alex, my name's Dylan. I'm Nora's daughter; do you know who Nora is?"

"No," I answer.

"Maybe someone he's closer to?"

"Do you know who Jess is?" she asks, pointing at the woman with the syringe.

"No."

"Who's he closer to than you?" Dylan asks.

"Maybe Elisha. Alex, do you know who Elisha is?"

"That name sounds nice," I say.

"Looks like this one's a miss, but let's try a few commands, just to confirm."

I stand when they tell me. Lift my left foot off the floor. Rub my stomach and pat my head. Dylan laughs, which makes me smile. I like when she's happy.

"That's enough." Jess looks at a clock on the wall. "We don't have all night."

She injects me with two more counteractives, which don't feel any different. I keep doing what they ask, but they seem disappointed. I don't know how to help them feel better, but I'm sure they'll tell me.

"Prototype E."

I wait while she injects me, hoping this is the one that makes them happy. At first, nothing happens. I sit still, like they want me to, and wait. Then, something begins to burn inside me. First my arm, then my chest. I breathe harder to compensate, feel the dampness of sweat on my hairline.

"How do you feel?" Jess asks.

"It hurts."

"Hopefully, that's a good sign."

The heat in my veins builds, searing through my body like molten lava. I hiss and clench my hand into a fist. "Ahh, fuck, fuck, fuck!" I jump to my feet and pull at my clothes. "I'm burning inside!"

"Oh my god," Dylan says. "He's going to take his clothes off."

"It's okay, Alex." Jess stands and walks toward me with her arms outstretched. "You're going to be fine."

Cool tears stream down my face. My eyelids sting, tongue prickles with pain. My fingers, toes, the deepest pit of my stomach. Like I've swallowed a fireball. "Water, please." I dig my nails into my shirt, as if I can claw the drug out of my chest.

"Okay, here you go." Jess hands me her glass.

I gulp it down in one long go, not stopping to breathe until the last drop shakes onto my tongue. I gasp. My head is screaming with pain as memories surface like a buoy forced underwater. "I remember," I say. "I remember the other injections. None of them did shit."

"No, they didn't," Jess says. "But this one is doing shit."

"Turn off the lights, please. My head is fucking killing me, goddamn." I sink back into my chair and bend over, until my face presses against my knees. The tears come involuntarily. Snot leaks from my nose.

When I can finally breathe without my throat feeling like the surface of the sun, I say, "Tell me to get up."

"Get up," Dylan says.

I don't.

"Prototype E it is."

"Should we test H, just to make sure?"

I begin to shake my head, but it hurts too much. "Augh. No need. I'll bring it with me, in case this one isn't a match for Abigail, but this is officially the worst, which makes it the best."

"Are you sure this is safe?" Dylan asks. "You've already hurt my family enough. I won't let you put Abigail through this if—"

"No," I say, my voice muffled by my shirt and the floor. "I'm not sure it's safe. But it's the best chance we've got." Dammit, I should ask her permission, too, even though I already have Elisha's. I sit up as far as I can. Lift my head as much as the pain will allow. "We won't inject her if you don't want us to. You're her family."

Dylan looks between us, hands fidgeting nervously at her sides. "Elisha wants this, so I do, too. Besides, this pain will be the first thing she's felt in a decade. Maybe that's better than nothing."

69

ELISHA

"Hey, Elisha, it's Alex. I'm sure you already know that because this is a voicemail and you have caller ID. Listen, I wouldn't call if it weren't important. Jess and I think we're ready to start testing our new treatment on your mom. Not sure we can make any more progress on our own, until we do. I don't know; this might be it, but it might not. If you can, let's meet at the safe house, after your shift. Dutch told me you got a job in the donations closet at Empower Maryland. I think that's really great." He pauses for so long, I almost hang up. "Anyway, text me when you're heading over with your mom. Don't know if you heard Dutch was fired, but he's not my conservator, anymore; it's some 'impartial' pencil pusher in the accounting department, so I'll do my best to get out of here and meet you. Okay, I lo—I'll talk to you then. Bye."

Mom walks the whole way from our apartment to the safe house without complaint. Not that I expected differently, but it's new walking down the city streets with her. Like we're going to the harbor together. I can't help but hope that we'll be able to. What if this is it?

I type the code into the front door and it unlocks. Mom waits while I close the door.

"Hello, Alex," she says.

"Hi, Abigail." Inside, Alex stands at the kitchen counter, in front of a row of bottles. Two stools, an end table, and a chair sit where a kitchen table would.

I don't know what to say to him. Everyone around Empower Maryland says that after you break up with someone, you're supposed to give yourself some space.

"If you want to sit down, one of those is for you," he says instead of *Hi,* or *I've missed you,* or *I almost said "I love you" when I left a voicemail.*

"Thanks." I stop halfway to one of the stools. "I'd rather stand."

"Okay," he says, turning back to his work. "I don't have long. Told my conservator I had a lunch date with Mariah, which, given that she's avoiding me, is either the best or worst cover story. So, want to help?"

I can't help but feel bad for him. I know what it's like to be monitored, even though it's not the same. "Sure," I say. I can work, now. He should know I'm useful. I join him at the counter.

"Grab a couple alcohol swabs, cotton balls, bandages, a disposable pad, and a pair of gloves." When he holds the box out to me, I do not think of what his hand would feel like in mine. "You can set them up on the table."

I take two gloves, careful not to touch him. Even though we've seen each other since Alex amended our contract, it feels like we're interacting as people for the first time. And he's telling me what to do, a—

"Thanks." He says it with half a glance. With sincerity. Like he'd say it to Jess while they work. He's treating me like an equal—a competent equal. The thought stops me where I stand.

Alex looks back at me when I don't move, and the worry grips me again. Will he think there's something wrong with me? That I still need hand-holding? Just because I still need help doesn't mean I'm helpless.

"Sorry," he says. "I didn't show you where anything is."

"It's okay. I can figure it out." If Alex can act like it's no big deal, so can I.

The supplies are in the cupboards above us. I open the first one to find cotton balls, alcohol, and bandages, which I set on the table. In the second, a stack of disposable pads. And Alex's jacket, folded like I left it. He must've seen. He doesn't move to take it, though.

Quickly, I grab a pad and close the cabinet. Alex doesn't look up; he keeps working while I do. Side by side. Like partners.

"Do you want to ask your mom to sit down?" he says.

"Sure." I move the alcohol wipes closer to the stool. He'll probably need those first. Everything's so close, the placement probably doesn't matter. But still.

Mom looks at me when I approach her, but not before. She's been standing silently, this whole time. I don't pretend she has the same needs as someone in a different state might. I know what it feels like to be content and fulfilled standing exactly where someone put me.

"Hey, Mom."

"Hello, Elisha."

"Let's go sit down."

"Okay." She walks with me, sitting in the chair when I gesture to it. "Thank you."

"You're welcome."

"Thank you."

I don't respond, again. It's a reflex for her. A reflex I'm still trying to shed.

"Would you please unfold the pad and drape it over the armrest," Alex says as he walks toward the stool, holding four capped needles.

I do so without responding.

"And open the alcohol wipe, if you wouldn't mind. I'd prefer not to touch anything I don't have to." He smiles and wiggles his gloved fingers. "This isn't exactly a sterile environment, but let's pretend."

I don't hide my smile. Alex Bishop is funny now that we can relax around each other. Now that our relationship is less life-or-death.

"What should I do with this?" I hold up the alcohol swab.

"You can rub it right there, on her arm, then get a cotton ball ready. Chances are we won't need a bandage, but better to be safe."

I wipe the cool alcohol over Mom's arm, from halfway to her shoulder down to her wrist. I don't know where Alex is going to inject and, like he said, better to be safe. She doesn't look at me while I work. I wonder if she'll notice the needle.

Alex stares at her arm.

"Is everything okay?" I ask, the swell of nervousness suddenly rising in my stomach.

"Yeah. I want to explain what we're going to do." He looks up at me. "When we tested these on me—"

"You tested these on yourself?"

"Yes. First, I injected Dociline. Then, the counteractives, one at a time."

Anger and confusion well up, inside me. "Why would you inject Dociline, after everything I've told you about it? After you've seen what it does?"

Calmer than me, Alex says, "I didn't want to test it on an on-med without their consent and we couldn't trust an off-med wouldn't tell on us. Dylan might have volunteered, but . . . I realize it's not ideal, but I couldn't bring myself to inject your mother with a drug that hadn't been tested in anything but a glass tube. Believe me, this is not the normal order of testing. I'm sorry I've distressed you. Jess tested my Dociline levels, afterwards; the Dociline is completely gone from my body. We only injected a small dose."

"Okay," I say, nodding my head more than necessary, as if I'm convincing myself. "I guess"—Alex and I won't always do things the same way. How could we, when we've experienced life so differently?—"I guess that was the best option. I appreciate you not stabbing my mom with an untested drug."

"I would never," he says. "Not after everything else my family has put yours through."

I pay close attention while Alex explains the specifics. What each syringe is for and what will happen and when. It's not until he uncaps the first needle that I start to feel nervous. I watch as he injects her, holding my breath as if something's going to happen. He already said it wouldn't, but we're so close I'm almost nauseous.

He watches her for a moment, then, when she doesn't react, moves on to C, then D. "I should warn you that this hurt when Jess injected me with it. I didn't bring anything to counteract the pain because I don't want any other drugs in the mix while this is still working. You'll want to hold her tight."

I nod and wrap my arms around her from behind the chair, pinning her as best I can. Eyes squeezed shut, trying not to throw up. This could be it.

"Abigail," Alex says. "I'm going to inject you with something that we hope will help you feel more like yourself. It will probably hurt, but that will fade. If you can remember me saying this, please do your best to hold still and remain calm. Your son, Elisha, is here, helping. You can feel him even if you can't see him."

I count the seconds that pass. One, two, three, four.

Mom's right shoulder twitches.

Five, six, seven.

Both shoulders.

Eight, nine.

Her chest expands.

Ten.

She screams.

"Okay, the needle is out," Alex says loudly and, somehow, calmly. "No sharps exposed. All we can do now is hold her, okay?"

"Yeah," I whisper, and readjust my hands over her arms and across her abdomen as hard as I can.

Alex moves to hold her legs. She screams like I haven't heard since I was seven years old. Not since the cops tried to take me, for our debts, but she went instead.

She's so loud. "What if someone hears and calls the cops?"

Alex grunts. "Let's hope no one does. Abigail, can you hear me?"

I feel the hard weight of my cuff press against my mother's struggling body and remember how Dad scolded me for letting Abby touch it. How Onyx clapped his hand over my wrist to stop me playing with it. I don't want Mom to be disappointed with me, if she comes out of this. Her son, still wearing the mark of his Patron, after everything.

"Abigail?" Alex shouts.

Her body goes limp.

I let go and hurry to look at her. "Is she—she's not—"

"She's breathing and her pulse is . . ." He's panting, two fingers pressed against her neck, eyes closed while he counts.

I hold my breath.

"Fine, her pulse is fine. Whether it worked, though . . ."

Her eyes open, lashes fluttering. Head still flat against the back of the chair, she looks between us. She pushes something like a whisper from her lungs. Air that wants to be words.

My heart feels like it's in my throat, quivering. "Mom?"

Her eyes land on me. Travel from my boots to my overgrown hair. Well with tears. "Elisha?"

My face is so hot, so full, I need to know before I explode. "Please," I say, the tears already leaking down my cheeks. I grab Alex's hand and squeeze it as hard as I can. I don't know if I'll be able to handle it if she doesn't come out of this. "Please say something real."

"You're so tall."

I drop to my knees beside the chair and rest my hands on her arms. "Are you okay? Can I—can I hug you?"

"I don't know if I'm okay, but you'd better hug me, right now, Elisha Wilder."

She throws her arms around me and I sob uncontrollably onto her shoulder. Hold her so tight it hurts. Until pain shoots up my legs from where my knees dig into the hard floor and I have to let go.

"Who's this?" she asks, looking at Alex.

He rolls his stool closer and sits in front of her. "You don't remember me?"

"Is that bad?" I ask, wiping my nose on my sleeve.

Alex makes an indecisive face. "She hasn't got her memories back, but it's too soon to tell; they could still return. I can't say she's fully rehabilitated, but I didn't expect that."

"Are you a doctor?" Mom looks from Alex to me, hungry for the answer.

"We met at your house, on the farm," he says, pushing his sleeves back up. "Several weeks ago."

This time, when Mom looks at me she's worried. "I don't remember. I'm sorry."

"That's okay. Please, don't be sorry. My name's Alex."

Bishop, I almost say. *His name is Dr. Alexander Bishop the Third, CEO of Bishop Laboratories. His family makes Dociline.*

"Do you mind if I ask you some questions?"

"Only if you tell me what's going on."

"Absolutely."

I pull my stool over and sit on it, beside Mom. She holds my right hand between both of hers, kissing it once, then resting back on the chair's arm.

"Do you remember injecting Dociline? It would have been some time ago."

"Fourteen years," I say. "It would've been fourteen years ago, when the cops came to collect on our debts."

Mom presses a hand to her forehead. "I remember."

I tuck my left wrist out of view, so she can't see my cuff, and squeeze her hand for support.

"And yes, I registered with the ODR, but don't remember my Patron. I'm sorry."

"That's okay; you shouldn't have many memories of them, anyway," Alex says. "That's what Dociline does."

"Do you know how long your term lasted?" I stare at her as if I can will the answer into her brain.

"Did it just end? Was it fourteen years?"

I breathe deep, trying to soothe another sob before it overcomes me.

"No," Alex says because, when I look at him, he knows I can't. "It ended four years ago. Your term was ten years long."

Mom's eyes dart around the room, panicked. "Then why—why do I not remember?"

Alex clears his throat. He knows this isn't his story to share. "I'm going to excuse myself. I need to head back to the Silo, anyway, before my conservator gets suspicious. Elisha, would you mind keeping me in the loop? I'm not sure how we'll manage without Dutch—maybe Jess would be willing to play traveling doctor. I'm guessing Abigail will need regular injections, so checkups are a must. Make sure you both document any changes, memories that return, unnatural obedience, and so on, in a notebook. Date the entries." Alex's head bobs side to side while he thinks to himself. "That's good enough for now. It was nice to meet you, Abigail." He offers her his hand.

She takes his hand and shakes it. "You too, Alex."

I don't know how to say goodbye to Alex, so I half-wave, on his way to the door, and say, "Thanks, again."

"Glad I could help," he says with a small smile and nod, before closing the door behind him.

Mom and I sit together in the empty house, alone. I worry that if we move, it will erase what just happened. As if she can't cross the threshold. That when I got home she'd be there, like always: docile.

I hug her again, startling her, "I'm so glad you're here."

She holds me tight. "I don't mean to push, Elisha, but—"

"Right, sorry," I say, letting her go. "I owe you an explanation."

"Please." She smiles and leans toward me, in her chair.

"The Dociline you injected fourteen years ago didn't leave you like it was supposed to," I say, my words finally vindicated. My truth, *the* truth. "You never detoxed, even though you stopped injecting it. It's like you've been on Dociline all this time, except you haven't."

Mom gasps, covering her mouth with her right hand. "What happened to my baby?"

Abby. She never really met Abby. She gave birth a little over a year into her term, and only saw her twice a year, for ten years—but Mom wasn't herself for most of those visits. She doesn't know. I feel tears in my eyes, again.

"She must be . . ." She does the math under her breath.

"Thirteen," I say. "Abby's a teenager, now. You came back in time for the good part." I laugh and wipe at my wet cheeks.

"That's her name? Abby?"

"Yeah, she picked it because of you."

Mom moves her other hand to her face and begins crying all over again. "My babies. I can't believe I missed you growing up. Tell me more. There's so much I don't know."

"We live in the city, now," I say. An inoffensive start. "Nothing happened to the old house—and I think Dad really wants to move back, eventually—but we're here for now."

"Wow!" A smile overtakes her face as she wipes away her drying tears. "We're fancy, now."

"I guess so." There's no way around the truth. I'm why we moved here. I'm why Alex is here. All of this is my fault—the good and the bad.

"You don't sound happy about it, Elisha." She leans forward and looks at me with the most caring eyes. When I was a kid, I always felt like she was totally interested in whatever I told her. She had a way of making me feel like the only person in the world.

"I should explain what's happened since you left. Well, what's happened over the last year, really."

"I'm listening."

I tell her how Dad was planning for Abby to sell off our debt. How I snuck out in the middle of the night and walked to the city. Sold all of our debt for a lifetime contract. How Dylan sold Nora and Riley's in exchange for a few years.

"So . . ." Hesitation laces Mom's voice. "Are you someone's Docile? Is this a temporary visit?" Her face tenses.

"No! No, I'm coming home with you. My Patron amended my contract to say that my debts were satisfied and we would continue to receive the stipend. He took me home after six months."

"Why don't you sound more excited? What happened?"

"I refused Dociline."

Her face tenses as she clutches her chest. "Goodness, Elisha. What were you thinking?"

"I was thinking I didn't want what happened to you to happen to me!" I say, louder than I mean. "I'm sorry. This is— A lot's happened. I'm still working through it all."

"I'm sorry, sweetie; we don't have to do all this now, if you don't want."

"It's okay. I'd rather now than later. In front of everyone."

"So, who was this man? Why did he amend your contract?"

I look at the floor. "You just met him."

"Alex?"

"His name's Dr. Alexander Bishop the Third. His family makes Dociline, so it didn't sit well with them when I refused. He . . . hurt me," is all I can manage. The thought of bringing everything back up with my mother is too much. "I haven't talked about it with anyone in our family. It's too personal. I'm sorry I can't give you any more, right now."

"It's okay, sweetie." She closes her hand over mine just as my phone rings.

We both look. Verónica's name shows on the display. "That's our attorney. I have to answer."

"We have an attorney?" Mom asks.

Before she can ask why, I answer. "Hi, Verónica."

"Hey, Elisha. Are you free? I've got some news—a settlement offer from Lex Bishop. We should look over this together."

"How're you holding up?" Verónica asks, as we settle in. The community room in my building is decorated with modern furniture and historic art. Scenes of the city from hundreds of years ago, when all the streets were cobblestones.

"Okay." I sit beside her at the end of a long SmartTable. "Never need to attend another deposition, again."

She snorts. "Tell me about it. Though I was pleasantly surprised by Dutch Townsend's testimony. He's since contacted me, volunteering to testify on your behalf during trial."

"That's great." I try not to look too surprised. "Hey, before we get started, I need to tell you something." I decided, while I was walking up here, that I was going to tell Verónica about my mother. She's my attorney. Even though she's with Empower Maryland, I want her to have all the cards. I don't want her to be surprised in the courtroom, on Monday.

I'm relieved when she doesn't get angry. When she says, "Maybe that'll finally force them to pay attention to her—assuming you don't want to accept this offer."

I look at her, waiting. I'm supposed to ask. Ask the question, dammit. "What's their offer?"

She pulls up an email on her phone and reads it to me. "'Plaintiffs will dismiss all claims against defendants on the following conditions. One, defendants agree to sign a nondisclosure agreement detailing that Elisha Wilder will not discuss, with anyone, his time as Alex Bishop's Docile, his relationship with Alex Bishop since then, or Abigail Wilder's experience with Dociline and/or her current medical condition.

"'Two, defendant Elisha Wilder will prepare a public statement, to be approved by plaintiffs, apologizing for taking advantage of Alex Bishop during the six months Elisha was his Docile, denying any alleged resulting relationship, and stating that Dociline is not harmful and is not the cause of Abigail Wilder's current medical condition.

"'Three, defendants consent to plaintiffs' filing a Protective Motion with the court, stating that all defendants will keep a specified distance, to be agreed upon, from plaintiffs.'"

Verónica sets her phone down. "Basically, plaintiffs want you to deny that they ever hurt you or your mother, keep the details to yourself, and stay away from them. In exchange, they'll dismiss all charges. Your debt remains resolved. I'm not sure about the monthly stipend, it's not mentioned, but if you're interested in this, I'll contact plaintiffs' counsel to discuss."

"Should I be interested in this?" I'm not, but what if I should be? We could lose this case. Eugenia said Empower Maryland would cover it, but not if I can't tarnish Alex's reputation thoroughly. It suddenly occurs to me that we never agreed on what that meant. How bad do I have to make the Bishops look? Eugenia is the real judge. If I take this deal, her judgment won't matter. My family won't have any debts. I could resolve this on my own.

"It's not a bad deal—not outlandish in terms of its demands,"

Verónica says. "But it would undo everything you've been working for."

Everything *Empower Maryland* has been working for. Not that I want to apologize publicly or deny what happened to me or sign something that means I can never see Alex, again. Maybe we are working for the same things—at least some of them. Maybe Verónica is right.

"Do you think we can win?"

She rests her elbows on the table and leans forward. "Most jurors will be working-class city dwellers. Bishop Labs' own CFO—well, former CFO—admits they're the ones at fault. Our expert is credible and his report on your behavior is a damning indictment of Alex. You're extremely sympathetic, Elisha. As is your mother, regardless of her current state. How anyone who meets her would think that's not Dociline's doing baffles me. So, yeah, we have a solid chance at winning."

"Then, no. Tell Lex Bishop we don't accept his deal." Even though I'm terrified—even though every nerve in my body is strung like a grand piano—this is right. I won't let another Bishop buy his way out of responsibility. We can do this. We can win.

ALEX

The morning of the trial, I dress in a forest-green suit, pale yellow button-down, and navy-blue tie with "ABIII" monogrammed with gold thread. I lace my brown leather oxfords on a chair by the windows, then select a matching belt. The leather pulls soft between my fingers and fastens with a cinch around my hips.

I do love it. I love these beautiful materials, their expert craftsmanship, and their history. I want to think of my family in the same way. *Wanted* to. I'm terrified of losing them—not as they are but as I want them to be. The idea of them. The stability, no matter how harmful.

The velvet curtains hang heavy and closed. These past few weeks, I've tried to pretend this was my home and not a cloister, but that got harder when Dutch was fired and my new conservator stopped approving requests for outings. I run my fingers down a vertical fold. Dust springs into the air, from where it had gathered in the thick fabric. I refused a Docile to clean up after me.

Today, I am done pretending. I am done playing along with my father's narrative and letting others hold my life hostage. Like a bandage, I rip the curtains back and force myself to look out at the thousands of people living anonymous beside me.

Today, like Elisha did months ago, I refuse.

ELISHA

The jeweler is hard to find. None of my working-class friends are familiar with the market for custom-printed precious stones, and if I know Alex, he wouldn't patronize an easy-to-find store. Not one I can search for on Empower Maryland's computers. Not one with price tags. When I cave and ask Dutch, he's only able to suggest a few addresses.

I know I've found the right one when I see a sign on the door that reads: "By appointment only." I don't have one, but I knock, anyway. I knock loud enough that someone in the back couldn't miss me if they were asleep.

An older white person wearing a sleek black dress walks slowly into view. They don't acknowledge me until after they've unlocked the door and cracked it open. "Our hours are by appointment only," they say, tapping the sign with a many-ringed finger.

"I know," I say, "and I'm really sorry. This is kind of a jewelry emergency. I have to be in court in two hours."

"A jewelry emergency?" They look me over for evidence.

I hold up my left wrist, hook a finger through the loop, and pull out the diamond chain. "Did you make this?"

Their body relaxes as they push the door the rest of the way open. "You're Alex Bishop's Docile."

"*Was* Alex Bishop's Docile," I say.

"Right, right. I read the news."

"So, can you take it off?"

They recoil. Their mouth forms a frown. Then, they reach out and take the chain from me. "May I?"

I allow them to hold my wrist. Smooth their nimble fingers over the opalescent rose-gold surface, up the length of the chain. With a long, deep breath they say, "I can take it off, if that's what you really want."

With conviction, I say, "It is."

72

ALEX

Walking into the courtroom feels like stepping into a holy place. Like a temple carved from mahogany. High ceilings, raised daises for the judge, jury, and witness. Benches like pews for the assembly. We sit at a long table in front of them—Reginald, Gabriela, my father, and me. Supplicants.

I see Verónica Vasquez, first, followed by Elisha and his parents. They sit at the next table, but ignore us as if there is a glass wall separating our parties. Once, Abigail looks at me and smiles. Reassuring, since several days have passed since I last saw her. I don't know how long the counteractive will last.

The judge enters. Then, potential jurors.

Our attorneys review and select jurors like trading cards. Reginald and Gabriela do not consult me; they consult my father. Verónica speaks with Elisha in hushed tones, pointing people out and asking his opinions. I sit quietly, waiting my turn.

It does not come next. Next are the opening statements. While Reginald stands to speak, I watch the judge. Was he the one who declared me incompetent? Elisha doesn't deserve this trial at all, but he at least deserves a fair one. I doubt he'll get it.

"Today," Reginald addresses the jury, "I am going to tell you about a good man who wanted to help debtors and was, in return, taken advantage of by someone he trusted."

Only if that someone is my father.

"His friends and colleagues will tell you Alex Bishop has worked for years to create a product that smooths out the rocky path to a debt-free life. That he is caring and kind and hardworking and honest. That Elisha Wilder targeted Alex and refused Dociline so that he could, during their time together, gain Alex Bishop's trust, in order to defraud him for his family's three-million-dollar debt— revenge for a perceived and slanderous accusation that Dociline harmed his mother.

"Our experts will report that it is Elisha's influence that led to such drastic changes in Alex's personality, that caused him to shirk his friends, family, work, and responsibility. To amend his and Elisha's Docile contract, such that Elisha was able to go home after only six months of a life term debt-free—and still receiving one thousand dollars per month, from Alex.

"There is no doubt that life is hard for many, in Maryland. Together with the Office of Debt Resolution, Bishop Labs has sought to salve the burn of debt—but Elisha Wilder would see that undone. His offenses against Alex Bishop will rip apart the very systems set up to help debtors like him recover their livelihoods and become productive members of society, once again.

"You esteemed members of the jury get to decide. Do you allow this to pass? For one debtor's misguided revenge to destroy our institutions for his peers? I urge you not to let this injustice go unpunished." Reginald sits.

Vasquez stands. She walks to the center of the floor, nods at the judge, then looks imploringly at the jury.

"That was a good story Mr. Moore just told you. During this trial, he's going to attempt to convince you of it with people who look important on paper. Who can afford credibility. Unfortunately, his story is fiction.

"Elisha Wilder will recount his journey with you. How, since returning from her contracted Docile term, his mother has continued to live as if she were still injecting Dociline. That, because of her condition, he decided before meeting any potential Patrons that he would refuse Dociline—his legal right.

"He will tell you that he did not know Alex Bishop in advance of signing with him, and that his reasons had less to do with Dociline and more with the unexpected promise of a stipend that would change his family's life, back home.

"More upsettingly, he, his family, our experts, and even Alex's friends and colleagues will tell you how Alex Bishop brainwashed Elisha slowly over a period of six months, chipping away at his sense of self until he was reduced to a state similar to his mother's. Elisha Wilder has been genuinely and irreparably harmed by Alex Bishop. Since the end of their relationship, he has suffered from depression and suicidal ideations, the latter of which he acted on, once.

"During the past few weeks, Elisha has worked diligently with debtor support organizations, friends, and family, to learn basic functions, again. He's learned how to ask questions. How to make his own choices, rather than defaulting to Alex's preferences. How to pick out his own clothes and feed himself."

She points at him. "A young man who was so manipulated that he literally could not live, on his own, is incapable of the level of strategy and manipulation that Bishop's lawyers would imply. How, if Elisha could not change his own clothes without direction, do they expect that he could change Alex Bishop's entire personality?

"This lawsuit is an attempt to destroy a young man even further than he already has been. To demonize Elisha and defend the man who abused him. During this trial, I ask you to pay attention. Do not let the Bishops' attorneys brainwash you like Alex did Elisha."

Shame burns through my body as Vasquez takes her seat. She's right. That's the true story. I hope the jury believes it.

Mariah is the first to testify on my behalf. As during her deposition, she tells the sad story of a friend who lost who he was because of time spent with his Docile. She makes me sound helpless. Pathetic. And I believe that she believes that's the truth. Mariah wants everything for me. For me to marry and succeed. For my Dociline dreams to come true.

I'm surprised my attorneys even subpoenaed Jess, after the way they treated her during her deposition. I'm even more surprised she maintains the same opinions as during her deposition. No one pushes her too hard, but when Vasquez asks whether, in Jess' opinion as a professional in the field of Dociline, Elisha behaved like an on-med, she says yes.

When Vasquez asks whose doing that was, Jess says, "Alex's." Ever so slightly, Jess nods at me. This isn't a betrayal; it's help.

Our expert certainly doesn't help. My doctor takes the stand with the same cool authority she projected at Ellicott Hart. She speaks clearly, describing in plain language about how I threw tantrum after tantrum, destroyed my suite, needed to be restrained. She compares my behavior to my earlier mental health records and makes her point: that after six months of near isolation with Elisha, I was a different man. Reckless. Besotted. Unkempt. Lost.

The jury must think, after the defense expert testifies, that both Elisha and I are pitiable, incapable shells of our former selves. The battle for our parties to undermine each other exhausts me and I haven't moved from my uncomfortable wooden chair since we entered. Haven't spoken.

When my name is finally called—when Vasquez says, "I now call Dr. Alexander Bishop the Third to the stand"—my body is in such shock, I cannot move.

I need to, though. I need to disprove everything my expert witness said. That Reginald and Gabriela and my father have pushed me to portray.

Standing is like pressing a weight over my head. Walking is like learning how for the first time. I climb up the steps into the witness stand and sit facing the court. I've never been so nervous in my entire life as when Vasquez asks my name, for the record. My mouth dries upon answering. I can't swallow.

I pour myself a glass of water, while she continues, careful to drink slowly. Like a normal person.

"In your own words," she says, "please describe what happened the morning you met Elisha Wilder."

"When I arrived at the ODR, I was provided a selection of

Dociles that the Bishop Labs Board had prescreened." Speaking becomes easier, the more I do it. "But I wasn't interested in anyone on their list. I'm a discerning person—any of my friends or family will agree with that. I knew what I wanted, so I asked my Patron Liaison for access to the larger database. Presented with more options, I selected Elisha myself. As soon as I read his profile, I knew I wanted him as my Docile, and I'd do anything to get what I wanted."

"Thank you, Dr. Bishop. We all know Elisha refused Dociline, so let's fast-forward. How did you respond? Tell us about your relationship with Elisha when he was your Docile."

I shift on the hard wooden chair and focus on Vasquez. If I don't look at my father, I won't be tempted by the memory of him. Of how he used to make me feel—how he inspired and validated me.

He doesn't, anymore. He's toxic.

"I wanted Elisha to be my companion. I set him up with tutors in the arts and sciences. He cooked and exercised regularly. I gave him access to my entire library. Even brought him to work, sometimes."

"Sounds pretty nice," Vasquez says.

"On the surface."

My words stop her. Slowly, she turns her head, the slightest of smiles appearing on her face. "What do you mean?"

"I was under intense pressure to show the Board, my family, friends—and pretty much all of Baltimore—that I could control a Docile without Dociline. I'd been informed before I signed with Elisha that my position as CEO was at stake, and I was further informed by my parents that his refusal to take Dociline was my failure. So, I set rules."

Vasquez holds up a hand to stop me. "I have something for you." She walks back to the defense table and picks up a small leather-bound book. As she nears, I blanch with recognition. The notebook I made Elisha keep when he was a Docile. I gave it to Tom to destroy. She holds it up for the jury to see and says, "Defense counsel enters Exhibit D: Elisha Wilder's—"

"I know what this is." I hold out my hand and Vazquez meets my gaze. Decides to trust me. "I'll explain." I close my hands around the creased leather cover, brush my thumb over the exposed paper edges, flip to the first page. "Exhibit D," I say. "Elisha Wilder's notebook, which I made him keep while he lived with me. I gave it to him, initially, to write down the rules I mentioned."

There they are, numbered 1 through 7 in his careful print. As I flip through the pages, his handwriting evolves. Letters join together more frequently throughout the hundreds of notes and supplemental rules. The thousands of lines.

"What kind of rules?" Vazquez asks.

I trace my finger over the dents his pen made on the paper. "I ordered him not to ask questions, to always answer me aloud, keep himself groomed, not to lie, gave him protocol on how to behave in public situations—sitting on the floor beside my chair, for example. But also to let me know if he ever felt sick or hurt. There were more—Elisha wrote them all down, so he'd remember them, even if I can't. They were things I'd say on the fly, like not to bite his fingernails or bounce his knee under the table."

Vazquez takes the notebook from me and walks it back to the defense table. She turns and faces me square. "What was the intention behind these rules?"

I feel like my heart is going to explode when I say, "To modify his behavior."

Murmurs fill the hall until the judge bangs his gavel and asks for silence. "Continue," he says.

"Thank you, Your Honor. Dr. Bishop, what do you mean by that? Can you explain?"

I look at her and only her. "I knew I would be humiliated and that the Board would take control away from me if I was unable to guarantee Elisha's compliance, so I trained him."

"Trained him?"

"Yes, like you would train a dog. I even used similar techniques." I risk a glimpse at my father. His jaw is set, eyes are trained on me. "He had no reason to trust me—I'm pretty sure he even told me he didn't like me. I didn't blame him, but I also didn't care. I was strict with him, following through on punishments when he broke a rule—no matter how small or accidental."

"Is that all?" Vasquez bites her lip. Her excitement emboldens me.

"No. The level of loyalty I was aiming for wouldn't be earned only with negative reinforcement."

"What else did you do?"

I shrug. "I made him like me. I showed him that I was willing to reward good behavior with more freedom, fun experiences, a more casual atmosphere, and so on."

"Your friends and experts have testified that Elisha changed you, is that true?"

"Yes," I say, "but not the way they'd lead you to believe."

This time, I look square at Elisha. I haven't since he entered the room. He sits on the edge of his seat, lips parted. Dressed like I haven't seen him in a while, in a suit. Brown tweed, well tailored, court appropriate, and yet earthy. He's clean shaven, but his hair is longer than I ever allowed. A strand hangs, ready to fall in front of his eyes as he watches me.

"I fell in love with him," I say to Elisha. A warm blush spreads across his cheeks before he looks down at his clasped hands. Those words don't mean what they used to. We both know we shouldn't feel that way, if we even do. But Elisha glances up at me and touches his hand to his heart. Something still remains.

"At your deposition," Vasquez continues, "you testified otherwise."

"I said that because I had to, in order to please my father and the Board. They'd taken everything away from me, overnight. I was only trying to survive."

"Objection, Your Honor," Reginald says.

"He's your client, counselor," the judge says, unimpressed.

Vasquez presses on, seamlessly. "Can you explain how you fell in love with Elisha?"

"It was my own doing. I bought him clothes I liked, gave him hobbies I enjoyed. Tailored him into the perfect lover. He softened into the role, over time. It was like making a boyfriend in my own image, only he never refused me and did whatever he was told. In that way, he wasn't a boyfriend at all—he was clearly a Docile—but I loved him like one."

"So why did you amend your contract and send Elisha home?"

"I was misguided for a long time—my whole life, actually. Even though I was raised around Dociles, including some that became my good friends, I never questioned anything. Never questioned myself. One day, though, late in our time together, I went on a date. In the back of my mind, I knew my feelings for Elisha were inappropriate, and I was desperate to prove otherwise. But my date mistreated him. Hurt him, physically, and discounted his role in my life. I woke up so quickly. In that moment, I saw what I had done. I knew that if I genuinely cared about Elisha, the right thing to do was to get him as far away from me as possible."

"What happened after that?" Vasquez asks, leading me gently forward.

"My dad showed up and told me he'd had a judge declare me incompetent—"

"Your Honor! What he's alleging—"

I don't stop, leaning closer to the microphone. "—put me under a conservatorship, and committed me to Ellicott Hart. I had no hand in this complaint, and would never have forced it on Elisha and his family. As far as I'm concerned, this whole lawsuit is a farce."

Reginald jumps to his feet. "This has gone on for far too long."

"Alex Bishop is his client, as Your Honor has pointed out. I have not led him on or asked any inappropriate questions. I have a right to—"

"Your Honor, I move to strike the testimony of my client. As he stated, he's been declared incompetent. He has no business on the stand."

The judge surveys us from his throne. "I'm going to let the jury decide how credible Dr. Bishop is. They have your expert reports and his deposition testimony. He's one of the plaintiffs. He is allowed to speak on the record if he wants."

Reginald sits with such fervor, the chair skids backwards with a loud screech.

"You may continue, Ms. Vasquez."

"Thank you, Your Honor." She returns to me. "Alex, before I dismiss you, I wanted to revisit your opinions on Dociline."

"Okay."

She picks up the transcript from her table. "During your deposition, you testified that Dociline is, quote, 'a wonderful invention that I'm honored to have participated in developing. It's changed a lot of lives. Helped a lot of people.' When asked about the new formula you said, 'We were making good progress, when I last worked on it,' despite your notes reflecting otherwise. You also said you 'still think there's a good version of Dociline.' Do you still believe that?"

I glance at Elisha again. "Yes and no. I think Dociline perpetuates a harmful debt system, rather than helping it, though I am sure that individuals have been relieved by the existence of Dociline. And, honestly, I'm not sure what our current debt resolution system would look like without Dociline. Is it more or less humane to ask that people pay their debts off, fully aware of the drudgery or horror they're experiencing? Our society is broken, and I don't know how to fix it. But I do know that Dociline can hurt people."

"You know as in you have a specific example?"

"Yes. Abigail Bishop."

"You testified during your deposition that even though you observed her at her home, you were unable to say for certain that Dociline had caused her disability."

"Since then, I've had a chance to meet with and further evaluate her."

"You have?" Vasquez looks pleasantly surprised, though I assume she's faking it. After all, Abigail Wilder is sitting with the other defendants, more aware and alert than she's been in over a decade. Surely he told his family rather than letting them believe she miraculously came out of it.

Harsh whispers draw my gaze to the plaintiffs' table. To my

father's scowl. After this, they'll probably lock me in my room. Might as well spill everything while I'm still able.

"Yes," I say. "When I met Abigail at her home, she exhibited several characteristics that on-med Dociles do: a willingness to obey, memory loss. Well, not memory loss, more like memory difficulties? And her eyes looked glossy, dazed. Like she wasn't fully there. On-meds can look 'off' like that, but not to the same extent. Abigail acted more like a broken doll than an on-med. I offered to examine her medically, but her husband refused my help."

"So, when did you . . ."

Forget locking me in my room; the second I reveal this, I'm fired. My time at Bishop Labs? Over. I'll be surprised if they let me back in to pick up my things. All I can do is omit Jess' and Dylan's names so they won't face the same or worse. Dutch has already been fired. I omit his name to spare him the "or worse."

"Several weeks later. I was able to visit Elisha for the first time after my dad committed me to Ellicott Hart, and offered the same help to him. He agreed and we secured a neutral meeting place, where I could run some tests."

"What did you find?"

"Honestly, the results were shoddy at best. You have to understand that, at Bishop Labs, we normally utilize control off-meds, a fully stocked and staffed lab, and so on. Elisha and I did this in an empty apartment building with scrounged supplies. The most I learned is that there was still Dociline running through her veins. Commercial Dociline is manufactured to maintain efficacy for two weeks before leaving the body. I have every reason to believe the Dociline in her blood contributed to her disability."

"Well, she looks better."

"She does." I breathe deep, sit tall, puff up my chest in preparation for what I'm about to say. I've already crossed a line, but that doesn't mean I can't cross another one. "Because I developed a treatment to counteract the effects Dociline has wrought on Abigail Wilder's body, over the last fourteen years."

Half the courtroom gasps, including Eugenia, who immediately stands up and dashes for the door, notes in hand. Her heels click down the aisle as those around her murmur, the volume rising. Even the jury—even my lawyers. Only Elisha's family and my father do not react. His, because they already knew. Mine, because the words are so blasphemous he cannot process them. How much anger and disappointment can one man contain?

The judge bangs his gavel and shouts, "Silence!" until the room simmers down.

Dad looks straight ahead, the whole time, as if I'm not there. I don't dare try to get his attention. Not now, anyway.

"Your Honor." Reginald stands. "Given this . . . *new* information, plaintiffs request to adjourn for the day."

"Defense, do you consent or oppose?" the judge asks.

Vasquez confers with Elisha and his parents, then says, "We consent."

"Good." The judge smacks his gavel down. "Then this court is adjourned until tomorrow at nine a.m. in this same courtroom. Dismissed. Dr. Bishop, you can go."

"Sorry," I whisper, before standing up and making my way clumsily out of the witness stand and back toward my seat. I keep my eyes on the empty wooden chair as if it'll disappear if I look away. My heart pounds in my chest, suit feels increasingly hot, as I join my father and attorneys. I busy myself with my jacket, while I wait, putting it on slowly, patting my pockets—not that I have anything.

I follow Dad and my attorneys from the courtroom, down the hall and the winding staircase. Still, no one speaks to me, nor do they speak to one another. Outside, a mob of press awaits, shoving microphones in our faces. I don't speak to any of them; I follow Dad to the car. He gets in the back, meets my eyes, and says, "Find your own way home." The door slams in my face.

73

ELISHA

Verónica and I are going over my expected testimony, that evening, when we see the news recap. Alex's face fills the television at Empower Maryland. I straighten up, abandoning our notes for the remote control. Several groups of people look between me and the television as I stand and the volume rises.

"Dr. Bishop!" Microphones thrust into Alex's space like weapons. He stands alone at the edge of the sidewalk, as his father's car pulls away. I watch, waiting for another to pull up, but it doesn't happen.

Below the image, a headline scrolls past: *Alex Bishop—"I quit."*

Verónica gives up trying to reclaim our attention and looks over her shoulder.

"Haven't we seen enough of him?" Dad asks.

"David," Nora and Mom say, both scowling at him.

Abby joins me as I walk closer to the television. "What's he doing?" she asks.

"I think . . ." On-screen, Alex beckons to a reporter I recognize. Chadwick Bell. "He's with the—"

"*City Paper,*" the reporter says.

"Alex hates this guy," I say. "He always hounded us."

"Doesn't seem to hate him, now," Abby says.

"Dr. Bishop, what did your father say?"

"He said to find my own way home." Alex looks past the camera, as if it's not even there.

"Why would he say that?"

"Because I just testified that—" Alex focuses, now. I watch him compose himself for the cameras like he's done thousands of times. Smoothing his hair back, straightening the cuffs of his jacket, fondling his tie clip. "Most of you don't know that I just testified that it's likely Dociline had an adverse effect on Abigail Wilder's health and that, when he was my Docile, I intentionally modified Elisha Wilder's behavior so he'd be easier to control."

Chadwick's face lights up like a kid who just got a pony for his birthday. "How do you think these revelations will influence your work at Bishop Labs?"

Alex snorts. *Snorts,* on live television. At least, it was live, this morning. I can't believe he didn't tell me his father kicked him out. I feel oddly proud.

"I don't work for Bishop Labs, anymore." He crosses his arms, confidently.

"You don't?" Chadwick asks.

"I'm pretty sure I was just fired, but if I wasn't, let me be clear: I quit. I can no longer work for Bishop Labs. I cannot unknow everything I've learned, this year, and I cannot continue on the same trajectory, given that knowledge."

"So, what are you going to do, now?"

"When he was with me, I told Elisha Wilder that we all change every day. I'm sorry I had to change him for the worse in order to change myself for the better. I'll never make everything up to him, and his mother, and the City of Baltimore, but I'm going to try. I have no idea how; ask me again in a month—or a year. Right now, I just need to figure out where I'm going to sleep." The horde of microphones shove forward, again, as Alex turns away from them, looks both ways, and crosses the street.

I press my hand over the pocket where my phone rests, resisting the urge to call Alex. What would I tell him? That I'm proud of him? It feels strange, but I am. He testified against his own family. He quit the job that consumed his life. Struck out on his own.

"Come on." Mom waves Abby and me back to the table. "Let's focus, so Verónica can finish preparing for tomorrow."

Before we can sit down, the news anchors pull back from Alex's footage and turn to a video of—"Wait, that's Mariah. Alex's friend Mariah VanBuren. She's a trillionaire. And she's awful." I turn the volume up.

"—I am dismayed to report that, tonight, during an emergency Board meeting, Bishop Laboratories voted to relieve Alexander Bishop of his duties as CEO. Though he was already operating on a provisional status, today's display, both on the witness stand and the steps of the courthouse, showed how unstable Dr. Bishop has become over the past year."

"Unstable?" Abby says, shocked. She's not used to the way Mariah twists words. Abuses her power. "I might not like Alex, but he seems more stable now than when—"

"Shh!" Verónica quiets Abby. "I want to hear what else she says."

On-screen, the interviewer asks, "Are you worried about this alleged treatment?"

"Not at all," Mariah says. "Bishop Labs maintains the stance that Dociline played no part in harming Abigail Wilder, assuming anything was ever wrong with her to begin with. Additionally, we would not consider any drug Dr. Bishop alleges to have created safe or viable. Only a few weeks ago, he was declared incompetent by a city judge, placed under a conservatorship, and involuntarily committed to a private mental health facility. Nothing Dr. Bishop says about Dociline or Abigail Wilder should be trusted." She turns to face the camera. "Alex, if you're listening."

"Dear god, she's good," Verónica mutters.

"Please seek help. Know that if you contact Ellicott Hart, there's still a room waiting for you. We only want the best for you and are sorry that meant ties needed to be severed—"

"I have an idea," Verónica says, pressing the mute button. She grabs a binder labeled "Medical Records" off the table. "I think Empower Maryland should release these to the public. I'm friendly with Chadwick Bell at *City Paper*—the one who interviewed Alex.

I bet if we hand these off to him, today, he could give us a damn good write-up. Push it tomorrow morning. Really throw plaintiffs' counsel off their game.

"Obviously, they'd need Abigail's consent," Verónica continues. "What do you think?" She's already getting out her phone when she looks to Mom for her answer.

Mom turns to me, as if I know better. I don't; Verónica's the expert. "It's up to you," I say. "This could be our only chance to prove to the world how unsafe Dociline is. Right now, people care. If they listen, we could help other debtors."

Dad takes her hand. "I'm not usually into this media stuff, but what Verónica and Elisha said make sense."

Mom nods to herself, then says, "Yes. Let's do it. I'll sign whatever you need."

74

ELISHA

The courtroom is silent except for the occasional turn of newspaper pages. Everyone seated here, today, heard Alex's interview and Mariah's follow-up. This morning, they read Chadwick Bell's profile on my mother. The tension in the room is deafening, breaking only when the judge enters and calls court to session.

Reginald Moore stands. "Plaintiffs would like to call Elisha Wilder to the stand."

I can do this. I knew this was coming, but now I'm so nervous the courtroom prickles to gray in the corners of my vision. I'm going to have a panic attack. I can't do this right now. Get it together, Elisha.

"Mr. Wilder?" the judge says. "Do you need a minute?"

"No." I stand and smooth the wrinkles in my suit. Instinctively, I reach for my cuff, for the diamond chain, but it's not there.

It's not there. I removed it.

I don't belong to anyone.

I rub my finger, instead, over the thick scar of a branding iron. The mark of a debtor. I can do this.

I walk slowly to the witness stand and sit, minding my posture and suit. Trying to look as credible as possible for these people judging me. None of them have enough debt to fully understand what it's like. You can't serve on a jury once you register with the ODR or go to debtors' prison.

Reginald approaches with a smug smile on his face and a piece of paper in his hand. He's the only one in the whole courtroom who looks pleased after the onslaught of news. "I'd like to submit for evidence plaintiffs' Exhibit E, Elisha Wilder's Multilineage Debt Resolution Consent Form, signed by David Burns and Abigail Wilder."

Oh no.

"Mr. Wilder, you stated in your deposition that you believe Dociline harmed your mother such that she still acts like an on-med despite having discontinued the drug four years ago. Do you stand by that testimony?"

"Yes," I say.

"And can you tell the court whether your mother was in her Docile-like state when she signed this consent form?" He points to where it rests, still, on the ledge.

"She was," I say.

"Did you consider that, like an on-med, she might be unable to read and understand legal documents such as this one when you gave it to her?"

"I—" I look at Verónica, but she can't help me, now. I can't lose this case for us over a permission slip and I can't disappoint Empower Maryland. "I didn't know for sure, either way."

"Did she know who you were?"

"Yes."

"After Dr. Bishop injected her with the alleged counteractive, did she know who you were?"

"Yes."

"What did she say?"

"She said, 'You're so tall.'"

"Safe to assume, then, that she did not remember you growing up."

"I don't know."

"Okay, that's fair." He holds his hands up in surrender.

"No, it's not fair," I say.

"Pardon me?"

"My mom stopped injecting Dociline when her term ended. She was supposed to detox within a month. She was supposed to come home to us, but she didn't. No one believed us or helped us, until recently. How was she supposed to sign anything over four years? How could we pay off our debts without sending her back to the ODR, herself? Would she have been allowed to sign for her own debts or was her only option debtors' prison thanks to Dociline? No, it's not fair. She might not have been able to read or understand that form—I don't know—but we had no other choice. Bishop Labs and the ODR made sure of that." I look at the jury, pleadingly. *Believe me.*

"Did you tell anyone at the ODR about your mother's condition when you submitted this form with her signature?"

"No."

"So, you submitted it aware of its fraudulent nature."

"I told you I didn't know whether she was capable of understanding."

"But her medical records state she behaved like an on-med Docile for years, after coming home."

"Yes."

"Would you trust that an on-med could understand and give consent to signing a legal document?"

"No."

"Your father signed this, as well. He's never injected Dociline, has he?"

"No, he hasn't."

"Was he aware of what he was signing?"

"Yes." Technically true. He thought it was for Abby, but I hadn't filled her name in, yet, and he didn't ask. Reginald doesn't either.

"Why should we believe you, Mr. Wilder? By all rights, you submitted a fraudulent document to a government office and, by Dr. Bishop's own admission, continued working with him on a back-alley drug to inject your mother with. Did you consider that you were tampering with an ongoing lawsuit?"

"N-no."

"That fraternizing with the plaintiff, without the knowledge of counsel, would compromise this case? You manipulated your way into the ODR, then manipulated Alex Bishop."

"That's not true!" I shout. My words absorb into the room. "I only ever wanted to help my family."

Reginald smiles. "I bet you did, Mr. Wilder." He turns and walks back to his seat. "No further questions."

Deep breaths, Elisha. In, two, three, four, five. Out, two, three, four, five. I've got this. The jury heard what I said. They'll understand. They have to. I'm not a fraud. They can't think I'm a fraud.

Verónica takes her time with me, asking questions I know the answers to. That give me confidence. That I've already answered to Empower Maryland and during my deposition and half a dozen others.

No, I didn't know who Alex was before I signed with him.

Yes, I refused Dociline.

No, it was not my goal to "seduce" him.

No, it wasn't my goal for my contract to be amended. I fought to stay with Alex like I was fighting for my life.

Then Verónica asks me, "What did it feel like?"

"I'm sorry?" The question catches me off guard.

"What did it feel like to be with Alex, from the time you signed the contract, until he amended it and took you home?"

How do I answer that? I felt more and less during those six months than I have during the rest of my life.

"I don't mean to overwhelm you," she says. "Let me break it down into more manageable parts. How did you feel during your initial time with Alex? During the first month or so."

"I felt a lot of things. Angry at Alex, in general. That he refused to see or care and could afford not to. That someone with as much money and power was even allowed to exist—I'd never met anyone that rich, before. But I was also angry at myself for giving in to him, doing what he said."

"You must've known you'd have to, since you'd planned to refuse Dociline, even before you met him."

"I did. I never planned to disobey—especially not with the threat of losing our contracted stipend. I'd accepted that I was a Docile. That was my life. Doesn't mean I liked myself for it. Alex was infuriatingly fair. All I had to do was follow rules. When I broke them, it was my own fault."

I pause, remembering the feeling of rice digging into my knees, the angry scratch of my pen over paper, and the loneliness of confinement.

"After breaking the rules, the first time, I became increasingly nervous that I would break them again. Then— Do you mind if I keep going? I think I understand your initial question, now."

"Please, go on," she says.

"At first I was nervous because I didn't want to lose the stipend. Then, because I didn't want to be punished, again. Then, because I started to care? I remember worrying, one night early on, that I would get to know him. What if he was nice? People can be nice to your face and awful everywhere else. I was afraid to lose my anger, but . . . I did. I lost myself.

"The more time I spent with Alex, the more I got to know him. He made me like him—he said as much, yesterday. It wasn't all punishments. He . . ." I bite my lip.

Verónica moves closer and gestures toward herself. "Look at me. You don't have to look at anyone else."

"I'd never experienced companionship like that before. After a few months, I was sleeping in his bed regularly. He was a good lover and he cared—I think he genuinely cared whether I was okay, when things went badly with my family or if I had a bad experience at a party. He said it was his responsibility. I began to care, too, until all I wanted was to make him happy.

"By the end, Alex was all I could think about. The stipend, my family, punishments—they didn't mean anything. I would have done anything for him. When he told me he was taking me home? I've never hurt more in my entire life. I still feel that ache in my chest, the dread and the longing, when I remember it. I felt like there was no point to living, anymore. I wanted to die."

Verónica lets my words hang in the open air of the courtroom. "I've heard you say you love Alex. Is that still true?"

"I can't give you a clear answer. I've thought so much about what love means, since he let me go. Do I feel strongly for Alex? Yes. Do I care deeply about him? Yeah, I do, whether or not I want to or think it's right or deserved. My mom spent ten years on Dociline and it lingered with her for the next four. I spent six months with Alex Bishop and I'm not sure my feelings for him will ever fully go away. Whatever you want to call them."

"Thank you, Elisha."

"Thank you."

When I sit down, Mom closes her hand over mine. We listen to Dutch confirm Alex's training methods and my feelings. He smiles at me when he takes down Bishop Labs, again.

I hope we've done it. As Reginald and Verónica give their closing arguments, all I can think is, Please let us have won. Please believe us. I watch the jury. If I could project my feelings into their brains, I would, I would, I would.

We sit in silence: Verónica, my family, and I. Nora, Abby, and Eugenia came over to hear the verdict, but since they're not named defendants, they won't be allowed to sit with us in the courtroom, so we sit together, now.

"Do you think we're going to win?" Abby asks Verónica.

"I think we have a good chance," she says.

By now, I'm used to disappointment, though. To an uncaring state. To judges who declare people incompetents because their parents can afford it. To trillionaires suing debtors.

"Even if we don't," she says, "we made a good case."

"You did," Eugenia says. "The details about Dociline and Abigail and what Alex did are all over the news. People know, now. Politicians and journalists—they're finally taking our calls, because of you. Reaching out. Sharing your story with the working class and folks in the counties. I don't want you to worry about the money, if you lose. You've done good, even if it doesn't work out in this instance. Your brother is very brave for what he's done."

"He is," Abby says.

"He is," Mom echoes, a hint of her Docile mannerisms.

"Yeah," Dad says, squeezing my shoulder. "He is."

We look up when the bailiff knocks on the door. "They're ready for you."

"Thank you." Verónica stands up and faces us. "Ready?"

"Ready," I say, and follow her back into the courtroom.

The judge and jury are already there when we enter. The benches crammed with spectators. Lex, Alex, and their lawyers stand behind their own table.

Up close, I can see the dark circles under Alex's eyes. When I pass, he mouths, *Good luck.*

"Madam Foreperson," the judge says, "have you come to a consensus regarding the matter of *Bishop, et al., versus Wilder, et al.*?"

She stands. "We have, Your Honor."

This is it.

"As to whether defendants Abigail Wilder and David Burns legally transferred their debt to defendant Elisha Wilder, in order to sell it to plaintiff Dr. Alexander Bishop the Third—"

This is it.

This is it.

"—we find that Abigail Wilder did not."

No.

"And that her outstanding debt, in the amount of approximately one million dollars—"

"No," I say out loud.

"—be reverted back to her name."

Cheers and objections rise up from the room, again. Increasingly loud chatter. I remind myself that Eugenia said Empower Maryland will pay the million dollars. I scan the crowd behind me, hoping to catch sight of her reaction, but I can't find her. She just said it, and they haven't even read the entire verdict. I can't help but worry this is a sign, though. That I'll be labeled a fraud and Eugenia will take it back.

"As to—"

The judge bangs his gavel down, silencing the court.

Please.

"As to whether defendant Elisha Wilder, with the assistance of defendants Abigail Wilder and David Burns, did knowingly and intentionally defraud plaintiff Dr. Alexander Bishop the Third—"

Please, please, please.

"—we find in favor of the defendants."

The courtroom erupts with noise—cheers and sighs and groans. I shudder, holding Mom's hand so tightly, it's the only thing that keeps me on my feet. Whisper, "We did it."

75

ALEX

When I return to the lab for my things, they're already packed in boxes, waiting at the security desk beside Dylan. "I packed up your shit," she says. "An intern was supposed to, but I volunteered."

"Thanks," I say, glad to see a familiar face in this building where I am no longer welcome.

"And I'm supposed to tell you that all your permissions have been revoked." She watches while I stack the three boxes on top of one another. I didn't have much, here, anyway. Not since I liquidated my apartment. "I'm sorry it played out this way for you, Alex."

"It's fine," I say, though I was surprised to hear her say it. "I chose this."

"Yeah, but family is supposed to love you no matter what," she says.

"Well." I pick the boxes up and peer around their side. "Doesn't always work out that way, apparently. Thanks for your help with this and . . . everything." She knows. This is as close to a heart-to-heart as Dylan and I will ever get.

"You know my rate, if you ever need it, again." She smiles and heads back into the Silo.

I walk out to Jess' waiting car, load the boxes into the trunk, then join her in the front seat. "Ready to go, boss?" she says.

"You know I'm fired, right?"

"Holy shit, you're fired?" Her face morphs from surprise to laughter in seconds. "Of course I know, doofus. I'm still allowed to call you boss, if I want." She pulls out into traffic.

"Fine with me," I say.

"Any idea what you're going to do?" Jess asks, while she swerves around stopped cars and buses on her way up Charles Street.

"Well, I don't have a house and I don't have a boyfriend and I don't have any money. I don't have a job and my résumé probably isn't worth much, after all this."

"Don't you mean your name?"

"That too."

"Well, you still have friends."

"Did you learn that from an after-school special?"

"No!" She looks at me a second too long and nearly flies through a red light. "Whoops. I just mean we'll help you."

"I know," I say. "Thank you for that."

"No problem, boss."

I haven't lived with a roommate, well, ever. Haven't stood awkwardly in someone else's house, unsure what I'm allowed to touch or where I'm allowed to go. I've stayed with Jess, before, but never like this. I'm not even paying her rent. I hate it. I hate feeling like I'm in someone's debt without the means to make up for it.

The next morning, I lie in bed, on sheets embroidered with my name—a name I don't even want, anymore—while Jess goes to work. This isn't like when I broke up with Elisha, the first time. I can't mope around in bed. Sell everything I own.

I can get out of bed, though, and I do. I can shower. I can put on real clothes—or not. I'm not going anywhere. After I make myself a strong black tea—Jess doesn't keep coffee in the house—I stack everything on her kitchen table into a neat pile and set it on the counter. No SmartTable, here.

I retrieve my personal tablet from the guest-room-now-my-room and plant myself in a flamingo-pink chair, wearing a pair of heather-gray University of Maryland sweatpants and a white tee shirt. There's enough color here to go around.

A knock interrupts my doodling.

"Coming!" I call as I make my way on bare feet down the narrow hallway. Jess lives in a historic building; I have to turn three locks to open the door.

I yank open the humidity-swollen door, ignoring the loud whine of sticky hinges. In front of me stands Elisha. Unlike me, he's wearing a pair of tight-fitting jeans, the denim worn, soft, and fraying. Over them, a long crimson tee shirt hangs. Over that, an unzipped hoodie.

"Going incognito?" I ask.

"What does that mean?"

I motion around my own head. "Don't want anyone to recognize you."

"Oh, no." His eyes rake over my body, in turn. "Don't want anyone to recognize you, either, I can see." Elisha smiles, looking between his scuffed leather boots and my bare feet.

"You got me," I say, sharing his smile. "Were you looking for Jess? She isn't home."

"That's okay." He squeezes into the narrow hallway, beside me. "I actually wanted to talk to you."

"Oh." We're so close. I scratch the back of my neck to occupy my hands, then realize that would be better accomplished locking the door. "Well, please, have a seat. The kitchen is mostly clean."

Elisha continues down the hallway, taking his sweatshirt off and draping it over a lime-green chair, before sitting down.

"Would you like some tea?"

"Sure."

I pick a blue floral teacup out of the cupboard and fill it. "Milk? Sugar?"

"Both, thank you."

I set the cup down in front of him, then sit one chair away.

"Are you afraid to sit next to me?" Elisha asks.

"No. Yes."

He raises an eyebrow.

"I want to respect your space."

"You don't have to treat me like I'm fragile; I'm not going to break. I'm not one hundred percent better and I probably never will be, but I am getting better. It's hard. Every decision I make, every conversation I have, I have to sort through what's mine and what's yours. Sometimes it's both—and I'm learning that's okay."

"Sorry," I say. "We haven't spent a lot of time together, lately, so I wasn't sure."

"I know. Looks like you've really hit rock bottom." He takes a long sip of his tea, attempting to maintain a look of concern, but he falters, smiling.

"Meet the new all-pajamas-all-the-time Alex." I hold out my arms.

He sets the teacup down. "I'm into it."

"Good, because I have two pairs."

"We can get you some clothes from the donation closet at Empower Maryland, if you're being serious."

"No, I'm good." The suggestion throws me. Empower Maryland did help, in the long run, but we still only barely trust each other. "Didn't really need as many clothes as I had, before."

"Okay, but if you need anything . . ." He peers at my tablet, still on the table. "What's this?"

"Nothing." I reach for it, but Elisha beats me to it. Not that I put up much of a fight. "It's just an idea," I say, leaning over while he reads my notes. "I don't actually have the means to—"

"This looks great," he says. "A clinic that specializes in helping debtors who've been affected by Dociline?"

"Yeah, I thought—" I rub my hand over my growing stubble. "I know a lot about Dociline and working with your mom made me realize that I could actually do something about it. I thought I didn't have anything to contribute without my bank account."

"I've been struggling to figure out the same—minus the newly broke part." Elisha sets the tablet back on the table. "I think I'm going to quit my job at Empower Maryland. I took it because I was looking to do something for myself, but Eugenia kind of stuck me with it, and I think I hate it?"

I snort. "I'm sorry, it's not funny."

"It kind of is?" Elisha chuckles, too. "I can do anything I want! And I have no idea what I want to do. When I think about that too much, I miss being your Docile." He lowers his voice. "Don't tell anyone I said that."

"Your secret's safe with me."

Elisha straightens up with renewed energy. "But, you know, this clinic looks pretty great."

"You did say that."

"I meant it. You could apply for a loan to get it started. I bet Empower Maryland would pitch in."

There's that name, again. "Think they're going to help the Third?"

"Almost all their money comes from Dutch. He's one of your best friends. In fact, I bet he'd love to get in on this. He was your CFO."

"True, but—"

"And Jess! She can help with the doctor part." Elisha flicks his hand as if he'll figure out her job description later.

"I can't ask all my friends to drop what they're doing and come work on a nonexistent organization." Elisha's never worked a job like this, before. He doesn't know how hard it is—how much risk—

"Yes, you can."

"At least one of us needs a real moneymaking job. Plus, if Jess quits, Dylan's stuck at the Silo all alone."

"True." Elisha slumps back in his chair. "I bet she'd invest, though. When does she get home?"

"Okay, maybe. Maybe I'll ask."

"Ask! It's a good idea."

"Okay, I'll ask." I take the tablet and set it off to the side. Have another sip of my tea, lukewarm from how long it's been sitting. Elisha watches me.

"What?"

He shrugs. "I've been thinking about what love is, since Verónica asked me, on the witness stand."

"Oh?" My face warms. I hide it behind my teacup.

"I meant what I said."

"You were under oath."

Elisha looks at me as if I've made a bad pun.

"Sorry."

He wraps both of his hands around his still-steaming cup and pulls his knees up against his chest, boots catching on the edge of the chair. "I had sex with someone else—after we broke up."

Not what I was expecting. I try to relax my face. Seem casually interested and definitely not jealous. "Oh?"

"Yeah. It was fun. Different. I like him and trust him, but I don't have feelings for him."

I assume he's talking about Onyx, but don't make him say it. I haven't forgotten that he confessed to having let Onyx hit him, before.

"Not like I do for you."

I'm forced to re-relax my face all over again, at those words. To pretend I'm not hopeful and interested. That I don't feel the same.

Oh, fuck it. "I still have feelings for you, too. I shouldn't. I know they're not based on a consensual relationship."

"It sucks," he says. "We definitely shouldn't act on them."

"It would be irresponsible and counterproductive."

"Here's what I'm thinking," Elisha says, putting his feet back on the floor and his teacup back on the table. He says it like he's worked out a heist. "Let's start your clinic, together. I want to be with you—want to be around you without the pressure. I liked when you showed me how to help my mom, in the safe house. Let's take some time, and let's make a deal."

"What is it?"

"Don't fall in love with anyone else."

"Okay?"

"Sex, fine."

"I don't see a lot of that in my future, but—"

"Then it should be easy for you."

"What about you?" I cross my arms. "You should be exploring, dating, falling in love with other people."

"I'm exploring myself, right now, and that's honestly enough," he says. "We can check in with each other, in a while. Until then, I would like to date our clinic."

"Any clinic would be lucky to have you."

Elisha stands and pulls on his sweatshirt. Walks down the narrow hallway toward the door. I follow, reaching past him to turn one of the dead bolts. Elisha reaches for another, exposing a scar I haven't seen since January.

"You removed the cuff," I say, surprised at myself for not having noticed.

"Yeah." He pushes up his sleeves and holds out his arms to me. "Wasn't easy finding your jeweler."

I reach tentatively forward. "Can I?"

"Yes," he says.

I slide my palms over his, until my fingers wrap gently around his wrists. With my right thumb, I brush the worn-down "US" once branded on his skin. Scar tissue I covered up with rose gold and opal and diamond. With my left thumb, the thin line across his wrist, still red. As if pressing too hard would open the wound—the *ache*—back up.

Elisha runs his hands up my arms, takes hold of my shoulders. Looks at me with his warm brown eyes. "Can I?" he asks.

"Yes," I whisper.

He rolls onto his toes and presses his lips gently against mine. I'm afraid to move. Afraid to push him, afraid to lose him. I wrap my arms around his back and waist. Feel his muscles tense under my fingers. He kisses me again, and again, parting so slowly I feel dazed. Heady.

Elisha leans his forehead against the base of my neck and I rest my chin on his head. When he finally looks at me, he says, "I'm not giving up on you, Alexander Bishop."

I don't answer him, because I want him to feel like he can go on without me if he needs to. He'll see me, soon, anyway. We're neighbors, now, and I think I promised to open a clinic with him. This isn't goodbye. It's a beginning—one we've agreed on. Together.

ACKNOWLEDGMENTS

To those I love most. Without my wonderful parents, Kathi and Ed, this book literally *couldn't* exist but, more so, it *wouldn't* if they hadn't always encouraged me to follow my (many and unrequited) dreams (see: dancing, singing, acting, archaeology, and academia). I can't possibly put into words how much I love you both and what your support—each in your own way—has meant to me over the years. And, Hilary, don't think I'm getting through this without saying something mushy and heartfelt about you, even though that is 100 percent not your style. There's no one I'd rather have shared my childhood with and I am enjoying the hell out of being an adult alongside you. (P.S. I'm definitely going to show this to your offspring, someday, and embarrass you, xoxo!)

To those who read the drafts no one will ever see. To Chase Jennings, my first-first reader! You're the reason I nailed down the debt/economics/political aspects of the book—and one of my oldest friends. Without you, I might not have evolved into my current form. To Faith Erline, I will never forget the day you told me, "That's what I want to read!" If you hadn't read the twelve chapters I sent you *that night,* and every incarnation of every chapter after that—hadn't spent hours spitballing and listening—I wouldn't have made it.

To those in Baltimore. To Sarah Pinsker, my parter-in-con-selfies-at-midnight. In driving to Canada and back. Writing in coffee shops and attending award ceremonies and saving seats on airplanes. Thanks for being my fellow Lawful Good. To Mike Underwood, I was a baby writer and you were not only a published novelist, but a publishing professional. Without your kindness and wisdom—without your taking me seriously—I may not have found a home amongst professionals. To Karen Osborne, who is my favorite Racecar Mouth.

To those who surround me. The writing community in the greater MD/DC/VA area. My fellow queers. Space Pirates. Blowholes. Vipers. Taken in the Terrarium. Vigorous Spring. Balti/VAcationers. Roses. Szparas and Honorary Szparas. The Kids Table. Hillen Road Gang. Hampdenites. To all those who've listened to me ramble, helped me plot, celebrated with me—and vented. To the Baltimore coffee shops I've haunted. To Marley and Piper for their company. To Hanson, for their music.

To those who turn words into books. To Jennifer Udden, my badass agent, who asked me to trust her. I always will. Thank you for helping me steer a six-inch-thick three-ring binder's worth of words onto the right path, and for your wisdom, snark, and insight along the way. Cheers to many more. To Carl Engle-Laird, who said my debut novel should be a complete thought. I feel incredibly lucky to be working with an editor who pledged to handle anything I throw at him. Thank you for overturning the right rocks, asking the right questions, and helping make *Docile* into the book it was always meant to be.

To the team at Tor.com Publishing and Macmillan. I knew it took more than one person to make a book happen, but I didn't realize just how many until now. To Irene Gallo, Jamie Stafford-Hill, Mordicai Knode, Caroline Perny, Katharine Duckett, Lauren Hougen, Jim Kapp, Esther Kim, Barbara Wild, Amanda Melfi, and Matt Johnson; thank you for treating my book-child with care and enthusiasm. To Lee Harris, Ruoxi Chen, and Christine Foltzer, for your energy. To Christina Orlando, Chris Lough, Bridget McGovern, Sarah Tolf, Leah Schnelbach, Natalie Zutter, and Emily Asher-Perrin, for your Internet wizardry. To everyone who took a chance on my Big Gay Book, sorry-not-sorry for all the sex scenes.

To everyone. Thank you. I can't possibly list all those who've gotten me and *Docile* where we are today. My family and friends and communities are not perfect but, like the words between these pages, they are mine.